The Bone
Chamber

Books by Robin Burcell

The Kate Gillespie Series
Every Move She Makes
Fatal Truth
Deadly Legacy
Cold Case

The Sydney Fitzpatrick Series
Face of a Killer
The Bone Chamber

The Bone Chamber

Robin Burcell

Poisoned Pen Press

Poisoned Pen Press

Poisoned Pen Press
6962 E. First Ave., Ste. 103
Scottsdale, AZ 85251
www.poisonedpenpress.com
info@poisonedpenpress.com

Printed in the United States of America

To
Cara, Alexa, and Brenna
Believe in yourselves and reach for the stars.

Acknowledgments

This book would not have been a twinkle in my eye without author extraordinaire James Rollins, who helped me come up with the first germ of a plot by showing me the back of a dollar bill and its relation to conspiracy theories. That plot grew with the help of my dear friend and writer Susan Crosby. Thanks also to my fellow investigator Arnd Gartner, history buff, who (not on duty—should our bosses read this) helped me with plot points. And to John Clausen; he knows why.

Any FBI agents depicted are not based on real persons. But if I were to include any qualities of real agents it would be those of my good friend Supervising Special Agent George Fong, for answering questions and coming up with a really cool plot idea when I needed something plausible with which to threaten the world. Any deviation from reality is my fault, not his. I also owe thanks to Peter Mygdal, MD, who helped vet one such idea to determine if it was still plausible two thousand years later when this book takes place.

Thanks also to my mother, Dr. Francesca Santoro L'Hoir, who accompanied me on my research trip to Rome and Naples, sharing her extensive knowledge of Italy and the columbaria. While in Rome, we dined at the Hostaria Antica Roma (one of her favorite restaurants); therefore thanks are owed to Paolo Magnanimi for the use of his name, his restaurant and the wonderful food he served. If you go, try the tiramisu. It's to die for.

Last but not least, thanks to my agent, Jane Chelius. To Barbara Peters, Robert Rosenwald, and all at Poisoned Pen Press who ensured a top-notch special edition hardcover. To all at HarperCollins for an awesome book and cover. To Wendy Lee, for all her help. And most of all to my editor, Lyssa Keusch, who let me try something different, embracing the idea for *The Bone Chamber* the moment she heard it.

For a Couple Worthy Causes

To my friends who contributed to the LHS cheer/drill team fundraiser, on behalf of my daughter: Special thanks to Dan Randolph of The Randolph Investigative Group for your sponsorship. And to HarperCollins for sending books for a raffle.

For the character auction: On behalf of the team, to Ron Nicholas McNiel II, for his son, Ron Nicholas McNiel III. To Natalie Bay and Kris Talley for their friend, Denise Woods. And on behalf of Sacramento DART (Drowning Accident Rescue Team), to Robin Morgan, for her daughter, Amber Jacobsen.

Chapter One

Sydney Fitzpatrick pulled out a small scale model of a crime scene from the metal cabinet at the front of the classroom, then eyed the clock by the classroom door. 9:40. Twenty more minutes and her Friday was officially kick-starting—once the students left and she completed the final paperwork. This was the last segment of a two-week forensic art course at the FBI Academy, with twenty-five law enforcement would-be artists from around the country. "Here," she said, setting the model on the table at the front of the class, "we have an interesting *and* controversial case. It dates back to the 1970s, before computers were all the rage in re-creating crime scenes, but it offers a good example of how a forensic artist can—"

She stopped when the classroom door opened. Special Agent in Charge Terrance Harcourt poked his head in the doorway. "You have a minute?"

"Sure." She excused herself to the men and women, then stepped from the room. Harcourt, a man in his fifties, gray-haired, dress shirt unbuttoned at the collar, sleeves rolled to his forearms, stood next to a man she'd never seen. He was taller than Harcourt, was maybe her age, mid-thirties, with a dark suit, a crisp tie, and a stance that screamed federal agent of the anal sort, she thought, closing the door tightly so that their conversation wouldn't be overheard.

"Sorry to interrupt your class," Harcourt said. "This is Special Agent Zachary Griffin. And this, of course, is our resident forensic artist, Special Agent Sydney Fitzpatrick."

"Good to meet you," Griffin said, shaking her hand.

"A pleasure," Sydney said. "What can I do for you?"

"I heard you were the go-to girl when it comes to recommending forensic anthropologists," Griffin said. "I know there are a few on the east coast, but my case is too important to draw one out of a hat. I was hoping if I gave you a wish list, you could give me a name."

"Depends," she said, glancing into the classroom—not that she expected her students to be throwing spit wads. Cops were, however, notorious pranksters. "What's your wish list?"

"Fast, reliable, the best in his or her field, and experienced in working with forensic artists."

"I know of two offhand. One in Vermont, one in D.C."

"The D.C. area would be more convenient."

"That would be Dr. Natasha Gilbert."

"How well do you know her?"

"We're good friends. I've worked a number of cases with her. If you want experience, she's the one."

"Any chance you can dig up her number?"

"You have pen and paper? I'll write it down for you."

He gave her a pen and small pad from his suit coat pocket. "And when might you be available for the sketch?" he asked, when she gave him the number.

No doubt Harcourt hadn't told him her plans. Or maybe, in typical federal agent style, SA Griffin hadn't asked her boss, just assumed she'd be available. "If you can wait until *after* Thanksgiving, I'm yours."

"That's two weeks from now. We're on a tight schedule."

"Unfortunately, as much as I'd love to work with Tasha, I'm tied up all day Saturday, then leaving Sunday for San Francisco to visit family for a much needed holiday vacation. If you'd like an artist sooner, my boss can hook you up," she said, nodding toward SAC Harcourt.

"Absolutely," Harcourt said. "We have a full list of artists available at a moment's notice. A number of them on the east coast."

"If there's nothing else," Sydney said, her hand on the door, "I have a class to get back to."

SA Griffin looked as though there was something else, but then he glanced into the classroom, stepped back, and said, "Enjoy your trip home."

"That should do it," Harcourt said. "Thanks."

The two men left, and Sydney returned to her class, not giving the matter another thought. At least not until she received a call at her office from the forensic anthropologist in question about an hour later. "Syd? Tasha. Just wanted to thank you for the job you sent my way."

"Not a problem," Sydney told her as she tucked the phone beneath her ear, balancing it so that she could continue sorting through the course evaluations left by her students in the forensic art class. SAC Harcourt was a stickler for making sure paperwork was completed, and she didn't want anything hanging when she left for vacation. "What sort of case is it?"

"Not sure. Yet. I heard you can't work it with me?"

"Flying to my mom's on Sunday. Too much to do between now and then."

A moment of silence, then Tasha said, "What happened to that workaholic I used to know?"

"Hit with reality on my last case. One that made me take a hard look at priorities," she said, not willing to go into details with her friend. It was one of the reasons she'd ended up back at Quantico. In the past, she would have taken this job in an instant, knowing her family would be there when she finished, no matter how long it took. Back then, she believed in what she was doing, believed that she had something to offer, to help. But she'd lost her edge on that last case and she needed to regroup, and flying home to be with her family for the two weeks preceding Thanksgiving was part of that effort. The sad reality was that the dead would be there for her when she got back. What she'd learned on her last case was that her family might not be. Deciding that she should offer her friend some sort of explanation, she added, "These days, family comes first."

"Don't blame you. Hold on a sec." More silence, then, "Sorry. My secretary's breathing down my neck. Listen, I was thinking that since you sent this forensic job my way, I could buy you dinner. Haven't seen you since—hell, what's it been? Six, seven months since you left here?"

"About that long. But let's catch up when I get back from vacation. Scotty's already asked me to dinner. He's helping me look for an apartment tomorrow and wanted to go over a few he found on the internet. I was hoping to find one before I left."

"You are not going to blow me off for an ex-boyfriend. I just got back from a dig and I *so* need to see a friendly face. Girls' night out for old times' sake."

"I really wish I could."

"You know we'll have fun, and Scotty will understand. Eventually. Ristorante Primavera at seven. I won't take no for an answer."

Tasha hung up before Sydney could object. And she wasn't even sure she wanted to. Scotty was undoubtedly using the apartment search to go out with her, and she didn't need to spend Friday night with him just to look at computer printouts of places they were going to see in person on Saturday. The question was whether to hit him with the truth, or come up with a reasonable lie as to why she was canceling dinner. She punched in his number, deciding that when it came to her ex, a lie was the much better option.

◇◇◇

Zachary Griffin hefted the large box to one side as he opened the office door of the Anthropological Division of the National Forensic Institute. The day had started off bad, and now the forensic artist wasn't available because she was taking vacation in the middle of a month he'd just as soon eliminate from the calendar. As a result he was forced to come up with an alternate solution—something he hadn't anticipated—and that was a mistake he shouldn't have made.

He refused to acknowledge that he'd had his mind on other things—this being November—and even if he did admit to that reason, it was not an acceptable excuse. There were no excuses, he thought, as he walked into the office. He nodded at the secretary, a round-faced, middle-aged woman with short blond curly hair, who was busy sorting through a box of papers. She smiled at him, then picked up the phone and called her boss' extension, saying, "Zachary Griffin's here...Very good. I'll send him in."

The secretary disconnected, whispered, "FYI. She's a bit frazzled from her trip. Something about a curse on the tomb." She angled her head toward the office door. Zach, figuring she was joking about the curse, crossed the reception area as she got back to her filing.

He stepped into the large office, one wall of shelves filled with reference books, the other filled with rows of labeled boxes—each containing bones, each waiting for IDs. Much like the box he now carried. "Your plan backfired, Tasha," he said. She seemed not to hear, intent on whatever it was she was reading on her computer screen, and he crossed the room, then stopped in surprise at her appearance. He hadn't seen her since her return from Egypt, only talked to her on the phone. The secretary's assessment was an understatement. Frazzled was not the word he'd use to describe her, he thought, noting the dark circles beneath her bloodshot blue eyes as she worked at her computer. Usually neat and meticulous, her blond hair was pulled back in a hasty ponytail. Her lab coat was wrinkled, and beneath it she wore a sweatshirt and jeans, also wrinkled, as though she'd grabbed everything from the bottom of some pile in her closet. "You did get my voice mail? Your *friend* is refusing to do the drawing. I don't suppose you have a Plan B." Because he sure as hell didn't.

"Already in the works. I got off the phone with Sydney not five minutes ago," Tasha said, glancing up from her computer. When she saw the box he held, she sank back in her chair, looking even wearier. "God, please tell me that's not what I think it is?"

"About your friend?"

"We're going to dinner tonight. Trust me. By the second bottle of wine I'll have her convinced to delay her flight to San Francisco and work with me on that drawing, though I think it would have made a hell of a lot more sense just to let her in on some of the details. This whole thing of you and me pretending not to know each other seems a bit much. If you would have let me just pick up the phone, tell her I had a job for—"

"That's not an option. Your work for me stays out of the public eye. Especially on this matter. Besides, it's a little late for that. She thinks I'm another agent, and I don't want the FBI involved beyond the means to complete this drawing." The only reason he even approached Special Agent Fitzpatrick was on Tasha's insistence that she was the best forensic artist on the east coast. And—more importantly—Fitzpatrick had been in San Francisco the last six months, too embroiled in the case involving her father's killer on death row to have paid any attention to what was going on in the capital with any real interest. Her return to the D.C. area a few weeks ago made her the perfect candidate. She wouldn't be up on the political scandal running in the newspaper a few months back, accusing a congressman of having an affair with a student at the University of Virginia. "For now," he said, "we will continue with things my way."

"Fine," she said, giving him an exasperated look. "As long as you realize you're a bit too paranoid. Surely you can trust the FBI?"

"I don't know who I can trust. And what I need is an identification without recognition." Anyone in this area during that time was bound to recognize Alessandra from those newspaper photos—should Alessandra end up being the victim. His gut told him that it was her skull in the box, though he wanted to believe otherwise. "So no government agencies. The last thing I need is to have Alessandra's name linked to the congressman, which could lead back to me."

Tasha eyed the box, taking a deep breath. "You really believe it's Alessandra in there?"

"I hope not. But until we know…How soon can you get on this?"

"I'd rather wait until I get Sydney on board."

"I'm not sure we have that luxury. Get started on the ID now. At least get me a preliminary report. Whatever else it is you can determine from a skull. Tonight, convince your friend to do the sketch for identification, make it out like it's a random murder victim—let's hope that's what it turns out to be—and we'll be that much farther ahead. If you can't get her on board, I'm going to have to take your report elsewhere and find another artist."

Zach set the box on her desk. Her phone rang, and she jumped, then gave a nervous laugh as her secretary picked up the other extension.

"You sure you're okay?" Zach asked.

"Fine. Simple jet lag."

That was when he glanced over, saw what she'd been looking at on the computer screen. Egyptian curses, just as the secretary had mentioned. "Tell me you're not serious?"

"Maybe just a little on edge. I was, after all, digging in an Egyptian tomb reputed to have a two-thousand-year-old curse. Half the time I was there, I felt like someone was watching my every move. The other half was exhaustion over the constant charade while I accompanied a crew who thought me nothing more than an anthropologist associated with an academic research dig."

"Do you think anyone suspected you?"

"Does it even matter? Because of that dig Alessandra is missing, and now you've found a body and—"

Her secretary poked her head in the door. "Some professor from the American Academy is on line one for you."

"The American Academy?"

"In Rome. Professor Francesca Santarella."

"Do me a favor. Take a message and tell her I'll get back to her."

"You sure you don't want to take it?" Zach asked. "I can wait."

She shook her head. "I contacted so many academic types on that dig that I can't recall if I should know the name. And the way I feel right now, I don't have the energy to keep playing my part."

Definitely stressed. He wondered if perhaps they were asking too much of her. "Tell me again about the Egypt trip."

She glanced at her computer, then back at him. "As I explained on the phone, more dead ends. If Carlo Adami set up that dig to cover for something, then he did a damned fine job. It looked like the real thing to me. Alessandra even thought so."

"You're absolutely sure?"

"Every person on the team was some sort of scholar. Frankly, I think Adami set up the dig as a way to deflect attention from something else. Maybe *somewhere* else. I was there for two weeks. The only weapons I saw were small-caliber pistols by the night security guards. As for a makeshift lab? Nothing in the vicinity that we could see. They definitely weren't shipping anything in or out. If there were any bioweapons, they were well-hidden among the artifacts being dug up, most of which would fit in the palm of your hand."

"And no idea why Alessandra left the dig for the States?"

Her gaze flicked to the box on her desk as she shook her head. "Alessandra said she wanted to check on some archeological facts."

They'd gone over all this before, but he was worried that maybe they'd missed something that might tell them what had happened to Alessandra. "What sort of facts?"

"I wish I could remember," Tasha said, looking troubled. "Something about three keys...The third key? Whatever it was, she said not to worry, that it was archeological research. Some biblical thing, I thought."

"Third key? You didn't mention that the first time."

"It was just such a strange conversation. At the time it meant nothing. Do you think it's important?"

He gave a shrug, brushing it off. "When did you last hear from her?"

"She called while I was still in Egypt, but I didn't get the message until several days later."

"That's what I don't like. No one's heard from her since." He rested his hand on top of the box. "And now there's this."

She didn't move, simply stared at the box. And even though she was a forensic anthropologist, and she had dozens more boxes like it on the shelves behind her, it was apparent that this one got to her. "Was it really necessary to do this?" she said. "A skull in a box?"

"If you saw her, yes. The pathologist is the one who insisted we go this route. Bring the skull to you. Trust me, we tried everything else."

"Maybe there's another way. Surely DNA…?"

"She was adopted."

"What about her apartment?"

"Unfortunately, the cover story we thought would buy us time actually created a few problems. In theory, telling everyone that she was sent home to her father's, and wasn't expected to return back to UVA anytime soon, should have worked. We didn't take into account that her roommate, short on cash, figured to make a quick buck by subletting Alessandra's room, or that her new tenant would carefully launder and box up the clothes left behind."

"No toothbrush or hairbrush?"

"Alessandra probably had them with her. In hindsight, we should have created the cover story after we'd searched her room. But at the time, we didn't believe she was dead."

"What about dental records?"

"Still looking. Because of her father's occupation, the majority of her dental history is spread about in countries that don't keep such meticulous records. The records we found were inconclusive. We need a forensic sketch. If it is her, her father will want to—" He stopped, ran his fingers through his hair. "How did I ever let her get involved?"

Tasha looked up at Griffin. "Maybe her disappearance has nothing to do with this? Like I said, it was a legitimate dig. And maybe it's not her in that box."

"The boss wants something a bit more definitive than *maybe* it is or isn't her. And if it does have to do with Adami, then we need to be careful. You're absolutely sure this friend of yours will come through?"

"Someday you're going to have to learn to trust someone else's judgment."

"I've gone that route. It didn't work."

A loud bang echoed just outside the closed door. Tasha's breath caught, and she paled, even as her secretary called out, "Sorry. Just a box of file folders."

Griffin looked down at Tasha's hands, saw they were shaking. "What the hell is going on?"

"Besides too much caffeine? It's nothing," she said, clasping her hands in her lap. He crossed his arms, looked her right in the eye. "Fine. But don't laugh. It was this curse. I know it sounds odd, but just hearing about the damned thing gave me nightmares, and I haven't been able to sleep."

"Okay, I'll bite," he said. Even though he didn't have time for this, it was clear that Tasha needed to talk about it. "What does this curse do?"

She gave a sigh, then tried to smile, as though she knew how silly it was going to sound. "Allegedly anyone who enters the tomb will be dead within a fortnight. At least that's the rumor according to the locals we hired." She stared at the box containing the skull, as if to say, *and Alessandra was in that tomb, so that proves it is true.*

"That is not why Alessandra died—if this is her."

"I know you're right."

He wasn't sure what else he could do or say. "Maybe you should start your report on the skull tomorrow. You look tired."

She shook her head. "Trust me. I'll be fine. I'll even put myself together properly before I meet Sydney."

"Call me after your dinner. Let me know how it goes," he said, turning to leave.

"Zach?" He stopped, knowing what she was going to say. "I can go with you, if you like. To the cemetery. I have time."

"I'll be fine." He left, said good-bye to her secretary who was busy sorting through the files she'd dropped. He continued on down the long hallway, his footsteps echoing through the dimly lit corridor. Every office door but the one he'd left was closed. Above him a fluorescent light flickered, then went out. He heard the swish of the elevator door, apparently just missing it, and not wanting to wait, he took the stairs three flights down. Once he'd reached the street he pulled out his cell phone to call his office.

When his boss answered, Zach said, "Did Natasha Gilbert say anything to you when she returned from that dig?"

"I haven't even seen her. Why?"

"She seems on edge." He thought about the ridiculousness of this two-thousand-year-old curse she spoke of. "Whatever it is, I'm not sure she's telling me everything. She did recall that Alessandra spoke of a third key, but that was it."

"You're sure that's what she said?"

"I'm sure that's what Tasha said she heard." He hesitated before adding, "And she thought there was some biblical slant."

"Biblical…?"

"*Don't* even go there. I don't trust Dumas."

"You don't trust anyone. Since he's the only religious expert we have, I don't see a way around it. We're going to have to contact him."

Zach knew that, but it didn't make things easier. Especially considering what day it was. "One more thing."

"What's that?"

"I need a complete dossier on an FBI agent working out of Quantico. Someone named Sydney Fitzpatrick."

"This that forensic artist you're trying to use?"

"Yes."

"Tell me you have a good reason for me to get my hand spanked poking around in Bureau files?"

"Tasha's meeting her for dinner tonight. If she can't convince her to do this drawing, I may have to intervene and I want to know who I'm dealing with."

Griffin disconnected, dropped his phone in his pocket, then looked at his watch. Just enough time to get to the florist before it closed.

A fitting end to an already bad day, and he wondered if it could get any worse.

Chapter Two

Sydney Fitzpatrick looked at the boxes stacked around the living room of her apartment, boxes she'd yet to unpack since her transfer to the FBI Academy at Quantico almost a month ago. She thought about digging through them to find her favorite cashmere sweater, only because Tasha usually dressed for dinner, even at the more casual restaurants. Then again, anything she pulled out of a box was bound to be wrinkled, and after the errands she'd been running this afternoon, she had just about enough time to brush her hair and race out the door as she was.

Tasha was waiting for her at a table in the Ristorante Primavera, an upscale Italian eatery. She stood when Sydney approached, her gaze locked on the door behind her, for what seemed a second too long, before suddenly smiling, then reaching out to give a hug. "Syd! You haven't changed a bit."

"In seven months? I hope not." Sydney eyed her friend as she took a seat opposite her. "How is it you have a tan, when the rest of us haven't seen the sun in weeks?" she said, when what she really wanted to ask was if Tasha was unwell. Beneath that tan, she looked tired, nervous even.

"Just got back from a dig. I'll pay for it down the road, wrinkled like an old prune, but that's the hazard of working in the sun."

"Where this time?"

"Egypt. Valley of the Kings."

They sat, scanned the menu, and almost in unison said, "Pizza Margherita!" A waiter approached, and Tasha ordered a bottle of cabernet to go with the pizza. "Unless you wanted something else?" she asked Sydney.

"Cab is perfect." The waiter left, and Sydney leaned forward. "Is everything okay, Tasha?"

"*Major* jet lag. I've only been back a couple days. But trust me. A couple bottles of wine, a taxi ride home, I'll sleep like a baby and all will be well with the world. How about you? I heard about all the mess with your father's old case."

"I'm fine. The case is fine," Sydney said, not wanting to get into the particulars of what had happened to her father. Not here at dinner. "So tell me about this latest dig of yours. Bones? Pottery? Ancient treasure?"

"Is the FBI spying on me?"

"Spying?" Sydney laughed. "Yeah, we've got a whole wing at Quantico devoted to the pyramids. Right next to the X-files. So give me the scoop. Find anything interesting?"

Tasha smiled. "Besides a few pottery shards? Nothing. What about you? How's this forensic art class you're teaching at the academy?"

"So far so good," Sydney replied, as the waiter returned with the wine. "Two-week course. Students are a mix of police officers and civilians working for law enforcement agencies from around the country. It's fun."

They spent the next hour talking about everything from Sydney's work to which fashion designer needed to die for bringing back some godforsaken style, like neon oversized flower prints that never should have seen the light of day in the first place. The closest they got to talking about Tasha's job was when she tried to convince Sydney to put off her plane trip and work the forensic ID case with her, which struck Sydney as odd—never mind that the whole time they sat there, Tasha's attention seemed to wander toward the entrance and the street front window. Sydney would have dismissed it as simple preoccupation, if it weren't for the fact that Tasha was definitely jumpy.

Maybe something was wrong at work. Stress, bosses, who knew? "You sure you're okay?" Sydney asked.

Tasha started to deny it again, but suddenly stopped, leaned back in her chair and said, "You'd never believe it if I told you."

"Told me what?"

"The tomb I was in? Supposedly anyone who entered was subject to a two-thousand-year-old curse and would be dead in a fortnight. So, call it bullshit, call it whatever. It gave me nightmares, and I haven't been able to sleep."

"Nightmares?"

"You know how vivid my dreams are. Like after I saw that Count Dracula movie and everyone in my dreams sprouted fangs and came after me, and I had to defang them?"

"I thought you said you were a kid when that happened?"

"I was. But I remember it like it was yesterday, and if I never see another Dracula movie again, it'll be too soon. Now give me the real dirt. Why is Scotty helping you look for an apartment? I thought you two broke up?"

There it was again. That turn away from Tasha back to her. Maybe it was best just to let it go. Tasha was a big girl, and certainly knew Sydney was there for her. "We're done."

"For good?"

"For good. But we're still friends." Scott Ryan, her ex-fiancé, was happily married to the FBI, which left no room for her. "Why? You interested in him?"

"Hardly, but there was that cute friend of his who worked in the same bureau. The one who just got divorced…" Tasha was three years divorced, and as far as Sydney knew, not in a particular hurry to settle down again.

"Carter?"

"Yeah. Too bad I'm going to Italy at the end of next week, which is why I need you to work with me on this drawing before I go," Tasha said, tipping the last of the wine into her glass, then signaling for the waiter to bring them another bottle. "If I hadn't already committed to this dig, I'd give him or any other eligible male some *serious* consideration."

"I'm sure Carter will be there when you get back," Sydney said, thinking that was the closest Tasha had come to talking about herself all night. "Me, I've sworn off feds."

"All feds, or just Scotty?"

"My opinion, Scotty's a good representative example of what they're like."

"He's damned cute, if you ask me," Tasha said, seeming more like her old self.

"And a really nice guy. But if you want a warm body sleeping in your bed each night, pick a man in the private sector."

The waiter brought a second bottle of cabernet, and as he walked off, Tasha leaned over and whispered, "Waiters are in the private sector."

Tasha's laugh was vivacious, infectious, and by the time they finished their second bottle, Sydney wasn't sure if she'd ever again look at a glass of cabernet without thinking of waiters in Italian restaurants.

The next morning Sydney wasn't sure if she'd ever look at a glass of red wine period. A textbook hangover made her head pound, and when the phone rang, the pounding increased tenfold. She hoped like hell it wasn't Tasha, because she had a hell of a time convincing her that she was *not* giving up her trip home.

"You ready to go look for apartments this afternoon?" It was Scotty, who, ever since her transfer back to Quantico, had made it his mission to get her out of her temporary apartment supplied for agents in downtown Washington, D.C. She'd done little to discourage his interest, because it gave her something to talk about with Scotty, telling him that she wanted to find a decent place to live.

It was really a smoke screen. She liked temporary. It meant she didn't need to make a decision. "Yeah, maybe...I don't know. I'm a little hung over."

"From what?"

"Tasha and I went drinking last night," she said, before she remembered the lie she'd told him about having a headache and just wanting to relax for the evening. "I started to feel better and she called. I'm sorry."

A stretch of silence.

"I figured you'd already made other plans," she said.

"Did I say anything?"

Did he ever? "Look, I've got to go take mass quantities of ibuprofen. I'll be ready in an hour."

◇◇◇

"Anything in the newspapers?"

Jon Westgate lit a cigarette, glanced over at his boss. "Not yet."

"Do not smoke in here."

"Sorry." But he made no move to put it out. Instead he walked toward the window, away from the man who sat in the leather wingback chair, drinking his coffee. Politicians. He wouldn't be working for one if the perks weren't so damned good. "I've checked all the papers, and the internet. Nothing."

"I find that odd. A young woman so brutally murdered… One would think they'd want her identified."

"If that were the case," Westgate said, "maybe one *shouldn't* have had her face removed."

An icy silence seemed to fill the room, and Westgate wondered if perhaps he'd been too sarcastic to the man who was signing his checks, until his boss said, "You're right. It seems the man Adami sent was a bit overzealous when I suggested that we didn't want her immediately identifiable."

"Adami is becoming a problem. He is obsessed with these Masonic symbols."

"Most Grand Masters are."

"Most Grand Masters don't carve pyramids on a girl's face. Clearly he ordered his man to do it. I think he needs to be reined in."

"I'll make that decision. For now, I'm curious to find out what this third key is. He insists that it'll change the course of bioweaponry."

"I thought you said it was nothing but a pipe dream?"

"I still think so. But I'm also smart enough to know that I don't know everything, especially when it comes to biblical history. I imagine that has something to do with this latest scientist Adami picked up, Dr. Balraj. His specialty is in the evolution of plagues." He shook the paper out, then turned the page. "I just don't get this. How is it this girl hasn't been reported missing? I have plans for this when she is identified, and it would be nice if it made the news. Are you sure there's nothing?"

"It's like the entire government has closed ranks around this case."

"That can't be good."

"There is one small lead."

"About?"

"Her skull," Westgate said, taking a long drag from the cigarette, then exhaling a plume of smoke against the cold windowpane. He looked out to the street below. Pedestrians hurried across the intersection, stepping over shallow snowdrifts from the previous night's storm. "My source thinks they'll take it to Quantico. We're looking into it."

"I want to know everyone who is even remotely connected to this case."

Westgate opened the window, flicked his cigarette into the dirty slush in the street below. "Arrangements are already being made."

◇◇◇

Sydney Fitzpatrick stepped off the plane that Sunday at San Francisco airport, looking forward to time with her family, especially her eleven-year-old sister. Her vision of two weeks of relaxation culminating in a home-cooked turkey dinner evaporated the moment she was greeted by SFO airport police.

"Special Agent Fitzpatrick?" the uniformed man asked her, after the flight attendant pointed her out.

"Yes."

"You need to call Quantico at once." He checked a piece of paper he held. "Contact SAC Harcourt."

"Thank you," she said, taking out her phone and powering it on, then hitting speed dial for Harcourt's cell phone.

"Hate to cut your vacation short," Harcourt said, once they connected. "But we need you for that drawing."

"What happened to that spiel about the full list of artists available at a moment's notice?" she asked.

"Think of it this way. You come do the drawing, and you're back in San Francisco before the turkey's thawing on the counter."

As much as she wanted to decline the job, if they'd gone to this much trouble to get her, she knew she couldn't. She'd accepted the transfer to Quantico for a reason. True, she needed the rest and respite from her last case that almost ended her career, never mind her life. She'd gone out of her comfort zone on that last assignment, and she wasn't about to venture out again. But the hard truth she didn't want to face was that she'd pushed the envelope so far, the Bureau was watching her, and wanted to know if she was a team player. Besides, Thanksgiving was nearly two weeks away. A drawing with a forensic anthropologist couldn't take more than a day, maybe two, depending on the condition of the body. "Let me check on flights and I'll call you back."

"We have a plane standing by. The officer will take you to it."

And that didn't make any sense. Since when did the Bureau have private planes waiting for something that could have, *should have* been dealt with before she ever left Washington, D.C.? Like they were expecting to fly her back?

Something was up.

Chapter Three

At precisely 9:53 P.M., Sydney's plane touched down at the Marine base at Quantico. She looked out the window and saw a lone jeep waiting on the tarmac. SAC Harcourt and Special Agent Griffin stood by the jeep. Other than that, the airstrip seemed surprisingly empty, especially considering the grounds were shared with the Marines...

She grabbed her overnight bag and briefcase, exited the plane, bracing herself against the chill of the mid November air. Patches of dirty slush lined the runway, remnants from the early fall snow promising that it wasn't about to get much warmer, even come morning. How had she ever thought of San Francisco as being cold during the few months she lived there? She was definitely going to miss the west coast.

The men standing by the jeep watched her, and as she approached, SAC Harcourt put his hand on her shoulder. "Thanks for interrupting your vacation and coming at such short notice."

"Not a problem," she said. "So we're starting first thing in the morning?"

"Tonight," Griffin said. "A lot to cover and little time. You brought what you need for the sketch?"

"Never leave home without it." She patted the soft-sided briefcase slung over her shoulder.

"Good," Harcourt said. "We have a room ready for you."

"I have a place in D.C.," she said, slinging the overnight bag onto her shoulder, trying to sound pleasant. Okay, so it was the standard apartment in the standard building used for temporary housing for agents. But even with the bare white walls and rented furniture and still-packed boxes, it was a damn sight better than what they had at Quantico in the Academy dorm, which consisted of a twin bed with a shared bathroom. "I'd rather be able to go home tonight."

Griffin held the jeep door for her. "Like I said, very little time and a lot to get through, so if you can manage one night here..."

She stood there a moment, looked him right in the eye. "Just out of curiosity. Why me?"

"I beg your pardon?"

"Of all the forensic artists, in all the towns, in all the world, you call me. Why?"

"The gin joints were closed, and you came recommended. Any more questions?"

"Not yet." Unless one pointed out that there were plenty of good artists on the east coast, so why the hell fly her all the way from the west when she was on vacation?

They drove her to the main building at the FBI Academy, had her check in her gun as was required with every agent, then escorted her to the basement, just down the hall from her own office. A sign on the door, one that hadn't been there when she'd left for San Francisco, read: "Absolutely No Admittance." Harcourt unlocked the door, allowing her to enter. Griffin stepped in behind her, placed his briefcase at his feet as she stopped before the only table in the center of the room where a skull sat, seemingly watching her.

"Something wrong?" Griffin asked, when she didn't move for several seconds.

She shook her head, not willing to discuss her thoughts about working with the dead. In typical cases, when she was called, it was usually because the investigators had exhausted all leads in identifying the victim. She was often the victim's last hope, the last voice. That was not something one explained easily—not without sounding like some narcissistic nutcase. For the obvious reasons, she kept her beliefs to herself. She'd worked from skulls before, but her instincts told her that all was not as it seemed. In fact these same instincts had been telling her so from the moment she stepped off the plane in San Francisco, then was flown back via special FBI transport.

Whatever was going on, she had no idea, and she eyed the room. There was only one chair. A coffeepot had been set up, and someone had thought to bring a box of granola bars. Other than that, the room was empty. If not for the skull, and the absence of a second chair, the place could double for a damn interrogation room, and she turned toward the men to ask what the hell was going on, but hesitated when Harcourt handed the keys to Mr. Federal, then made some excuse about being late for an appointment before rushing off.

Sydney set her overnight bag near the door, then walked to the table, depositing her briefcase at its base, examining the evidence before her. The skull had been boiled clean, a standard procedure that in her mind always seemed to depersonalize the victim, by removing the last vestiges of his or her being. What was left, the empty orbs and corporeal grin, were never recognizable as who the person had been—though often in far better shape than how that person had been found. Ever since she'd been trained in forensic art, she'd never looked at a skull or skeleton the same. Before, she'd seen them as bones, simply bones minus the flesh, never imagining who they were or what they'd been thinking. Not so anymore.

She pulled on a pair of latex gloves from a box on the table, picked up the skull, examined it. There were no obvious signs of trauma to the head. "I thought you'd lined up a forensic anthropologist," she said, turning the skull about in her hands. "Dr. Gilbert."

"We have her notes and measurements," Griffin replied, handing over several sheets of paper, handwritten. "We just need you to do the drawing."

"We usually work in concert."

"In this case, we, uh, made other arrangements."

She glanced at the papers he gave her, saw the notations in pencil, some of them haphazard, as though these were the notes from a report that had yet to be completed. "These are Natasha's notes?"

"She was the forensic anthropologist you recommended."

It took a moment for his answer to register. Tasha Gilbert was neat, fastidious. "Are you sure you have the right report? This isn't like her, never mind she'd want to be here."

"Like I said, we had to make other arrangements. Time is of the essence, so how soon can you have a drawing done?"

"Hard to say until I know what I have to work with." She looked over Tasha's notations, the measurements of skin and flesh thickness, based on height, weight, race and approximate age of the victim, all things that a forensic anthropologist would relay to Sydney through the examination of the skeleton or remains, helping her to proceed in recreating the victim's face. It was a complicated process, certainly not an exact science, but a science nonetheless. She flipped through the few pages, curious as to why Tasha, a perfectionist if there ever was one, would allow her rough draft report to be turned over. "Crime scene photos?"

"In another file."

"This is highly irregular."

And Special Agent Griffin said, "For a reason."

She glanced over at him, and for all his calm exterior, there was something about him that made her think he was worried, harried, not so unruffled after all. Interesting. "Clothing? Hair? I need a photo of the body as it was found. Blow it up, eliminate whatever you don't want me to see, just get it to me if you want me to do my job. If you can't release that, a frontal shot of her, pre-autopsy, before the skull was cleaned, will suffice. Again, the same. It will help me finalize the drawing, make sure it's accurate."

He nodded, unlocked and opened his briefcase, and pulled a single photo from a manila folder. "Crime scene only. I can get you the other tomorrow. This I'll need back." He handed it to her, then started pacing the room.

Apparently this was a case that wasn't to be discussed, wasn't to leave this room. Maybe that's why Tasha had agreed to pass on her notes as rough as they were. Even so, had Special Agent Griffin just presented the damned photo with the skull, then let Sydney do her drawing at a normal hour, she wouldn't have given any of it a second thought—probably wouldn't even remember it as anything significant. At least that was her train of thought up until she viewed the crime scene photograph. It wasn't as if anyone could view such a photo with hopes the image would fade. One look made it easy to understand why it was necessary to boil the skull. The victim's face—along with her fingertips—had literally been removed. Peeled away. And it was more than someone simply not wanting the victim ID'd. There was something clearly ritualistic about the way the face had been removed, the shape of the wound. A triangle with its point at the top of the forehead, its base at her chin.

Damned hard to make that pattern on a skull, but there was no doubt about the shape, and she forced herself to look beyond it to what she needed for her work. The woman had dark, wavy, shoulder-length hair. Her shirt had been ripped open, exposing well-developed breasts which put her past the age of puberty. The condoms trailing from her front jeans pocket gave her the appearance of being at least near the age of consent, and Sydney glanced at Tasha's report and found that the victim was probably in her mid-to-late twenties.

She took out a pad of lined paper, started writing her own notes, when Griffin stopped his pacing, looked at her. "What are you doing?"

"Taking notations for my drawing. From there I intend to do a rough sketch of the victim's hair length, noting the color, details about it, as well as the clothing. If that's okay?"

He stepped back, didn't ask any more questions, and she told herself that it wasn't her place to decide how the drawing was done, or why the drawing was done. She was here to follow orders—something she used to be good at.

Three hours and five cups of coffee later, leading to several *escorted* trips to the restroom, she decided there wasn't enough caffeine in the world that was going to allow her to concentrate on the developing sketch. At the moment it resembled a scientific study one might find in a scholarly journal. She'd drawn the frontal view of the skull on her sketch pad, then overlaid it with vellum, upon which, with the aid of a small metric ruler, she drew precise markings to indicate the specific measurements given in Tasha's report to note the thickness of the flesh upon the skull. The vellum, like tracing paper, would simply overlay the drawing of the skull, then once the sketch was finished, be removed for photocopying and distribution to the investigators—whoever they might be.

Sydney stifled her umpteenth yawn, stared at the skull, the orbs that seemed to watch her in return, wondering about the victim, hoping she hadn't suffered greatly before death—before she'd been disfigured. One could only hope it had all been done postmortem. She thought of the condoms, wondered if they were brought there by the victim, or left by the suspect. "Was this a sexual assault?" she asked.

And just as Zachary Griffin had avoided answering every other question she'd posed that might directly lead to the case, he didn't respond to this one, either.

Fine. He might not need sleep, but she did, and if he wasn't willing to talk to her, help her keep awake, then tough. "I'm sorry," she said, pushing her chair back. "I can't work any longer tonight."

"You're certain?"

"So you do remember how to communicate?"

He didn't reply.

"Yes, I'm certain. I'll need *several* hours of rest if you want a decent drawing, and then I'm going running. I presume you want everything to remain here?"

"Yes."

Sydney left her briefcase, drawing tools, and sketch pad behind, walked over, picked up her overnight bag, then stood there, waiting for him to unlock the door, let her out. When he hesitated, she held up her arms. "Either search me, or open the damned door. I'm tired."

He glanced back at her things on the table, perhaps to assure himself she took nothing with her, then unlocked the door, letting her out before locking it behind him. And if that wasn't secure enough, he escorted her to the elevator, then to the front lobby, where the guard who had taken her gun for safekeeping gave her the key to her room for the night. When it seemed her self-appointed escort intended to accompany her to her dorm, she held up her hand. "I can take it from here, thank you. Know the place well."

A nod and he stepped back, allowing her to enter the elevator on her own. In her entire twelve years in law enforcement, the last four in the FBI, she wasn't sure she'd ever experienced security this tight. Definitely not for a drawing, she thought, feeling the agent's gaze on her even as the elevator door slid shut and she began her ascent.

Her room was on the third floor, a short walk through one of the many glass-enclosed hallways that connected each of the buildings. The glass enclosures reminded her of the tubes in a hamster cage and were often referred to as the same by the recruits housed there. Outside, a light dusting of snow covered the moonlit landscaping below, and all looked peaceful—as long as she didn't think about the crime scene photo. It bothered her. She'd seen plenty of crimes over the years, plenty of violent scenes and photos. But this one was different. Forensic artists weren't usually ushered into Quantico under cover of darkness, secreted away to a room where no one had entry, then guarded the entire time…

So who was the woman? Clearly someone of significance. Or a case of significance.

The photo had showed a woman who was made out to be a prostitute—or something similar, if the condoms were to be believed. Over the years, Sydney had seen dozens of sexual crimes, and this had all the earmarks of such a case. Until one thought of the overkill on security while she did her drawing.

Which certainly made her think twice when she unlocked her door, stepped into the room.

She tossed her bag on the twin bed, then shut and bolted the door behind her, slipping her phone from her belt and calling her former partner, Tony Carillo, back in San Francisco. He answered on the second ring, his voice sounding as though she'd woken him. She glanced at the clock, after two A.M. eastern time.

"Sorry," she said, then looked around the room, taking stock of the Spartan surroundings. "Just missing everyone back home. How are you?"

A slight hesitation. "Fine. Everything okay?"

"Yeah, yeah. Just trying to unwind. You know. If I can't sleep, why should you," she said, walking into the bathroom, closing the door. She checked the door leading to the dorm room on the other side, made sure it was empty, told herself she was just being paranoid, then locked it, before turning the shower on full force, trying to keep her voice low. "You ever hear of a guy named Zachary Griffin? Special Agent?"

"For the Bureau?"

"So it seems. Do me a favor. Find out what you can on the guy? Code Two," she said, giving the old cop term for "without delay."

"Yeah, sure. What's going on?"

"Other than they've got me locked up with this drawing tighter than an alchemist's formula for gold at Fort Knox? I haven't the foggiest. Call you tomorrow."

She hung up, thought about calling Tasha to find out what she could offer on the case, but realized it was too late, she'd be in bed. Then again, Sydney could leave a message on her voice mail at her office, and called that number instead. When she heard the doctor's voice mail kick in, she said, "Hey, Tasha. This is about that case I recommended you for. Give me a call on my cell. I have a couple questions. Oh, and if you're free tomorrow, let's do a late lunch, before I fly back to San Francisco."

That done, she turned off the shower, exited the bathroom, tossed the phone on the bed, then began a top-to-bottom search of the room, finding nothing, and telling herself that she really was being paranoid if she thought they'd go to the trouble of placing a bug in her room when all she was here to do was a drawing.

The next morning, as she dressed in her running clothes, she decided her paranoia was merely a result of being tired, until she opened her door at ten A.M., and found Special Agent Griffin standing there as if he'd been waiting outside her room all morning. Then again, maybe there *was* some camera or listening device hidden somewhere. She almost laughed at the direction of her thoughts, then stepped into the hallway. He gave a questioning look at the sweats she wore.

"Sorry," she said, with an apologetic shrug. "I'm not doing anything before I get in my run, then eat breakfast."

"You can run after you finish."

"My brain functions better this way," she said, trying to keep her annoyance at bay. She failed. "And unless you want to jog along beside me and hold up that sketchbook, or you feel like employing another sketch artist, you'll have to wait."

She double-checked that her cell phone was clipped to the waist of her sweatpants, then swept past him. "Lock the door behind you," she said, since there was nothing of interest in her things, in case he was so inclined to search through them.

Outside, the air was crisp, cool, but not too cold, even with the snow. Truth be told, she enjoyed the vast parklike grounds and the woods that surrounded Quantico's academy, and missed the fireflies in the summer. What she didn't miss was the summer humidity, she thought, choosing a path that led into the trees, away, she hoped, from prying eyes and ears, and allowing some shelter against the light, but melting snow. About ten minutes out, she slowed her pace, and phoned Carillo.

The first thing out of his mouth was, "What the hell are you working on?"

"Why?"

"I'm having a hard time finding any info on this guy. He seems familiar with the Academy? Maybe he's some muckety-muck investigator with the Marines."

"He was introduced as a special agent, so I doubt it."

"Yeah? Well, there's a lot of agencies out there that use that title. What sort of case is it?"

"At the moment, I can't give you details, other than it looks like some ritualistic killer. Like I said, the security around it is tight, and they won't let me talk about it. But when I can divulge anything, I'll let you know."

"If it's your basic serial killer, why all the secrecy?"

"The million-dollar question." Sydney thought she heard something behind her. "Hold on," she said, then paused to listen. It was the slightest of sounds, but it sent a shiver through her. When she turned, she saw nothing.

"What is it?" Carillo asked.

"Probably a deer. Anyway, do me a favor, and keep checking on this guy. I get the feeling that he's not one of ours."

"Will do."

She disconnected, started jogging, and again had that sensation of being watched. When she slowed, she heard nothing, so she quickened her pace, wanting out of the woods now that she no longer had need of privacy. Fifty yards later, she was sure someone was following her. She eyed a swath of needles on the ground where the snow had melted, veered off the path into the trees, making sure she left no tracks, then waited, trying to slow her breathing, hoping not to be overheard. A moment later the cadence of joggers approaching from the opposite direction caught her attention. Two young men wearing FBI Academy sweats ran into view. She stepped out, nodded. "Mind if I join you?"

"Feel free," one of them said.

She fell in beside them, jogged for a bit, then looked back. And could've sworn she saw a figure slip into the woods.

◇◇◇

Sydney showered, changed, then headed down to grab a bite to eat at the cafeteria, where Zachary Griffin was waiting. The dining hall wasn't crowded, the morning rush long since past. No recruits in their blue shirts. Probably all in class. The patrons who remained were probably employees on a break. She recognized no one, and turned to her shadow. "You weren't following me while I was out running, were you?"

"No. Why would you think that?"

"Thought I saw someone out on the trails. It's a big base. Suppose it could've been anyone."

His gaze flicked to the expanse of windows, then back to her. "I'd like you to finish as soon as possible."

"That makes two of us." She set an apple, juice and yogurt onto her tray, then stopped for coffee. "You bring that autopsy photo?"

"You can eat downstairs while you work," he said, ignoring her question.

"Or you can try drawing it yourself," she replied, choosing a table at the far end of the hall near the windows. She opened her juice and took a sip. "The photo?" she asked again.

"It's en route. Do you really need it when you have the other?"

"Maybe not," she admitted. "What branch of the government do you work for?"

He didn't respond.

"So this case is not a sexual assault? Or are you investigating some senator committing heinous serial murders on prostitutes that he's paid for with federal tax funds?"

The slightest of smiles from him, and she thought: not just a sense of humor, but a warped sense of humor. She was tempted to make a joke about looking for bugs in her room, but decided now wasn't the time, and so she finished her yogurt, drank down her juice, then took her coffee and apple with her. "Ready when you are."

He gave a slight tip of his head, then held out his hand, indicating she should precede him.

Down in the basement hallway, their footsteps echoed. She stopped at the door, waited for him to unlock it, stepped in, moved directly to her sketch while he secured the door behind them. And finally she had to ask. "Why all the secrecy?"

He leaned against the door, crossing his arms, saying nothing. Which was when she noticed that unlike her, he was armed.

"Wait, I know," she said, picking up her pencil, eyeing her sketch. "If you told me, you'd have to kill me."

"Actually," he said, "if we told you, someone else might kill you."

She looked up to see if he was joking.

Apparently he wasn't.

Chapter Four

Sydney examined the sketch pad, the nearly finished drawing. She'd been sitting in this damned room for the last couple of hours, and the autopsy photo had yet to materialize. Still, Sydney doubted she'd need it. The original crime scene photo contained the necessary elements such as the hair, and she made a rough sketch on a separate sheet of paper. She'd complete it from that—wanted to complete it from that, as anything was better than looking at the crime scene photo, the memory of which was bound to stay with her far too long.

Her cell phone vibrated. Thinking it was probably Tasha returning her call, she pulled it from her belt, saw her ex, Scotty Ryan's number showing on the screen, then looked over at Griffin to see if he would object.

"Who is it?" he asked.

"My boyfriend. He's an agent out of HQ," she said, figuring Griffin was in the business, and undoubtedly knew she meant the Washington, D.C., office.

"I was under the impression the two of you had broken up."

"Delving a bit on the personal side, aren't you?"

"This is a sensitive case."

"So what *do* you know about me?" she asked, ignoring Scotty's call for now.

"You're thirty-three, five-nine, brown hair, blue eyes—"

"Besides the obvious?"

"You were a cop in Sacramento for eight years before joining the Bureau four years ago. According to SAC Harcourt, you're one of the best forensic artists the Bureau has. You transferred from Washington, D.C., to San Francisco when you and your boyfriend broke up, and you were recently looking into your father's murder, which took place twenty years ago. His murder case is why you took the transfer back to D.C."

"Maybe I should have asked if there was anything about me you *don't* know."

"Red wine or white."

His answer surprised her, and she was tempted to quip that apparently he hadn't seen her and Tasha drinking the other night, or he'd know it was red. Instead, she merely stared at him, noted there was actually a spark of amusement in his previously unreadable gaze, and it wasn't until her phone vibrated again that she was able to look away. "I need to take this call. Scotty's a little on the possessive side. But then you probably already know that if you've done a complete background."

As quick as that spark appeared, it was gone. "*Nothing* about this case."

Sydney ignored him, flipped open the phone. "Hey, Scotty."

"I called your mom's house, and she said you were already back at Quantico. Are you okay?"

"Just a crime sketch. I'm flying back to my Mom's this afternoon."

"I mean about Tasha."

"What are you talking about?"

"The hit-and-run."

Sydney stilled, felt her heart beat several times as she absorbed what she was hearing. "*What?*"

"I figured you knew, why you flew back to D.C. It was in the papers. She was crossing the street and—"

"Oh my God," she said, since that was all she could think to say.

"I'm sorry, Sydney. I know you were good friends."

"I can't believe it…"

He was quiet for a moment, then, "Call me when you're done. I'll pick you up, and you can decide what you want to do."

"Thank you…"

He disconnected, and she closed her phone, staring at it, unable to believe any of this was real. They'd just gone out drinking…

And then it hit her. That's why Griffin had handed over a set of notes that weren't included in a finished report. Tasha had been killed before she'd been able to complete it. It was also why Tasha wasn't present, because she would've insisted on being here.

What was it Griffin had said to Sydney, why they'd refused to tell her what was going on? Because someone would kill her if she knew…

She spun around in her chair, looked right at him, very much aware that he'd heard the entire conversation, knew that she knew. "How dare you keep me in the dark about my friend's death."

"This case takes priority."

"Was Tasha killed because of it?"

"At this time, we have no proof that there is any connection."

"And being that it's a hit-and-run, how would you know?"

He didn't answer.

She turned away in anger and disgust, closing her eyes against the pain and confusion. Was it her fault her friend was dead? Sydney had recommended Tasha. She was—had been—one of the best forensic anthropologists on the east coast. But if she was killed because of the case, then it stood to reason that anyone Sydney might have recommended would have come to the same fate…"Were you aware of the danger in this?"

"Not all of it."

It was said with such quiet conviction that she believed him. "Then why keep it from me?"

"Because we had to reevaluate. If Dr. Gilbert was killed because of this case, then we had to protect anyone else we had working on the identification. You think you were followed on your run this morning? If you were, it was by someone who can gain access to these grounds. Someone who knew we were bringing the skull to Quantico. You can understand why I didn't want to involve yet another artist. And why we let you go home to San Francisco to preserve the illusion that you were not connected to the case at all."

"Hence the private jet to bring me back?"

"Exactly."

And that she could appreciate. Because if someone came after her, they could certainly do it while she was visiting her family. "I need a few minutes, if you don't mind."

Griffin hesitated. "I'm sorry about your friend."

She nodded, waited until she heard the door close behind him, then stared at the skull through a blur of tears, wishing that Tasha had left for her dig in Italy a week earlier.

By the time Griffin returned about fifteen minutes later, she had composed herself enough to attempt finishing the Jane Doe sketch. Pencil poised over paper, she suddenly doubted herself and her hurried sketch of the victim's hair. "I need to see the crime scene photo one more time before I finish."

He picked up the briefcase, unlocked it, removed the folder, set it on the table in front of her. She opened the folder, tried to force her gaze past the woman's visage to the surroundings, everything she needed to remember. It was not an easy task. Look at any photo of a person, and one's gaze is drawn to the face. Look at a photo where the face has been savagely removed, and it's just as hard not to stare at where the face is supposed to be.

But do it she must. An ID of Jane Doe was imperative, assuming that Jane Doe's killer had also killed Tasha. Eyeing the photo, and making a few tentative strokes on the paper, Sydney tried to mentally take in everything from the obvious to the not so obvious. She noted what the victim wore, blue jeans and a zippered sweatshirt. She noted the ground, the neatly manicured lawn, and more importantly the absence of snow, which, if the murder had occurred in this area, meant it was at least a week or more ago. To the right of the victim was what looked like the base of an old-fashioned streetlamp, black iron, and beyond that the corner of a building made of massive blocks of hewn stone that, other than the reddish color, reminded her of the historic brownstones seen in the New York area.

"How much longer?" he asked.

"Almost done."

She finished up the hair, another ten minutes to get the basics, try to emulate the style she presumed the woman would've worn, judging from what she could tell in the photo, what wasn't matted in congealed blood. Brunette. She'd been a brunette. After that it was simply shading to give the sketch depth and realism. An hour later she was done.

"All yours," she said, eyeing the sketch of the young woman she'd drawn, and then the skull. She lifted the vellum from her sketch pad, the drawing of the skull beneath it, then held up the vellum sheet with the actual sketch on it, to size up the real skull behind her rendering. It fit. When she held up the sketch pad so that Griffin could view the drawing, he looked at it. And had she not been watching his face, she might have missed the flash of emotion. Guilt, maybe even pain. He knows this girl, she thought, but just as quickly as that look appeared, it was gone, and she couldn't help but wonder who the girl was, where she had been found.

And who killed her?

Sydney knew better than to ask. Instead she handed the sketch on vellum to the agent, and then the skull drawing from her sketch pad.

"I'll need the entire sketch pad," he said.

She didn't bother to ask why. She knew. They were taking no chances that she might be able to reproduce the sketch at a later date using any sort of technology that might enhance what was compressed on the pages beneath. She simply flipped through the sketchbook, made sure there was nothing written on the other pages, then handed that over to him as well.

"You worried about the pencil?" she asked.

"Feel free to keep it."

"Gee, thanks."

"But I'll need the notepad."

She slid the yellow lined tablet next to the crime scene photo and the skull. "All yours," she said, dropping her pencil into her drawing briefcase, which, unlike his, didn't lock.

She phoned Scotty the moment she was out of the basement and up in her room, keeping the call brief. She was finished, and he could come pick her up. She packed, took her overnight bag and briefcase, turned in her key, retrieved her gun from the guard, then looked at her watch. Scotty wouldn't be there for another forty-five minutes. So instead of sitting patiently in the reception area waiting for him, she walked to the outdoor range, trying to stay in the sun where the snow had melted and the path was clear.

The range master put her at the end of a group of recruits who, judging from the coins atop their weapons as they stood poised to fire, were honing their breathing and trigger-pull skills. The coin would be knocked off with the recoil of each shot. But it also meant the range master had loaded the magazines with one or two dummy rounds somewhere in the fifteen live rounds, and the recruits had no idea what order. If the recruit was firing with proper trigger pull, breathing, etc., when he reached the dummy round, whether it was the first, third, or fifteenth round, the penny would remain atop the weapon when he pulled the trigger, quite simply because no shot had been fired. More often than not, the coins jumped, because the recruits anticipated the shot and recoil, then jumped themselves—one of the primary reasons for bad shooting.

Sydney focused on her own target hanging at twenty-five yards. She needed this after working on the Jane Doe sketch. It was mentally taxing enough doing a drawing under ordinary circumstances, but there was nothing ordinary about this case. Her friend had been killed, quite possibly because of this case. And beyond that, there was a young woman with a triangle carved where her face was supposed to be. A young woman who was nameless, who could no longer tell anyone what had happened. In concert with the other investigators, Sydney's job as a forensic artist was to speak for the dead, give them the voice to help discover who they were, and in the case of homicide, who had killed them. The sketch of her Jane Doe was so clear in her mind. Maybe too clear, perhaps because of Tasha's death… Anger surged through her about being kept in the dark over that, and she knew she needed to expunge it if she was to think with a clear head. Just breathe in the cold air. Calm. Right now she needed calm.

Calm and some damned answers, she thought, firing off two rounds, then deciding the other thirteen needed to go as well. She emptied the magazine, reloaded, then concentrated on her target, knowing it would do her more harm than good to let any anger get the best of her. The target swayed slightly as the other recruits shot, but Sydney stared ahead, raised her weapon, and cleared her mind. There was something meditative about outdoor range practice, focusing your gaze on the front sight and aligning it with the target. Evening out your breathing, then gently pulling, pulling, hearing the slightest of clicks before the gun went off. And if you did it right, you barely heard the report of your weapon, or any other weapon out there. Nothing but you, the target, and the slow, even pull of the trigger. Just breathe in the cold air. Calm.

But there was no calm for her. She had to know if Tasha's death was related. And to do that, she thought as she walked to the cleaning station to begin the process of field stripping her weapon, she had to know who Jane Doe was, and then who killed her.

She was wiping the cleaning oil from each piece, reassembling it, when who should walk up but Mr. Federal himself, Special Agent Griffin. "We have a plane available to take you home."

She glanced at him, deciding it would do little good to unleash her anger on him. "Not going home yet," she said, holding out the barrel of her semiauto so she could look down inside, make sure there was no residue, before dropping it in place. "My ex is picking me up. But feel free to take the plane yourself. You could use a vacation."

"Your ex can't make it."

She looked at him. Saw he was serious. "And why not?"

"Bank robbery. Suspects are holed up in the surrounding area, may have hostages."

She decided that he was telling the truth, dismissed the absurd thought he'd set up the robbery as part of some plot to get her on that plane. "Guess I'll catch a ride into the capital and wait for him to get off. Sometimes you have to go the extra mile for a chance at true love."

"And sometimes love is really, really blind."

"What's that supposed to mean?"

"I've met your ex. He's not your type."

She laughed. Not kindly, either. "And how would you know?"

"Your plane is waiting."

"To hell with the plane. I'm not getting on it."

"That your target?" He nodded at the bull's-eye on the table next to her. Every round but one was in the Ten X.

"What's it to you?"

"I beat you, you get on the plane."

She said nothing, merely finished the reassembly. "And if I beat you?" she asked, pointing her weapon into the clearing barrel, slapping in a fully loaded magazine and pulling the slide back to load it.

"Then I'll take you where you need to go."

"Sorry. I don't play games. But have fun." She holstered her weapon, smiled, and walked off.

He followed her back to the main building's reception area. She ignored him, until he said, "I'm driving past your place, if that's where you're headed."

"Actually, I'm going to wait for Scotty at his place."

"I'm driving past there, too."

"Why am I not surprised?"

"I'll bring the car to the front." He walked off, and the only reason she didn't stop him was that one could learn quite a bit when sequestered in a car together. Assuming she could get him to talk.

Ten minutes later, Sydney saw his gold Ford Crown Victoria pull up. She walked out into the bracing cold, carrying both her briefcase and overnight bag. A dark-haired man stood off at the distance, smoking, well away from the building per government regulations, his arms tucked close as though warding off the chill. He watched her walk over to the car until a group of young female recruits strolled past, giving him something better to look at apparently.

Zachary Griffin got out, walked around and opened the rear door, allowing her to put both her briefcase and overnight bag in the back, then opened the front door for her.

"A gentleman after all."

"There are a few of us left."

Once they'd driven past the Marine stationed at the gate, she said, "I'm assuming you know where he lives?"

"Vaguely."

"You mind filling me in on why all the secrecy? The background?"

"The case is important. We needed to know that everyone involved could be trusted."

"Thought that was why the Bureau did the backgrounds before they hired us."

"People change."

The conversation ended there, and they drove in silence. About ten minutes later, her phone vibrated. Carillo. "Hey," she said, answering.

"Not only is your guy *not* with the Bureau, but any record of whatever you're working on? Your Jane Doe? It's not there. Like you're not even in Quantico right now."

"So I'm beginning to find out." She kept her gaze straight ahead, tried to keep her voice conversational, pleasant as they sped past the barren trees, the gray winter sky.

"Can you say OGA?"

OGA stood for Other Government Agency. Only problem was that term ran the gamut, and if there was one thing the government had, it was lots of agencies and shadow agencies, some above board, some so far undercover that even the legit agencies didn't know they existed. "I'd rather not."

"I'm thinking CIA, but I haven't gotten a verification on that yet. Can't get shadier than them. When you coming back to your mother's?"

"Tomorrow. I'm spending the night at Scotty's."

A long pause followed. "Fine. It's your life. Just don't forget he's no good for you."

"One of our friends was killed in a car accident."

"Oh."

"Gotta go." She eyed Griffin as she tucked the phone on her belt. "You don't work for the Bureau."

"Never said I did."

"But you never denied it."

"No one asked."

And she had to agree, it had only been implied. "You were willing to let me believe you worked for us."

"Why do I get the feeling we picked the wrong forensic artist?"

"A little late for that direction." She crossed her arms, trying to figure out what agency he possibly worked for.

"Everything in your background that we conducted alluded to you being…compliant. The sort who doesn't ask questions."

"Well, like you said about backgrounds. People change."

"In a couple months?"

"Trust me," she said, trying to rein in her anger, since it would do her little good to get on his bad side. "It was a hellish couple months. So, what are you? CIA?"

"That bothers you?"

"Uptight as you are, Secret Service fits better. Presidential detail."

He glanced over at her, then back at the road, signaling for a lane change. "I used to work for them."

"Figures."

A slight smile creased the corners of his mouth, but then just as quickly faded back to the staid, unexpressive personality he'd exhibited throughout their short tenure at Quantico. Definitely a Company man.

◇◇◇

Zach Griffin glanced over at Sydney Fitzpatrick. It would've been better had she returned to San Francisco, so that no one would suspect she'd been working on the case. Then again, maybe it was just as well. Keep a better eye on her here. Find out what she knew or suspected. She'd said nothing the last ten minutes, just watched the passing scenery, no doubt grieving for her friend. Unfortunately, he'd been ordered not to tell her, even though he'd argued that her compliance might be greater if she knew the risks up front. Now she had even more reason to distrust them, and she didn't know the half of it.

He turned his attention back to the rearview mirror, saw the smoke-gray Honda. He'd watched it for the last dozen miles, thinking about how Fitzpatrick had said she was followed on her run this morning. He wondered if the Honda was a tail, a bad one, or if he was just being his usual paranoid self.

Turned out he wasn't the only paranoid one, because Fitzpatrick nodded toward the mirror. "Either that gray Honda's been following us the last fifteen minutes, or the driver's got some obsessive-compulsive complex that requires he stay exactly two cars behind us."

"Or," he said, "the car we're in looks like any other unmarked police car, and he's worried about getting a ticket."

"He'd be inching up on us if that were the case. Peeking into the window to find out if we really were cops." She was quiet a few seconds, then, "So what sort of case is this that you have people following you when you leave Quantico?"

He wasn't about to answer that, but he decided to find out if they were in fact being followed and he pulled behind a particularly slow motor home. The Honda swept past, and he noted the license number as well as the physical description of the dark-haired male who drove. He continued trailing the motor home, right up until his exit, satisfied that no other vehicle seemed to be tailing them.

Then again, if someone knew where he was headed, there was no reason to tail him, a point brought home as he made a left turn toward the office, stopped at a red light—directly behind said Honda. Fitzpatrick crossed her arms, glanced over at him. "Now what?"

"On the off chance this guy is part of a tail, I don't think you want me dropping you off at your ex's place until we lose him. How about we stop for coffee first?"

"Coffee works for me."

The light turned green. The Honda continued through. Griffin made a hard right, took several more evasive turns, all with no idea if the vehicle was or wasn't following. For him it was just in case. Old habits die hard. When he was certain he was in the clear, he pulled into a driveway of a nondescript warehouse, then hit a remote control on his visor. A bay door opened and he drove into an enclosed garage, the door closing as he pulled in. "Get your things," he said. "We'll be changing cars after we get our coffee."

Fitzpatrick made no comment, merely got out, opened the back door, and took her possessions.

He popped the trunk, gathered his briefcase and bag, then slammed the lid shut, hanging the keys on a wall hook. "This way," he said. She followed him to an innocuous-looking scarred and battered door at the rear of the bay, bearing a sign that read "Janitorial Supplies." He lifted the air-conditioning thermostat cover set in the wall adjacent to the door, revealing a biometric scanner and keypad. He placed his right index finger to the scanner, then punched in his code. The door buzzed open, three inches of solid steel.

Fitzpatrick eyed the door, then him. "Must be some damned good coffee you keep in there."

He indicated she should precede him, and she stepped through the threshold, onto the top landing of a stairwell, the steps faintly lit by unseen lights at the base of the walls. At the bottom, a brick tunnel stretched off in either direction, and the same base lighting illuminated the concrete floor.

"Which way?" she asked as they neared the bottom.

"Turn right. My office is the second door down. The one marked 'High Voltage.'"

"How apropos," she muttered. The rumbling of a passing Metro subway train reverberated through the walls, then quickly faded. "Why not just walk in the front door?"

"After the tail, I'd rather not take a chance."

"And this door?" she asked as they passed one that was unmarked.

"A convoluted exit into the Metro. Comes in handy sometimes."

The "High Voltage" door appeared just as unassuming as the garage bay door, until it, too, was opened, revealing the several inches of solid gleaming steel. The small space looked like any high-voltage electrical room. The only voltage within, however, was the hidden biometric keypad in one of the boxes, which once engaged, caused the back wall to slide open, revealing a normal-looking elevator. They stepped in, the door slid shut, and up they went. It stopped on the fifth floor of his building. "My office," he said.

She looked around, taking in the monotonous off-white walls, standard industrial linoleum flooring. "I give. Where are we?"

"The *Washington Recorder*."

"A newspaper?" She laughed. "Mild-mannered reporter, à la Clark Kent? I thought federal law prohibited intelligence agencies from having cover identities as reporters."

"Reporters from American media. Unlike Clark Kent, I'm not a reporter," he said, pulling a business card from his pocket and handing it to her. "I'm an editor."

"Of course." She looked at the card, which read *International Journal for World Peace.* "Convenient. Offices throughout the world, no doubt?"

"Would you expect anything less? My boss is the publisher. Not that he publishes or I edit."

"A shadow paper."

"Precisely. It just so happens that the *IJWP* rents space from the American newspaper that occupies this building."

"The American paper you rent space from wouldn't also happen to be owned by the agency you work for?"

"We need a place to go to work every day without raising suspicion that we're drug dealers or earning a salary without means of support. Unlike the *IJWP*, our American paper has a staff that fully mans, reports, and publishes on the floors below ours, and we use the AP. A lot."

"So you're a covert operative," she said, walking to the window, looking down to the street below. "Running a paper."

"A *foreign* paper. You'd be surprised what we learn from the letters to the editor." He unlocked his desk, grabbed a set of car keys, then checked the messages his secretary had left for him. When he looked up, he saw Fitzpatrick trying to make a call from her cell phone. "You'll have to use a landline. No signals in, no signals out on this floor." He pushed the telephone toward her.

She picked it up, punched in a number. "Hey, Scotty," she said, then listened to whatever it was her ex told her. "Yeah, I've still got a key. Be careful." She hung up, looked at him, her expression unreadable. "He's still out on the robbery. They've holed themselves up somewhere in the downtown area."

"Hostages?"

"Only one bank teller, and she escaped when they tried dragging her into their car."

"Lucky for her," he said, picking up the inside line to call his secretary and let her know he was back. "Done. We deliver the briefcase, then we're out of here."

They stopped for a cup of coffee in the break room, then, coffee in hand, continued on to the director's office. Griffin knocked, waited for the "come in," then opened the door. His boss, Ron Nicholas McNiel III, was talking to one of Griffin's team members, James "Tex" Dalton. Griffin introduced Fitzpatrick to both men.

Tex stood, and with his usual shit-eating grin, said to Fitzpatrick, "You doing anything tonight?"

"She's visiting her boyfriend," Griffin said.

"Doesn't hurt to ask."

Fitzpatrick smiled at Tex. "If plans change, I'll let you know."

"You do that, darlin'," Tex said, laying on a thick drawl he used to impress the ladies. Like many on Griffin's team, Tex spoke several languages, but with an added skill of having accents down to an art. He'd recently finished a stint in the Boston area. No one could've told he wasn't Boston born and bred.

"We should be going," Griffin said, then directed Sydney toward the door.

"Zach?" his boss called out. "Have a minute?"

Fitzpatrick gave a neutral smile. "I'll wait out here."

Griffin stepped back in, shut the door.

"They recovered the car that ran over Tasha Gilbert. It matches the description of the vehicle that hit Dr. Balraj's car a couple weeks ago. They're doing an analysis on the paint transfer. The color matches."

"So she was targeted by the same people?"

"So it seems. Why Tasha, though? She has absolutely no connection to Balraj or his assistant."

A good question, Griffin thought. Dr. Balraj was a microbiologist who was working on the evolution of plagues. On the day in question, Balraj had lent his car to his assistant, who later died in a solo car wreck after the car allegedly blew a tire and went off an embankment and into the river.

At least that was the official story released.

The real story was not for public consumption. There was no doubt that Balraj was the real target, but it wouldn't do the public any good to know that someone was picking off the world's foremost scientists one by one, especially when those scientists were known for their work in biowarfare research. As to who was doing it, a print found at the scene of one of the murdered scientists had been matched to a suspect they knew worked for Carlo Adami, an American crime boss based in Italy.

Unfortunately, Adami had the man killed before they could prove a connection in any court of law.

"Any word on Balraj?" Griffin asked.

McNiel's secretary called on the intercom before he could answer. "Congressman Hoagland's on the phone."

"Put the call through," McNiel said. When his extension rang, he said, "Martin, what can I do for you...? No, sir, we do not believe there is any truth to the rumor that Alessandra was having an affair with Congressman Burnett...No, we haven't heard from her yet, but I'm sure we will, soon. Yes, sir, I do agree that it's best to clear his name. We are looking into that, but at this point, it won't help matters to bring it out in the open..."

To which Tex whispered to Griffin, "Clear his name my ass. Hoagland would like nothing better than to publicly humiliate him and gain the chair when Burnett resigns."

Griffin wasn't interested in politics at the moment. "What about Balraj?" he asked Tex. "Anything else on that investigation?"

"We don't know if he's been kidnapped or killed, but knowing Adami, I'd have to guess the latter."

"So much for hope," Griffin said, not that they'd ever held much. He'd been in this business far too long to think that Balraj's fate would be different from that of the other microbiologists who'd been murdered. The only consolation—if one could call it that in a twisted sort of way—was that it was because of Dr. Balraj that they'd found Alessandra's body. After his assistant had been killed, two agents were assigned to watch Balraj. They'd lost him somewhere in the vicinity of the Smithsonian, and it was during their search for the microbiologist that they'd found Alessandra—and why they'd been able to keep her murder from the police and the press.

Griffin looked down at his briefcase, thinking about the forensic sketch within. Alessandra had never told them about any meeting with Dr. Balraj—they couldn't even imagine a reason why she would have contacted him—and so it took them quite some time before they realized she was missing and the body might have been hers. But now, thanks to Sydney Fitzpatrick, there were no doubts…

"Of course, sir," McNiel said into the phone. "We'll put every effort into the investigation." He slammed the phone into the receiver. "Congressman Hoagland is a pompous idiot." He leaned back in his chair, eyed Griffin. "You have the sketch?"

Griffin opened the briefcase and took out the drawing.

Tex saw it as he pulled it out. "Hell."

Griffin laid the sketch on McNiel's desk, and he saw the moment of recognition, the pulse pounding in his neck. "Sometimes I hate this job," McNiel said. "Alessandra. And now Tasha."

"What about this third key that Tasha mentioned?"

McNiel turned the drawing face down. "With what we can gather from the chatter we've picked up, our best guess is that the third key is some code for a new super-plague that Adami's scientists are working on. I'd have to guess that's why he's hell-bent on killing off anyone in the business."

To which Tex said, "Knock off the competition and the possibility that anyone can counteract whatever the hell his scientists are coming up with."

"Exactly," McNiel said. "All the more reason to concentrate on finding his lab, which, thanks to Tasha, we know isn't in Egypt." He looked at Griffin. "After you notify Alessandra's father, *that* is your main objective. Find his lab, destroy it."

"Understood."

McNiel straightened a stack of papers on his desk, clearly bothered by the drawing, and doing his best not to show it. "I'm afraid it's public transportation en route. Tex will be using the jet as part of his cover. Marilee has your ticket on her desk," he said, referring to his secretary. "And speaking of planes, I thought this artist of yours was to be on a plane back to San Francisco, not on a private tour of our building."

"She had other plans."

"That wasn't part of *our* plan. I agreed to her involvement because she played by the book, which made her predictable and compliable. Someone who would do as she was told, and not ask questions."

"What we didn't count on was someone calling her and informing her that her friend was killed in a hit-and-run." It was as close as he would ever come to telling his boss, *I told you so,* about keeping her in the dark over Tasha's death. "Short of hogtieing her, I didn't think it wise to force the issue. She's already asking questions. And that was before her partner told her I was CIA."

Tex laughed. "CIA?"

Their boss threw Tex a dark look, then tapped the drawing of Alessandra. "This forensic artist. Do you think she's made any connections?"

"That's exactly what I intend to find out." Griffin turned to Tex. "You busy? I might need your skills in the next hour or so."

Chapter Five

Sydney unbuckled her seatbelt when Zach Griffin double-parked his black Chevy Tahoe in front of Scotty's apartment building with the confidence of someone who wasn't worried about traffic tickets. "Thanks for the lift," she said, sliding out, then hauling the straps of her bag and drawing case over her shoulder.

He lowered the passenger window after she shut the car door. "If you need anything, day or night, my cell is on the business card."

She gave a small wave, then turned toward the building. The doorman opened the heavy glass door, and she walked in, taking the elevator to the third floor. Once inside, she threw her things on the couch, then called the D.C. field office to have the secretary let Scotty know she was going to borrow his personal car.

"He just came in for a quick break," the secretary said. "I'll put you through."

"Catch the bank robbers?" Syd asked him when he answered his phone.

"They're holed up on the south side, and MPDC's doing a door-to-door search right now. They called us the moment it went down. Some serious shit going on. They were armed with assault rifles. I'm thinking Russian mafia, if the accents are any clue."

"Any leads?"

"Why? You coming down to volunteer your time on the case?"

"No. But if I get bored, maybe I could borrow your personal car. Mine's still at the airport."

"Keys are on the kitchen counter...You doing okay?"

"Yeah, thanks. Have you heard anything about the funeral?"

"I believe her parents are having her body shipped home. I was thinking...if I get off in time, I'll take you to dinner?"

"Sure," she said, hoping that he had no illusions about making it anything more than what it was. Scotty had always entertained the idea that their breakup was only temporary, which was partially Sydney's fault, because she hadn't wanted to hurt him, and in the end, she'd had to do just that. "Scotty, you do realize—"

"Hate to cut this short, Syd, but they're signaling me. SWAT's getting ready to move in. Love you."

He hung up, and she stood there, staring at the phone, his "love you" echoing in her mind, making her think she shouldn't have come here after all. There was a time when she used to be like him, black and white, by the book. It was why she'd fallen for him. She always knew where she stood with Scotty. Life was predictable.

When they'd lived together, that was precisely what she'd needed. Structure and order. He'd been good for her at a time when she'd needed it. Back then she would've never questioned the government's need for secrecy about a forensic sketch. And, as Griffin had indicated, that was probably why they'd chosen her out of the several forensic artists they used around the country. It was probably stamped across her files, maybe even across her forehead, her belief that if the government needed her to know, they'd tell her.

Just like a good little FBI agent destined for promotion.

Now that seemed like a world away, a lifetime ago. A time when she'd believed that there was a clear demarcation between the good guys and the bad guys.

Back before she knew many of the details of her father's murder. But she wasn't about to let the past cloud her judgment, and right now, she had to admit that there was something suspicious about Zachary Griffin. She called Carillo. "You find anything else on this guy?"

"Didn't we just talk? I've got cases, you know."

"What's more important? Your caseload, or my curiosity?" Phone to her ear, she walked over to the kitchen, looked around for Scotty's car keys. "Are you saying you haven't even heard what this guy did for the Agency?"

"They weren't exactly forthcoming when I tried to inquire. Not to worry. You remember that PI friend of mine, helped me solve that case a while back? Dan Randolph of the Randolph Investigative Group?"

"Used to be a cop in the central valley."

"Yeah, him. Might have almost as many connections as Doc Schermer does. Turns out he knows someone at DOJ, who knows someone at CIA, who told him that your guy was involved in the investigation of a bunch of microbiologists who had died suspiciously all within a few weeks of each other. Taken randomly one could dismiss the suicides, plane crashes, and a couple murders. Considering they all occurred within a few weeks after 9/11, it smacks of conspiracy, and even though it was played down in the press, his agency felt it needed looking into. Couple that with the fact that no one keeps better tabs on every microbiologist on the face of the earth than the CIA does, and it tells me he was at least, at that time, with them. He still with you?"

"Dropped me off at Scotty's. I need to schedule a flight home and I might just go out to grab some lunch."

"You want something more than the peanut butter Scotty keeps as a staple?"

"Aren't you the funny one. Call me if you hear anything else on this guy."

"Good luck with the lunch thing."

"Thanks."

She hung up, switched on Scotty's computer to schedule a flight home, then arrange to have flowers sent to Tasha's parents in Kansas. The moment she did, she was tempted to look up any news articles on Tasha's hit-and-run, as well as any Jane Does found in the area in the last couple of weeks. But then she talked herself out of it. She knew the risks. She'd gone that route before—getting involved in something best left alone—and had nearly gotten her family, her young sister killed in the process...

Besides, maybe Tasha's death had nothing to do with the case.

Her gaze swept over the computer screen. What could be the harm in just looking? Seeing what sort of information might show up on the hit-and-run? No. She wouldn't do it. She didn't trust herself enough. Not after the danger she'd dragged to her very doorstep while looking into her father's murder...Scotty's web browser home page was set to the metro area news. There was the typical uprising in the Middle East, the current breaking-news hunt for the bank robbery suspects, a married CEO from a top Fortune 500 company apologizing for his inappropriate affair with a college student, and the latest stock news.

After a quick scan of the headlines, she perused the flights home, trying to decide between a late morning and an early afternoon flight. She needed to decide how much time she was willing to spend with Scotty, and wondered if she should settle for a red-eye flying out tonight.

What she should have done was accept the free flight home that Griffin offered, then she wouldn't be sitting here trying to decide, while her stomach protested that she hadn't had a bite since breakfast. She got up to find something to eat. Just as Carillo guessed, peanut butter and jelly was all Scotty seemed to have in the house. Some things never changed, she thought, staring out the window, absently pulling the crust from her sandwich. A light sprinkle misted the sidewalk and slush piles below, the few pedestrians rushing to their destinations in case it turned into a real rain.

She liked this neighborhood, and for a moment she contemplated the idea of finding an apartment somewhere nearby—once she finally got around to actually looking. She'd lived here a short time with Scotty before they'd broken up, and she missed the area, the older tree-lined street, the Heavenly Java coffee shop on one corner and Raja's Star of India restaurant on the other. In the summertime, you couldn't see the sidewalk through the trees, but in the winter, with nary a leaf in sight, there was a clear view up and down the street. Peaceful, she thought, biting into her sandwich as a telephone utility truck pulled up, double-parked in front of the building.

Maybe she could convince Scotty to move, let her have this place. In her selfish dreams, she thought, watching as two workmen got out, placed safety cones on either side of the work truck, then started unloading what looked like phone repair equipment from the back. Losing interest in the view, she returned to the computer, deciding she'd go late morning, sort of a compromise. Just enough time for breakfast and little else.

Absorbed in her search, she heard Scotty's telephone ring on the desk beside her. "Hello," she said, noting the number from the caller ID read "Restricted."

"It's Zach Griffin."

"What a surprise."

"Just wondering how you're doing."

She eyed the flight times on the computer screen, looking for late morning. "Well, aren't you the concerned federal agent. I'm doing great. So why are you really calling?"

"Just wanted to remind you, this case is not for public consumption."

"And here I was thinking of holding a press conference. Thanks for the reminder."

She heard his laughter as she disconnected, and she was bothered by something she couldn't quite place. She stared at the telephone. Scotty's number was unlisted. She hadn't given it to Griffin, and he wasn't FBI, so how'd he get it? He would've called her cell phone, should've called it. She got up, walked to the window, saw the men in the phone truck packing up. It was either the fastest phone repair in history, or the CIA, or OGA, or whoever the hell they were, had just installed listening devices in Scotty's building, and Griffin had just called to see if they were working.

Sydney watched until the phone truck disappeared from view, trying to stay calm. To hell with calm. She used her cell phone to call the police department, the traffic investigations unit, asked the particulars on Tasha's case, discovered there were no leads, nor was there anything that made them think it was anything but a "run-of-the-mill hit-and-run." If it had been "run-of-the-mill," why had Griffin not said something about working from the notes because the forensic anthropologist had been killed in a car accident, and the report hadn't been finished?

Because she and Tasha had been friends? There had to be more to it than that.

She paced the room, told herself that she needed to think logically about this. But there was no logic. Griffin, ergo the government, had gone to great pains to keep Sydney in the dark, allegedly to protect her, even though she was a federal agent, armed and trained, better equipped to handle the dangers of whatever cluster they'd thrust her in the midst of. But what about Tasha Gilbert, a woman whose passion was old bones? What protection had they offered her by keeping her in the dark? If this case was so damned dangerous they couldn't even let Sydney know what was going on, what business did they have letting an anthropologist walk around unprotected so that she could be hit by a car?

Anger anew over her friend's death spurred her back to the computer. She had recommended Tasha for this case. Tasha knew her, *trusted* her. The least Sydney could do was repay that trust and make sure that Tasha's killers were brought to justice.

Having lost her appetite, she tossed what was left of her sandwich in the trash. The best way to solve Tasha's murder was to find out who their Jane Doe was. Between the sudden call out, the government involvement and secrecy, the surveillance, and now Tasha's death, there was no doubt in Sydney's mind that the murder of this Jane Doe was connected.

She tried looking for the girl's identity on the internet, but came up with too many hits of missing young women. A better lead might be trying to figure out the location of that crime scene photo she used in her drawing, where the victim had been found. She tried to remember the details. The girl's clothing had been unremarkable. No help there. Too bad there hadn't been more of the building and streetlamp to make an accurate guess of where the crime scene was located, but she doubted that Griffin was about to pull out a full crime scene shot for her benefit.

Everything about the locale had appeared old. Not just old, but historic, right down to the cast-iron lamppost. Plenty of reproductions like that in this area alone, so she doubted that would clue her in. The building definitely had an old feel to it, with the large red blocks of stones, very similar to the brown-stones commonly used in the northeast. She returned to the computer, typed in "red stone buildings" and the first site that came up was titled "A Web Gallery of Stone Buildings and Their Building Stone."

The site showed not only the photos of the structures, but also close-ups of the stones used. She scrolled down, paused about midway at the description of "red sandstone" and felt fairly certain the paragraph described the stones in the building she'd seen. At the bottom of the page was a "Related Links" section. She clicked on "Building Stones of Maryland," a logical guess since she'd been flown to the east coast to do the drawing, which told her the victim was probably from this area. Or the crime scene was in this area. Tasha's death had certainly been in this area, she thought, leaning back in her chair and focusing on the screen.

Seneca red sandstone was listed, and she read how that very sandstone had been used in 1847 to build the Smithsonian Institution Building in Washington, D.C. She typed "Smithsonian buildings" into the search bar. The official Web site popped up, one announcing their latest displays: Campana collection on loan from the Louvre, and something about the Holy Crusade. Her crusade was a bit different. It wasn't the collections she cared about. What she wanted to see was the grounds, and she clicked on "Images." A view of the Smithsonian castle came up, and she searched that site and others for close-up photos. There was one of a grassy area with a black streetlamp, a very old-looking black streetlamp...

"Almost too easy," she said, because hell if that didn't look just like the crime scene.

She typed "murder Smithsonian" into the search bar. The only thing that came up was a book someone had written in 1990. Estimating her age, she typed in "murder Washington DC 24 year old woman," and again ended with so many hits, she gave up. But the Smithsonian was as good a start as any, and she pulled open Scotty's printer, removing several sheets of paper from the paper tray, then a pencil from his desk. If she was going to figure out what the hell was going on, why her friend was killed, she'd need a fairly good likeness of the Jane Doe she'd sketched in Quantico. And there were two things in her favor. One, she was a good artist. Two, she had an excellent memory of what she'd already drawn. Now all she had to do was complete another sketch of her Jane Doe.

"For you, Tasha. I'm going to find out who did this."

Chapter Six

Sydney called the D.C. police department from the car. Amber Jacobsen, the records supervisor, was a cultivated contact from Syd's days working in the capital. Cultivated because Amber's finger was on the pulse of what was going on in that town, and it always paid to have a friendly face when it came to dealing with the local law enforcement. Sydney had always been careful to reciprocate any favors.

"MPDC, Records, Jacobsen speaking."

"Hey, girl. It's Fitz."

"To what do I owe the honor?"

"I was hoping you might be able to clue me in on any unsolved Jane Does in your area?"

"Not a one that I know of, why?"

"Just handled a forensic sketch, and was curious if the victim came out of your area. It was pretty brutal," she said, and left it at that, since the case was CIA's and she had no idea what was going on with it. She'd already had one friend killed, she didn't need another. "Might have occurred at the Smithsonian or nearby."

"Now that I would've heard about. I'll double check with Dennis, but believe it or not, for D.C., we've been pretty quiet. Well, up until the bank robbery today. Nothing but the usual, and a couple gang killings the past few weeks. Since they're only killing each other, not even the reporters are getting excited. Hey, that's my other line," she added, the phone ringing in the background. "I'll call you if I hear anything on any Jane Doe murders."

"Thanks."

By the time Sydney arrived at the Smithsonian castle parking lot, doubts had hit her about this being the location. The color of the building was right, but surely there would've been some sort of rumor. All doubts fled the moment she saw the building up close. The large blocks of stone looked very much like what she'd seen in the crime scene photo.

She carried two sketches in her soft-sided briefcase, one of the woman's face, the other of what she recalled from the crime scene. It was this one she looked at, trying to get a feel for its location on the property, and she walked around, stopped only once by a security guard who suddenly appeared through a side door from the building. The grounds were undoubtedly monitored, and she was off the beaten path.

The guard was a good six inches taller than her five-nine frame. His uniform shirt was strained at the buttons and at the pants' pockets, as though he'd gained considerable weight since he'd purchased the uniform. His smile was guarded as he looked her over. "May I help you?" He had a slight accent, something eastern European.

She pulled her credentials from her briefcase, held them open for him. "I'm looking into a report that a woman might have been assaulted here, possibly even murdered."

He tucked his thumbs in his belt, shaking his head. "If there was any crime on these grounds, we'd be notified, especially something that serious."

"Nothing in the past few days? Weeks...? Months?" she added when she received no reaction.

"I've only worked here a few weeks. If anything happened before that, I have no idea."

"Mind if I have a look around?"

"You have a card? I'll call my superior, let him know."

She handed him one from her briefcase, then pulled out the sketch of the Jane Doe. "Do you recall ever seeing this woman around here?"

He eyed the sketch, his gaze narrowing as he shook his head. "With so many tourists, it's hard to say. Would you like me to make a copy and ask around?"

"No, thank you."

He held up her card. "But if I think of something, I'll call you."

"I'd appreciate it."

He left and she continued her perusal, definitely at a loss. This appeared to be the crime scene she'd seen in the photo, but if so, it told her little. She stood there, eyeing the lamppost, the red sandstone on the building, but there was nothing that stood out, and she thought of the photo she'd seen in Quantico. She was no homicide detective, though she'd assisted on several serial murders during her few short years with the FBI, and the occasional murder while an officer with Sacramento PD before that. Perhaps that was why she hadn't made the connection to what she *hadn't* seen in the photo. Blood.

It had been there on what was left of the woman's face, to be sure, but head wounds are known to bleed profusely, and the removal of a face from a body was bound to leave some blood evidence, if not massive amounts of blood evidence.

Which meant the woman had been killed elsewhere.

Sydney walked around a bit, finally ending up at the front of the building, with the distinct feeling that someone was watching her. She looked up, saw a tall, dark-haired priest eyeing her, a look of curiosity on his face, perhaps because she was coming from an area where the tourists didn't usually venture. He was standing next to a group of people who were waiting at the entrance to the front of the very building Sydney had been searching around. She glanced at a sign, saw it was a display on the Holy Crusade, which no doubt explained the priest's presence, and when she saw nothing else out of the ordinary, she returned to the parking lot. Okay, think. What would the homicide guys do if they were investigating a Jane Doe murder? Two things, she thought, both of which might help identify the victim. Missing persons reports and towed abandoned vehicles. If someone was missing or dead, she could very well have left a car somewhere, a car that was towed because she failed to return for it. And that could give her a good starting break.

Syd pulled out her cell phone, called Amber Jacobsen at MPDC Records. "You have time to do one other favor for me?"

"Depends. I get off in thirty. My favorite band is playing tonight. Scars on Broadway."

"Hoping this won't take too long. I need info on towed abandoned vehicles in the downtown area."

"Time frame?"

"Last couple weeks, up until now. And if you can tie one of them to a missing person's case, preferably a woman, that's even better."

"Piece of cake. When do you need it?"

"I'm on my way to the PD now."

"I'll have the listing for you when you get here."

"Thanks," she said, then looked up, surprised to see the security guard was standing just a few feet behind her.

"Sorry," he said. "I didn't want to interrupt your call. There's another guard who may have heard something a few nights ago. I thought you might like to come back, perhaps to speak with him."

"Heard what?" she said, standing there, her hand on the car door.

"A man arguing with a woman. A lovers' quarrel."

"Did he say what night this was?"

"Three nights ago, I think. He's tied up at the monitors, and said to come inside to the office and he'll go over the details with you. He thinks it could be what you're looking for."

"Thanks," she said, then tossed her briefcase into the front seat, not wanting to sound too ungrateful, since he had gone to the trouble to check for her. "Unfortunately, I have an appointment. If you could give him my card and have him call me, I'd appreciate it." And she slid into the driver's seat, started the car, then drove off, catching sight of the security guard in her rearview mirror. She dismissed the information he'd given her, not worried about this lovers' quarrel thing, especially if it occurred that recently.

There had been snow on the ground three nights ago, and in the crime scene photo, there was no snow, which meant the murder had occurred sometime before that.

About twenty minutes later, she was walking up the front steps of the Henry J. Daly building of the Metropolitan Police Department. Amber was waiting for her at Records. Petite, she stood about five and a half feet tall, brown hair, blue-green eyes, and a dusting of freckles across her pretty face. She smiled as she held up two stacks of printouts.

"I'm assuming," Amber said, "that you didn't care about any of the normal tows, drunk driving, that sort of thing. Only the unoccupied tows?"

"Good guess."

She tapped the closest stack. "These are tows that were claimed by the registered owners. And these," she said, tapping the second stack, "are for tows that the ROs didn't claim. Not as many, but if you're dealing with a dead registered owner, might explain why they didn't claim their cars?"

"Certainly one explanation." Sydney took the first stack, looking them over. "Don't suppose any of them are actually linked to a missing person?"

"One actually, but to a man, and I thought you were interested in missing women."

"At this point, I'll take anything suspicious."

Amber dug the report off the bottom of the first stack. "Originally it was entered as stolen. I remember it, because the girl came in and gave some convoluted story about people following her boyfriend. One of those truly paranoid types, government plots, tinfoil, the works, but the real story was that she was pissed off because her boyfriend borrowed the car, and he hasn't been seen since. She reported it stolen, but it had really been towed. Boyfriend's still missing, though. As whacked as she was, I'd hazard a bet he took off on purpose."

"Probably nothing, but I'll check it out."

"This one, however," Amber said, removing another report, "was towed a few days ago not two blocks from the Smithsonian. Figured since you were asking about that particular locale, it might fit."

Syd eyed the car's description, a Ford Tempo, then the registered owner, a young woman who lived about ten minutes from the Smithsonian. She thanked Amber, took the reports, and after a quick stop at the ladies' room, headed there first.

A dead end. The car was towed due to "No Parking" signs erected for some road construction, something the owner hadn't caught, because she had been out of town on a business trip. The next several on Syd's list were similar, and the owners present and accounted for. It was dark out now, and she was getting hungry. She looked at the other registered owners, eyeing the tow sheet from the so-called whack job Amber had told her about, a young woman named Penny Dearborn.

Everything about the tow was wrong. From the location, the farthest from the Smithsonian in comparison to all the other cases, and an ex-boyfriend missing, when Syd needed a woman missing. What it did have going for it was that it was somewhat closer to Scotty's apartment, which meant she could swing by, talk to the woman, then wait for Scotty to get back, since she was starved and had no intention of eating peanut butter for dinner.

Penny Dearborn's apartment was dark, at least the upstairs windows. The two downstairs windows were boarded over, and she wondered if anyone still lived there. Sydney parked Scotty's Jeep about two doors down, then walked up the well-lit street. She kept to one side of the front door, knocked, and looked up at the darkened window upstairs. A few moments later, Sydney heard what sounded like footsteps descending an interior staircase, and then the door opened, revealing a tall, thin blond woman with a gaunt face.

Sydney held open her credentials. "Special Agent Fitzpatrick, FBI. Are you Penny Dearborn?"

The woman glanced up and down the street before looking at Sydney, then nodding. "Yeah, why?"

"I have a few questions about your car being towed, and the missing person's report on your boyfriend, Xavier Caldwell."

Penny gave a cynical smile. "Not so paranoid, am I?"

Syd figured that remained to be seen. "Do you mind if I come in?"

Again the woman gave that look up and down the street, then stepped aside allowing Sydney to enter. The room reminded Sydney of her own place, filled with boxes stacked around the walls, some taped shut, others still open, filled with books, newspaper-wrapped items, and other possessions tossed in with less care.

"You're moving?"

"Tomorrow. Which isn't soon enough. I haven't had electricity in two weeks, and I've been broken into twice in the last week, never mind the drive-by shootings from the gang war. Used to be a nice neighborhood. But I have to draw the line when bullets start flying through my living room window," she said, nodding toward the boarded-up windows on either side of the TV. "Goddamn landlord says he's deducting it from my deposit. Bastard."

"I'm hoping this won't take but a couple of minutes."

"Mind if we talk upstairs. I'm a bit paranoid these days…"

"Upstairs is fine." Sydney followed her into a bedroom, unlit, except by the glow from a streetlamp outside. Like the downstairs, this room was filled with boxes stacked around the perimeter of the double bed in the center of the room.

The woman sat on the bed, and Sydney stood near the dresser next to the window that looked out over the street below. "I understand you made a missing person's report on your boyfriend?"

"Not sure why I bothered. I should've figured out what he was up to, ever since he hooked up with Miss Hoity-Toity."

Sydney had the sinking feeling that this was nothing of any consequence. Spurned lover. "What happened?" she asked, more as a way to urge the girl to get on with the story so Sydney could get out of there.

"Happened? Xavier hooks up with this girl from his religion class or political history, or whatever it was, and wants to borrow my car. They're going to go talk to someone about a conspiracy theory," she said in a voice that told Sydney that the only conspiring was that which was taking place in the backseat of said car. "I used to think he was so profound. We'd sit and talk for hours over coffee about how every country's governments were all working to keep the people in the dark, how everything from 9/11 to the Catholic Church was all part of some big conspiracy, just like the conflicts in the Mideast. And then he met *her*. They were in the same class." She looked away, wiped a couple tears from her face with the back of her hand. "And she said she had proof on the back of a dollar bill that it was all being run by shadow governments and the Freemasons."

There were a lot of nuts out there thinking that Freemasons were taking over the world, and the proof was on the back of the dollar bill. Amber undoubtedly had the right of it about this particular case, when she'd put together the reports for Sydney. Whacked. Even so, Syd was sympathetic. The woman had lost her lover to someone who told a better story. "Proof?" Sydney asked. "On the dollar bill?"

"Yeah. Like the eye on the pyramid. And the Star of David that points to the word MASON. He just got all into it. Found his kindred spirit, he says. Hope you don't mind, but it's fate, he says. Fate that he forgets to give me his half of the rent money, and the utility bill. I have no power, no phone, and I got evicted when I couldn't come up with the rent. And then maybe two weeks ago, he calls up and says they're in trouble. That they want to borrow my car again, because he's got to get to the airport, and he thinks they've been following him and her both."

"Who was following them?"

"He didn't say."

"This girl, she have a name?"

"Hell if I know. I never actually met her. She was an assistant to some professor in Xavier's history or archeology class at UVA."

"You know the professor's name?"

"Woods, I think. Anyway, Xavier started meeting her for coffee, just like he used to take me. Only with her, he became twice as paranoid. He actually believed this crap." She sat down on the bed, looking up at the ceiling. "I know it's stupid, and I even used to agree with him, but once he met her, all that stuff he spouted just sounded…annoying. Like a cop-out. Everything that went wrong in his life, he blamed on the government. The fact we got evicted from this apartment? Government plot. His checks kept bouncing, because his deposit was lost? Government plot. All of it proved his point that they were going to take over world banking. At one point he had tinfoil on every window and wouldn't talk without the water running. He let them turn off the phones, because they were tapped. I swear he had escape routes planned," she said, sweeping her hand around the room to point up into the closet, now emptied. "The attic, the bathroom. I couldn't take it any more. It's one thing to rail against the government over coffee, but at some point you still have to pay your rent."

She shrugged, tried to smile, and added, "So I kicked his ass out, got the landlord to give me an extra two weeks to get the rent money together, and what good did that do? Nothing, because I had to use my rent money to get my car out of hock, because that son of a bitch sweet-talked me into borrowing it, then left it parked in a construction zone after he ran off with his new girlfriend. It got towed."

Syd was tempted to tell the woman she was better off without the guy and was almost glad when her cell phone vibrated. Whatever Penny and her boyfriend were about, it wasn't related to her case. "Excuse me," she said, when she saw it was Scotty.

"You ready for dinner?" he asked. "I thought we could meet at King Yen's."

"Can I call you back in a few?" she said, moving away toward the window for a bit of privacy.

"I've already made the reservations."

He'd proposed to her there and, no doubt, had chosen that spot for tonight in hopes that they could discuss their relationship. Her fault, she supposed, for not squelching the dinner thing. That didn't mean she wanted to hurt him, give him any ideas. Unfortunately, this wasn't the time or place to discuss it. "Give me five minutes. I'll call you right back."

"Yeah, sure," he said.

She disconnected, was just tucking her phone on her belt when she noticed a man in a long overcoat looking into the window of Scotty's Jeep parked just down the street. "You get a lot of car thefts in this area?" she asked Penny.

"Don't even get me started on this crappy neighborhood."

The man straightened, started walking up the sidewalk. He was white, clean-shaven, too healthy-looking to match the profile of some dirtbag hoping to smash a car window for a stereo. Even so, Sydney kept her eye on him, then noticed a second man across the street, also in an overcoat, paralleling the first man. The second man started across the street, and she noticed a vertical ridge running down the length of his coat. A ridge about the length of a long barrel of an assault weapon hidden beneath. The momentary thought that these were the missing bank robbers fled when she realized Scotty would not have called her for dinner if the robbers were still out there.

Her gaze flew to the man on this side of the street. The one walking toward Penny Dearborn's front door.

Syd glanced at Penny. "Where's your phone?"

"Downstairs. But it was shut off."

Every telephone in the U.S. was supposed to have 911 access, even if it was shut off for nonpayment, and 911 access meant instant address relayed to the cops, far superior to using a cell phone. "Please tell me you have a phone up here?" she asked, looking around.

"Packed," she said, pointing at all the boxes. "Somewhere."

Syd drew her weapon, stepped back from the window, then pulled out her cell phone. "This paranoid boyfriend of yours," she said to Penny. "He happen to show you any of these escape routes?"

Chapter Seven

"Damn it, Tex!" Zach Griffin paced his office as far as his landline would allow without pulling the phone from the outlet. "You were supposed to be tailing her."

"We were. She left the Smithsonian. Archer was on her like white on rice."

"Apparently not close enough."

"Close enough to hear the security guard telling her that there was some fight between lovers, maybe that was the assault she was asking about. He wanted her to talk to some other security guard, but she left, went straight from there to the police department. She was getting reports on towed cars. That was when we lost her. Delivery truck got between us and her car, and Archer lost the point."

He had to figure out Fitzpatrick's logic if he was to have any hope of finding her. "The police have been kept out of the loop, she's got to know that by now, so why go there at all?"

"Because she's thinking like a cop, a fed, not a spy."

Zach paced in the other direction, but the phone cord stopped him from moving farther. "A cop...Towed vehicles..."

Hindsight forced him to see the consequences of letting Fitzpatrick believe she had recommended Tasha for the job, all because he didn't want Tasha's connection to his agency known. But as a result, Fitzpatrick believed she was responsible for recommending Tasha for the drawing, which meant guilt over her death. And if a by-the-book FBI agent wanted to allay that guilt?

Bring the killer to justice.

By looking up towed cars...? For what?

She used to be a cop, so think like one...

She had reason to believe Tasha's murder was connected to the drawing. If so, she'd realize she needed to identify her Jane Doe—Alessandra—to determine if there was a connection. But his agency had taken over the investigation, had kept it from the local police once they realized the connection and what it could do to their operation. In essence, there were no records of the case at the police department.

Unless they'd overlooked something...

But what?

Towed cars...

Hell. "Get back to MPDC. Run an audit on every towed car that clerk ran."

"What kind of connection could she possibly make?"

"If Alessandra was in a car before she went missing, that car might very well have ended up towed, because she never got back to it."

"But Alessandra didn't own a car."

"No, but she certainly could have borrowed one. And who the hell knows what happened to the person she borrowed it from. Maybe they're watching that person now, to see who comes calling."

"I'm on it."

He stared out the window watching the bright headlights zip down Twelfth Street. No doubt they'd been hasty when they'd chosen Fitzpatrick, even though she had been the logical choice because of her preoccupation with her father's killer in San Quentin. Once she completed the sketch, he'd firmly believed that she'd want to get back to San Francisco and her family for Thanksgiving, which meant she probably wouldn't give the sketch more than a passing thought.

Her former relationship with Special Agent Scott Ryan was another factor. The guy was heading to the top of the administration ladder, liked to do things by the book, and liked his women the same, just what Zach needed for this op. Administration says jump, subordinate says how high. Tasha had led him to believe that Sydney Fitzpatrick had been cut from the same cloth as Scott Ryan.

Apparently she was wrong.

And now, because of this miscalculation, Sydney Fitzpatrick was out there, God knew where, playing cop in a game that was out of her league. A game that had one rule: kill or be killed.

◇◇◇

The only escape route Penny's ex had ever truly planned was the attic. Penny, however, refused to go up there by herself. So Plan B it was, and Sydney hated Plan B. It was such a misnomer, like one had some other plan waiting, ready to go. She stood just inside the slatted closet door, peering out, cell phone in one hand, weapon in the other, hoping this didn't get them killed, because there wasn't enough time to think of something else. Before someone even answered the 911 call on her cell phone, the front door crashed open downstairs. After that, the only thing Syd heard was the pounding of her heart. Cops announced their arrival. These guys weren't cops.

And no one was answering the damn 911 call on her cell.

She looked between the crack in the closet door, to the stack of boxes, the bulky figure—a decoy—covered by a blanket behind the boxes. She prayed Penny would keep quiet.

Someone moved downstairs. She heard the opening of doors. One man or two?

And then the quiet footfall. Someone ascending the steps. The squeak of a floorboard down the hallway. Closer. Now outside the bedroom. On the threshold.

"Nine-one-one, what is your emergency?"

The voice sounded like a loudspeaker. Unable to talk, she shut the phone, aimed her gun.

She peered through the closet door slats. Saw the man take a step in, knife in one hand, assault rifle in the other. He spied the thick bundle behind the boxes, brought the rifle up, then suddenly swung it toward the closet.

Syd fired through the slats. Wood splintered, the blast deafened. The man hung in the air, then crumpled to the floor as Penny screamed.

"Quiet," Syd ordered. She used her foot to push open the closet door, kept her gun trained on the body.

"Ohmygod, ohmygod, ohmygod." Penny stared through the closet door in horror, sank to the ground, started rocking back and forth.

"Shut up…*Please*," Syd added, figuring no matter how paranoid the girl's boyfriend had been, killing someone in their apartment was probably never part of their discussions. To Penny's credit, she clamped her mouth shut, stifled the sobs, and Syd listened to the house. Tried to. There were no other footsteps, no sounds coming from below, but off in the distance, she heard a siren from an emergency vehicle, figured it was too soon to be related to their shooting.

Syd stepped from the closet, kept her gun trained on the man she hoped was dead. She moved closer, caught sight of his face, his lifeless eyes. The uniform beneath his overcoat.

The security guard from the Smithsonian.

Chapter Eight

Amazing how quickly MPDC officers swooped down on that apartment. And amazing how quickly Sydney and Penny were separated, and Sydney hustled away by some "detective" to an interrogation room at some "outstation" that didn't look remotely like it belonged to the MPDC cops at all. She thought of Zachary Griffin's cover and resources that allowed him to walk into Quantico without any problems. Whoever he worked for could certainly pull off something like this. The guys who brought her in definitely had that federal feel, as did the questioning. It was enough to make a girl think that not only was this related to Tasha's hit-and-run, but something bigger was going on.

And definitely enough to make a girl think that she wasn't leaving this area until she found it.

Unfortunately, it seemed everyone else had different ideas, her ex being one of them. "You need to go home," Scotty told Sydney, hours later, after the cops, if that's who they really were, finally let Scotty come pick her up and take her to his apartment.

"You're the one who told me I shouldn't sleep alone after the shooting."

"I don't mean your apartment, I mean San Francisco. You're supposed to be on vacation, on your way to Thanksgiving at your mom's place, and after tonight, you need it."

"How can I possibly go home without answers?"

"Answers to what?" Scotty dropped a pillow and blankets on the coffee table, since she refused his offer to share his bed, insisting on the couch instead. "Go back to your mom's. Don't put your career in jeopardy by being stubborn."

"Jeopardy? For what? Not rushing home to finish my scheduled two-week vacation? Are you saying that someone is ordering me home?"

"No, but if this is another federal agency, as you claim, you know that they'll pull strings and have you moved to where they see fit."

"Last I heard, it was my business where I spent my vacation time, not the Bureau's or any other agency out there."

"No one's ordering anything. All I'm saying is that before you get all fired up to investigate, remember what happened the last time you got involved. The reason you jumped on the Quantico position to begin with…"

He let that hang in the air, and she suddenly doubted herself, wondered how it was she'd even contemplated looking into Tasha's death, because, in a way, he was right. This was out of her league. She came back to Quantico to regroup. She didn't need this sort of trouble…

Syd leaned back on Scotty's couch, closed her eyes. It had been a long night of intense questioning by her interrogators. Suspect number two was nowhere to be found, which was part of the reason she had no desire to sleep in her empty apartment. Suspect number one was DOA, and determined *not* to be a security guard at the Smithsonian at all.

That part she believed, that he wasn't a guard. It was the rest of the story that didn't fit, and she was having a hard time letting it go. "Don't you find their theory that this guy stole his security guard uniform so he could rob unsuspecting victims in a series of home invasions a little too pat?"

"No."

"Well, I do."

Scotty picked up the TV remote and flicked through the channels until he found the late night news, which was when Sydney noticed something else odd. Their shooting hadn't even made it to the media yet.

"He targeted me," she continued. "No doubt once I'd walked onto the Smithsonian grounds and began asking questions, I was marked. Was probably marked from the moment I started that forensic sketch."

"I checked into it," he said, his gaze fixed on the TV. "You're way off base."

"Meaning what?"

"This drawing. It's being kept quiet because they think the victim might be a foreign diplomat's daughter. If it gets out, the press will turn it into an international scandal."

"They happen to mention this victim's name?"

"No, and I didn't ask. If they'd wanted me to know, they'd tell me."

She watched the TV in silence for a few moments, thinking that there were still too many unanswered questions, even if it was some diplomat's daughter. And what about this "guard"? Had he stolen the uniform and stationed himself at the Smithsonian in order to see who might come poking around in the Jane Doe murder? Unfortunately, she couldn't very well voice her suspicions to Scotty, since she wasn't supposed to be working on the case at all. She could, however, voice her suspicions about the shooting that she was involved in. "Don't you find it strange that the cops were there so fast?"

"Someone probably heard the shots. They were close by."

"I heard sirens before the guy hit the floor, Scotty."

Scotty turned off the TV, tossed the remote onto the coffee table, then looked over at her. She couldn't quite make out his expression in the now darkened room. She didn't need to, though, because she could hear the disapproval in his voice. "What's up is your overactive imagination. You're making a federal case out of something the locals need to handle. They think this guy has targeted others the same way. The unsuspecting come into the Smithsonian, he follows them home, he robs them. The last thing they need to do is advertise that the Smithsonian has turned into a crime-infested blight. Tourism is down enough as it is."

"Fine. You're right, I'm wrong. I'll go home. Be a good girl."

Scotty stood, leaned over, kissed the top of her head, gentling his tone, as if that would make up for his disbelief in her whacked-out theory. "You're doing the right thing. Get some rest, quit worrying. You have a long flight in the morning."

"Good night," she said, then sat there for several minutes in the dark, long after he'd disappeared into his bedroom and shut the door. Doing the right thing…That was what she was all about these days. The prudent thing would be to go home, let the authorities here handle it, forget about everything—everything but Tasha…Besides, why couldn't it be a home invasion robbery, as the "locals" called it?

Because for one, regardless of what Scotty thought, it was clear the locals weren't handling it. This shadow agency, whoever they were, was. And two, home *invasion?* It was more like a home *assassination* than some robbery attempt. She pictured the guy looking into Scotty's car, as though he'd been watching it, probably followed her there. That part she believed, that they'd followed her, probably from the moment she'd left the Smithsonian, but what sort of crook follows a victim, an FBI agent, to the PD and doesn't back off? Most crooks liked their victims unaware, unassuming, and uninvolved with the police.

Too many connections to other seemingly unassociated matters. Her secret sketch sanctioned by the CIA, or OGA, her discovery of the Smithsonian grounds as the crime scene, the "phone company" showing up at Scotty's, the towed car leading to the missing paranoid boyfriend who thought people were following him, never mind his unaccounted-for paramour, and the now dead Smithsonian security guard. She still wasn't sure what all the connections meant, only that her hunch on the possibility of a towed car leading her to a potential victim had landed her here. These were not the sort of coincidences Sydney believed in. And if it wasn't coincidence then what the hell was it, and what did it have to do with the forensic sketch? Was there any connection to this foreign diplomat's missing daughter?

She got up, walked to the window, looked out to the street below, wondered if she was being watched at this very moment, figured she probably was. If there was one thing she had faith in, it was the various U.S. intelligence agencies' methods of surveillance. After all, the FBI shared a number of those techniques. She'd been trained in some of them, and certainly been a part of them in the past—the very recent past. If one of these other government agencies had been following her, it explained why the cops had arrived so fast. What it didn't explain was why two armed men were allowed to get that close to her in the first place.

Unless a mistake had been made somewhere along the way?

She wasn't supposed to look into the case, and the CIA/OGA had suspected she might, which was why they'd taken the steps they had when she'd left Quantico. But the CIA, if they were following her, had lost her. The bad guys, whoever they were, had definitely followed her. But if they were ready to take *her* out that quickly, if they were the ones responsible for Tasha's hit-and-run, then how was it that Penny had escaped their notice? As whacked out as Penny's theories had sounded, she certainly had some information that could be considered vital.

Then again, maybe they had ignored Penny, assumed she wasn't a threat, because her only connection to her missing boyfriend and his new girl had been the loan of her car, and that had merely been left in a construction zone, towed, and subsequently returned…They might not have even realized there was a connection to Penny, via her boyfriend, until Syd had stepped in, followed up on the lead herself.

Clearly no one had suspected that a lowly domestic FBI agent would connect the dots and stumble onto the Smithsonian and right into the lap of one of the players…

She closed her eyes, because that was, in essence, what she'd done. Stumbled across them. That was not how she liked to operate. She needed control. Today had not been a controlled situation, and she'd almost gotten killed as a result.

She was not about to let that happen again, and that begged the question of what to do next.

The smart thing—the right thing—to do would be to go home as ordered, let the big boys handle it, the Mr. Federals of the world. And she might have, but for two things. One, she was somewhat responsible for her friend's death, since she was the one who'd recommended Tasha for the job. Two, she'd killed someone tonight, someone who no doubt meant to kill her.

Hard not to take that personally, especially knowing that there had been *two* men approaching Penny's apartment. Which meant there was someone else out there, someone she couldn't identify, who probably had the same agenda: kill her.

She'd given her card to that security guard. That meant they knew who she was. One up on her, since she still didn't know who they were, and if she went home to San Francisco, they could very well follow her there. She'd be doing exactly what she'd swore she'd never do, never allow to happen again. Dragging danger to her family's doorstep. *Never*, she thought, turning away from the window, unable to see if anyone was sitting in any of the darkened cars parked below.

Grabbing her blanket and pillow, she settled on the couch. She'd never been very good at the whole let-sleeping-dogs-lie thing. No, she liked her dogs up and barking, the better to find out which were the vicious ones.

There were going to be some upset males come morning. Scotty for one, but also the alleged Special Agent Zachary Griffin, and this last thought made her smile. Served him right.

"Might want to work on those point-counterpoint surveillance techniques tomorrow," she said, just in case they were listening. "Oh, and FYI, my favorite red is cabernet. California cab."

The same as Tasha liked...

A shaft of light spilled into the hallway when Scotty opened the bedroom door. "You say something?" he called out.

"Just talking to myself."

◇◇◇

At eight the next morning, Scotty unlocked his Bureau car and held the door open for Syd. She slid in, and he stood there a moment, smiling. "I think this is the right decision you're making, Syd. Go home, let the locals deal with it."

"I'm stubborn. Not stupid." When he got in, started up the car, she added, "Since we've got a few hours to kill, mind if we make a quick stop before we head to my place and then the airport?"

"Where to?"

"UVA."

Scotty threw her a strange glance. "The university?"

"Old professor friend I haven't seen in a while. Just want to drop in, say hi. See if he remembers me."

He glanced at his watch, then shrugged. "Guess we have time."

"Thanks."

Syd leaned back in the car, checked the side view mirror. A Dodge pickup pulled out after them, but turned off a block later. She hoped the fact it was broad daylight would keep suspect number two from coming after her for the moment, and her right elbow automatically pressed against her side. She felt the hard edges of her temporary replacement sidearm the FBI had issued her. The minions who had interrogated her last night had taken her weapon, allegedly to book it into evidence for the requisite testing after the shooting.

Scotty was also armed, always a plus, since two guns were better than one, she thought, stifling a yawn. Scotty caught it, said, "We should stop for coffee first," and she didn't argue. She hadn't slept well, tossing and turning over the whole affair, thinking about what she might have missed, then coming up with today's battle plan, not saying anything inside Scotty's apartment for fear that not only would he try to talk her out of it, but Griffin would swoop in and physically escort her to that damned plane himself.

When they got to the university, she asked Scotty to wait in the car while she checked with the administration staff to locate the professor.

"I'll go in with you," he said.

She didn't want Scotty to see her pulling out her credentials and making this an official visit, since that sort of ruined the whole "old friend" scenario she'd woven for him, especially when she didn't know what department or what class. "It'll only take me a second to see if he's in. If he's not, I'll be right out and we're off to breakfast."

Scotty leaned back in his seat, gave her his best "hurry up" look, and she was off. There was only one Professor Woods who taught at the university, Denise Woods, and apparently *she* had a nine A.M. class and was presently in her office. Maybe Scotty wouldn't notice Sydney's slip up on the professor's gender. The girl at the counter gave Sydney a map of the campus, pointing out a parking lot closer to the professor's building.

Five minutes later, she was knocking at the professor's office door, with Scotty at her side. The door opened, and Syd eyed the beautiful, petite, blond-haired woman and smiled. "Professor Denise Woods? I'm Sydney Fitzpatrick. I'll bet you don't recognize me."

She gave Syd a thorough appraisal. "You're right. Should I?"

"Yes, you should." Syd turned to Scotty. "Can you give me a couple minutes here, Scotty? It won't take long, I promise."

He didn't trust her, she could see it in his expression, but he did give her the privacy she requested, perhaps because she had promised to be on that plane, and he stepped away from the door. "Make it quick."

"Scout's honor."

Syd stepped inside, closed the door of the small office behind her, then pulled out her credentials. "I'm Special Agent Sydney Fitzpatrick, FBI, looking into the disappearance of one of your students."

"Xavier Caldwell?"

"Yes. You've been contacted about his disappearance?"

"No, but I did wonder at his sudden absence."

"When was that?"

Professor Woods walked over to her laptop computer on her desk, cluttered with stacks of papers, books, manila folders. She ran her finger across the mouse pad, tapped something into the computer, then said, "Almost two weeks ago."

Syd took out the sketch she'd made of her Jane Doe. "Does this woman look familiar to you?"

"She bears a striking resemblance to my assistant, Alessandra Harden."

"Is she here?"

"With her father. May I ask what this is about?"

"As I said, a missing person's case. On Xavier Caldwell. Other than that, I'm not at liberty to say." Primarily because she had no damned clue as to what it was about. Even so, she now had a name to go with the face. "Did either of them approach you about anything odd? Conspiracy theories?"

The professor hesitated, her gaze narrowing slightly. "As a matter of fact Xavier did, and I can honestly say that at the time I figured it was an excuse for not turning in his final draft report, which happened to be on the very same subject. Telling me he was in the midst of the biggest conspiracy theory in modern history is no excuse for not turning in his report on conspiracy theory in past history."

"Any idea what this big theory of his was?"

"Something about criminals using secret societies to control politicians, thereby controlling the government, thereby controlling the world banking system. Alessandra might be a better person to ask."

"Why is that?"

"They were pretty friendly. Tight. Of course, you'll have to go to Italy to talk to her. I was informed that her absence was due to her sudden return home to take care of family matters. I think that translates to she was sent home in disgrace after she was caught in dishabille with the congressman."

When Syd finally found her tongue, all she could say was, "The congressman?"

"Congressman Burnett. You do read the papers, don't you? It made all the headlines about two months ago."

"I don't pay too much attention to the D.C. scandals," she said.

Professor Woods walked to a tall box marked "Recycle" parked in the corner of her office, dug down a bit, and came up with a newspaper and handed it to Syd. "Here you go. Big conspiracy theory. She's playing hooky with a politician instead of grading papers for my class. Too bad, too. She had a remarkable career in archeology ahead of her, maybe even a position here. She took the assistant's job with me until one opened up in the archeological department."

Syd stared at the grainy newsprint photo of a woman who resembled her sketch. Said woman was either whispering political figures or sweet nothings in the representative's ear. Hard to say unless one was actually there, listening to it. What was it Scotty had told her? The explanation for all this? Diplomat's daughter being sent home to prevent an international scandal in the press?

That whole coincidence thing again. Easily bought if one didn't look too closely at the more obvious circumstances, the biggest being that if the girl in the photo was the girl in her sketch, then she was very much dead. "Did Xavier ever mention any specifics on this conspiracy theory of his?"

"He offered up several theories, the main gist being that Freemasonry was running amok in our country, about to start wars or ruin the banking system and government all in one fell swoop. One of his main points was that a Masonic Lodge called the Propaganda Due, or P2, had emerged again, after being shut down in Italy back in the 1980s for political corruption. This time, however, he thought it was happening right here in the capital. Oh, and they were instrumental in the deaths of a number of microbiologists, who were working on bioweapons research. In other words, classic conspiracy theory stuff you can find on any internet site."

Microbiologists? What were the chances that field would crop up a second time in as many days? "So how far out there was he?"

Professor Woods gave Syd a somewhat patronizing smile. "Do you ever read your horoscope?"

"Occasionally."

"Ever wonder how it is that your daily horoscope can fit into your life, as though there is some truth to it all?"

"Because it's so general."

"Exactly. The theories I teach are more a way of illuminating history throughout the ages. They're themes that recur over and over, but when looked at very closely are no different than what is going on today. Conflict in history revolves around the same issues. Money and power. And those without, blame it on those who have it all.

"I liken the conspiracy theorists," she continued, "to those who read the Bible and interpret it to suit their own needs. One can look anywhere, grasp a word that is vague in one context, or might have a dual meaning in another, and twist a phrase to mean something completely different from what the author intended. Xavier's paper was returned to him for being too general. I asked him to do a little more research on the start of Freemasonry, and why the Catholic Church was so opposed to it back when it first surfaced. You could say he came back enlightened."

"How so?" Syd asked, wondering what, if anything, this would tell her about her missing student.

"He discovered a theory that Freemasonry started much earlier than the eighteenth century as originally believed. It was, he said, a means of hiding and protecting the Templar Knights who escaped the persecution, imprisonment, and execution by Pope Clement V and Philip IV of France in 1307. According to Xavier's research, the Templars went underground, only to emerge in the early 1700s as Freemasons, a group that believes in a supreme being, but does not affiliate itself with any church or specific religion. What this new secret society did espouse was something the church found extremely dangerous at the time: freedom of religion, the separation of church and state, the education of children by laymen, and the right to choose one's own government. You might recognize those as the very tenets that this nation was founded on."

"So Freemasons aren't the mastermind behind all evil in this country?"

"If you'd asked my mother back when I was a kid, she'd tell you it was rock-and-roll. Don't get me wrong. The church was right in some respects. If you have a secret society and they meet in secret and there is an inner circle of powerful men running it, and one or more is corrupted, it doesn't matter if they are church members, Freemasons, or politicians. There will be conspiracy and unless it is caught, bad things can happen, just as history has proven again and again."

Which told her exactly nothing. But her list of names had grown to two. "Mind if I keep this article?"

"Feel free."

"Any chance you have a copy of these conspiracy theories Xavier was working on?"

"I'll print one up for you. My students are required to turn a draft in electronically before the final draft is due. Gives me a chance to look it all up on the internet, see if anyone's doing too much cutting and pasting," she said, returning to her computer. She scrolled through some files, then printed out a copy, handing it to Syd. "Unfortunately, he never did turn in the final draft, so I don't know if he ever found the proof he was looking for."

"Proof of what?"

"That there was a conspiracy going on in our government at this moment, and someone in power should know. He said he needed a few days to get the information together. Whatever that might be, I have no idea, as he never returned to class. But I recall that when he and Alessandra were walking out, I over-heard her telling him that he needed to leave this harebrained scheme of his alone, as he had no idea what he was getting into and it was going to lead to—her words exactly—'a big bunch of nothing and a whole lot of trouble.'"

"Thanks," Sydney said, flipping through the pages, too numer-ous to quickly scan. "Can I call you if something else comes up?"

"Sure," the professor said, digging a card from her desk drawer, and writing her numbers on it. "My home and cell.

Normally I don't give them out, but I find the fact the FBI is asking questions a bit intriguing."

Sydney opened the door, then hesitated, turning back. "You don't happen to have the address of your assistant who had to return to Italy?"

"She lived on campus."

"I mean her home address."

"Should be easy enough. She's the daughter of the U.S. ambassador to the Holy See."

"The Holy See?" Syd stared at the newspaper photo, not sure what to think. "As in the Pope?"

"Yes. So you can imagine her father wasn't too pleased when he heard the rumors of her…involvement with a married man. No doubt that's why he ordered her home."

"No doubt," she said, though that wasn't what she was thinking at all. She folded the newspaper and report, putting both in her purse. "Thank you very much for your time, professor."

Scotty was leaning against the wall, his arms crossed, when she exited. "Are you ready to go to breakfast?"

She pulled out the card Zach Griffin had given her. Breakfast was the last thing on her mind.

Chapter Nine

"About breakfast?" Scotty asked again when they reached the car.

Sydney slid into the front passenger seat, glanced at her watch. "I need to pack a few things I forgot the first time around. Maybe you could drop me off at my apartment, grab us some fast food, come back, get me, and we can head straight to the airport."

"Special requests?" Scotty asked, backing out of the parking space, then having to stop for two young women who darted in front of the car, probably late for a class.

"Anything."

Which seemed to suit Scotty fine, especially the part about heading straight to the airport, no doubt because he thought it would keep her out of trouble. The moment he dropped her off in front of her building, she ran upstairs with her briefcase and overnight bag, shoved her key in the lock and threw open the door, tossed everything down, then opened her cell phone. Several phone calls later, Sydney was no closer to learning Zach Griffin's true identity. He wasn't answering his phone, and his so-called boss at the "newspaper" he worked for said he was leaving the country on an editorial assignment. Her next call was to a contact at CIA, which netted her zero results. If Griffin was CIA, they weren't admitting any association to him. But Griffin definitely worked for a governmental agency because someone had to fund all the bells and whistles to his so-called newspaper job, and no way could he step onto the grounds at Quantico, arrange for a private plane, and a forensic drawing, never mind the cooperation of her bosses if someone high up the food chain wasn't pulling some strings.

Right now the only thing she'd deduced was that he was leaving the country. So where the hell was he going?

Rome, Italy.

Had to be. If the victim's father was the ambassador to the Holy See, then Sydney's money was on Zach Griffin flying to Rome. She scrolled through a list of names in her cell phone, finding the number for Jonathon Levins, her contact at Homeland Security. "I need a favor. How quickly can you check outgoing flight records and see if there's a Zach Griffin departing on any of them?" she asked on a hunch, since she didn't know if that was his real name, a cover, or even a name he'd use for travel.

"From which airport?" Levins asked.

"Dulles? Probably an international flight, and if you want it narrowed further, to Rome."

"What am I putting down for the reason?"

"You want the unvarnished truth or a close proximity?"

"Since when are you one for skirting rules?"

"Since circumstances dictated it. Look, I can't go into anything, but you know me, and you know I wouldn't be asking if it weren't important. Everything's on the up-and-up, I'm just going about it in an…abstract manner. So, if anyone asks, the case is a missing person, probable kidnap, possible homicide."

"Victim?"

She thought of the article, decided it wouldn't be a good idea to publicize what the CIA, or whoever the hell they were, didn't want publicized. Even so, no one seemed too worried about the man Alessandra had been with at the time of her death, no one except Penny Dearborn. And since he was still missing, that made it legitimate. "Xavier Caldwell."

"Got it. I'll call you back."

The next call Sydney made was to Tony Carillo in San Francisco. "Good morning, merry sunshine," she said.

"Morning, yes. Good, it depends on why you're calling. Can't you let a guy finish a cup of coffee first?"

"You didn't happen to hear the rumor about the security guard at the Smithsonian who tried to kill me last night, did you?"

"Missed that one. So fill me in."

"I can't. I just want to let you know where I'll be, in case something happens."

"Why can't you tell me?"

"It's possible I could face disciplinary action, maybe even just by telling you what happened. Not only that, but I need some things looked into that might also lead to…issues. Things on the QT."

"Let me get this straight. You're keeping secrets from the government to assist in something that, as far as I know, might be questionable, and might result in disciplinary action?"

"Pretty much, yeah."

"Something that if you discuss with me, I could also face disciplinary action?"

"Yep."

"Like being-terminated-type action?" When she didn't respond, he said, "I'll take that as a yes. Which is why you don't want me involved."

"Exactly."

"Okay. I get it. So what exactly am I not getting involved in?"

She told him the information about her anthropologist friend, killed in an alleged hit-and-run, and her upcoming trip to Rome.

"Why Rome?"

"That forensic drawing I did? It was a girl with a missing face. A girl whose father happens to be ambassador to the Holy See."

"The Holy…shit. You're kidding me, right?"

"I'm about to head to the airport to get on a plane to Rome to follow some guy who works for some as of yet unknown branch of the government, so, no, I'm not kidding. What I really need is for you to either talk me out of this, or find out what you can on a certain congressman that this girl was with before she was killed."

"Congressman?"

"A couple months ago, there was a newspaper article linking the ambassador's daughter with a married congressman. She was allegedly sent home to Italy when it was rumored the two were having an affair. Might be interesting to talk to the man. It wouldn't be the first time a girl was found dead after an affair with a married politician."

"You think that's why everything's being kept so hush-hush? Someone trying to save this congressman's career? Wait. Don't answer that. I'm not supposed to be getting involved. Remember?"

"Remember what? A conversation we never had? Don't suppose you have any investigations that would take you to D.C.?"

"I'm sure I could scrape up something."

"I don't yet know *where* she was killed, but her body was found at the Smithsonian. One of the guys that came after me was wearing a Smithsonian security uniform, and he stepped out of the very building located next to said crime scene. Makes me wonder if she wasn't killed inside, and the body moved. Another part of me wonders if this security guard wasn't stationed there as a means of watching who might come poking around about her death."

"And you walked right into it?"

"There were extenuating circumstances."

"You don't think the guy was stupid enough to kill her in front of some security camera?"

"We could only hope," she told him. "Actually I'd be happy just to trace her last steps. Pull those security tapes, see if she's wandering around, admiring the artwork, or if she's there for a purpose."

"Or if she's there at all."

"Which is why we need to look into this congressman connection."

"Call me when you get to Rome. Let me know where you're staying."

Chapter Ten

The moment Tony Carillo disconnected with Sydney, he called his friend, Michael "Doc" Schermer, who was literally the go-to guy, when it came to discovering obscure information. "You at your desk?"

"Yeah."

"Guess who I just heard from?"

"Your soon-to-be ex, who realizes she made a big mistake and is begging your forgiveness, but you told her to pound sand, because you just came into a major inheritance, and the girls are lined up outside your door?"

"Whatever you spiked your coffee with, save me some. And no. Fitzpatrick just called. She's on her way to Italy."

"And what's she doing there?"

"Being that she's an upstanding agent, she couldn't discuss it with me, for fear I'd end up in front of the OPR tribunal alongside her," he said, referring to the Office of Professional Responsibility, the Bureau's internal affairs watchdogs. "So you can see my dilemma."

"So what is it you can't discuss with me, for fear I'd be drawn and quartered alongside you?"

"You mean the part about the ambassador to the Holy See's daughter being murdered, after having her face and prints removed to prevent her ID? Or something about a possible affair with a congressman and the pontification of whether or not the death was related?"

"First," Doc Schermer said, "I'm impressed you can use pontification in a sentence. Second, in light of the case matter relating to the pope, I'm wondering if you did it on purpose. Third, if I'm going to get fired, I'd rather it wasn't for a bad pun. So what is it you're not really asking me?"

"To find out everything you can on this congressman. I want to know every skeleton in his closet, and every committee he's ever sat on. I want to know about the girl and what she's involved with. And last but not least, I could use a legit reason to get on a plane to D.C. ASAP, so I can get the Bureau to pick up the tab. If I'm going to be unemployed soon, I'd rather not be out the airfare."

"I'm sure I can dig up an old case for you that needs follow-up in the D.C. area," he said, and Carillo heard the click of his keyboard as Doc Schermer started typing. "Give me the names of all the involved…"

◇◇◇

Sydney looked around her apartment, trying to figure out all she'd need for the trip. Everything except her work clothes was still in boxes. Her indecision on where to look for an apartment was now costing her time, and she wished she'd just let Scotty pick out a place. A few minutes later her contact at Homeland Security called her back.

"What's the good word?" she asked Levins.

"Your guy's flying to Rome, Fiumicino, via Dulles at seven P.M."

"What are the chances you can book me on that flight in the seat next to him?"

"Can't. But I can put you in the row right behind him."

"Works for me."

"*Ciao.* And you owe me. Credit card number would be a good start. I'll think of a proper extortion after you get back."

Perfect, she thought, looking around at all the boxes, searching for the one marked "Important Papers." Time to pull out her damned passport.

◇◇◇

Zach Griffin's seat was near the rear of the plane, far enough back to be able to see what was going on up front, and the best way he knew of scanning and profiling each passenger on board. It was one of the reasons he was always the last to board, when circumstances necessitated public transportation. He preferred knowing whom he shared a plane with, because he didn't like surprises.

And he didn't like finding unexpected passengers seated one row behind him.

He stopped at his seat, eyed Sydney Fitzpatrick, who occupied the middle seat right behind his. "What are you doing here?" he asked.

"Good to see you again, too." She smiled.

He didn't smile back. Instead, he looked at the twenty-year-old kid sitting next to her in the aisle. He dug a few bills out of his wallet and waved them in front of the kid's face. "Yours if you switch seats with me."

The boy shrugged, grabbed the bills, and got up to switch seats.

Zach swung his bag in the overhead bin, then sat next to Fitzpatrick, who sat with her hands folded on top of some file folder in her lap. He eyed it, then her. "What the hell are you doing on this flight?" he asked.

"I'd ask you the same, but I figure it has something to do with this." She opened the folder, then slid out a section of a newspaper, the article and accompanying photograph on Alessandra Harden, while making sure no one else could see it.

"How did you discover who she was?"

"How was it you didn't?"

"Besides the obvious?" he asked, referring to the victim having no face. Or fingerprints. "We had a suspicion, but needed confirmation. Hence the need for your services. As you can appreciate, they are no longer needed."

Sydney tucked the article back in her folder. "Well, here's the thing. A couple guys tried to Ten X me last night, and, just a quirk of mine, I tend to take those sort of things personally.

The way I see it, with one of them still at large, it's in my best interest to figure out what the hell is going on."

"It would have been in your best interest to fly home on the plane we'd provided. Had you done so," he said, keeping his voice low, "and not involved yourself in something you shouldn't have been nosing around in, you wouldn't have been made into a target."

"Well, it's a little late for that now, isn't it? And speaking of being in my best interest, how is it I had to learn from someone else that my very good friend, whom I *personally* recommended for your case, was killed. What if her parents had decided to hold a local service?"

"Like I said, on the off chance it was something more than a hit-and-run, we didn't want you there for the obvious reasons."

"The off chance?" she whispered. "Had you informed me of everything from the beginning, last night's events could have been completely avoided."

He glanced over at her, saw she was staring straight ahead, doing her best to keep her temper in check. "You're welcome to get off the plane."

"Not going to happen."

"How'd you get permission to fly out?"

"Simple. I called the Security Officer at HQ, told him I had hankering to go to Italy, because I got a real good deal on a flight, but only if I leave now. He told me I knew the drill. Leave my gun at home, and see him when I get back for a security briefing. Italy's not way up there in the countries of concern, you know."

"So you lied." That was something he hadn't expected, not based on her background.

"Bent the truth a little. I'm thinking about visiting the Vatican. You?"

Griffin buckled up his seat belt as the flight attendant made her rounds for the preflight check. "Haven't decided yet. But wherever I go, it'll be without you. You lost your friend, and for that I'm sorry. But that makes you emotionally involved. It's something I can't afford." He leaned back, closed his eyes. "So how was it you found her?" he asked.

"The crime scene photograph. The red sandstone. Looked it up on the internet and discovered the Smithsonian was built with it. From there it was basic. Looked up vehicles towed in the area, found one that was connected to a missing person, who happened to be a student in a history class she assists with," Sydney said, patting the folder on her lap. "Their professor confirmed it this morning."

Impressed by her powers of observation and deductive reasoning, he was still bothered that she'd found the connections so easily, primarily because it had put her in danger. Even so, she'd handled herself well, better than the two agents he'd assigned to follow her. "Sorry about losing you last night."

"Yeah, well, it all worked out in the end."

"Except you let the second guy get away." He opened one eye, smiled at the dark look she gave him. "Would've been cleaner had you gotten him, too."

"Win some, lose some."

He laughed. Sydney Fitzpatrick was nothing like he'd been led to believe. That didn't mean he was keeping her on, but at the very least, it was going to make his flight less tedious.

◇◇◇

The plane touched down at the Leonardo da Vinci Airport in a smooth landing, and the moment the seat belt lights were shut off, the passengers rose from their seats and started digging for their carry-ons. Zach retrieved his and Sydney's, then they both remained seated, waiting for the passengers in front of them to depart. Sydney unzipped her bag, dropped in the folder of the conspiracy report, then sat back to wait, thinking that Griffin might actually let her in on his investigation after all.

That illusion lasted until he said, "When we get off the plane, you're going back on the next flight to the States."

"You can't order me," she told him. "I'm on vacation."

"Watch how fast I get you ordered back."

She didn't doubt for a second that he could do it. "At least let me see Bernini's Daphne and Apollo at the Villa Borghese. Not letting an artist see Bernini is like...like not letting a cop shoot a gun."

"That's the lamest analogy I've ever heard."

"I'm sleep deprived."

"Fine. Daphne at the Villa Borghese tomorrow. And then you're out of here. Where are you staying?"

"I haven't gotten that far."

He took out one of his business cards, wrote the name of a hotel on it and below that a number, then handed it to her. "This place will be perfect. Modernized and secure. And the number is my emergency contact number while I'm here. And I mean emergency. When I get off this plane, we are simply two passengers who chatted on the flight over. You do not know me, and I don't know you."

"Fine. But I guess you'll never know if I get on that return flight."

He glanced over at her. "Good point. I'm booking, paying for, and personally delivering you to that plane. Come to think of it, I'll deliver you to your hotel room."

"What hotel are you staying in?"

"I'm not."

The row in front of them started forward, and the two of them followed the other passengers to passport control.

The terminal at Leonardo da Vinci was crowded with travelers speaking a babel of foreign languages. Following Griffin's lead, she dug her passport out, then stepped into the line for non-European Common Market passengers, careful to listen as he was questioned, though she was certain he wasn't giving accurate answers.

"Business or pleasure?" the short and rather sour-faced Passport Control Officer asked in English, eyeing his passport, then him.

"Business."

"Nature?"

"Newspaper. A series on vacationing in Italy."

"Destination?"

"Rome."

"Length of stay?"

"A week."

"Fast writer?"

"Very."

"Thank you." He stamped Griffin's passport, then waved him through.

Sydney went through the same drill, but when he asked her the nature of her visit, she nodded toward Griffin and said, "I'm illustrating his articles." Her return ticket was for a week as well, since Levins had booked it to match Griffin's.

As they walked off, Griffin said, "Quite the cover story."

"No worse than yours."

If she had any hopes that Griffin might forget about babysitting her until her plane, they were crushed as he took her by her arm and led her to the Alitalia departure desk. "When is the next flight back to…" He glanced at Sydney, then the attendant as he said, "San Francisco."

The woman tapped at her keyboard, eyeing her screen. "The soonest we can get you on a connecting flight via New York is tonight—"

"She'll take it."

"She won't," Sydney said. "She has some *illustrating* to do." Then to the clerk, asked, "What do you have day after tomorrow?"

"We have a mid-afternoon flight that leaves at two-forty."

"Perfect," Griffin said. He took out a credit card, slapped it on the counter. "Give her your ID and your ticket, Fitzpatrick."

Sydney tried to keep her expression neutral as she handed over her passport and plane ticket. The clerk eyed the ticket, punched in some numbers, and said, "It'll be an additional one hundred dollars for the change, not including the charge to get to San Francisco."

To which Sydney told Griffin, "You should just save your money and time. I can do this myself."

"You could, but I get the feeling you won't."

The clerk dutifully ignored their conversation as she finished up the reservation, printed out the ticket, then gave everything to Sydney. Griffin reached over, took possession of the new plane ticket as if he didn't trust her at all.

"Gee, thanks," Sydney said to Griffin as they walked away.

He didn't respond, and judging from the expression on his face, she wasn't sure she'd have wanted him to. Deciding it best not to push him further, thereby ruining any chance she had of changing his mind, or at the very least, making a break, she slung her bag over her shoulder and walked quietly beside him as he stepped out to get in the long line of passengers waiting for a taxi.

After five minutes they arrived at the head of the line. As soon as Griffin gave the driver the name of the Albergo Pini di Roma on the Aventine, they were off. The taxi careened through the flat marshlands that bordered the airport and veered in and out of the insane traffic that congested the roads leading to Rome, past the rather nondescript modern apartments. Cabdrivers in the States had nothing on this guy. She gripped the seat to keep from sliding around, while the driver gave a monologue of the sights in heavily accented English: the Baths of Caracalla to the left, the Palatine Hill with its sprawling Palace of the Caesars to the right, a glimpse of the Colosseum in the distance as they turned into the sycamore-lined Viale Aventino. He was proud of his knowledge and probably hoped for a substantial tip. Sydney, more frightened than impressed, wondered if she'd be killed in a taxi before she had a chance to find out who had murdered her friend, then tried to murder her.

As far as she knew, the moment she stepped back in the United States, they'd come after her again. Too late to take back that burning curiosity that compelled her to find the murder scene, determine what they were covering up, and follow the trail here. Now she'd be damned if she would sit back and put her life in some other government agency's hands. At the moment she knew of only one person who held her best interests at heart, who cared about what happened to her and those she loved. That person was she.

"Have you ever been here?" Griffin asked.

"A few times as a kid," she said, noting that he seemed unfazed by the wild taxi ride. "My parents brought me to visit some of my mother's relatives. She actually lived here for a few years before she married my father."

"You speak Italian?"

"Not enough to traverse the country without a dictionary and some very patient natives who don't mind me massacring the language, but my mother can."

"Massacre it?"

"Speak it. Pretty fluently."

The taxi drove up the steep Via Santa Prisca and turned into the wide and surprisingly traffic-free piazza, stopping in front of the Albergo Pini di Roma. Griffin, who apparently spoke fluent Italian, instructed the driver to wait for him while he checked Sydney in. They exited the cab, and Sydney took a good look around the hotel. With its terra cotta-washed stucco façade into which a gleaming glass entrance had been set, The Pines of Rome Hotel managed to look rustic and modern at the same time. Two low travertine steps led into the marble-floored lobby in which comfortable armchairs had been grouped at intervals around red Turkish carpets. A long reception desk ran the length of one wall.

"Nice place," she said.

"You'll need your passport to book the room," he told her when they reached the desk.

Sydney surrendered her passport to the desk clerk, who punched the information into her computer. When she finished, she slid Sydney's key across the counter and said, "Enjoy your stay."

Her room was on the fourth floor, tastefully decorated and refurbished, a mix of vintage 1920s, the height of the Fascist era, and modern updates. A large oak wardrobe occupied a corner and she set her bag on a chair beside it, then walked to the window. Her room looked out toward the Tiber river and across to the Gianicolo Hill. "Wish I really was here to paint. It's gorgeous."

"Perks of the job," he said. "Drawbacks are that you don't get much time to enjoy the perks." He didn't move from the door. "You think you can stay out of trouble until I come by for you?"

"As much as I'd love to get out there, the first thing on my agenda is a nap."

"That makes two of us. I'll give you a call this evening after I visit the ambassador for the death notification."

"You know, I might be able to help. With the ambassador."

"Thanks, but no thanks. Mind if I use your bathroom before I leave?"

"All yours." She stepped out onto the narrow balcony to get a better look at the immediate area. The pine-scented air was brisk, but she found it refreshing.

After a few minutes she felt his presence before he made it known, and finally she turned, saw him staring at her. "Something on your mind?"

He didn't answer right away, just eyed her, giving her the feeling that he could see deep within her, guess that she had no intention of remaining uninvolved. "I should warn you, if you go out, don't carry a purse. If you do, watch out for the light-fingered gypsies in designer clothes."

"I'll keep that in mind," she said as he left.

Sydney didn't move from the balcony. She waited until she saw him emerge four stories below. Just before he got into his waiting cab, he glanced up, as though he'd been aware she'd been watching him. He didn't wave, just looked at her, then slid into the backseat and the cab drove off. A small red sedan pulled out from the curb after him, honking its horn at a woman who stepped off the sidewalk, then jumped back.

Only then did she return inside, deciding that as much as she really wanted to see the sights, what she really desired was a soak in the tub and a long, long nap. The spacious bathroom had been updated, including a large Cararra marble tub with gold dolphin-shaped faucets. She ran the water, then got out some clean clothes and the report on conspiracies that the professor had given her, and was about to head back into the bathroom when she spied a small refrigerator. On impulse, she opened it and found an assortment of beverages. When in Rome, she thought, withdrawing an ice-cold mini bottle of *prosecco*. She poured it into one of the flute glasses sitting on top of the small refrigerator, then carried that into the bathroom. When the tub was filled, she undressed, slipped into the steaming water, and sipped her sparkling wine.

Not too bad, she thought, picking up the first page of the report, trying to give it a thorough read. Maybe it was the lack of distractions from passengers or from Zach Griffin's presence, or that she was more relaxed, but she was having a hard time keeping her eyes open as she scanned Xavier Caldwell's report. It was your basic conspiracy theory on Freemasons and the New World Order; Caldwell's version stated they were running Washington, D.C., New York, and the entire banking system. Definitely nothing new. Flipping through several more pages, she decided that Caldwell was a bit heavy on a few key words like Illuminati, Vatican, and the P2 Italian Freemasonry lodge.

Grade B for effort, in that it took some time to type up, or at least cut-and-paste the dozens of pages from various conspiracy Web sites, but D-minus for originality. Even so, she continued to read, just in case there was something there. But jet lag finally caught up with her. Having no energy, she got as far as dressing in her underwear, then bundling up in the thick terry robe hanging in the wardrobe. The bed was soft, inviting, and she picked up Caldwell's report, thinking she'd read a few more pages before sleep finally overtook her. She nodded off twice, then woke again trying to grasp what the professor had told her… something about Xavier Caldwell speaking to Alessandra about finding proof of a government conspiracy, but she had warned him off…and now she was dead and he was missing…

Her last thought before the report slipped from her grasp and she fell asleep was that she needed to call Carillo.

Chapter Eleven

The private residence of Alec Harden, Ambassador to the Holy See, was situated across from the American Academy on Via Giacomo Medici. Zach Griffin parked his car down the narrow street, passing a white van with a man sitting inside, then noted the other white van opposite, making them for the two armed *carabinieri* guards assigned to watch the residence under the heightened security. The residence itself was surrounded by a high wall with glass shards stuck into it to keep out unwanted visitors. Zach, who had actually worked out of Harden's office in the past year, had called ahead, and so he passed the *carabinieri*, and walked up to the gates, where the *portière* admitted him through and into the villa with its square tower. From there, a black-and-white-uniformed maid escorted him upstairs to the ambassador's private study.

Alec Harden was expecting a report on his missing daughter, and Zach did not relish the duty of informing him that her status had changed from that of missing to most likely dead. Despite the forensic drawing that solidified their suspicions of it being Alessandra Harden, they lacked the evidence such as DNA or dental for that one hundred percent verification, the sort that told a waiting family member that there could be no mistake.

"Mr. Griffin, a pleasure as always," Ambassador Harden said, rising from a wingback chair to shake Zach's hand. He was in the midst of late afternoon tea, a steaming cup by the window with a view of the spacious gardens of the American Academy across the narrow street. A group of Fellows of the Academy were playing croquet under the tall parasol pines, and their laughter drifted into the high-ceilinged room.

"Mr. Ambassador. Thank you for seeing me on such short notice."

"What can I do for you?"

Zach waited until the maid left the room. Once they were alone, he said, "It's about your daughter."

"You found her? Thank God."

"I—" He took a breath, knew there was no good way to impart such news, then said, "She was murdered."

Alec Harden's face paled. His mouth parted, but no words came, and Zach let him be, allowed the words to sink in as he dropped into his morocco leather chair, closing his eyes. Outside, wooden mallets clicked on wooden balls, and one of the Fellows shouted that another had cheated on his shot. Finally, through eyes blurred with tears, Alec asked, "How? Why?"

"We don't have all the answers yet, sir, but we're working on them."

"Why so long?"

"We only just identified her. A forensic artist had to be brought in."

"A forensic artist? For what? What does that mean?"

"Whoever killed her didn't want her identified."

The ambassador stared in mute silence. And then he rose, walked over to a side table, and poured himself a glass of what looked like whiskey from a crystal decanter. He drank it down in one shot, then poured another. When he finished that one, he faced Zach, saying, "That's why you asked for my DNA—why there was an issue when you found out she was adopted? It wasn't just a precaution—you knew?"

"We suspected. We had no way of knowing for sure."

"How many weeks has it been? You should have informed me then."

"And what if it wasn't her? Torture you while we waited to learn the truth?"

"My daughter has been missing for that long. That was torture enough, the not knowing."

And Zach could say nothing. He had no children of his own. He could never imagine what it would be like to report a son or daughter missing, never mind learn that they had been murdered. But the request for the ambassador's DNA had been a precaution, because it was possible they were wrong. And that was when they'd learned that the ambassador and his late wife had adopted Alessandra from Romania when she was an infant. There were no clear records, no chance of a family member's DNA to be found, so that avenue of identification had been fruitless. Because she had traveled so much with her family, finding any dental records that could be used had been harder than Zach had thought possible. "At this point, our only identification is from the forensic artist's sketch."

"I'd like to see it."

Zach removed it from his briefcase, handed it over.

Alec stared at it, blinking back tears. "That's her."

"It would help if we had some of her DNA. For a positive match."

"It's her."

A moment of acquiescence, allowing that he was grieving, and not likely to be thinking in terms of investigations and conclusions. "Of course, sir. But we intend to prosecute once we find who did this, and for that…"

Alec eyed the drawing, then handed it back. "I—I'd forgotten, but she stopped by here during her break a few weeks ago, off touring Rome, or rather visiting the columbaria of Imperial Rome with her friend Francesca, from the Academy across the street." He took a deep breath, glanced out the window at the croquet game, which was winding down.

"Maybe there's something in her room, something she left behind…"

Alec shook himself, said, "Yes, I'll take you up."

"Perhaps one of your staff can show me, if you'd like to have a moment to yourself, sir."

Alec nodded, and Zach opened the door, saw the same woman who had escorted him up, waiting a discreet distance away. He hesitated at the door, turned, saw the ambassador staring out the window. Zach hated to disturb his thoughts, but figured now was better than later. "Was there anything she discussed with you over the phone the last few weeks? Anything unusual? Maybe something she sent home?"

"I was so busy. We didn't speak but once or twice a week, and it was she, asking about my health…"

When nothing more was forthcoming, Zach let himself out and started down the hallway, the closed door and his footsteps doing little to muffle the strangled sobs of a grieving father.

◇◇◇

Leonardo Adami had come to the decision that watching the ambassador's residence was a waste of time. He was tired of the waiting, even more tired with sharing a car with Alonzo, and was half tempted to switch places with Benito, who watched the ambassador's residence through his binoculars from the rooftop of one of the nearby houses. In fact, he'd picked up his phone to make the call when Benito announced that Griffin had arrived at the ambassador's. That was not something they'd anticipated when they'd started watching the place. The three of them had been there all afternoon, as they had been for the last two weeks, waiting to see if any out-of-the-ordinary deliveries were made. None of them had expected Griffin to walk into the midst of their surveillance, and of course now they had to wonder if he knew what they were waiting for, and perhaps had come looking for it himself. This long, they had to wonder if it was going to arrive at all, but where else would the girl have sent it?

"You're sure that's Griffin?" he asked Benito once again. After all, Benito was several houses away on a rooftop.

"Positive. He went in almost ten minutes ago, and hasn't come out yet. Maybe you should call the boss."

The last thing Leonardo wanted to do was call his cousin and give the impression that he couldn't handle this on his own. Adami did not like weak links. Instead, Leonardo thought about the other reasons why Griffin might be there. "They must have her identified. He's come to make the death notification."

"Now what?" Benito asked.

"You're sure Griffin's alone?"

"Positive."

"Let us know the moment he leaves," Leonardo said into the phone. "We're going to follow him. When he stops, we'll take care of him there. If we're lucky, he'll lead us to his safe house. Adami will no doubt be extra grateful if we eliminate Griffin as well as those bastards he is working with."

◇◇◇

Washington, D.C.

Carillo waited until he saw the congressman leave the building, then walk toward a waiting car, before he approached. While he was here in D.C. on a legitimate case that Doc Schermer had dug up for him, his contact with the congressman was unofficial, and he needed to step lightly.

"Congressman Burnett?"

The man looked up, appearing mildly annoyed at being stopped. "Yes?"

Carillo held up his credentials. "Special Agent Carillo, FBI. You have a few moments?"

"I'm in a— What is this about?"

"Alessandra Harden."

The congressman took a deep breath, this time looking more than annoyed. "I've answered these questions ad nauseam. Someone is trying to discredit me. There was no affair, for God's sake, and I didn't divulge anything about the committee. Isn't it time you let this thing go?"

He started to walk away, and Carillo decided a different tack was needed. Maybe a subject not quite so threatening as an affair with a girl now dead, and he thought about what Sydney had told him on her most recent call, thinking this kid might have contacted the congressman. That, she thought, might give them a clue as to why Alessandra was murdered.

"Actually, I'm interested in learning about a student in a class that she was in. A friend of hers who is missing," he said.

"Fine," the congressman said. "You don't mind if we talk in the car? I'd rather my business not be overheard so I can read about it in the paper the next morning."

Carillo glanced into the interior of the town car, saw the driver, and no one else. "Not a problem."

The congressman got into the backseat, and Carillo followed, closing the door, shutting out the noise from the street beyond.

"Where to, sir?" the driver asked.

"I need a cup of coffee."

The driver nodded, and the moment the car took off, the congressman leaned back in his seat, closing his eyes. He looked haggard, his brown hair flecked with gray, his skin covered with fine lines around his eyes and mouth. This was not the man who'd graced the posters at election time, the doctored pictures that took ten years off his face. This was the man worried about scandal and career-ruining photos plastered all over the nation's newspapers.

"Did you ever speak to a student named Xavier Caldwell?"

"I believe that was his name. This kid was a nutcase. He said he was a friend of Alessandra's, and that's the only reason I agreed to talk to him. He tried to say that the photo of she and I, that the government leaked it to discredit me. A government conspiracy."

"Any truth to that?"

"No doubt in my mind that it was done on purpose, and to discredit me. But I think he's out there if he thinks my own government did it as part of a national conspiracy. Especially when he added that it was all due to the government's involvement in Propaganda Due."

"Which would be what?"

"You may have heard of it under the name P2. A Freemason lodge in Italy, shut down in the eighties, after it nearly toppled the Italian government and crippled the Vatican bank. He said he had proof that they were active again, this time in our country, and there would be biological warfare involved."

"Okay. So he was out there. About Alessandra?"

"What about her?" the congressman asked, his voice short. "Regardless of what appeared in the paper, there's nothing to tell."

"Why did it appear?"

"The photo in question? Someone got a lucky shot, figured they could pin a quote beneath it, and somehow it made its way to a real newspaper. But when you think about it, is it any different from what you see on the cover of any supermarket tabloid? Make up crap and sell a story?"

"Why don't you tell me?"

"*Nothing* happened."

"You realize she's dead?"

"Dead?" His jaw dropped, and the blood drained from his face. One couldn't fake that sort of reaction. "How?"

"Murdered."

"Oh my God." The congressman closed his eyes a moment, took a deep breath. When he looked up again, he said, "Stop the car, Thomas. I need some air."

"Yes, sir." The driver made a right turn, then pulled over, allowing them to exit the car. "Where would you like me to pick you up?"

"I'll walk from here. I'll call if I need you later today."

The car drove off, and Burnett stood there, his hands shoved in his pockets, staring after the car. After several seconds, he turned to Carillo. "I'm sorry, I really am, but nothing happened between us. I didn't kill her if that's what you're asking. For God's sake, I regret the day I agreed to be on that committee."

"What committee?"

"Atlas. That's the reason our photo appeared in the paper. She had learned from her father that I was on the committee, and she wanted to know if we were looking into the death of the UVA professor, that microbiologist who killed herself. I sure as hell wasn't about to admit to her it wasn't a suicide. I had to say it was investigated thoroughly, but they were friends and she wanted to know if I could have it reopened. Nothing more, I assure you. Unfortunately, it wasn't like I could go to the press and clarify details."

"Atlas?"

The congressman looked over at Carillo. "Do you agencies ever *talk* to one another?"

"You'd be surprised how much we don't talk."

"Hell. I really don't want to end up in jail for breaching national security secrets. I'm sorry, but I can't discuss any more of this with you. I—I was rattled about Alessandra's death. I wasn't thinking." He looked more than rattled. A sheen of sweat covered his brow and upper lip. A vein pulsed at his temple. He might not be guilty of Alessandra's death, but he was certainly worried about something more than a simple photo in the paper.

"Look. My partner may be in danger, and it has something to do with whatever Alessandra was working on."

"I'm sorry. I really need to go." He stepped to the curb, held up his arm, calling out, "Taxi!"

A cab pulled up, and Congressman Burnett got in, barely sparing a parting glance in Carillo's direction.

Carillo stood there at the curb, going over the conversation. It wasn't unusual for politicians to sit on committees that weren't necessarily common knowledge to the rest of the world, but at least he had one more lead that hadn't existed a few minutes ago.

He pulled out his phone, called his personal font of knowledge, Doc Schermer. "You ever heard of Atlas?"

"Are we talking cartography or Greek mythology? A map versus the guy who was forced to hold up the sky?"

"I thought he was holding the globe."

"Common misconception, which may be why a map of the world was called an atlas."

"Figures you'd know this. But no, I'm referring to an OGA with that name. Just got done talking to Congressman Burnett, who mentioned it in relationship to that other matter I'm not allowed to discuss. The guy froze up on me. Was worried about breaching national security."

"That's a whole different ball game," Doc said. "But it fits with what I found out about the congressman on that background you asked me to do. He was sitting on a national security task force, so..." Carillo could hear him clicking away on his keyboard. "Not Atlas, but ATLAS the acronym."

"As in...?"

"As in Alliance for Threat Level Assessment and Security. It's a global task force that assesses terrorist threats, and when necessary deploys a highly trained strike force to eliminate those threats."

"And why is it no one's ever heard of it?"

"It wouldn't be very effective if everyone knew about it, would it?"

"So they're a covert agency?"

"Extremely covert. Most of their operations are NOC, non-official cover. Plausible deniability is standard procedure, if you could even get the government to admit there was such an organization."

"How come you know about it?"

"Hello? Didn't you just get done asking me to research the congressman less than a day ago? That and I was able to finally dig up something on this Griffin. He's running an international paper that's more than likely a cover for CIA."

"I'll keep that in mind should someone mistakenly nominate them for a Pulitzer. Back to the OGA."

"It's a multi-agency, multi-country task force, populated by brainiacs in specialized fields, along with your average spies and your not-so-average special ops types on the strike force, of which Griffin is one. From what I've been able to deduce, each country involved has their own team, but they work cooperatively. It came about after 9/11."

"So how much plausible denial are we talking?"

"Remember those CIA agents who were arrested in Italy a few years back for some shady operations?"

"Vaguely."

"Put it this way. The government will not admit any involvement whatsoever. If Fitzpatrick involves herself in anything not above board and gets caught? Not only is her job at the Bureau history, but she's probably looking at jail time."

"That's assuming she survives whatever it is she's doing. I'm starting to have a real bad feeling about all this."

"As well you should. They don't send out guys like Griffin on the strike force, unless there's a damned good reason."

◇◇◇

Sydney woke from her nap, wondering if Carillo had gotten ahold of the congressman, and if so, had the man actually been contacted by Xavier Caldwell. She picked up Caldwell's papers, scanned the last sheet, then found it. World governments all searching for some key that would lead them to the missing Templar treasure. That was enough to make any sane FBI agent realize that the writer of this paper was reading way too much fiction and internet propaganda. And that's precisely what she'd thought at first, except for that niggling memory of the latest display on loan to the Smithsonian. Something to do with the Holy Crusades…Templar Knights were involved in the Holy Crusades.

For the second time that day, Sydney called Tony Carillo's cell phone, having the hotel operator place it on her hotel bill. Italy being six hours ahead, she glanced at the clock to determine what time it would be in Washington, D.C., assuming he'd gotten there by now. It was almost five in the evening, not quite dark here, which would put it almost eleven A.M. there. "Give me good news," she said.

"I haven't made it out to the Smithsonian yet, but I did get in touch with the congressman. You ever hear of an agency called ATLAS?"

"No."

"That's where your boy Griffin works."

"What is ATLAS?"

"Alliance for Threat Level Assessment and Security. Griffin's on the strike force team. As in the special ops guys who go out and deal with the really, *really* bad boys. Doc Schermer thinks you need to get your butt out of there and home, if you want to keep your job." He gave her the rundown of the team.

"As it turns out, Griffin is insisting I return home, to keep me from becoming involved, so that shouldn't be a problem. Tomorrow, in fact. I suppose if necessary, I could leave earlier. He's all for it, Scout's honor."

"Where is he now?"

"Making the death notification to the ambassador. Back to the congressman. You asked him about the missing student?"

"I did. He says the kid is a nutcase, talking about how the Freemasons and Propaganda Due are running the U.S. government, and that's why they manufactured his photo with Alessandra and allowed it to be published. Hard to imagine that lead going anywhere."

"Except that she is dead and he's still missing."

"Maybe he killed her and fled."

"Or maybe he was killed, too, and we haven't found his body yet. In a nutshell, I think we need to find out if there's anything in this conspiracy paper he wrote, and if that's why this girl was killed."

"Okay, let's say it is why she was killed. How the hell'd she and this Xavier stumble across this on some conspiracy Web site, and end up dead? It's not like other nuts out there haven't made a similar connection, and yet they're still walking around searching for the Templar treasure and spouting off that the Illuminati is about ready to take over the world. No one's killed them."

"What did she do different, you mean?"

"Exactly."

"Like I said, her body was found at the Smithsonian, where they recently had a display on loan having something to do with the Holy Crusade."

"As in the Templars?" Carillo said. "Maybe you shoulda taken this vacation a lot sooner."

"Bear with me a second. This conspiracy paper I'm holding mentions Templar treasure, and some key that leads to it, which certain world governments are searching for."

"Does it say why?"

"No. But like you, I'd have dismissed it in a heartbeat, if not for the dead girl with the missing face, whose body was found just outside the very building where this display was located."

"Or maybe it has nothing to do with the display. Either way, I'll head to the Smithsonian next."

"I'll keep in touch, let you know what's going on here."

"Likewise. Stay out of trouble, Fitz. And do not, under any circumstances, get yourself involved with whatever these guys are involved in. Doc Schermer's a pretty laid-back guy, and if he's insisting you get out, I think you should listen."

"I'm holed up in a Roman hotel room in my bathrobe. What sort of trouble could I possibly get into?"

Chapter Twelve

Sydney walked to the balcony and threw open the door, realizing there was little she could do about this information until Griffin's return. The air had warmed somewhat, probably due to the low gray clouds that now filled the sky, threatening rain. Warm enough, she decided, to sit outside with something to drink. She thought about getting dressed, but was comfortable in her robe, and she cinched the belt tight, retrieved another small bottle of *prosecco,* when the phone rang.

It was Griffin. "I hope you're awake?"

"Yes. And I'm glad you called. There's something I found out—"

"No time," he said, his voice sharp, clipped. "I'll be at the hotel in about one minute. I'm being followed. Have been since I left the ambassador's residence."

"What do you want me to do?"

"I don't want them to know I'm on to them, and I can't have them follow me to the safe house. Meet me out front."

It wasn't until she caught her reflection in the mirror that she realized there was a flaw or two with this plan. "*Now?*"

"Something wrong?"

"I'm not exactly dressed at the moment."

"Nice visual," he said. "I need you out there to see what they're doing. Don't contact me. Just observe."

"Out where?"

"The lobby should do nicely."

He hung up before she could protest, and she glanced at her clothes, then out the window, saw him pulling up. "One minute? Try thirty seconds," she said. No time to dress, she ran out the door, still carrying the little bottle of *prosecco*. It wasn't until she stepped onto the elevator that she realized she'd forgotten her key and she was barefoot. Okay, so maybe she'd be dismissed as a crazy American waiting for a friend. If that was the worst of her problems, she could deal with it, she thought, dropping the little bottle of *prosecco* into her pocket as the elevator stopped and the door opened. She stepped around a young woman who was busy trying to catch a towheaded toddler, who tried to run toward the open elevator.

Sydney ignored the polite but direct stares of the hotel staff, as well as the few tourists lounging about in the chairs. Had this been Florida, no one would have given her a second glance, probably assuming she was on her way to the beach or the pool. But this wasn't, which made the whole experience somewhat awkward. She only hoped it didn't get her booted out of her hotel, and she did her best to ignore the looks, waving off the concierge, who asked if she needed assistance.

She headed for the doors, exited, and tried to remain unobtrusive—as if that were even possible, dressed as she was—beside a column just as Griffin got out of a Peugeot that he apparently had picked up after he'd dropped her off. He handed his key to the valet, as though he were a guest, waited for his ticket, gave a casual glance toward Sydney, raised a brow at the sight of her robe. He walked past her, dropped his ticket, and as he bent down to retrieve it, his back to the street, said, "Do you see a blue BMW?"

"It's pulling up now."

"Keep an eye on them. Maybe they're only here to see where I'm staying. I can deal with that."

"And if it's not that?"

"Plan B. I'm open to suggestions."

"I *hate* Plan B," she muttered, glancing past him as the BMW came to a stop. She watched as the passenger exited, following Griffin toward the lobby doors. The man was tall, wearing dark slacks and a sport coat, his pale blue shirt open at the collar. Mirrored sunglasses masked his square face and reminded her of the guard from the Smithsonian. The BMW pulled up the street slightly, just out of sight, with only its back bumper in view. She didn't like the way this looked, the driver waiting, ready for takeoff. Quiet area, few witnesses...

The man approached the lobby doors, his hand poised inside his jacket, and she decided that if this was a hit, if he did have a gun, he could easily take out Griffin, then her and the doorman, who paid them little attention. Time for a distraction, she decided, loosening the belt on her robe, allowing the terry to fly open, revealing her black underwear and bra as she walked. "Darling?" she called out, loud enough for the man to hear. "Is that you?"

All at once, the doorman, Griffin, and the man tailing him turned her way, and she put a little extra swing into her step to make sure her robe stayed open. "Darling?" she called again, seeing the man reaching into his coat toward the small of his back. "I seem to have left my *key* somewhere."

The man following Griffin hesitated, and she caught a glimpse of the butt of his gun in his waistband. Griffin turned on his heel, but stopped as the lobby door opened, and out stepped the woman with the little towheaded toddler, who fled from his mother's arms, laughing as he ran right between the suspect and Griffin. His mother ran after him. "*Gianni! Gianni!*" she called out. "*Vieni a me subito!*"

Sydney's heart thudded at the sound of the child's laughter. Directly in the line of fire. Griffin stepped toward the man, stopped when he saw the boy, no doubt worried about the same thing. And what could she do, armed with nothing but a bottle of *prosecco*? Maybe she could throw it at him, distract him enough to give Griffin a shot—assuming Griffin was armed. Instead, she strode up to the man, shouting, "You're late!" He looked at her in confusion, his gaze flicking down to her exposed skin. "You promised to meet me."

His expression hardened. Dismissed her. He turned away. Again started to draw his weapon. She came up behind him. Grabbed the bottle of *prosecco* in her pocket. Shoved the top of it into his back. Grasped his arm with her free hand, and hoped the Bureau's reputation extended to this country. "FBI. *Capisce?*"

He froze. The mother ran up, grabbed her child, then retreated back into the hotel, blissfully clueless.

"Reach for that gun," she said, "and you die."

"You're making a mistake," the man said in English, his accent thick.

"Not as big as yours," Sydney replied. The understatement of the year, she thought, pressing the *prosecco* harder against his back as Griffin appeared at her side, taking the man's gun, slipping it into his own waistband. He raised a brow at the sight of the small bottle, but otherwise said nothing, and she dropped it into her pocket, cinched her robe closed, as Griffin placed the man in a discreet wristlock. From the corner of her eye, she saw the driver step into view. He looked as though he was ready to approach, investigate. "What about his friend?"

Griffin looked that direction just as the driver ran back to his car, sped off, wheels screeching across the cobbled drive. "Looks like your friend abandoned you."

"He'll be back."

"But you'll be gone. In the meantime, walk quietly into the lobby," Griffin said, with a slight twist to the man's wrist to ensure compliance. The doorman opened the glass door, let them in. Griffin said something to him in Italian, and Sydney overheard the word *carabinieri* and assumed he was asking that the police be called. That and no doubt something about an office, since the doorman ran up to the desk, and the well-dressed man from behind the counter rushed forward, and ushered them into a room just off the lobby.

Griffin said something to the manager, who nodded, then left them alone. The moment the door closed behind him, Griffin shoved the man in the chair, drew the gun on him, and told Sydney, "You don't happen to have a spare pair of handcuffs to go with that lethal weapon, do you?"

She smiled. "Unfortunately, no. Budget cuts have really taken their toll." She withdrew her sash from her robe. "Will this do?"

"As good as anything." He handed her the gun, then took the belt. "At least tell me you caught a license number on that car?"

"Sorry. I was a bit occupied."

"Probably stolen anyway." He walked behind the suspect, pulling his hands behind him, tying them to the back of the chair with the sash. "My suggestion? Be very careful. The lady has no qualms about blowing your brains out. The wine goes to her head pretty quickly." Griffin pulled the belt tight, asking, "Who are you, and who do you work for?"

The man said nothing.

Griffin didn't bother questioning him further. He searched his pockets, found no ID and no more weapons. Five minutes later there was a knock at the door, and someone called out Griffin's name. He opened the door to four men.

They stepped into the room, remained near the door, conversing quietly in Italian, every now and then glancing either at the prisoner or at Sydney, who had taken up residence in an armchair, where she could keep watch on the man. Earlier the man seemed calm, unruffled over his capture. But the longer the group spoke, each time they glanced his way, he seemed more disturbed. A sheen of sweat soon covered his brow and upper lip, his jaw clenched, and a vein in his temple seemed ready to burst. When two of the men walked over, switching out Sydney's sash for handcuffs, then each taking one of his arms to escort him out, his face paled. So be it, she thought as they left.

And no sooner had they stepped out the door, when a tall, stocky man walked in after them. She recognized Tex from Griffin's office in D.C. He gave her an appreciative glance, smiled in greeting, then said to Griffin, "Why is it I never get the pretty girls in bathrobes on my assignments?"

"Luck of the draw. But watch yourself. She's dangerous."

"And," Sydney said, "she'd like to go up to her room to change. Or is that too much to ask?"

"We'll walk you up," Griffin said. "Your hotel has been compromised."

"Which means what?"

"You won't be staying here tonight. It's not safe."

Tex held the door, and she cinched her robe even tighter, feeling very conspicuous as the two of them walked her across the lobby to the elevator. "One minor problem. No key."

Griffin left her and Tex at the elevator, walked up to the manager, whispered something in his ear, nodded toward Sydney, and the man went behind the long registration desk to retrieve a duplicate key.

Once up in her room, she gathered her clothes and stepped into the bathroom to change. When she came out, the men were standing before the window, and she heard Tex say, "She really took him down with a bottle of *prosecco* from the minibar? You know, Griff, we could use her—"

"She's not available."

"But—"

Whatever Griffin interjected was in Italian, and judging from the tone of his voice as he argued with Tex, not a subject he wanted to discuss, a fact confirmed when Griffin walked out onto the balcony, apparently frustrated with whatever Tex was telling him.

"Is something wrong?" she asked Tex, sitting down to put on her shoes.

"Guess that depends on your point of view. Mine's thinking you might be perfect for the party at the Adami villa. Lots of dignitaries, and you'd look a damned sight better on my arm than he will, no matter what his disguise, since my so-called date never made her flight out here."

"A party? You're kidding, right?"

"We're using the party as a cover to get me in the door. Have a—"

Griffin stepped back in the room. "Enough!"

"If she's going, she has a right to know what she's getting into."

"And who said she's going?"

"You have a better idea? The Lodge aside, I'm supposed to be a rich American, looking to buy art. We all know rich Americans like to have beautiful women on their arms. And her presence will take notice off of me."

"It's too damned dangerous. I don't want her involved."

"Maybe," Sydney said, "someone should ask me?"

"Much like you asked if it was okay to hop a plane to Italy, involve yourself in an investigation you shouldn't have involved yourself in?"

"And it's a damned good thing I did," she said, grabbing the folder of university papers and shoving them in the small suitcase. She zipped it shut. "Or they'd be scraping your sorry ass off the pavement."

Tex laughed, until he saw her pick up the bag, then her purse, and walk to the door. "You're not going to let her take off, Griff."

"Actually, I am, because I can guarantee that once she finds out this covert operation isn't sanctioned by the government, and that she could very well jeopardize her position with the Bureau, she'll refuse."

Sydney stopped cold, thinking about what Carillo had told her about this team Griffin was working on. She'd been tired, wasn't making the connection until now. "ATLAS is black ops, not special ops?" she said, eyeing them both.

Griffin crossed the room, stood face-to-face with her. "How do you know about ATLAS?"

Anger surged through her. "Tasha died for some black op gone awry? Find another guinea pig, because whatever game you're playing at isn't one I want in on."

"Since you're not in on it, no worries."

Tex put his hand on the door to prevent her leaving. "Sounds like she does want in on it, Griff. Or she wouldn't be protesting so much."

"Let her go, Tex."

But Tex didn't move. "Can I apologize for whatever he did?"

"Or what he didn't do?" she said, her hand still on the door, thinking about how Griffin had kept Tasha's death from her.

"I'll admit he isn't the easiest man to work with."

"Work with?" She glanced over at Griffin, who stood there with his arms crossed, glaring at them both. "I didn't even know who the hell he works for until about an hour ago, and even then, I wasn't sure. What I do know is that from the moment my plane touched down in Quantico, he's managed to—"

"Be a royal pain in the ass?"

"Something like that."

"He's a tortured soul."

"Tell him to get in line. A few of us have the market cornered."

Tex gave her an empathetic smile. "That we do, darlin'. But we get on with our lives. So, give us a chance to convince you to change your mind?"

"You heard her, Tex. She doesn't want any part of this."

Tex ignored Griffin, saying, "I'd really like to plant this device in that bastard's office. You're perfect for my cover. You studied art, you know the classics, and I'm allegedly there to buy a painting."

She wasn't surprised he knew her passion for fine art. Not with the background Griffin had done on her. And as much as she was tempted by the thought of getting to see some actual paintings, it wasn't worth the price. "Sorry. I only packed business casual."

"See?" Griffin said. "She can't do it."

"We have connections, darlin'."

"Doesn't matter," Sydney replied. "There's nothing you or anyone else in here could say that would make me change my mind. Nothing."

To which Tex said, "You want to nail the group we think killed your forensic anthropologist friend?"

It seemed several heartbeats passed as his words sank in. "Nothing except that."

◇◇◇

Before they left the hotel, two of Griffin's Italian team members, both special agents in the *carabinieri*, returned to acquire the proper dress and jewelry for Sydney. Her measurements and shoe size were taken, followed by some rapid transactions in Italian via the phone. Within a half hour, a delivery was made directly to the hotel from Salvatore Ferragamo on the Via dei Condotti, consisting of black satin pumps and a low-cut, black evening dress that gathered just below the bodice into a shimmering fall of crepe and velvet that brushed at her toes. Tex left for the safe house to change into his formalwear, and while they waited for him to return, she was briefed on what they expected of her, while Griffin paced the room, clearly not happy with this latest turn of events.

"Calm down, *amico mio*," Giustino, the shorter of the two *carabinieri*, said to Griffin, as his partner, Marc, helped Sydney fasten a diamond bracelet, then showed her how to work the transmitter and receiver. "She will be fine. It is not as if you are taking some unsuspecting citizen off the street and dropping her into the den of the lion."

"No," Marc said. "We are dropping an unsuspecting FBI agent into the den."

"But a beautiful and well-trained one, *non è vero?*" Giustino said.

Griffin threw the two men a dark look, then said to Sydney, "It's not too late to back out."

"If this gets me closer to finding out who killed Tasha and the ambassador's daughter, and who tried to kill me, then I'm in."

Marc said, "You do understand, *signorina*, that if something happens, if you or Tex are caught, we cannot acknowledge you? This is NOC." He pronounced this last as "knock," which meant nonofficial cover. No ties to any governments. Everything under the radar.

"You mentioned that twice."

"We cannot even go in after you."

"You *are* giving me a gun?"

Giustino said, "There is a small-caliber pistol in your evening bag. But as with everything else, if you get caught with it in Italy, you are—how do you say—on your own?"

"Even if the *carabinieri* give it to me?"

"*Mi dispiace, signorina,* we are not involved in this affair, just as Griffin and the Stati Uniti are not involved in this."

Truly on her own, then. About to embark on her first unsanctioned black ops mission. And hoping she wasn't about to make the biggest mistake of her life.

Chapter Thirteen

A shaft of moonlight broke through the clouds, allowing Sydney a glimpse of the pungent baytree forests, as Tex drove the Lancia Thesis up the winding narrow and steep road in the Alban Hills. Their destination was the sixteenth-century Villa Patrizia. "Wait till you see this place," Tex said. "Built on a crag overhanging the volcanic circle of Lake Nemi by one of the more eccentric Orsini Dukes. Probably why Adami bought it."

"So how is it no one ever came after this guy?" Sydney asked Tex.

"You can't topple a well-loved public figure like Adami without irrefutable proof."

"He's American?"

"As apple pie as a gangster can get. Born Carl Adam in New Jersey. Moved to Italy and became Carlo Adami. That's his identity now, and since he's lived the past twenty-something years in Italy, married his wife and made his fortune, or rather, increased hers, he's become untouchable. He's handsome, rich, and the king of philanthropists. Donates millions of euros. Travels to Africa and Sudan, fights for orphaned AIDS babies, even holds and kisses them. That's the figure the public sees. No one wants to look too closely at how his numerous international holdings in energy and construction companies prosper anytime there's a war or civil unrest in the Mideast or third world countries. Or how some of that philanthropic money being thrown around the globe is funding terrorists, who keep that civil unrest going.

That's why our operation is unsanctioned. We, being Italy and the U.S., need the evidence before we point the fingers. And he has too many important people from both countries in his pocket for us to be able to get it via the normal investigative route."

"So why would he have Alessandra murdered?"

"That, darlin', is the million-euro question. Something we haven't quite pieced together. We're fairly certain it had to do with his arms smuggling, or a cover for it."

"So she was working with your team on this?"

"She's the one who brought it to our attention. She seemed to think that Adami was working on finding the source to some plague he could use for his bioweapons. Unfortunately we couldn't convince Alessandra not to go on this expedition he was financing. She insisted it would look better if she went herself. When she tried to contact Griffin about a week before she was murdered, he was working an operation in Tunisia. Didn't get her message until too late."

"Any idea what she wanted?"

"None. She only said it was urgent he contact her. A few days later she went missing, and we've been scrambling ever since," he said, flicking on the high beams as they approached yet another steep uphill curve.

"But you were able to make a connection between her and Adami?"

"Last summer she stayed with her father at the Vatican embassy residence, and at a party, Adami approached her, asking if she knew of any good archeologists, as he was financing an expedition. Naturally, we assumed this was a cover for his arms smuggling. We got word that he was looking to start building up bioweapons. So far no proof. Can't even find his damned lab. But a few weeks after she returned to the States for school, she telephoned the CIA, saying that she had some information she thought they might be interested in. Something called the third key, which translates to *la terza chiave* in Italian. We figured it had to do with a Freemason lodge in Italy called C3, if only because the initials are the same."

"C3?" She thought of Xavier Caldwell's conspiracy paper. "Any chance it's connected to something called Propaganda Due?"

He looked over at her, then back at the road. "A big chance. How'd you come up with that?"

"A kid in Alessandra's class at UVA wrote a paper on Freemasonry right before they went missing. He thought P2 was still going strong and had infiltrated the U.S. government."

"Not sure about that last part, but we do think that C3 is possibly an offshoot of the old P2, Propaganda Due, a clandestine Masonic lodge that was shut down about twenty years ago. The Italian government nearly collapsed when it was found that P2's members consisted of *numerous* top officials in Rome, all corrupt and on the take. Everyone from the highest-ranking politicians to the police and judicial officials, even a number of high-ranking Vatican officials, all commingling with the Mafiosi." He slowed for a turn, and Syd caught a glimpse of the steep cliffs and the lake below. "The downfall caused the collapse of the Banco Ambrosiano, a major financial institution that was controlled by the Vatican. And that's not even counting the murders connected to the whole affair."

"Was Adami part of that operation?"

"Damned straight he was. As usual, he managed to survive the scandal. Claimed he didn't know the P2 Masonic lodge wasn't the social club he'd thought. Which is how we came up with my cover. A rich American Freemason, looking to buy some artwork from him."

Xavier's conspiracy paper aside, it seemed the Freemason connection certainly opened doors, she told herself. "And all you intend to do tonight is to plant a listening device?"

"An undetectable device. It's our best chance to figure out where he might be making and storing bioweapons. We want to prove it, destroy them, and shut him down."

As they neared the villa, Sydney smoothed her dress, adjusted the diamond bracelet at her wrist, then pulled the visor down to look in the mirror. "How about a test," she said, turning her head from side to side as though looking at the diamond earrings, but in reality checking to make sure the tiny transmitter in her ear was not visible. Griffin, Giustino, and Marc were holed up in a van farther down the hill near the small town of Nemi, monitoring their progress. Once at the villa, Tex would have to leave her to break into Carlo Adami's office to plant the listening device.

"Testing, one, two, three," came Griffin's voice.

"Perfect," she said.

Tex stopped at the tall wrought-iron gates, adorned with the Orsini coat of arms, and showed his invitation to one of the uniformed guards, who took it, leaned down, looked into the car, eyed Sydney, then returned the invitation to Tex. "Enjoy your evening, *signore è signorina*," he said, waving them through.

The gates slid open, and Tex drove up the long winding drive, lit on either side by torches set into shallow pans. The flickering flames cast eerie shadows across grotesque moss-covered statues of satyrs chasing nymphs. The drive ended in a broad ellipse before the great renaissance mansion, and Tex pulled up to wait their turn behind a Ferrari that had stopped behind a Mercedes. Angry clouds threatened rain, but the stylishly dressed guests seemed not to notice. Not one umbrella or raincoat marred the perfection of the Fendis, Versaces, and Armanis worn by the men and women emerging from the various luxury vehicles. A few moments later, two of several crimson-liveried valets walked up to the Lancia, one opening the door for Sydney, another for Tex. The keys were left in the vehicle.

"You be careful with that there car, son," he said, in a thick drawl. He didn't wait for a response, just took Sydney's arm possessively, playing his part of the rich Texan. Sydney, keeping up her role as arm candy, laid her hand over his, and gave her best ingénue smile, having to look up at him. At six-three, with shoulders that looked like a linebacker's, and thick wavy blond hair shimmering in the torchlight, he was an impressive sight in his tux. He led her up the steps to mingle with the guests, as they waited for their introductions to the Count.

A white-gloved waiter bearing a tray of *spumante* approached. "*Prosecco, Signorina? Signore?*"

"*Grazie,*" Sydney said, taking a glass.

Tex took one as well, leading her through the gilded columns of the cavernous salon, whose baroque mirrors reflected light onto the fanciful parrots that darted in an impossible flight across the frescoed ceiling. Sydney, in her black velvet and crepe Ferragamo gown and simple diamond earrings, blended in with the other women, who, according to Tex, included *contessas* and *principessas* among the guests. A discreet servant informed them that an *al fresco* supper as well as their host, Carlo Adami, awaited them in the Raphael Loggia, which she discovered was the name of the great veranda that overlooked the gardens and Lake Nemi. There were propane heaters set up to keep the guests warm. A long table, draped with the finest damask, had been covered with plates of canapés, bowls of iced caviar, and other delicacies of antipasto. Mingling among the guests was another waiter, this one holding a tray of frosted vodka glasses, which Sydney declined. Tex immediately went for the vodka, leaving his wineglass on the tray. At one end of the spacious loggia, a tall, dark-haired man, perhaps in his late forties, broke away from a cluster of guests and approached them.

"Ah! Signore Jamison," he said to Tex, who was using the name Roger Jamison instead of James Dalton. "I am so happy that you and your charming friend could attend my small gathering." He turned his attention to Sydney, saying, "I do not believe that I have had the pleasure of making your acquaintance."

"This here little lady is Cindy Kirkpatrick," Tex said, putting his arm around Sydney. "And this, Honey Pie, is our host, Carlo Adami." Sydney eyed the man who was allegedly behind the killings. He didn't fit any stereotypes, unless one was trying to pigeonhole the suave, debonair multimillionaire murderer. His dark eyes swept over Sydney, and she imagined that if one didn't know his background, one might easily be charmed by his easy smile and the slightest of dimples on his chin.

But she did know his background, which made it all the harder to appear pleasant, neutral.

"Your home is magnificent," she said, falling on the only truthful statement she could think of at the moment, and she held out her hand. "Thank you so much for inviting us."

Adami took her hand in his, bowing over it, before turning his attention back to Tex. "I cannot wait to show you my Tiziano. I am certain that once you see the painting, you will not regret your journey. Perhaps after I see to my guests?"

"Looking forward to it," Tex said, lifting his vodka glass, then downing it.

Adami excused himself, and continued welcoming new guests as they arrived. After about a half hour of Tex making a show of drinking more alcohol than was good for him, with much of it discreetly poured into the potted persimmon trees that were conveniently located at the corners of the loggia, he made a loud declaration of going off to find the "little boys' room." And since his words made little impression on the guests, who were unfamiliar with the term, he announced in stentorian Texas Italian, "*Dough-vay Eel Gaaby-Netto?*" The *principessas* and politicians politely pretended not to hear, and one of the waiters immediately ushered Tex out of the salon and presumably to the room in question. Sydney was thus left to wander and to gather bits and pieces of conversation that could be recorded by Griffin and the others monitoring her and Tex from the van.

A number of fine paintings had been hung between the mirrors of the salon, and Sydney decided she'd use them for her cover. She stopped to view a portrait over the marble fireplace of a girl in red velvet, wondering if it was really by Leonardo da Vinci. If it was merely an exquisite copy, she'd have no way of knowing. She'd never seen a real Leonardo outside a museum. Moving on, she strolled the perimeter of the salon, admiring each work of art, pausing by first one group of guests, then another. Tex's pretended ignorance of Italian had the desired effect. The guests continued their conversations, paying her little attention. Unfortunately, Sydney's limited understanding of the language made it difficult to know if she was picking up anything useful. She figured Griffin would notify her via the receiver if something came up, so she continued on, perusing a painting or statuette, attempting to stand close enough for the transmitter to pick up what the guests were saying, before moving on to the next piece of art. Finally she spied Carlo Adami with several men near the winding double staircase, and wandered in that direction, hoping to capture something there as well.

Adami held court among a group of distinguished-looking men, and no one glanced her way. As she stopped to admire a marble bust of the Emperor Nero set on the left balustrade of the double staircase, the conversation seemed to change course, more of a hushed whisper, urgent, and one word caught her attention. *Massonico.* Considering that part of Tex's cover was that he was a Mason, and Adami was suspected in dealings in the P2 Masonic lodge, that made this particular conversation something she wanted to overhear. The men had other ideas, however, and moved beneath the giant arch that spanned from one side of the staircase to the other. Probably just as well, and so she crossed the room to the other staircase beneath the great parabolic arch, which allowed her a visual on the men, but was far enough away to appear as though she had no interest in anything they were discussing, even if she could understand it.

And it might have been left at that, had she not noticed a rare bust of the Emperor Gaius Caligula in the far corner beneath the arch, something she might not have known had her history of art professor not been almost fanatical about teaching them Roman art. She wandered over to get a better look, discovering that though she was thirty feet away and on the opposite corner from where Adami stood, the acoustics now worked in her favor. Like the arch in New York's Grand Central Terminal, even though she stood well away from the men, and far enough away to seem uninterested in anything but the marble statuary, their whispered conversation sounded as though she was standing right behind them.

Keeping her back to the men, she pretended great interest in the bust of Caligula, all while listening. She understood little of it, hoping it was loud enough for the transmitter to pick up, especially when she caught the phrase, *la piramide grande*. Immediately she thought of the ambassador's daughter and the crime scene photo, the gruesome triangular shape carved from the young woman's face. Attempting to put the image from her mind, Sydney tried to concentrate on what they were saying, noting that one phrase seemed to pop up again and again, something that sounded like "cheetray."

Suddenly the conversation stopped, but she didn't move in case it resumed.

"*Mi piacerebbe mangiucchiare i tuoi capezzolini squisitissimi…*" This was no echoing whisper. Carlo Adami had moved up behind her, spoken into her ear, his hot, wine-soaked breath caressing her neck. Her instincts told her that he wanted to know whether she'd been eavesdropping, and if she understood any of it.

She turned, smiled. "Signore Adami. You startled me."

"My apologies, *signorina*. And please, call me Carlo."

"Carlo," she repeated. "I'm embarrassed to admit that I don't speak Italian, so whatever you said…"

"It is I who should be embarrassed, *cara mia*. For taking advantage of the vulnerability of a *bellissima donna*—a beautiful lady left alone."

"We're hardly alone."

"Something that can be immediately remedied if you but say the word." He gave a mock sigh. "But being American, you are probably one of those ladies who are faithful to their… *fidanzati*, no?"

She merely smiled, casually glanced past him, noting the other men had moved from beneath the arch.

"Such a waste," he said. "This idea that one must have but a single love in one's life."

"What about your wife?"

"Giulietta? She is the understanding sort," he said, leading Sydney by the arm up the stairs, and no doubt out of hearing of the men he'd been conversing with. He stopped her midway, then turned toward the salon. "Do you see that delightful young man standing by the bust of Augustus Caesar? The tall blond man? He's been her lover these past three years."

"And it doesn't bother you that she has a lover?"

"What is it you Americans are so fond of saying?" he asked, apparently forgetting his own heritage. "Variety is the spice of life?"

"Something like that."

"Here, we say, '*Ogni medaglia ha il suo rovescio.*' There are two sides to every coin," he translated. "He makes my wife happy. That makes me happy." No doubt because she was the one who bought him respectability in this country. "But what I am more interested in is what makes you happy."

Somehow she doubted that. "For one, your stunning art collection."

He eyed her, his expression filled with skepticism. "I have noticed your admiration. You seemed particularly fascinated by the Roman busts beneath my staircases."

"Because I have a penchant for art history, which is what drew me to the busts in the first place. Especially that of Caligula. My understanding was that the majority of his likenesses had been destroyed after his assassination."

He looked at her with somewhat renewed interest. "Perhaps because of his reputation, at least that written by his detractors."

"And what was that?"

"That he was considered cruel, insane, and," he said, leaning in close to her, and lowering his voice, "he indulged in sexual aberrations that offended Rome." He straightened, watching her closely, and she had the feeling that whatever these aberrations were, he enjoyed thinking about them. "But Caligula's errant reputation aside—"

"Errant or repugnant?"

"That would depend on one's point of view," he said, as he once again ushered her up the stairs, placing his hand at the small of her back to guide her. "What I find interesting is that very few of my acquaintances, certainly none here tonight, could look at any of these pieces and be able to discuss them with any authority. Perhaps that is why Signore Jamison brought you with him? To determine if the Tiziano he intends to buy is real or a forgery?"

"Hardly. My knowledge comes only from haunting museums and taking art history classes. These could all be forgeries or the real thing for all I know." She hesitated at the top of the stairs. "Where are we going?"

"To show you what makes me infinitely happy." His sweeping gesture included the vaulted frescoed ceiling—and as Adami and Sydney rounded the corner of the first landing, she looked up and saw naked Cupids flying after thinly draped Psyches with butterfly wings. They flitted among curving acanthus vines that ran over the breadth of the ceiling. Farther on, Pygmies wearing conical hats and wielding long spears hunted crocodiles, and ibises fluttered on a lotus-studded Nile, which seemed to cascade down over the cornices that separated the ceiling from the staircase walls on either side of the great hall. As Sydney's eyes followed this painted Nile to its logical source above the center balcony that joined the twin staircases, the elegant grace of Greco-Roman temples gave way to the squared, but equally elegant, trapezoidal Egyptian temples with red and gold columns. At the very top, two sphinxes faced each other on either side of a great pyramid. From its central door, the tributaries of the Nile poured, dividing into two rivers, both of which went their separate ways, tumbling down on opposite sides of the double staircase.

Arriving at the top of the stairs, Adami escorted Sydney through the double doors, just under the pyramid. These led into another gigantic oblong room, elegantly furnished. Here, however, the artwork changed dramatically and was clearly a tribute to all things phallic. On the wall were paintings of satyrs with full erections, chasing naked wood nymphs, and young women mounting their lovers. A curio held wind chimes shaped like penises, as well as small statues of creatures and men, erections evident. Adami swept right past the displays and a conveniently placed chaise longue from which to view the artwork, as though barely noticing, and led her to some tall glass doors that opened onto a large travertine-paved balcony. Pushing one of the doors open, he said, "We are now standing above the Raphael Loggia." As she stepped through the door, she was stunned by the view. The balcony overlooked the formal gardens that ended at a balustraded cliff that dropped sharply into the volcanic lake. Except for the marble nymphs and satyrs, the gardens were now deserted, perhaps because the wind had picked up, bringing with it a few scattered raindrops that mixed with the spray from the fountains and vanished into the winds of the lake.

"What's on the other side of the fountain?" she asked, pointing to a winding path of moonstone that led to what appeared to be a garden house that overlooked the lake.

"A very, very special place," he said, watching her as he spoke. "The collection in the room we passed through is but a small part of it. Perhaps one day I will show you…sooner rather than later. What do you think?"

"About your gardens?" she said, deciding that was a safer subject than the one he was intimating. "They're magnificent."

"Almost as magnificent as you are," he said, his voice low, smooth.

"*I'm in.*" She froze at the sound of Tex's voice in her ear, almost didn't expect it.

"You are, perhaps, uncomfortable with my attentions," Carlo said, eyeing her still.

"I— Yes," she said, realizing that was as good a cover as one could ask for.

"*Che peccato!* I shall take you back to the *festa.*"

"Not yet," she said, lifting her face, taking a deep breath, grabbing at any chance to stall Carlo. Tex needed at least five minutes in Carlo's office to set up the listening device. "Don't you love the way the air smells just before it rains?"

"*Sì,*" he said, moving closer to her, so that his arm brushed up against hers. "I do." His voice caressed her, made her think perhaps she'd taken this a step too far, especially considering the room they'd passed through to get here. She was saved from responding when someone stepped out on the balcony.

"Signore Adami?"

Carlo stepped back, looked toward the open veranda door. "*Cos'è?*"

"*C'è una telefonata. È urgentissima!*"

He hesitated, then, "*Starò lì, subito!*" He took Sydney's gloved hand. "You will forgive me, *signorina*, but I have some annoying business that I must attend to. A phone call."

He bowed over her hand, turned it and pressed his lips to her palm. "*Ci vedremo presto, cara mia!*"

She forced a smile, watched him leave, then turned her back, pretending to look out over the gardens, ignoring the fat rain-drops brought in on the wind. Leaning on the balustrade, her hands clasped together, covering her mouth, she said, "Hope you heard that, because he left in a hurry."

"I did. He's got an urgent phone call." Tex's voice came in clearly through her earpiece. "Which means he's probably headed right for his office. You can't stall him for thirty more seconds?"

"I can try," she said, then turned on her heel and hurried through the offending room and down the winding double staircase. Carlo was weaving his way through his guests, heading through the main hallway toward the back of the house, when she finally spied him. "Carlo?" He didn't hear her, and she pushed her way through, calling out again. "Carlo?"

He'd just reached the back passageway, stopped, turned her direction.

Suddenly she doubted herself, doubted her ability to handle anything about this operation. She didn't know what to say, what wouldn't tip him off. "I just wanted to…thank you. For showing me your gardens." Lame, but she was at a loss here.

Carlo gave a perfunctory smile, his gaze sweeping over her as he said, "The pleasure was mine, *signorina.*"

He left her standing there as he strode out of the salon, then down the hallway toward his office, and she breathed a sigh of relief when she heard Tex's voice saying, *"All clear*. I'm out the window."

"Thank God," she said, snatching an iced flute of vodka from a passing waiter, who smiled at her, undoubtedly thinking she was grateful for the alcohol. She took a sip of the burning liquid, then nearly spit it out at as she caught sight of a man walking through the front doors. The driver of the BMW who had followed Griffin from the ambassador's house to the hotel. And he was walking directly toward her.

Chapter Fourteen

Leonardo Adami glanced at his watch as he crossed the *grande salone* of his cousin's *palazzo*, crowded with insufferable guests. The whole thing should have been canceled, propriety be damned. But Carlo would not hear of it, or rather his wife wouldn't. She had too many friends to impress, too much of a reputation to keep up, and too tight a rein on the family finances. Had it been up to Leo, he'd have eliminated that little difficulty years ago, he thought, looking up to see a woman in a black Ferragamo dress, standing near the grand staircase.

Something about her seemed familiar, but before he could determine what it was, she turned away, walking toward the *loggia*. No doubt he'd seen her on the arm of one of the visiting dignitaries, probably in a more intimate setting, the sort they didn't bring their wives to.

He put her from his mind, weaved his way through the guests to the far wing, up another flight of stairs to the third door on the left, then knocked sharply, before opening the door. His cousin was speaking on the phone, so he walked over to the bar and poured himself a drink.

"You have the money," his cousin said. "And three days to make it happen, *capisce*. No more mistakes. And if the doctor balks, show him the picture of his mother's house in India. That should gain you some cooperation." His jaw tensed as he listened, then gave a curt "*Ciao*," before dropping the phone in the cradle and turning his attention to Leo. "You're late."

"We had a few problems."

"Where's Alonzo?"

"That would be one of the problems. We followed Griffin from the Ambassador's residence to a hotel. It should have been simple..." He shrugged. "A woman got in the way."

"Griffin is still alive?"

"And Alonzo is in his custody."

Carlo walked over to the decanter, poured himself a drink. "Tell me exactly what happened, Leonardo," he said, walking to the window, looking out to the courtyard below.

It was moments like this that reminded Leo why Carlo was still in charge of the family. No show of emotion, no indication that anything was wrong, nothing but the slight tightening of his jaw as he sipped at his drink.

When Leo finished, Carlo said, "What does Alonzo know?"

"He knew nothing. Not even why we were watching the ambassador's villa." Leo waited in silence for him to make up his mind.

"It's time we sent a strong message. If they choose not to keep Griffin out of our business, then perhaps we can convince them another way."

"How?"

"Do you still have her face? The ambassador's daughter?"

"Of course not," Leo said. "Your American counterpart didn't want her identified too readily. He was not pleased with the method chosen to delay that identification."

"And now they have her identified. In hindsight, it might have hastened the ambassador's departure from Rome."

"I would think that he will be leaving now."

"See that he does."

Leonardo tipped his head, turned to leave.

"One more thing, Leo."

"Yes?"

Carlo's gaze remained focused out the window. "Find out who that woman was. The one who prevented Griffin's death. Let us send *her* face to Griffin. Perhaps then they will realize the full import of our demands."

◇◇◇

Sydney watched from the alcove as the driver emerged from the hallway. "Mr. BMW," she whispered. "He's out."

She listened for Tex's voice, but it was Griffin's she heard over the transmitter. "Why the hell isn't anything transmitting from the office?"

A slight hesitation, then Tex saying, "I couldn't activate it. I'm still outside the window."

"We call it off. I want you two out of there. Now."

"I can do it, Griff."

"That's an order, Tex. Out."

"Carlo's leaving," Sydney said. "I can see him in the hallway."

"Let me finish it, Griff."

"Negative," Griffin said. The driver walked directly toward Sydney, and she moved around the column as he strode past. When he continued on into the salon, she breathed a sigh of relief, only to step right into Carlo's line of sight just as he looked up.

"Hope springs eternal?" he said, when he neared her. "Dare I believe that you have changed your monogamous ways? Perhaps my enchanting little room changed your mind?"

"Or maybe that the wine has gone to my head and I've lost my way from the ladies' room?"

"I should have forgone the phone call, and brought you a bottle myself."

"I see you're the incorrigible type."

He grinned. "I try my best. More wine? I have a very special bottle of *Vino Nobile di Montepulciano, Carpineto*, 1991."

"As much as I'd love to, I'm waiting for my boyfriend, who just left to get me a drink of something cold and nonalcoholic."

"Then I'll wait with you."

"You should attend to your guests."

"As you can see, they're attending quite well to themselves," he said, looking up, waving his hand across the room. "Ah, my cousin," he said. "No doubt taken by your beauty."

Apparently his cousin and Mr. BMW were one and the same, and he was bearing down on them, a frown darkening his expression. In case he might recognize her, she turned away, keeping her back to him, hoping that he didn't see her. "I think I need a bit of fresh air. I've had entirely too much to drink."

"Carlo!" Mr. BMW called out, and she took off just as Carlo turned to find out what it was his cousin wanted.

She wove her way through several people, glanced over her shoulder, and saw the man running toward Carlo, a definite look of recognition on his face as he called out again. "I've been made," she said, hurrying toward the door.

"Tex?" Griffin's voice sounded scratchy. "Where the hell are you?"

"Almost done, just making the connection."

"Fuck the connection. Get out and get Sydney out. Now."

"Done. Hitting the window as we speak."

Sydney ran out the doors, grabbed two fistfuls of dress, yanking it up as she bounded down the steps. Heavy drops of rain hit her in the face. She glanced behind her, saw Carlo and Leonardo emerge through the doors. They hadn't yet seen her, and she ducked behind a sedan. "I could use a little help here, guys. They're on the steps, looking for me now."

Griffin said, "Get her the hell out of there. *Now.*"

"I'm working on it."

She heard Carlo shouting out to one of the valets, just as the sound of an engine revved. A moment later, a black Mercedes pulled up. "Hop in, darlin'," Tex said, as he threw the door open.

"Stop them!" she heard Carlo shout.

She jumped in, closed the door as he took off. Wheels screeched across the paved stones. She buckled her seat belt. "This isn't the Lancia we came in with."

"I was a little pressed for time. And this was parked in front of it. Lucky for us, all the keys are conveniently left in the ignition."

He sped toward the gates. Sydney glanced behind her, saw Carlo and Leonardo running toward the BMW that the valet was bringing around for them.

"We're going through," Tex said.

She turned, saw the gate, their car bearing down on it. Solid, massive. A guard stood front and center, his gun out, pointed at them. Tex stabbed the gas pedal. The guard jumped back, fired.

The driver's window shattered. The Mercedes hit the heavy wrought-iron gate. Metal crunched. The gate flew off, tumbled over the car, bounced onto the roof, then landed behind them, taking a couple of torches with it.

Tex slowed into the turn, maybe a bit too much. She glanced back, saw the BMW gaining on them. The Mercedes swerved, and Sydney grabbed the dash. "Tex?" She looked over. Saw him slumped in his seat. "Tex?" she yelled.

He didn't move. The car continued forward. The one working headlight lit up the curve in the road, the cliffs, and the lake below. She shook Tex's arm. No response. "Tex!"

"*What's wrong?*" Griff's voice in her ear.

She grabbed the wheel as the car gained momentum. Rain splattered against the windshield. She steered into the curve. The back end started sliding. Just reach the trees.

Please, not over the cliff. Anywhere but the cliff...

Chapter Fifteen

Griffin stood on the cliff overlooking the sheer walls of the deep crater lake, the rain beating down on his coat. He brushed the water from his face, tried to keep his vision and senses clear as the *comandante* of the Nemi police questioned him in heavily accented English. "And what is it you are doing at Lake Nemi at such a late hour?"

"Writing an article on travel," Griffin called out over the wind. He'd already given the officer a fake U.S. passport with the name Roger Reynolds, and apologizing up front for not being able to speak a single word of Italian. "I saw the car go over the cliff and came up to see if I could do anything to assist."

"A gracious effort," the *comandante* replied. "But as you can see, there is nothing to be done."

An answer Griffin would have to be content with. Not even Giustino or Marc, two high-ranking *carabinieri*, could step in, make their presence known at this time. Hence the delay in Griffin's arrival. He'd had to leave his team down in Nemi before coming up to investigate. By the time he'd arrived, the local police were already on the scene, and everything he'd gleaned was from overheard conversations and eavesdropping on their radio traffic. Apparently Carlo Adami was being questioned back at his villa. Adami's only admission was that a car was stolen and the guards shot at the driver. He was, however, allowing the police access to his grounds, small consolation, since the locals embraced Carlo, not realizing what he was truly involved in.

For now, all he could do was watch and wait. And hope Tex and Sydney were not lying at the bottom of the steep-cliffed volcanic lake.

There was no sign of the car, no sign of either of them. Just the report of a lone unidentified witness seeing the car with a single headlight go off the cliff.

"*Signore?*"

The *comandante* stood there in the driving rain, waiting for Griffin to acknowledge him. But Griffin couldn't take his eyes off the lake below. Tex knew the dangers, knew what he was getting into when he'd come into the unit three years ago from the NSA. But they were wrong to assume that Sydney Fitzpatrick had the faintest idea, even if she was FBI. He should never have allowed her to assist.

"Signore Reynolds," the *comandante* shouted over the wind. "You should step away. There is nothing you could have done. Nothing."

He laid his hand on Griffin's shoulder, tried to draw him away, but Griffin refused to move. "You'll send down divers?"

"As soon as the storm abates. For now you should go back to your hotel. If you like, you may call our office in the morning."

"Thank you."

Griffin stood there several minutes more at the cliff's edge, staring out over the lake, not even bothering to brush the rain from his face, wondering if Tex had left when ordered, perhaps this entire catastrophe could have been averted. "Damn you, Tex," he whispered, his voice lost in the wind. "Why didn't you listen?"

When there was no answer, he turned away, not giving up hope that his friend might still be alive, that Sydney might still be alive. The lights of the villa farther up the hill were visible, and he thought of Tex racing down the hill, recalled with acute clarity the panic he'd heard in Sydney's voice as she cried out for Tex to respond. What the hell had happened up there?

Hell, he couldn't even figure out what had happened here. Between the rain and the cops trampling everything in their haste to respond to something they thought was a simple car accident, there was nothing left of the crime scene. Just mud and grass, he thought, walking back to the van, pulling open the door, sliding in, his mind turning about Sydney's panicked cry, again and again, trying to make sense of it.

There was no sense in death.

"Damn it, Tex," he said, then slammed his hand on the top of his steering wheel. It didn't lessen the pain, and knowing he still had a job to do, he turned the key in the ignition, switched on his headlights, and turned on the windshield wipers, listening to the rain beat down on the roof of the van. And that was when he saw the sparkle of something, like broken glass in the road in a place where no glass should be.

This was supposed to be a solo car accident.

He pulled forward slightly, and whatever he saw disappeared, so he shifted to Park, engaged the emergency brake, then got out, kept his gaze fixed to the wet road. He walked up. His heart pounded in recognition.

A diamond bracelet. The one Sydney had been wearing when she'd dressed for the party. Here on the side of the road near the stand of bay trees. Not near the cliff where the car went over. Not anywhere it should have been, he thought, looking in both directions, before bending down, picking up the piece of jewelry from the pavement, noting the open clasp.

"Did you find something, *signore?*" the *comandante* called out, walking over.

Griffin palmed the bracelet, shook his head. "No," he said, casually dropping it into his pocket. "I thought I had, but it was a bottle top." He made a show of kicking at something, giving a shrug.

The *comandante* nodded, went back to his work, and Griffin looked at the area just off the side of the road, saw the water sluicing down, turning the shoulder into mud. He strode back to the van, then took off, driving down the hill, when what he really wanted to do was drive up to the villa and search it room by room.

Only when he was out of view of the police did he pull over, turn on the cab light, and examine the bracelet. He had no idea if Sydney Fitzpatrick was still alive, but he was fairly certain of one thing. If this bracelet didn't go over the cliff, chances were good that neither did she.

She was smart, resourceful. Too resourceful at times.

The question now was had she survived?

◇◇◇

Leonardo waited until the uniformed officer left Carlo's presence, and then, when he was sure they wouldn't be overheard, approached. "There was no identification on the woman. Just a small-caliber pistol in her purse."

"You are certain she was the same woman you saw at the hotel? The woman who assisted in the capture of Alonzo?"

"Yes."

Carlo smiled at a few of the guests still lingering about in the *salone*. "No one saw you bring her in?"

"No one. The reports are saying she went over the cliff."

"Prepare her for the Caligula room. The white robe."

"For you?"

"Tempting. But once we have her identified, I believe she will turn out to be someone I desire to link to one or more of our important initiates before her demise," he said, nodding toward the *loggia*, where a group of men stood smoking cigars and drinking iced vodka, watching the rain beat down.

Leonardo eyed the men, no doubt discussing their common bond, world banking. "And her friend? The driver of the car?"

"Let me think on this. Considering his *alleged* Masonic background, perhaps we should make him a warning to our distinguished guests on what they can expect should anyone violate the oath of secrecy and our activities find an audience outside of our circle."

◇◇◇

Sydney opened her eyes, or thought she did, but saw nothing. Her head pounded, a sharp pain—unlike anything she'd ever felt—zinged across the back of her scalp when she tried to move, and she hurt all over. More importantly, her limbs failed to obey her commands.

She was either paralyzed, dead, or dreaming. The fact she felt pain in her head pretty much eliminated the last two choices as a possibility, and pain or no pain, since she could struggle, only not move, she was discounting the whole paralyzed thing. At the moment, a couple of those choices seemed preferable to what her instincts were telling her, especially when something scuttled across her legs. Though her head pounded with the movement, she tried kicking out, hoping to discourage any more visiting creatures. She hated the dark.

"Tex?" Her whisper seemed to echo off the walls, then disappear into hardening silence. The damned dark kept her from seeing whether they'd brought Tex in. He'd either been shot or knocked unconscious when the gate hit the car, and she knew he needed help. But who would come here looking for them, wherever here was? Maybe she was in a hospital, sedated after the crash. Unfortunately, this sure as hell didn't smell like any hospital bed she'd ever been in. It smelled of must and mold of some long-forgotten place. And she felt stones beneath her on the floor, cold and hard. Once again she tried to move, gritted her teeth against the pain, only then realizing what was wrong. Her arms were tied behind her, trussed to her feet. She'd survived the crash of the car, only to be taken captive. She tried scooting across the ground, scraping her arm and leg in the process. Her foot hit the wall, then something leaning against it. It fell across her legs, clattering to the ground with a ringing echo.

A shovel, she realized, and wondered if it was going to be used to bury her.

This was a black ops mission, something she knew before she'd agreed to assist Tex and pose as his girlfriend. They were warned there'd be no rescue. She and Tex were already written off. Hell, she wasn't even sure that Tex was alive. Griffin couldn't publicly search for them, would have to create a cover story to account for the accident, even their visit to Carlo Adami's party, all to cover the planting of the bug in his office, which may or may not have been successful.

She had to get out of here. Her best chance was in the bracelet she'd dropped in the road after they'd dragged her from the car. At least that was her thought until she remembered that no one was going to come looking for them. Which meant that if she couldn't depend on Griffin or his team, then she was going to have to find a way out of this herself.

Hard to do when one is trussed up like a Thanksgiving turkey.

◇◇◇

Griffin took his gear bag from the trunk, then left his car at the edge of the woods on the east side of Adami's property. He climbed the hill, not wanting to drive past the police working the accident scene. Normally Adami would have dogs patrolling the grounds with his guards, but because of the party, the dogs were kenneled. The guards, he hoped, were busy with the commotion at the front; if not, he'd have to deal with them. Once the cops left, once the last guests left, the dogs would be released. And once that happened, the odds of him getting in and out without firing a shot diminished significantly. He'd rather use a knife or his hands. Quiet kills were always more efficient. Right now he needed efficiency, he thought, making his way up the hill through the trees.

The property on this side was surrounded by an eight-foot wall topped by thick shards of glass, and he traversed the perimeter until he came to the back of the *palazzo*, and the formal garden that would allow him access to the property with some cover, with its hedges, topiaries, and statues at every turn. Getting over the wall was the easy part, because Adami had overlooked a few beech and chestnut trees growing in the midst of the bay wood forest, some with branches extending right up to the property. He threw a rope up into the closest chestnut, used it to climb the wall, rappelling up one side, waiting to make sure he wasn't observed, then using the leather gear bag to cover the top of the wall, before rappelling down the other side into the empty gardens as the rain continued down in a steady patter. He didn't venture toward the house, because he was fairly certain Adami wouldn't risk moving a body inside, not with the cops, never mind the guests, still present. But neither would the man leave any evidence somewhere where any of the cops or guests could accidentally come across it.

He looked up at the house, saw the lights in the *salone*, nearly empty, a few people standing around, men and women in their finery, along with a handful of men in the *loggia,* no doubt gossiping at the horrors of the shooting and the accident, probably wondering if it was safe to drive home. And he could well imagine Adami consoling them, telling them that they were welcome to stay until they were sure the roads were safe. Adami's finesse was unrivaled. He had the police department fooled, the politicians in his pockets, and the people at his feet. No one knew what he was really capable of.

Which was why Griffin was working alone tonight. Tex knew what his duty was, knew the risks, just as Griffin knew. The operation came first. His superiors would consider Tex's and Sydney's loss collateral damage, a by-product of the greater good. And the main reason he'd been reticent to have Sydney join them. It was one thing if you knew the risks from the beginning, knew what you were signing into. And even though they'd informed her, told her, he doubted she'd fully appreciated what it was they were asking of her when they sent her into Adami's villa.

By the time he made it halfway across the massive grounds, the rain slowed to a drizzle, and the wind diminished considerably. Unfortunate. The inclement weather had masked any noises he might make. But it also worked both ways, and he soon heard the sound of heavy boots crunching in the gravel as a uniformed security guard made his rounds. Griffin pressed against a conical hedge, then circled around a statue of a satyr playing a pan flute, as another guard walked up, joined the first. They stood not three feet from where Griffin hid, and he kept watch, waiting for them to exchange a few words and hopefully move on. Apparently they were enjoying the break in weather. The first guard, the swarthier of the two, took a pack of cigarettes from his pocket, tapped one out, offering it to the other man, who shook his head, saying, "Don't let Adami catch you smoking out here, or you're likely to end up in the bottom of the lake."

"Always he wants the perfect show for his guests. But he can't see here from the house." He lit his cigarette, cupping the flame from the drizzle, took a long drag, then blew out a stream of smoke. He nodded toward the satyr. "I keep the cigarette butts in the bush by that statue and pay the gardener a few euro to clean them each night for me."

The only bush near the satyr was the one Griffin stood next to, and he glanced down, saw several cigarette butts. Definitely not good. There was no place to back out, nowhere to turn without alerting the guards to his presence. And the moment the one guard tossed his cigarette into said bush, he was bound to notice that the satyr had grown an extra set of legs…

Had he been dressed in a tux, he might have masqueraded as a drunk guest. Dressed as he was in all black, he doubted he'd pass muster as anything but an intruder. And since it didn't look as though he was going to be able to avoid discovery, he decided that he'd have it occur on his timetable. Drawing his knife from its sheath, he leaned down, grabbed a handful of pebbles, getting ready to toss them so that they'd hit the guards from above. An intended distraction, make them wonder what was going on. He hoped.

He brought his hand back, ready to toss the pebbles, when the second guard said, "I'm going to finish the perimeter. Enjoy your cigarette."

"I'll meet you at the fountain."

The second guard walked off, his footsteps fading in the gravel. Griffin held on to his stones, decided the farther away the other guard was, the better for him, and so he waited, while the first guard smoked alone. A minute went by, and the guard looked at his watch, not seeming in a real hurry to join his comrade. He took another long drag, the cigarette glowing, then suddenly turned toward the statue. Griffin's only hope now was that he'd simply toss the cigarette, then be gone. But no. The man walked the two steps over to the conical bush, bent down and knocked the lit end from his smoke on the ground, then flicked the butt underneath the lowest branches.

Griffin saw the man's shoulders tensing.

He rose, sidled around the statue, pointed a gun at Griffin. "Who are you?"

Griffin palmed his knife, kept it out of sight. "I was at the party. I'm just here to find a friend."

The guard motioned with his gun. "Get your hands where I can see them."

Griffin threw the gravel in the guard's face. In the same movement, he moved his arm up, knocked the gun away. The guard lunged. His left hand arced toward Griffin. A glint of steel, the whistle of a knife. The guard plunged it toward his gut. Griffin grabbed the guard, spun with him, heard a loud hiss. Felt his side freeze. *Gas knife.*

The guard stepped back. Griffin moved with him, not giving him any space to plunge that knife. It would explode his insides in an instant. One step to the left, Griffin followed. Eye to eye, each with a knife. The guard smirked. He might have missed the first time. But he knew he had a partial burst of gas left. Enough to do some serious damage. Griffin hefted his knife. Another step to the left. Griffin did the same. The guard, heavy on his feet, telegraphed his moves.

The moment he lunged again, Griffin stepped back, came around him, brought his knife to the man's throat. The guard refused to give up, and Griffin grabbed him by the hair with his other hand, swung him around, and brought his head crashing down onto the base of the statue. Still alive, the guard slumped to the ground, unconscious. He took the guard's handcuffs, cuffed the man's hands behind his back, then looked around, figured he had maybe five–ten minutes before the other guard made it around the perimeter and realized that his partner wasn't waiting at the fountain as he'd said.

No time to waste.

Griffin sheathed his knife, stepped out, kept to the shadows, made his way through the gardens to the side of the house, and just beyond that, the garages and outbuildings. Two other men emerged from a side door of one of the outbuildings: another uniformed guard and a man wearing a white shirt, dark jacket. Griffin was too far away to determine who the man with the guard was, but the way he stood there, looking around, indicated to Griffin that he hoped they weren't seen.

Which meant that was precisely where Griffin wanted to look first.

◇◇◇

There were still twenty cars parked between him and the garages, a few with "CD" plates belonging to the *corps diplomatique*, which meant Adami was going to play host until his most important guests left. And there, near the front, was the Lancia that Tex and Sydney had arrived in. After checking for guards, Griffin scurried to the closest car, ducked down behind it, then carefully weaved his way through the vehicles to the side door of the outbuilding where he'd seen the two men standing. The door was closed, and of course, locked. Question was, attempt to get in there, or through a different door? And more importantly, if he did go through, was it alarmed?

It was a series of locks, breached in seconds with a lock pick. Once inside he looked around, saw no indication of an alarm panel. There were stairs that led up, probably to the servants' quarters, and stairs that led down. Nothing else but the two staircases. He chose down, figured they wouldn't risk any servants seeing anything, no matter how much they paid them. But at the bottom of the steps, there was only one door at the end of a short, stuccoed hallway, and when he opened it, it led into a room filled with cleaning supplies. The first thing he thought was that this was an odd place to have just one room, and so he checked for hidden doors. And found none. So upstairs it was, he thought, closing the door, then backing out.

That was when he felt a slight breeze, or maybe he heard it, like the faintest whispers of air moving where there shouldn't be any air moving. He listened. There it was again. A rubbing sound, or something scraping. He turned back, ran his hands along the bricks, feeling for anything that seemed off, and then he felt a ridge, pushed, and a door swung open.

He stepped in, closed it partway, and only then dared to use a small blue cell light, one that wouldn't be as easily seen from a distance. He shone it around the room, saw the space was cut from stone, and small, barely ten by ten, completely empty but for a pile of muddy rags in the corner. He started to walk toward it.

"Syd?" he whispered.

From the corner of his eye, he saw something flying down at him. He raised his arm, deflected the blow. Pain shot through his limb. Something metal clattered to the stones. He stepped back, pulled his knife. Turned. A quick flash of his light.

Sydney.

She backed away.

"Syd. It's me. Griff."

"Oh my God. I thought you were one of them, coming back."

"Are you okay?"

It took her a moment, but finally she nodded. "I hurt like hell. Cut my hand on that shovel I tried to hit you with. I used it to cut the rope."

He flicked the light across the shovel's blade, saw it covered with rust and dirt. "Where's Tex?"

"I don't know. I'm sorry…"

"Let's get out of here. We need to hurry. Can you walk?"

"I have no idea."

"Try," he said, putting his arm around her. Her knees shook, but she seemed okay, no broken bones that he could see. She looked like hell, covered in mud, never mind there was enough blood on the floor to concern him. "You're bleeding."

"My hand. God, it hurts." When she tried to walk on her own, her knees gave out. He lifted her in his arms, carried her out of the room and up the stairs. At the entrance, he opened the door leading to the grounds, stepped out into the night air. He glanced right, then left, before crossing the distance to the remaining cars parked between the outbuilding and the main house. He was fairly certain he couldn't carry her out the back way, the way he'd entered. Maybe he could get to the Lancia that she and Tex were forced to leave behind.

"We're almost there," he told her, glancing down, seeing her eyes were closed. He could feel the blood soaking into his shirt.

"Stop right there."

Griffin froze. He was ten feet from the Lancia. Ten god-damned feet. He looked up, saw the same two men he'd seen exiting the outbuilding, realized who the second man was. Leonardo Adami. "Perhaps you didn't notice. The lady is hurt and she needs help."

"Perhaps you didn't notice the gun pointed at you."

"And what?" Griffin said, looking around, trying to see if there was anyone there who might help. No cops in sight, only one of the diplomatic drivers, asleep behind the wheel of his sedan. He glanced at the weapons Leonardo and the guard were pointing at them. Nine-millimeter Berettas. "You're going to shoot me here with the police on the grounds? How the hell are you going to explain that?"

"I'm sure we'll think of something."

"Look, it's me you want. She's got nothing to do with this."

"And what did you have in mind?"

"I let her go, she walks out of here. You get me."

"An interesting offer. But I have the advantage. My gun pointed at you."

"And no less than four police you'd have to explain the gun-shots to, and how she ended up here, when they're looking for her down there," he said, nodding at the police vehicles still visible down at the edge of the cliff, never mind those parked in the drive at the front of the house.

"My cousin was wrong about you. You do have a weakness." Leonardo smiled. "Throw your handgun toward me, and your offer is accepted."

Sydney stirred in his arms. "What are you doing?" she whispered.

"Doing what you did for me this afternoon." Louder, to Leonardo, he said, "I'm going to lower her down. If you want my cooperation, you'll get me the key to the Lancia, then let her walk over to her car, get in, lock the doors, then drive off."

"Why not let her go back inside?" Leonardo said with a smirk.

"With her gown muddied and torn? You know how vain women can be. The key?"

"It's in the car."

He lowered Sydney to the ground, held her gaze, then nodded toward the Lancia, afraid that if he said anything further, they'd try to stop her, maybe even suspect his next move, which, considering he didn't know what the hell he was going to do next, was laughable. Right now, he wanted Sydney safe.

Keeping his hands up and visible, he watched as Sydney ambled toward the car, using the other vehicles to balance. She opened the door, sat inside, then pulled the door closed. He heard the lock engage, then turned his attention to Leonardo and the guard.

A second later the car alarm pierced the air. Startled, Leonardo and the guard pointed their weapons at Sydney, who had opened the door, engaging the alarm. She slammed it shut as Griffin dove, scrambled for cover.

"We'll kill her!" he heard Leonardo shout to him over the alarm.

Griffin ducked behind the front end of a limo, angling himself so the engine block stood between him and them. His weapon drawn, he watched their reflections in the rear windshield of the car to the front of him. They were walking forward, searching for him. When they passed by the car he was hiding behind, he moved toward Sydney and the Lancia. He was a car length from it when several uniformed police came running out of the house to investigate the cause of the alarm.

Their shouts in Italian alerted Leonardo and the guard, who turned just as Griffin stood, tucked his gun at the back of his waistband, then raised his hands. He glanced toward the house, saw that several of the guests had followed the police out, as had Carlo Adami.

Griffin continued to walk toward the Lancia. "My wife had a little too much to drink," he said in Italian, loud enough for the cops to hear. "She stumbled and fell and accidentally set off the car alarm." One hand held high and visible for the police, he slowly lowered the other, and opened the car door. "The alarm," he told Sydney. When she shut it off, he looked up at the men on the porch, and again in Italian, said, "My apologies, Signore Adami, for giving everyone a scare. But after tonight's earlier accident, you wouldn't want her to drive home alone, now, would you?"

Adami glanced at his cousin, then back to Griffin, his gaze narrowing. After a moment of sizing up the situation, Adami smiled. "You are wise to be concerned for her welfare, Signore Griffin. But perhaps she should not be behind the wheel?"

"Of course." Griffin leaned into the car, not about to let Sydney out, exposed in her condition, and have someone point out that she looked like the woman who ran from the party and jumped in a stolen car. "Do me a favor, dear. Could you slide over the console into the passenger seat?"

Sydney scooted up onto the console, then over. The moment she was in her seat, Griffin waved to Adami, and in English, said, "Good night, and thank you for the invite."

Adami gave a brittle smile, then turned back into the house. Leonardo glared at Griffin as Griffin closed the door, locked it, started the engine, then drove off.

"Thank you," he told Sydney.

"Likewise. Don't suppose you have any aspirin?"

"You're probably going to need it. Don't suppose you remember when your last tetanus shot was?"

"No."

"Lucky you. Hear they hurt worse than anything else. We're going to the hospital, have you looked over."

She didn't argue.

As they drove past the guardhouse, he saw one of the guards on the phone, watching them as they drove past. No doubt he was speaking to one of the Adamis, letting them know they'd driven by. He checked his rearview mirror. So far no one was following them. He didn't think that would last; even so, he drove carefully down the winding road as they approached the turn to the cliffs, slowing at the flares the police had set out to warn other drivers of their presence.

He glanced over, saw Sydney look out the window at the police cars, then turn away, closing her eyes. He didn't ask her about it, figured she'd tell him when she was ready.

And he was right. When they were halfway down the hill, she said, "The guard shot at us as we drove through the gate. The window shattered, but I thought it was okay. He was still driving..." He heard a deep intake of breath before she continued. "He wouldn't answer me—"

Griffin looked over at her, saw her staring out the windshield, her gaze empty. "He was shot?"

"I don't know. It could have been the gate, we drove through...Hit the roof. I don't know."

"What happened?" he finally asked.

"When he didn't respond, I steered the car into the trees. I didn't want to go over the cliff...Next thing, someone was dragging me from the car. That's the last thing I remember until I woke up in that room."

"You did the right thing."

"But that's just it. I shouldn't have done this...I didn't want to leave him."

"I know," he said, checking his rearview mirror to see if they were followed. So far nothing.

"Why did you come back for me?"

"I found your bracelet in the road."

"I thought—"

"Sometimes we break the rules that need to be broken."

He checked the mirrors again, still no sign of a tail. Normally that would be a good thing, but right now it bothered him. Adami wasn't one to give up so easily. So what was his next move?

And then it struck him.

The car might be at the bottom of the lake, but Adami had Tex.

Chapter Sixteen

In the security room of the Smithsonian, Special Agent Tony Carillo scooted closer to the monitor, trying to get a better view of the woman standing near a display on the Templar Knights in the Smithsonian. She was young, early twenties, wearing a UVA alumni sweatshirt, similar to what Fitzpatrick had described. The girl seemed particularly interested in something in the display case, but from his angle, he couldn't see what. After a couple of minutes, she walked a few feet, asked a security guard a question, and he pointed in the opposite direction. She turned, walked that way, was met by a man of East Indian descent, and both disappeared into a doorway. That was the last time either was seen on any of the tapes.

"What was she looking at? Or for?" he asked the head of security for the Smithsonian.

"This would have been a traveling display..." He consulted a calendar. "Templar Knights and the Holy Crusade. Relics, armor, that sort of thing."

"Anything the world hasn't seen before?"

"Not that I could tell. The display will be here a couple more days, if you want to see it, then it's back to France."

"And what's that she's holding?"

"The catalog. She would have purchased it from the gift shop. I have a copy here," he said, handing Carillo a catalog on the display.

It was slick, glossy and Carillo looked through it, didn't see anything earth-shattering, but figured it couldn't hurt to compare the catalog to what was being shown, and once he was taken directly to the display, he checked off each item, figured everything was there. She'd seemed particularly interested in something at the end of the last case. There was an illuminated map, and next to that a belt buckle depicting the Templar cross, a ring with the same cross, an old coin showing the double Templar knights on horseback, and then a very worn cross engraved with the Crucifixion.

But then he looked at the catalog again, saw the price stamped on the cover. "I don't suppose you have security tapes of the gift shop, do you?"

"Actually, we do. Just never thought about that."

"I'd like to have a look."

◇◇◇

Sydney woke with a start, looked around, not recognizing the darkened room. There was a second of momentary panic as she recalled the accident, her basement prison, and she thought about Tex, wondered if they'd found him yet. If they were even looking for him. Griffin had come after her, saved her in direct defiance of any orders. What she wanted to know was, orders from whom? What obscure branch of the government did he work for? Was ATLAS a shadow branch of one of the most covert branches? Very much like her father's work. Before his death, he'd worked special ops, even black ops for the army, and kept it from his family, work that wasn't always on the up-and-up.

Was what she'd been doing on the up-and-up? She had only Griffin to assure her it was. Only his word that Carlo Adami, a man with legitimate ties to the U.S. and their allies, one of the most respected businessmen in the world, a man who funded numerous global charitable organizations, was up to his neck in murder and terrorist funding. Publicly accusing such a man of conspiring with terrorists to further his business interests would have been as welcome as someone accusing the Pope of conspiring with the devil to help the church.

"You're awake."

She glanced over the edge of an eiderdown quilt, saw Griffin watching her from the arched doorway. "Yeah," she said.

"How do you feel?"

"Sore all over. Groggy from the painkillers." She remembered nothing after the stop at the hospital, other than sleeping on the long drive. "Where are we?" she asked, eyeing the wooden-beamed ceiling.

He walked into the room, stood at the side of the large double bed. "Our safe house. Your CT scan was clean, so other than a few bruises and scrapes, the cut on your hand from the shovel—"

"The least of my worries…Tex?"

"Nothing yet. But it doesn't look good."

"I'm sorry."

"It wasn't your fault."

"But he recognized me. Adami's cousin. From the hotel. He came after me."

Griffin didn't respond.

"Is anyone going to look for Tex?" she asked.

"Tex didn't follow orders. He should have left. He knew the rules." Before she could think of what to say, he turned, walked toward the door, and with his back to her, said, "I'll see you in the morning."

"Where are you going?"

He didn't answer. He didn't need to. She knew. Rules or no rules, he was going to look for Tex.

◇◇◇

Jon Westgate exited the sedan that pulled up in front of Adami's villa. The morning sun lit up the hillside. It also blinded him as he was approached by one of Adami's goons, who patted him down for weapons. If Adami weren't so bloody important to their operation, he would never have submitted himself to such humiliation. Surely the man knew that all Westgate needed to do was make one phone call, and for all Adami's millions, he would never survive the next day.

But that was just it. Adami knew. And he also knew that as long as he held the cards he did, Westgate would never make that call. They'd needed him. But that was about to change.

Weapons search over, the goon escorted Westgate up the travertine stairs, through a large salon, then past the impressive double staircase, and a length of windows that looked out over a massive veranda, which bore the remnants of the previous evening's festivities. They continued on up a back set of stairs that led to a private balcony with an unparalleled view of the lake, where Adami sat eating his breakfast. He looked up, smiled at Westgate, then indicated he should sit.

Westgate pulled out a chair, taking a seat across from Adami.

"Would you care for something to eat or drink?" Adami asked him.

"No, thank you. Tell me about the party."

Adami took his damned time, sipping at a glass of orange juice, keeping him waiting. "An unexpected visitor," he finally said, then proceeded to tell him what had happened the night before.

"Griffin was here? How did he get in?"

"The back wall, apparently. The guard who was working it is no longer in my employ."

No doubt now residing at the bottom of Lake Nemi, Westgate thought. Adami's penchant for killing aside, he turned his thoughts to what had transpired at the party before Griffin had arrived. "This woman, do you know who she was?"

"Unfortunately, not yet. I sent someone out to the hotel where they first ran into her, but apparently the records were sanitized. We learned from a maid that a woman of her description checked in, but as for any names…" He shrugged in that insolent way of his, as though he couldn't be bothered by such minute details. "A shame we lost her, though. I had some high hopes of using her to bait some of the attending dignitaries."

And there was the crux of Adami's power. He had taken the lessons learned from the old Propaganda Due Masonic lodge disbanded over two decades ago, and used them to his advantage. On the surface he was the king of altruism. Beneath, he had a number of high-ranking politicians and dignitaries from countless countries in his pocket. Most were brought into the fold by way of Freemasonry, a common bond exploited by Adami. He was careful to nurture this connection until he had them where he wanted them. Some were there due to simple bribery on a grand scale. Others because they believed in the cause, domination of the world's banking system. A few very powerful heads of state, however, needed a bit more coercion, and therein was the key to Adami's success, because he had dared to find out what their innermost fantasies were, then presented them with such, only to blackmail them once their wishes were fulfilled.

Surprising how many of them were sexually deviant, when presented the right opportunity. Not surprising how many caved, once they were faced with reality and a few choice photos or tapes of their escapades. And the Freemasons were the perfect venue with which to hide and manipulate those men. The inner circle of a secret society lent itself to corruption, because there were no checks and balances, no oversight. The Catholic Church got that part right when it condemned Freemasonry all those years ago. So yes, aside from the plain, greedy power mongers, or the bribed officials, the new C3 Masonic lodge also had its share of extremely powerful deviant members who would go to great lengths to ensure that their intimate lives didn't cross over to their public personas.

It was perhaps this, more than the bribery and blackmail, that made Adami such a distasteful partner in crime. And the very thing that made him such a dangerous one. As much intel as Westgate's boss had available at his disposal, he had yet to learn exactly who had been lured into this sexual den of Adami's. Certainly a number of top-ranking C3 members, but who else?

He smiled at Adami, decided it best to change the subject. "My boss doesn't seem to think that this little plan of yours to stir up tension will work. He thinks you should just stick with supplying the bio arms that we agreed upon."

"Little plan? Trust me. If we find what we're seeking, it will do more than stir up tension."

"Well here's the thing—"

"The thing…?"

"Cut the I'm-Italian-and-don't-understand-your-Americanisms crap. You're as Italian as I am."

"I haven't been to America in well over twenty years."

"Your loss, our gain," Westgate said, tiring of always having to kiss Adami's self-made "foreign" ass, when everyone knew he hailed from New Jersey. Which made him relish what he was about to do, because it was about damned time someone put Adami in his place. "As I was saying, here's the *thing*. This map? We want it."

"I was under the impression that your boss called it a pipe dream, one that generations of men before me have searched for in vain."

"That was before he started looking into it. He is interested in knowing how you came about this knowledge."

"As a philanthropist, I have funded a number of scholarly works and studies. Several were of particular interest, involving the studies of ancient temples, burial sites, and religious artifacts. But why does he care how I came about this knowledge?"

"Let's just say he had a change of heart, and he shares in your vision of what this thing can do."

"And what if I don't want to share?"

"You and the little empire you've built here using the Freemasons will cease to exist. C3 will be exposed for what it is, an offshoot of Propaganda Due's Masonic Lodge, and you their Grand Master in charge of corrupting public officials for illicit gain."

"You think you can touch me?"

Westgate leaned back in his chair, enjoying this much more than he thought. "If you think otherwise, it would be a fatal mistake on your part."

Adami looked him in the eye, as though contemplating just how seriously he should take this new threat. Then he smiled. "I am not so foolish to think that I wouldn't be here if not for the help of my friends. What did your boss have in mind?"

"He will be sending two of his men to assist you in the recovery of the map to ensure its safe arrival into his hands."

"And if something but the desired result occurs?"

"It would be in your best interest to guarantee the desired result. Any other outcome, and you may find certain past hidden allegations of your business dealings coming to light in a very public way. Allegations about C3 that will make the Propaganda Due scandal twenty years ago pale in comparison." Westgate stared at him over steepled fingers, smiling at the sudden pulsing of a vein in Adami's temple.

"You do realize," Adami said, "that we aren't the only ones searching for the map?"

"You're speaking of Alessandra's friends?"

"Yes."

"Then take out some sort of insurance policy to ensure their cooperation. Your future and that of C3 depends on it."

"Done. About Alessandra. My understanding is that she may have brought some information to the Smithsonian."

"Did you ever find out what this was?"

"Niko, the man you helped me to set up at the Smithsonian, followed her and Dr. Balraj. He thinks she may have posted it before he was able to stop her. We believe she sent it to Rome."

"Her father's residence?"

"We know of nowhere else she might have sent it. And Niko was not able to get what it was or the location from her before he killed her."

"And do you know who killed Niko?"

"I suspect it was that FBI agent who came to the Smithsonian asking questions. Niko telephoned me right after she arrived—a fortunate thing he stayed on after we picked up Balraj and had Alessandra killed. Niko was supposed to kill the agent as well. Apparently he failed."

"Apparently." Westgate tossed an envelope on the table. "Think of this as a present."

"What is it?"

"A photograph of your FBI agent. Sydney Fitzpatrick."

"Why bring it here?"

"She flew into Rome yesterday."

Adami reached over, opened the envelope, and slid out the photo. That vein in his temple started pulsing again. "She was here at the party last night. The woman who Griffin carried out."

"Why do you think they were here?"

"Seeing this photo, I presume they were looking into Alessandra's death. Hoping to find someone who might talk."

Westgate leaned back in his chair, sighed. "I have a flight to catch. In the meantime, you might want to make sure this insurance is foolproof. We want that map."

Adami said nothing.

Westgate glanced at the photo on the table of the FBI agent. "Interesting that they showed up here. Were they ever out of your sight?"

Adami hesitated. "Of course they were. I didn't realize who they were until my cousin recognized the woman. A shame we lost her. She would have been easier to interrogate."

"And you've gotten nothing out of the man as to why he was here?"

"Nothing at all. I don't even know who he really is."

"Maybe you haven't tried hard enough to find out." He pushed back from the table and stood. "But I'm sure you'll remedy that little problem."

◇◇◇

Adami picked up the photo of the woman that Westgate left behind. There was much to think about. An FBI agent? Something was off there. FBI wasn't typically involved in international covert operations of this sort. Then again, what if they were? What if the man he held in the chamber was the unwitting party to all this, and the agent had used the poor schmuck?

But then he thought of the way the man was able to withstand his interrogation. This was no milquetoast nouveau riche businessman. Which altered things considerably.

Adami didn't like being played—by either side—and he tossed the photo on the table, then picked up the phone to call his cousin. He needed to make sure that when the endgame was played, when the map was found, he was the winner. "The visitor in the chamber."

"Still breathing. Why?"

"There's been a change of plans."

◇◇◇

The late afternoon sun poured in through the double terrace doors of the safe house, bathing the terra cotta-tiled floors in honeyed light. Wanting to banish the dank chill of that chamber in Adami's villa, Sydney basked in a white linen chair, soaking in the warmth of a Rome autumn. She was fascinated by the safe house, a flat that occupied the entire fifth floor of a seventeenth-century palazzo on Via della Grotta Pinta in the heart of Rome's historic center. Marc, one of the two *carabinieri*, had told her that the palazzo used to be a monastery, and the bricks of the double arch in the living room, which had been brought up from the basement, dated back to 57 B.C. The thick walls were whitewashed; the ceilings were held up by wooden beams, of such an age that they were pitted with wormholes; and the apple-green door with its several Byzantine brass locks might look ancient, but it was actually reinforced and completely soundproofed. All in all, the flat consisted of three bedrooms, a bathroom, a radio transmitter room, a long hall, and a kitchen. The living room and kitchen opened up on to a splendid terrace garden, complete with fishpond and bell tower.

None of them had heard a thing from Griffin since he'd left, apparently at first light. All they could do was watch and wait. And though Sydney wanted nothing more than to take a nap, she didn't move from the small salon next to the radio transmitter room where Marc sat watching the monitors for each security camera positioned at pivotal locations outside the safe house. Every now and then his glance strayed to a TV positioned next to his workstation, the channel tuned to the local news. Giustino also watched the monitors, but his job was to listen to the receiver for anything that might come out of the device that Tex had planted. It had been quiet since the initial transmission, and they were beginning to wonder if it still worked.

Sydney paid little attention to the security monitors, since she wouldn't know what did or did not belong on the busy street outside. Instead, she watched the news on the TV, saw the view of the Tiber River, with the familiar sight of the Vatican in the background. The camera shot moved to a close up of a bridge in the foreground filled with pedestrians walking past statues of angels. The words Ponte Sant'Angelo appeared on a banner at the bottom of the screen. It meant little to her, and she turned her attention to the front door. "We should have heard something by now."

"He will call when he can," Marc said, intent on the news. He took a drink from his water bottle, then used it to point at the television. "Another one on the Ponte Sant'Angelo. What is that, three suicides this month?"

Giustino adjusted his earphones, then held his hand up. "Quiet. I think I have something." Sydney looked over, saw him adjust a slide control. "We're still in."

Marc shut off the TV. He and Sydney walked up, listened in as Giustino put the audio on speaker, and she could make out someone speaking Italian. Giustino took notes as a backup in case the recording equipment failed. "We're definitely in," he said, then gave a gratified shout, and slammed his hand on the table.

"What's he saying?" Sydney whispered to Marc, watching as Giustino took notes.

"Something about a shipment to Tunisia, once the money is transferred. They expect their new scientist to help in the preparation, as he is now being cooperative...It's Balraj. They have Dr. Balraj..."

"Balraj?"

"He was kidnapped. We thought he was dead. It is, as you say, very big. That's what we were looking for. We knew Adami was trying to build bioweapons. We didn't know where he—" His face paled as he looked at Giustino. "Did I hear that correctly?"

"What is it?" Sydney asked, just as she heard laughing on the monitor.

He waved for her to be quiet, while Giustino played back the digital recording. She listened to the rapid Italian, understanding next to nothing, until an echo of what she'd heard on the news, the Ponte Sant'Angelo stood out.

"They laugh about this report of a suicide off the bridge, and then they discuss what will happen when we—I assume they speak of us here—investigate this death at the…how do you say it? Morgue. And this other man, he asks how will they get us to look for the agent there. The first man says that when news of the death is out, we will know. They stripped him and removed his face."

"His face…?" she repeated. "Tex?"

Giustino said, "What else can we believe? They say agent. They must have guessed as much when Griffin arrived at the villa to find you."

Marc sank into his chair, burying his face in his hands. "We must verify this."

She stood there for several seconds, while the news washed over her, bringing with it an enormous load of guilt, even though she couldn't have known that the guy from the BMW was Adami's cousin, or that he would recognize her. Had Griffin not come back for them, she'd be there, too…

Sydney walked to the front window, stared out at the great baroque cupola of Sant'Andrea della Valle, trying to recall what Marc had told her of it—anything to get her mind off Tex. After several seconds she turned to the men in the radio room. "Can we get in touch with Griffin?"

"I've already tried," Marc said. "All we can do is wait for him to check in. We can, however, let HQ know." He picked up the phone, hit a number on speed dial. When the phone was answered on the other end, he asked for Ron McNiel. She wasn't sure why she should be surprised that he answered to the same boss as Griffin, which made her wonder who McNiel answered to. When Marc finished his conversation with HQ, he hung up and seemed to sink in his chair.

"*Cosa è?*" Giustino asked.

"Griffin is due to check in with the director in about an hour. McNiel wants to be the one to tell him."

"For that we thank God. I do not look forward to sweeping up broken glass."

"In the meantime, we prepare for Tunisia come morning," Marc said. "We need to destroy the bioweapons."

And for the next hour, the three of them sat in that room, waiting for word, and Sydney's stomach knotted every time she heard a noise on the monitor, wondering if it was Griffin. Finally the phone rang. Marc pounced on it, answered, "*Pronto! Giornale Internazionale per la Pace Mondiale. International Journal for World Peace,*" he repeated in English. They were supposed to be a small free-press newspaper that ran out of several countries. Marc listened to whoever the caller was, said, "*Grazie,*" then hung up. "It was the director, Signore McNiel," he said. "Griffin knows. He will be checking the morgue himself to make the identification of Tex."

The news did nothing to lessen the tension in the room, something that increased tenfold when Griffin walked in the door two hours later, strode past the three of them to the garden doors without a word, his face grim, his eyes cold, hard. He opened one of the double doors, stepped out to the terrace, then pushed the door shut behind him with enough force to warn the others off. If any of them harbored the thought that it might not be Tex at the morgue, their hopes were dashed as they watched Griffin.

For thirty minutes he didn't move, just stood there with his back to them, looking out at the forest of television antennas—transmuted into gold by the November sun—toward the cupola of San Carlo ai Catinari in the distance. Across the courtyard, two cats were stalking a pigeon on the weed-choked tiles of a rooftop. Inside, no one said a thing. Sydney and the others pretended great interest in the radio monitors, even though there had been no traffic since the last report of Adami's men talking about the morgue. But when Griffin didn't move after a half hour, Sydney said, "Someone should go to him."

"One must stay at one's post," Giustino said.

"And what if he needs help translating?" Marc said.

"Translating what?" Sydney said. "You all speak Italian."

Marc shrugged. "You never know when a foreigner might walk into the room. Why don't you go?"

"It should be someone he knows. And likes."

The two men looked at each other, both shaking their heads. "His temper I know well," Marc said. "*Fa arrabbiato!*"

Giustino said, "With his bare hand we have seen him break a man's arm."

"What's another trip to the hospital?" Sydney said. "I'll go."

She walked up to the terrace doors, hesitated at the thought that Griffin might blame her for his friend's death. One look at him told her otherwise. It was clear he was blaming himself. Steeling herself for whatever might happen, she opened the door and stepped out.

"Leave."

Sydney ignored his order, closing the door behind her. At first she merely stood beside him, shoulder to shoulder. The sun had slipped behind the bell tower that graced the terrace garden of the safe house. Silhouetted against the silver incandescent sky, chimney swifts were darting into their nests. Gradually the sky's luminescence was dissolving into azure, and finally she dared a glance, looked up at him, saw his attention fixed on a bat flitting in the distance. "I'm sorry," she ventured.

"I said leave."

"If you wanted to be left alone, you wouldn't have come back here."

He didn't respond, but neither did he tell her to leave again, and after several long moments, she reached up, put her hand on his shoulder. He stiffened, as though her touch repelled him, and she wondered if he really did blame her. And then he reached up, grabbed her wrist, his grip strong, sure, and she thought of what Marc said, about him breaking a man's arm when he lost his temper…

But Griffin didn't move, just held her wrist in his hand, held it tight, as though he couldn't let go.

"Do you know what happened?" she asked.

Several seconds ticked by and she thought he wasn't going to answer, then, "Do you know that Freemasons take an oath of secrecy? 'To all of this I most solemnly and sincerely promise and swear—'" His voice caught. She glanced up at him, saw his eyes closed, his face taut, his jaw clenched. But a moment later, he continued, saying, "The oath is supposed to be metaphorical. The metaphorical penalty of having one's throat cut across, one's tongue torn out by its roots and buried in the rough sands of the sea at low-water mark, should one ever knowingly or willingly violate that oath."

Sydney froze. "Tell me they didn't…?" She couldn't even finish the thought, felt sick to her stomach.

"They did. And like Alessandra, his face was removed, as well as his fingertips. The medical examiner said it was postmortem. He died from a gunshot wound. They stripped him. All they left was his ring. The desecration was no doubt a warning, but—"

"It's my fault. I shouldn't have run. Drawn attention to myself. I panicked."

"Panicked? What were you supposed to do? Stand there and let them capture you? The fault lies with me…I shouldn't have allowed this…" Again he tensed, tried to swallow, tried to breathe, and she wasn't sure what happened next, if she stepped toward him, or he toward her. But a moment later, she was in his arms, and he held her, his face pressed into her hair, until his breathing evened. She tried to pull away, but he said, "Don't. Not yet."

And so she waited, let him hold her, hearing nothing but his heart beating against her, slowing, finally relaxing. After several minutes, she whispered into his chest, "I'm sorry." When she looked up at him, he was staring off into the distance. She stepped back, and he reached out, let her hair drift over his fingers as though he was reluctant to let her leave. But he didn't move to stop her this time, and so she left him there, returned inside as the night deepened into purple velvet. As she shut the terrace doors, she saw him silhouetted against the rising moon, rust red, as if it had been spattered in blood. And then he sank onto the garden bench, buried his face in his hands, consumed by his grief.

She turned away, saw Marc and Giustino looking distinctly uncomfortable. Marc was back to watching TV. Giustino was busy monitoring the equipment. She told them how Tex's body had been desecrated, his face removed, just like Alessandra's. Both men looked sick.

"Any more traffic?" she asked after a while, hoping for some sort of a distraction.

"None," Marc said. He nodded toward Griffin, then asked Giustino, "Do you think the director told him about Tunisia?"

"He'll want to go."

"Can't be helped."

"In his state of—"

The veranda door suddenly opened, and the three of them turned to see Griffin standing there, eyeing them. "My state of what?"

"The traffic from Tex's device. Bioweapons in Tunisia. Adami's lab. They have Dr. Balraj."

Griffin didn't move for a full second, as though the very mention of Tex's name pained him, then, "You have the details?"

"Yes, sir. I reported them to the director."

"Let me know the moment the orders are back to us. I want to get an early start."

"Sir—"

"You heard me." He didn't even look at them, just walked off toward his own room.

No one opposed him, and Sydney waited a beat, then followed him down the hall. "Do you really think you should be running off to some other country in this state of mind?"

"Speaking from experience?"

"What about what you told me on the plane? The whole emotional involvement thing?"

"I'll be checking all emotions at the door."

"Did it ever occur to you that that might be worse?"

"I need to do this. It's clear I can't place my trust in others."

"Are you even listening to yourself?"

He stopped so suddenly, turned to face her, that she nearly ran into him. They stood there like that, in the darkened hallway, so close she could hear him breathing. He didn't move, just looked at her, apparently waiting for her to protest, step back, make some sort of move. When she didn't, he said, "What the hell is it you want from me?"

The force of his question stunned her, even more so when he closed what little distance remained between them, taking her chin in his hand, holding it, forcing her to look at him. "What do you want from me?" he whispered.

"I—" She couldn't answer, could barely swallow as she looked up at him, saw the darkness in his eyes.

And then he said four words that started her heart pounding. "Don't leave me tonight."

◇◇◇

The next morning, Sydney opened her eyes to the sound of bells pealing from the towers and cupolas of hundreds of Roman churches. A soft morning light filtered through the sheer curtains on the window. She stretched out, feeling relaxed for the first time in days. And frustrated, too. Griffin had asked her not to leave him. She didn't. They slept together. Platonically.

Her senses had been on overload. She was attracted to him, but he apparently had no intention of taking it further, and she wasn't about to push the matter. He'd just lost his friend, after all. But hell if she hadn't realized how very much she'd missed sleeping with a man until last night. And how very much she missed having sex.

She sighed, got up, walked to the window, and looked down onto the waking city. An old lady was feeding spaghetti to some wiry cats, who were rubbing up against her legs in gratitude. In the house across the street, a maid was hanging some washing out the window. Iron grates creaked as shops were opened, horns hooted, alarms shrieked. Then she realized just how quiet the house was. She looked around.

Griffin. *Tunisia?* "Son of a bitch. He left me here."

She ran her fingers through her hair as she strode down the hall to see if anyone remained behind. Giustino was sitting at the desk, cappuccino in one hand, earphone held to his ear with the other. He glanced up, nodded a good morning, then turned back to the equipment. "They left before dawn."

"He did that on purpose."

"Did what on purpose?"

"Didn't wake me," she said without even thinking about what her words implied. The moment she realized what she'd said, she felt her face heat up, and hoped it didn't show.

Apparently it showed quite well, because Giustino gave a quick grin, then swept it off his face as though worried it might offend her. She hurried out of there down the hall to the bathroom, where she showered and changed, then emerged to the scent of espresso, which Giustino had prepared for her in the kitchen, along with some fresh *cornetti*, crescent-shaped pastries. After breakfast, she walked back to the radio room. Now that she was awake, he had the radio turned up so he could listen without the headphones. No traffic sounded on the monitor. Adami's office was quiet, just as it had been since last night.

"You make espresso *and* monitor radio traffic?" she said, trying to keep the conversation light as she set the plate of *cornetti* on the table. "A man of multiple talents."

"So my wife tells me." He waved off her offer of food. "You have plans, yes?"

"One part of me figures I should just fly home. The only reason I'm still here is Tex wanted me for his operation. And now…"

"Tex was a good man. The fault is not yours."

"I don't think Griffin wants me to stay regardless."

"Perhaps why he left your plane ticket," he said, just as the telephone rang. He glanced over. "If you could answer that. It's the Journal office line."

"I don't speak much Italian."

"This is no problem. The Journal, she is mostly for the American cover."

Sydney walked to the desk, picked up the phone. "*Pronto!* International Journal for World Peace, may I help you?"

"I'm looking for a Mr. Griffin?" Female speaking English, no trace of an accent.

"He's…on a business trip and I'm not sure when he'll be available." She glanced over at Giustino, about to ask if she should take a message, but then thought better of it, saying instead, "I'm a close associate. Is there something I can help you with?" She ignored Giustino's bemused look, turning her back to him.

"Perhaps. My name is Francesca Santarella. Alessandra Harden asked me to contact Mr. Griffin regarding something she wanted him to have."

"Alessandra Harden." She glanced at Giustino, motioning for him to come over to the phone, then hit the speaker button. "As in Ambassador Harden's daughter?"

"Yes. This number was in her note, saying I should call it when the package arrives. I would have called sooner, but I was away on a dig. The package has apparently been sitting here for about a week."

Giustino held up his hands, as though to say he knew nothing about it, so she said, "And where is here?"

"The American Academy in Monteverde Vecchio."

Sydney muted the speaker function, asking Giustino, "Suggestions?"

"Get the package, *immediatamente*."

To which she asked Francesca, "Do you think we could come by to pick it up?"

"Alessandra did specify that I give it to Mr. Griffin, and only Mr. Griffin. I'll know him when he gives me the code."

Giustino grabbed a pen, wrote: "Get it."

"As I mentioned," Sydney said into the phone, "he's away on a business trip. He has asked us to handle all his matters while he's gone. This way, it'll be here when he gets back, and you're relieved of all responsibility."

Judging from Francesca's long hesitation, it seemed she recognized a line of bullshit when she heard one. "In light of Alessandra's instructions in her letter, it's a responsibility I'm willing to shoulder."

"I'm a close associate of Mr. Griffin's, Ms. Santarella."

"Then you shouldn't have any trouble relaying my message. Please have him call me as soon as possible."

The dial tone filtered through the speaker when the woman hung up. Sydney dropped the phone into the cradle, bringing silence to the room. Before she had a chance to consider her next step, a bell sounded. Giustino checked the security monitor. "Your taxi is here," he said, as he got up, walked to the door, and pressed the speaker button. "*Chi é?*"

"*Tassì!*" a voice answered.

"*My* taxi?"

"To the airport. Griffin ordered it before he left."

"Always the efficient one."

"Don't take it personally."

"No problems there." She walked into her bedroom, stuffed the few things she had into her bag, glanced around the Spartan room, then left.

Giustino stood as she walked out. He held out his hand. "I don't think Griffin would have conveyed this, but our team, we are grateful for your assistance."

"Thank you," she said, shaking his hand. "And I'm deeply sorry about the way things turned out. I don't know if there is any way you can pass that on. Let Griffin know…"

Giustino clasped both hands around hers, as though to let her know he understood. What he said was, "Signore Griffin. He is not an easy man, *signorina*, especially these last two years, but he is a good judge of character."

"I'm guessing that means something profound?"

"I have worked with Griffin for a lot of years since this team formed. He is a good man."

The taxi's horn blared again, and Sydney picked up her bag, walked to the door, but, unable to shake Griffin from her mind, she asked, "Does he have anyone significant in his life?"

"There used to be a woman who—" He stopped suddenly, then said, "She is—was— He does not like November. That is all I should say."

When nothing further was forthcoming, she started out.

"Your ticket, *signorina*."

He walked over, gave it to her. She took it, thanked him, then walked down five flights of stairs, trying not to look back, not to think that if she were to stay, things might turn out different.

Perhaps because of the warmth from the sun through the car windows, she drifted off as the taxi got stuck in a traffic jam on Ponte Garibaldi. Hers was not a solid sleep, but one filled with images and bits of dreams that ran into each other. Griffin watching her, then Tex's image, holding up a glass of iced vodka, which he dropped, and she watched the glass tumble down the cliff, to the water below, and when she looked in, a skull stared back at her, its eyes reflecting a pyramid. When Sydney turned to see where the reflection was coming from, she saw her friend Tasha saying something to her about the pyramid, then asking her not to forget her.

"I won't," Sydney said, surprised to hear it coming from her lips. She opened her eyes, tried to reconcile the sight of the tree-lined boulevard, the trams, and the milling pedestrians that she saw from the taxi's windows with the images from her dream.

"Did you say something, *signorina?*" the taxi driver asked, looking at her in the rearview mirror.

"Do you know where the American Academy is?"

"*Sì, signorina.* On Via Angelo Masina; in Monteverde Vecchio."

"Take me there, please."

"What about your plane, *signorina?*"

"The plane can wait."

"As you wish, *signorina. Fortunatamente,* l'Accademia Americana is just up the hill." With these words, the cab emerged from the traffic-glutted Viale di Trastevere, turned sharply into Via Dandolo, and after careening around a dozen hairpin corners, finally arrived at the iron gates of the imposing edifice of the American Academy.

Now all she needed to do was to convince Francesca Santarella to let her see what it was that the ambassador's daughter had mailed to her just before she was killed.

Chapter Seventeen

Francesca Santarella stood at the massive windows of her studio, located over the main entrance to the American Academy, watching as the electric iron gate swung slowly inward. Roberto, the gatekeeper, had just phoned to tell her an FBI agent was there to see her, something she assumed was related to the strange package that her friend Alessandra had mailed to her from the States. And though she was tempted to tell Roberto not to admit the woman, she wasn't sure if she could. After all, FBI was FBI, even if they were slightly out of their jurisdiction.

If only she'd been able to reach Alessandra this morning. But she hadn't, and then, before she could change her mind about this unexpected visitor, Roberto emerged from his cubbyhole, walked up to the gate to admit the woman, mid-thirties—about her own age—dressed in slacks and a dark blue blazer, with a soft-sided travel bag slung over her shoulder. Pointing up to Francesca's studio, Roberto escorted the visitor around the massive travertine fountain and led her up the front stairs.

When Francesca heard the footsteps in the hall, she walked over to her desk, closed her laptop computer, then crossed the polished terra cotta tiles to open the door, even before her visitor knocked.

Roberto hovered behind the woman, who flipped open a credential case containing an ID card and a gold shield. Her left hand was bandaged, and there were a few scrapes on her face. "I'm Sydney Fitzpatrick, Special Agent, FBI. And you're Francesca Santarella?"

"Yes. Come in." She glanced at Roberto, smiled, and said, "We'll be fine. Thank you."

Roberto, ever protective, nodded, then headed back down the stairs as she smiled at the agent.

Even though Francesca had never come into contact with a federal agent before, she had no reason to doubt her visitor's identity. Francesca might be American born and bred, but this was Rome, and during her prolonged stay, Francesca had rubbed elbows with famous scholars, notorious novelists, the embassy crowd—many of whom she suspected were spies—minor royals, even foreign ministers of hostile countries, whom she had guided on special tours of Rome's ancient monuments. It was all part of what Francesca counted as "Roman experiences."

Of course that didn't mean she didn't examine the ID; she did. And then she asked, "And what brings the FBI all the way to Rome?"

"Alessandra Harden."

Francesca glanced over toward the package, still sitting on her desk, then back at the agent, stating the obvious. "You're the person to whom I spoke on the phone this morning…"

"Yes."

"Mr. Griffin's associate."

"Yes."

She wasn't sure what to make of the FBI's interest in Alessandra, but she wasn't about to make a decision about it until she'd had her morning tea. "Would you like a cup of tea? I was just on my way to the kitchen, when you arrived. The Academy won't let us have hot plates in our studios. Might burn the place down, and where would we all be?"

"I'd love a cup."

Francesca led the agent out the door, locking it behind them.

As they rounded the corner of the long hall, the agent gazed up at the forty-foot-high ceilings. "Amazing building. It reminds me of the Metropolitan Museum in New York."

"Probably because it was designed by some of the same architects. A bit of a mystery surrounds them, in fact, because one was murdered. Stanford White," she explained, as they walked past open bedroom doors where various Fellows of the Academy were lolling about. "Jealous rival. Trial of the Century, circa 1906. Actually White was dead when this place was built a few years later, but his name was still used by the firm. Kitchen's at the end of the hall. We can talk there, since most of the Fellows won't be using it at this hour."

The kitchen—another huge room with tall windows—was happily empty, and Francesca immediately filled a battered teakettle with water, then set it on the stove. Dishes, some washed, were piled haphazardly in the dish rack, others with congealing egg were piled in the sink. Francesca moved the offending plates with a clatter. "Sorry about the mess," she said, filling a clean teapot with hot water from the tap, then setting it aside.

As the teakettle came to a boil, Francesca started rinsing some of the dishes in the sink. That done, she dumped out the water used to warm the teapot, then spooned in two heaps of Darjeeling. "So, what is it you need to know?"

"How did you and Alessandra meet?"

An odd question. But since she was curious as to where this was leading, she decided to answer. "We first met when she was visiting her father during spring break last year. The ambassador held a party—just across the street there; you can see the garden from the window—and invited some of the senior Fellows from the Academy. My interest in ancient history and archaeology mirrored Alessandra's own academic interests. Of course, that wasn't the only interest we had in common. We both held a distinct distrust for big government," she said, pouring boiling water over the tea leaves to let them steep for a few minutes.

"As in government conspiracy?"

Francesca returned the kettle to the stove, glancing over at the agent, somewhat surprised. "Yes. How did you guess?"

"I spoke with her professor at UVA. Did she ever mention anything about any conspiracy that came from personal knowledge?"

"No. I think her suspicions had more to do with rigged elections and dicey world diplomacy."

"And your suspicions. Where do they come from?"

"Thucydides—history," she said, pouring the tea into two clean china cups. "A lesson for mankind, which since human nature tends to be rotten, mankind never learns. The present mirrors the past."

Agent Fitzpatrick accepted one of the teacups, sipped from it as she looked around the plainly furnished high-ceilinged room with its old-fashioned stove, white formica and wood table and chairs.

"Sorry, not much to look at," Francesca said.

"But at least you have a view," the agent replied, walking to the tall windows that looked across the street directly into a large square garden with manicured lawns and trimmed hedges. A shaft of morning sun peered through the parasol pines, powdering gold dust onto a large terra cotta urn in the center of the ambassador's garden. "How long have you lived here?"

"I've been in residence for about two years."

"Almost as long as Ambassador Harden?"

"I arrived a few months after he did."

Agent Fitzpatrick sipped her tea, as though contemplating her next line of questioning. "So that's the ambassador's residence there, across the street. The one with the square tower?"

Francesca joined her at the window, wondering what was really behind her visit. What had the FBI so interested? "Yes, you're looking at his garden. The house is to the right. He's not in residence now."

"How can you tell?"

"The *carabinieri* vans are gone. They're usually in that little alley, next to the garage. And the American flag is down."

"Is the place secure now?"

"Always. There are guard dogs and caretakers, and when Ambassador Harden is in residence, the *carabinieri* guard both sides of the house. Some of the younger Fellows think it's fun to try and engage them in conversation. Personally, I think those

Uzis the *carbs* carry mean business, so I tend to ignore them when I go on my morning walks." Francesca noticed a dark-haired man, clad in black, strolling up the hill under the tall umbrella pines, approaching the ambassador's gate. When he stopped, she caught sight of the clerical collar as he pulled out a small book, the white paper reflecting the bright sunlight. "And there you have the typical visitors," she said. "Pope's business, I presume. Or morning tea," she said, watching as he turned a few pages as though referencing something, perhaps an appointment. Glancing up and down the street, he returned it to his pocket, walked to the gate, and rang the bell.

"If the ambassador's not there, why would he stop for tea?" Agent Fitzpatrick asked.

"Maybe he's friends with someone on staff." The *portière* came to the gate, and after a few words, let the priest in.

"That small gray car farther up the street," Agent Fitzpatrick asked. "With the two men sitting in it. Is that part of the police detail?"

Francesca peered out the window in the direction indicated. "Hard to say. I saw it there yesterday, but since I was away for a couple of weeks, working down in the columbaria, I don't know whether it was there previously."

Agent Fitzpatrick nodded, sipped her Darjeeling, then glanced over at Francesca. "Why is it that Alessandra mailed this package to you instead of her father?"

She hesitated, not sure how much she should divulge, since she had yet to decipher what the agent was searching for. "I think that there was someone in her father's service whom she didn't trust. A servant, assistant, maybe even a friend," she said, as a woman wearing bottle-lensed glasses walked into the kitchen. Francesca tried to remember her name, couldn't, then nodded in greeting as the woman made a beeline for the refrigerator. "For whatever reason," Francesca continued, as the agent focused on the street below, "Alessandra thinks it's important that this information reach Mr. Griffin, and until I hear otherwise from her, I intend to honor her request."

Agent Fitzpatrick frowned, and Francesca imagined she was about to protest, about to attempt to persuade her to hand the package over. Instead, the agent stepped back from the window, set her teacup on the table, and asked, "This special detail to the ambassador's residence. Have you ever known them to use sentries on the neighboring rooftops?"

◇◇◇

Griffin opened the door of the safe house, taking in the aroma of freshly brewed espresso. Giustino drank the stuff like water, all day long, and sure enough, was sipping a cup when Griffin walked into the salon. He threw his keys on the table, poured himself a large glass of water, then sat, glad the morning was almost over.

"Did Marc arrive in Tunisia?" Giustino asked.

"Should be landing there any moment. How about our wayward FBI agent? She make it to the airport?"

"The *signorina* left in the cab about two, two and a half hours ago." He glanced up at the clock. "The plane should be taking off any moment."

"No trouble?"

"She gives many apologies," he said, reaching over to adjust the controls on the monitoring equipment. "I think if she could, she would stay."

"Pick up anything this morning?" Griffin asked, not wanting to think about what Sydney was involved in the past few days. Truth be told, he was relieved that she'd left. Less to worry about.

"*Niente*. Unless one counts the fax."

"Intercept it?"

Giustino nodded toward a paper on the table. "A catering menu. Commendatore Adami must be having another party." Griffin reached for the menu, curious to see what a multimillionaire ordered for his guests, when Giustino added, "But we did receive a call on the Journal line. From a *professoressa* Francesca Santarella. She speaks of a package and some code.

Signorina Alessandra mailed it to her at the American Academy two weeks ago."

"We?"

"The Signorina Fitzpatrick took the call."

"The same Fitzpatrick who is allegedly on her way to America?"

"There is, perhaps, another one?"

"Damn it!" Griffin slammed his hand on the table.

"*Cosa c'è?*"

"Do we even know if she ever got on board that flight?"

"You would like me to inquire?"

"Don't bother," he said, grabbing his keys. "I already know the answer. Get a landline to Professor Santarella's office. If she picks up, patch it through to my cell." He stormed toward the door, cursed himself three times over for not personally putting Fitzpatrick on that plane himself.

◇◇◇

Standing at one side of the window, Sydney studied the man on the rooftop a few buildings down from the Ambassador's residence, someone she wouldn't have noticed had it not been for the sunlight reflecting off what appeared to be the lenses of binoculars. She pulled Francesca back, out of sight, even though she was fairly certain that the object of the surveillance was the ambassador's grounds and not anyone at the American Academy. "I've changed my mind about the tea," Sydney said. "I think we should return to your studio."

Francesca looked at Sydney as though she'd lost her mind. "Is something wrong?"

"I'd rather explain it back at your room."

The professor shrugged, set their still full teacups in the sink, then led Sydney back to her office, which was obviously intended to be an artist's studio at one time. Francesca had her work sorted out neatly on a long white table in the center of the room, with photographs and charts tacked to one wall. These seemed to focus on maps of underground chambers of some sort. A large drawing of a map of Rome was taped to another wall. A laptop sat on a desk next to the huge windows, which must have been a good fourteen feet in height. And beside the computer was a clear vase of yellow autumn crocus. What held Sydney's interest on the desk, however, was the U.S. Global Priority Mail shipping label on the small box. What the hell was in it, and why had Alessandra sent it here? And just when Sydney had decided what line of questioning she wanted to follow in hopes of gaining her answers, the professor's phone rang.

Francesca answered it, with *"Pronto?"* Listened a moment, then said, *"Grazie*, Roberto." Then, turning to Sydney, she asked, "Now what was it you wanted to explain to me here, instead of in the kitchen?"

"First, I'm wondering if anyone knew of your friendship with Alessandra."

"An odd question. I'm assuming that this has something to do with the package she sent?"

"I'll explain it in good time," she said, since Alessandra's murder wasn't yet public knowledge. "Just believe me when I say it's important."

"It wasn't a secret," she said. "Her father knew, and I presume most of his household staff did. I've been to several parties across the street over the last two years, even on occasions when she was back at school in the States."

Footsteps echoed on the tiles outside the door. "Are you expecting someone?"

"Father Emile Dumas," the professor said. And a moment later there was a knock. Before Sydney could stop her, Francesca opened the door to a tall man, his dark hair flecked with gray. His white clerical collar contrasted sharply against his black suit, something that might have put the average person at ease had it not been for one thing.

Sydney had seen him before.

At the Smithsonian museum standing next to the building housing the Holy Crusades display.

Chapter Eighteen

Sydney looked around the room, grabbed an unopened wine bottle from a table, positioned herself between the priest and Francesca. Priest or no priest, she wasn't about to take a chance with the professor's safety. "What do you want?"

"It's important I speak with the professor. Urgent," he said in impeccable English, but with a slight French accent.

"Why?"

"The professor has something I've been waiting for. Something of great importance to me. You do not realize the danger she is in."

"I think I do."

"Well *I* don't," Francesca said.

"Mademoiselle Alessandra meant for me to receive the package. She would have explained this in her letter." He took a step closer, and Sydney raised the bottle in warning. "She did not mention a code?"

Francesca stared in disbelief. "How did you know?"

"It's our code."

The shrill ring of the telephone interrupted the discussion, and the priest raised his hand in warning. "Don't answer it," he said. "They may be checking to see if you're home. I think they're watching the ambassador's residence, maybe even this place as well."

"And who are *they*?" Sydney asked.

"Those who'd think nothing of killing any one of us."

That she did believe. And still she hesitated. Until the sound of screeching tires on the street below brought her to her senses. She strode toward the window, looked out, saw the small gray sedan pulling up out front, then the driver leaning out, asking the guard something. "Now would be a good time to take a back exit," she said, while the telephone continued to ring. "Don't suppose either one of you have a car nearby?"

◇◇◇

Griffin turned into Via Angelo Masina, drove up, parked just down the street from the Academy gate, then phoned Giustino. "Any word?"

"No answer. Phone just rings."

He disconnected, pulled on an SIP jacket, deciding that the phone company was the best disguise for the institution, as that would allow him to walk around unnoticed. He grabbed his toolbox, then walked up the street just as a small gray sedan pulled slowly away from the academy gate. Griffin stopped at the gate to speak with the guard, identifying himself as the telephone repairman, a plausible pretense, since Italian telephones were perpetually *guasti*—on the blink.

Toolbox in hand, Griffin said, "*Il telefono di professoressa Santarella è guasto. Cos'è il numero del suo studio?*"

The guard glanced at the SIP logo on his jacket, then telephoned up to the professor's studio, but after several seconds, told Griffin there was no answer, and that he couldn't let him in, to which Griffin responded that there couldn't be an answer if her phone wasn't working.

The guard muttered something about too many people looking for the professor, and that set Griffin's senses on alert. "*Duecentocinquantasette!*" said the guard, pointing to the great windows over the Academy doors. "*La scala alla sinistra!*" Number 257. Up the stairs and to the left.

Griffin nodded, then strode toward the building, just as the guard called out that if she wasn't in her room, she might be in the kitchen. Once inside, Griffin headed straight for Professor Santarella's, climbing the stairs two at a time. When he turned into the hall, and saw the partially open door, he lowered the tool chest to the ground, drew his gun. Pressing himself against the wall, he stopped just before the threshold, listened. He heard nothing.

Not necessarily a good sign, and gun at the ready, he stepped in, scanned the room.

Empty.

He saw papers dumped on the floor, and a wine bottle lying beside them. The bottle, he figured, could have been used as a makeshift weapon, one that was dropped, perhaps at the sight of a gun. Or maybe it had simply been knocked over. Even the papers on the ground weren't enough to make him think there was a struggle. But there by the door was Sydney Fitzpatrick's travel bag.

So they either left willingly, or something alerted them, sent them running.

The best bet, he figured, was to rule out one or the other scenario. With the exception of Sydney's bag, maybe the papers on the ground, there was nothing inside the studio that shouldn't be there, at least nothing he could see. He glanced outside, saw the Academy entrance, the fountain, the street beyond the gate. The gatekeeper had the iron gate closed, and Griffin doubted anyone was getting in or out without the gatekeeper's knowledge—unless they'd taken a back way. Perhaps they were still on the premises, in the kitchen as the guard had surmised.

Griffin retrieved his toolbox, set his weapon just inside it, then left the studio, walked down the long hall. None of the residents milling about in the upstairs halls paid him the least attention in his SIP jacket. Apparently telephone repairs were commonplace at the Academy. At the end of the hall, he turned into an open door that led to the kitchen, where a heavyset woman in thick-lensed glasses was cooking something that looked indigestible. No one else present there, or in the adjoining television room.

"*Telefono!*" he said to the woman at the stove, and she hardly glanced at him as he walked over to the red telephone by the window. "Professor Santarella was having problems with her phone, but I can't find her."

"She was here a minute ago, but left in a hurry."

Not exactly a telephone repairman's business, but he sized up the woman, decided she wasn't paying too much attention to give his questioning much notice. "Was she with someone?"

"Yes. Another woman."

"Problems with the phone here?" he asked, picking up the red phone, and placing it to his ear.

She shrugged, then went back to her cooking.

He hit the flash a few times to make it look good as he glanced out the window and saw there was a clear view of the Ambassador's residence across the street. He also noticed the guards were gone, and the flag was down, which meant the ambassador wasn't there—he'd returned to the States to claim his daughter's body.

Either way, he saw little that seemed to present a threat. Perhaps Fitzpatrick and the professor had gone for a stroll on the premises, though judging from the papers scattered on the floor, it seemed they left in a hurry, and why would they leave in a hurry for a casual stroll? The events of the past few days and his instincts told him otherwise. He had to assume that Fitzpatrick's training gave her an advantage, perhaps let her notice something that wouldn't stand out to the ordinary person. His gaze swept the street, the garden beyond, and then the ambassador's residence, first the windows on each floor, and then the rooftop. Nothing there, and he kept searching. And that was when he saw the man in the palazzo two doors down, standing in an open tower room, watching the ambassador's residence and the street around it through binoculars. No doubt it was how Griffin's arrival was observed at the ambassador's residence his first day back in Rome. And how he'd been so easily followed back to the hotel by the assassin that Adami had sent after him.

He hung up the phone, stepped back, not sure if he'd been seen in the apartment, if they were even watching the Academy. Either way, if the two women had come into the kitchen, and Fitzpatrick had looked out the window, seen the rooftop surveillance, it could very well have spooked her enough that she'd left in a hurry with the professor, and perhaps left her bag behind as a sign.

And now all he had to do was find her.

Griffin walked past the goggle-eyed woman who was now carrying her meal toward the table. His "*Arrivederci!*" went unnoticed, and he walked the long hall back to Professor Santarella's studio, grabbed Sydney's bag and walked out, pulled the door shut behind him. He descended the stairs, asked the guard if the professor had any visitors who might have used the phone, and was told that the professor had not one, but two visitors. An FBI agent and a priest who came by to use the Academy Library. When the guard was called away by the arrival of a young woman, Griffin glanced at the guard's clipboard, saw the name *Dumas* written upon it.

Griffin walked casually to the SIP van, then drove off down the street, trying to see if there were any more sentries watching the area. The Academy didn't appear to be the main object of the surveillance, which meant it was more than likely the ambassador's residence—but they might notice the comings and goings here at the Academy as well.

He had to think about this. What reason would Adami have to still be watching the ambassador's residence?

To await Griffin's arrival, and take him out? He doubted that. He was fairly certain that on that first day in Rome, his appearance at the ambassador's and the ensuing assassination attempt on his life had been an opportunity of circumstance. No one had known he was en route to Rome. Even he hadn't known until the last minute, once Fitzpatrick had finished the drawing, confirmed that Alessandra was, in fact, the victim.

So what was the purpose of still manning the operation? What were they waiting for? And why had Dumas suddenly showed?

It struck him then. They had figured the same thing he had figured. The day he'd made the death notification, he'd asked Alessandra's father if she'd sent anything home. Why would Adami think anything different? And how had Dumas known to retrieve Alessandra's package from Professor Santarella?

Quite simply, no one had suspected that Alessandra would send the package to her friend, Professor Santarella, across the street, or that her friend wouldn't discover it until later, because she had been out of town.

Until now.

And just when he was convincing himself that Adami's men were focusing on the ambassador's residence and not the academy, and that he was worrying for nothing, a faded red Peugeot, driven by a priest, pulled out of the lot down the street from the academy. There were two passengers in the car, and though he had no doubt as to their identities, that wasn't what concerned him. They were being followed. By the same gray car he'd seen at the academy gate.

◇◇◇

Tunisia

Marc di Luca headed toward the Medina—the old quarter, which dated back to the Middle Ages. He thought about Griffin, wondering if he shouldn't call HQ, mention that maybe they should pull Griffin from the case. It was no small feat that Marc had managed to convince Griffin that he needed to stay in Italy, that they had enough operatives to manage the mission to destroy the bioweapons that Adami was trying to smuggle into Italy via the Tunisia warehouse. The last time he'd seen Griffin that upset was after that operation two years ago…The ambush. He hadn't been the same since. As it stood, the only reason Marc hadn't called HQ was that miracle of miracles, Griffin backed off at the last minute and told Marc to head the bioweapons mission.

Marc glanced over his shoulder, checked for the umpteenth time that he wasn't being followed, then turned into the wide Avenue Bourguiba, where a small regiment of shoeshine boys, sheltered from the sun by shaded arcades, called out to him in French, apparently oblivious to the fact that he was wearing suede-topped hiking boots. He made his way into the narrow-laned maze of the Medina. With its rough-hewn paving stones, the quarter had lost none of its charm, despite the number of tourist shops peddling red carpets, brass hookahs, and fezzes of all colors. A spice shop displaying huge bowls of powdered saffron, cumin, and harissa filled the air with pungency.

Just before the covered *suq* displaying leatherwork, he turned into an alley away from the tourist path. Here men in fezzes and women with shawl-covered heads and more traditional dress occupied the street. With a quick glance over his shoulder, he ducked into another alley, where his Tunisian contact, a microbiologist and French agent named Lisette Perrault, lived above an herbalist's shop. He stopped at a faded and peeling blue-green keyhole-shaped door, which with its artfully studded hobnails looked as if it belonged in the *Arabian Nights*.

A few moments later, the door opened. The shabby exterior masked the bright tiled courtyard, where a fountain splashed in the center, but he didn't have time to admire it. Lisette motioned for him to follow her up the inner staircase to her apartment.

Marc had to duck through the low doorway as he entered the apartment. It took a few seconds for his vision to adjust to the dark interior after the brightness of the sun on the white stucco before he could really see Lisette. He'd known she was going to be here, but even so, the sight of her after all these months hit him like a rock. She looked past him, out the door, then back. "How was your flight?"

Not *How are you? How have you been? Good to see you're still around.* Just how was your flight? "Rough."

Lisette nodded. If she was disappointed that it was he and not Griffin or even Giustino who had come, she didn't mention it. "We heard about Tex."

Marc nodded, unable to discuss it. Thinking about Tex all night, he hadn't slept, and the short doze on the quick flight to Tunisia did little to ease his exhaustion.

"I'm sorry," she said, then reached out, touching his arm.

The feel of her cool fingertips against his skin shocked him, and he looked down at her hand, an onslaught of memories of nights together flashing through his mind. He shoved those thoughts aside, gave a brisk nod, then asked, "Where are the others?"

Moment over. She dropped her hand. "They're already on point, waiting to hear from us," she said, leading him to a high-ceilinged room at the back of the house, where crimson oriental rugs on the polished terra cotta floors gave the space a look of elegance. An open window let in a soft breeze, bringing with it scents of lavender and sage from the herbalist's shop below. "Rafiq set out for the compound the moment we received word. He should be back any moment. This is big. A bioweapons lab in Adami's Tunisian warehouse, one he allegedly uses to ship food and first aid to war-torn countries. Should your information prove accurate, it will be the first time we've ever had knowledge of their activities beforehand."

"His warehouse aside, what have you heard on your end?"

"The same as you," she said, motioning for him to have a seat on the divan. "The Black Network is active again. We've heard it's centered in Rome and Washington, D.C." Aptly named, the Black Network was the deadly enforcement arm of a vast and powerful network of criminals, politicians and businessmen, all board members of the Bank of International Commerce Trade and Trust, or BICTT, one of the largest and most profitable—yet illegal—world banks. While BICTT had been shut down after an almost successful run on the U.S. banking industry twenty years ago, a good portion of the money was never recovered and the power brokers who ran it—Adami being one of them—were still in business. They met under the guise of Freemasonry, which gave them a way to conduct their meetings in secret.

"What are they after?" he asked, watching as she took a small kettle of mint tea from a samovar. She poured the steaming liquid into glasses that contained pine nuts. "Besides brokering information and selling weapons, that is."

"You mean you haven't heard the rumor of *la terza chiave*," she said, handing him a glass of the tea.

"Is it possible you mean C3?" She gave him a blank look, and he added, "Ci-Tre. We heard it the other night at Adami's villa. Someone mentioned it in conjunction with P-Due."

"Propaganda Due," Lisette said. "You think this C3 is a clandestine Masonic lodge in the same vein?"

"After the way Tex's body was desecrated, there is no doubt in my mind."

"I do not believe *la terza chiave*, this third key, has anything to do with P-Due, which is, to our knowledge, still running under Adami's watchful eye. But that Adami mentioned C3, it confirms our suspicions that he is after the third key, perhaps for the very reasons we feared. We have overheard chatter that this third key is a means of unlocking the sources of plagues not seen on earth for two thousand years. Biblical plagues."

"Isn't that a little far-fetched?"

"According to the academic studies I have read, the possibility is very real. Does the actual source of these plagues still exist? That I do not know."

"If it does exist, what is the possibility that these sources could remain viable after that long?"

"If contained under the right conditions, it is a very real threat. And what makes it particularly dangerous is that, if true, these plagues have remained untouched for that many years and have survived, whether dormant and intact in their original form or evolving in a protected environment for so long…The possibility is great that it will devastate a population, since there are no vaccines for something that hasn't been seen on earth in two thousand years."

"Is that why Adami kidnapped Dr. Balraj?"

"Undoubtedly. Balraj is probably the world's foremost expert on the evolution of plagues. If Adami is able to gain his cooperation—and under duress, who is to say Balraj won't cooperate?—Adami is that much closer in his attempt to create a super-plague."

"Do you think he has any chance of succeeding?"

"Unfortunately, yes. His past attempts to genetically modify the plagues to better control them have failed. We're certain that's why Dr. Zemke was targeted. Her expertise was on genetic engineering."

"You do not believe she's dead? Killed like the others?"

"We have yet to find Dr. Zemke's body, and right now we believe she is worth more to him alive than dead. Her expertise fits with his plan to genetically mutate these plagues and combine his current bioweapons with this new, or rather much older plague, to increase its virulence."

The news worried Marc. They knew Adami intended to create bioweapons, but this was much worse than any of them had dared imagine. "And if he is successful?"

She stared into the cup of tea before looking up at him, her dark eyes reflecting her worry. "Past attempts to weaponize plagues and viruses have been largely unproductive, due to heat and shock from explosives, never mind simple exposure to sun. And any biomatter that survived and found its target in the population was quickly contained, because the disease did not spread fast enough. But if Adami is able to develop this super-plague—genetically engineer it so that it will survive the heat, retain its virulence, in fact make it hypervirulent—he could wipe out whole cities before the world is able to do a thing. Adami is trying to create a hypervirulent antibiotic-resistant airborne plague. Airborne pneumonic plague would spread from person to person, and by the time the first fever appeared, it would be too late. Within days, thousands would be dead and the remaining population would be dying. The only answer would be to isolate the city, restrict travel so that no one could leave—hope no one has left—then let the population die out."

"And since he is eliminating all the microbiologists one by one, if we uncover what he has done, we can't control it?"

"That is one of the most frightening aspects about this. By the time the world caught up with what was happening, by the time they even realized the need for massive antibiotics—if such measures even worked with this new super-plague he intends to develop—it would be too late. Even more frightening is this: What if Adami's scientists can't control it? If he is effectively eliminating anyone in the free world who has a hope at containing such a threat, and he controls the scientists who have developed this new strain, who will put it back in the bottle once it is released?"

"Then let's hope this information we've gotten about his lab being here in Tunisia is accurate. We can at least eliminate that part of the threat. What is your next step?"

"The warehouse is located near a small private strip at a compound south of here, used by Adami's Tunisia corporation. Should they suspect that we are on to them, they could possibly move their lab and we are back to square one, so whatever we do, we'll have to move quickly. We've had our eye on this place since you called. They're very meticulous about who they let in, turning anyone away who is not on their schedule of deliveries. If we can't figure out a way to get to that schedule and get the proper IDs, we won't be able to pass the guards into the compound."

"And what is it you need me to do?"

She sipped her tea, then smiled that smile he knew so well. "Break into their security building and get a copy of the schedule, of course."

Chapter Nineteen

That old saying of not getting in the car with strangers circled the back of Sydney's mind as Dumas started his car and drove away from the Academy. He hadn't exactly convinced the professor to hand over the package, but he had given a good argument for the two of them to accompany him to a very public location away from the ambassador's residence, and they could discuss the matter there. The professor had agreed reluctantly, which meant Sydney had no choice but to remain with them or risk losing sight of the professor's briefcase that now contained the package Alessandra had mailed to her.

Which is why Sydney sat in the back of the car, the better to watch Dumas.

Then again, if something happened, she needed to know where they were, so it was one eye on Dumas, and the other trying to pay attention to her surroundings. As he sped down the street, then slowed for a turn, she saw the street name set into the side of a corner building reading "Via Giacomo Medici." As he turned, another sign read "Via Garibaldi," and then he slowed around a curve, past a massive marble edifice with a magnificent series of baroque arches, where water gushed from fountains into a pool. A bride and groom stood in front of the fountain, embracing, while a photographer snapped photos. "Where are we going?" Sydney asked.

Dumas replied, "Passegiata del Gianicolo. There are enough people there for safety." By the time Dumas drove through the gates of the Passegiata del Gianicolo, she'd relaxed slightly. Had they been driving toward some dark, deserted alleyway, she might have reason to be more concerned, but it seemed Dumas was keeping his promise, to take them to somewhere open and public. This was definitely public. Up the hill she caught sight of a carousel with children riding horses, giraffes, and even a Cinderella's pumpkin-coach. Just beyond that, a handful of boys and girls were riding in a cart drawn by a quartet of red Shetland ponies. All the trappings of an amusement park, she thought, except for the tall and somber marble busts, who stood like silent sentinels on either side of the street. No one seemed to pay the statues the slightest bit of attention as entire families strolled under the giant plane trees with their dappled trunks, and everywhere one turned there were children, some holding cones of gelato, others clutching the strings of helium balloons.

"What makes this location better than, say, the police station?" Sydney asked, as Dumas circled around a huge statue of a man on horseback. She thought about asking who it memorialized, then caught sight of the cityscape beyond it, one of the most magnificent views of Rome, to rival any postcard she'd ever seen. Too bad she didn't have time to enjoy it.

"Passegiata del Gianicolo," Dumas said, glancing at her in the rearview mirror, "is a good place to get lost in the crowd, while we attempt to sort this matter out."

Professor Santarella looked out the window, focusing on a group of children clustering around the puppet hut. "We could have stayed at the Academy and waited for Mr. Griffin there. After all, we do have a guard and electric gates."

"I told you, professor. I shall explain all, if you are patient," Dumas said, pulling neatly into a parking space just vacated by a Ferrari. "We can have a little chat at the wall. It will be my pleasure to buy you a *gelato*—anything you wish."

Both women decided on coffee, and Sydney got out of the car, feeling reassured by the presence of so many people milling about, as well as the *carabinieri* mounted on white horses. When she glanced over at the skyline of Rome, visible just over the low stone wall, Father Dumas suggested that Francesca take Sydney to claim a seat there, while he ordered coffee for them from the kiosks.

The two women walked over to the wall, and Sydney was again taken aback by the magnificent view of the city and the Alban Hills beyond. Francesca rested her briefcase on the wall, then directed Sydney's attention to some of the major points of interest, the cupola of Sant' Andrea della Valle, the rotunda of the Pantheon, and to the right, the white elephantine Vittorio Emanuele monument and the Forum and Palatine beyond.

"And what's that ugly brick building with the tower just down the hill?"

"That's the Regina Coeli—the Queen of Heaven Prison," she said, taking a seat on the wall as Father Dumas walked toward them with their drinks.

On his return, Sydney told Dumas, "I think it's time to get down to business. Why, exactly, are you involved, and what are the Vatican's interests in this matter?"

"The Vatican's interests are to protect that which belongs to the church. My interests are to do what is right."

"You were at the Smithsonian," Sydney said, taking a seat on the wall next to the professor. "I saw you."

"True," he finally replied. "I was at the Smithsonian. Alessandra was supposed to contact me after she'd been there. The last time I spoke with her, she told me that if we missed each other, it meant she'd had to leave in a hurry and that she'd send the information home."

"And do you know what happened to her?" Sydney asked.

"I understand she was murdered."

"Murdered?" the professor said, her face blanching. "Alessandra?"

He looked over at her, his expression filled with compassion. "I am sorry you had to hear it this way, professor. But it is as I explained, a dangerous situation, and we had no time."

"Alessandra's murder is what brought me to Rome," Sydney added. "That's why I need to know what it was she sent to you."

Francesca sat on the low wall and hugged the briefcase to her chest. A few tears coursed down her cheeks. "Alessandra wanted this to go to Mr. Griffin."

"And I work with him," Dumas said, handing her his handkerchief.

Sydney looked at him in disbelief. "You? And Griffin?"

"You seem surprised."

"You don't exactly fit the image of a government spook."

"It's complicated," he said with a quick glance at Francesca, as though to say that this was not the place to go into the particulars. "I think it's time we found out what it was that Alessandra died for."

"I'm sorry," Francesca said, dabbing at her eyes. "If Alessandra was murdered as you say, and her last wishes were for this to be given to Mr. Griffin, then that is exactly what I intend to do."

Dumas lowered his voice, said, "I told you she would have mentioned a code in her letter?"

Sydney recalled there being something about a code, and Francesca said, "And once again, I ask how did you know what was in the letter?"

Dumas replied, "Alessandra called me when she couldn't get in touch with Monsieur Griffin. She said she was at the Smithsonian to meet someone and had discovered something. More importantly, she saw someone at the museum, someone she'd seen at one of her father's dinner parties, and for this reason she couldn't send anything to her house. She decided to send whatever it was to her friend. Before she could give me this person's identity, she said that she had to go, she was being followed. And that's the last I heard from her."

"And do you know who it was she thought she saw at the Smithsonian?" Sydney asked.

"No. But I flew out there earlier in the week in hopes of retracing her steps." The priest's words answered Sydney's question as to why she'd seen him there. "When my search proved fruitless, I returned to Rome and decided to have a talk with one of the embassy maids to see if there had been any word on

Alessandra's whereabouts. The maid is the one who informed me that Alessandra had been murdered, and that the ambassador was flying back to the United States to claim her body. It was the perfect opportunity to learn if Alessandra had any friends here in Rome. Professor Santarella was one the maid named, and I knew that the American Academy being just across the street from the ambassador's residence would be the logical place to send whatever it was that Alessandra had found. I also knew that if I could determine the destination of the package so easily, whoever murdered Alessandra could also discover this."

Francesca lowered the handkerchief and looked at the priest. "Surely you aren't trying to say that whoever killed Alessandra would come after me?"

To which Sydney said, "I have to agree with Father Dumas. If he figured out your presence so easily, those watching the ambassador's residence could easily do the same. They already tried to kill Griffin after he made a visit to the ambassador's home. Which means they could very well have noted Father Dumas' arrival there, and may have even followed him to the Academy."

"Like it or not," Dumas said, "your life is in danger, certainly as long as you possess whatever it is that Alessandra sent."

Francesca looked at each of them, then lowered her briefcase to her lap.

Chapter Twenty

Tunisia

Marc and Lisette hiked through a tangle of narrow streets and back alleys to where Rafiq, their other operative, waited by a Jeep parked outside the Medina. They drove toward the Sahara compound. Considering the place was supposed to be used strictly for charity, shipping food and first aid to needy countries, why all the cement barricades? They dropped Marc off around the corner from where the compound and security offices were located at the edge of the desert. Marc watched as Lisette draped a colorful scarf over her dark hair, just before Rafiq drove the Jeep up to the guardhouse. The guard stepped out of his hut, approached the vehicle, looked into the window. When Lisette exited from the passenger side, bringing a map with her and spreading it out on the hood of the car, Marc made his approach, crouching low behind the stone wall barrier.

He didn't like making broad-daylight entries, but time was of the essence. As he arrived at the guard's station, keeping low behind the cement barricade that ran the length of the road, he could hear Lisette's voice, her halting use of her native French, designed not only to perfect her role as a lost Italian tourist, but as a delaying tactic to give Marc the opportunity to get into the guardhouse and search for the security schedule they'd need. The moment he heard her ask how they could find the Sahara Douz Festival—his cue that it was safe—he moved to the doorway.

Unfortunately, the guard had locked the door, which meant time wasted while Marc took out the necessary equipment from his bag, and hacked the electric door code. Finally the lock disengaged and the door opened. The room was the size of a walk-in closet, with a desk, chair, and closed-circuit TV monitor, showing not only the entrance and exit, but also the remote airstrip and the warehouse that was the focus of their op. He took a moment to view it, determining the best position to set up. Each screen flashed to a new view after several seconds. Intel always appreciated, he thought, resuming his search for the schedule of deliveries.

Of course the damned schedule wasn't anywhere easy, or out in the open, and it was damned hard to keep so low in such a small confined space that was surrounded by windows on all sides, even if the glass was mirrored one-way, not allowing anyone from the exterior to see readily within. Outside, Lisette and Rafiq continued their pretended bickering over the direction they were allegedly trying to travel for the festival. While they kept the guard distracted, Marc eyed the room, knowing that the security schedule was probably in the locked cabinet. Just in case, though, he tried the desk drawer, hoping the guard was the lazy sort.

He wasn't.

The drawer was empty.

The cabinet was secured with a standard key lock, and Marc took a pick from his tool bag and slid it into the keyhole, teasing it until the tumblers clicked. He pulled open the door, reached in, just as the phone rang.

He froze. Listened. Heard the guard excuse himself as the phone continued its ringing.

Marc grabbed the clipboard, shut the cabinet door, then scrambled beneath the metal desk, just as the guard stepped up to the door, punched his code in the lock. Marc slid a knife from his boot as the door opened.

From his position, he could see the reflection of the security monitor in the glass from the window. One camera was apparently positioned directly outside, and in it he saw Lisette glance at Rafiq, who was slowly reaching for the gun hidden in his waistband. Lisette gave the slightest shake of her head. Gunshots would draw immediate attention and jeopardize the entire operation, especially if there was a dead guard on the ground.

Think of something, he willed. And then, in the monitor, he saw Lisette walk up to the guard shack, calling out, "Allo?"

The guard turned toward her and said, "*Un moment, s'il vous plait.*"

"I'm not sure," she said loudly, "but I think my husband is having a heart attack."

The guard looked out the window, saw Rafiq clutching his chest. He hesitated, but the phone continued ringing. "I must get this," he said, signing his own death sentence, because there was no way the guard could answer the phone unless he came to this side of the desk.

◇◇◇

Rome

From just up the street where Sydney sat with Dumas and the professor, Griffin had parked where he could watch them. Twice he'd seen the small gray car pass slowly, then disappear around the bend. It was the same car he'd seen parked up the road from the ambassador's residence, and it began following Dumas' vehicle the moment it took off from the Academy. He called Giustino to run the vehicle's license plate through the *carabinieri* database.

"The plate is, how do you say? Cold?"

"Not a good sign," Griffin said.

"What is happening?" he heard Giustino say into his earpiece.

"Nothing. The car's left the area." He glanced at Dumas, saw him shaking his head, handing something back to the professor.

"Perhaps the occupants of your vehicle were only sent to follow the professor and report her whereabouts?"

"I'd believe that, except for what happened when someone from Adami's crew followed me the other day, and the fact the professor has what they no doubt want."

"And Monsignore Dumas is with them."

Another fact that bothered Griffin. Why was Dumas there?

"Where did you say you followed them to?" Giustino asked.

Griffin had parked his SIP van on the other side of the equestrian Garibaldi statue, as though taking a noon break. Consequently he had an excellent view of the wall across the street, where Dumas sat with Fitzpatrick and the professor. Only in Rome would it be possible to enjoy a day outdoors under the November sun. "To the Piazza Garibaldi."

There was silence on the other end.

"What do you make of the location?" Griffin asked.

"I am hoping to understand why Dumas would choose that locale. Perhaps he thinks Adami would not dare to send a car in to do a hit in full view of the public."

"I think he underestimates Adami. His men are good, they'll utilize any weakness to their advantage. You know the place, what would that weakness be?" he asked, eyeing the piazza, trying to determine it for himself. The area began filling with tourists and locals alike, enjoying the view, or strolling through the park.

"Since I do not have the advantage of your view, it would be difficult to say."

"For Christ's sake, tell me what you know about the place, besides there being too many tourists and a thousand busts lining the street, therefore a thousand places to hide."

"Of course! It is almost *mezzogiorno*."

"Thank you. Something more besides it being noon."

"No. Every day at noon, there is a cannon blast."

"Damn it," he said, glancing at his watch. So much for worrying about Dumas and any cover he might be using. He got back in the van, hit the gas, and drove around the statue, as close to the wall as he could, his wheels screeching as he skidded to a stop. Two girls close to the street screamed. Dumas and the two women looked up in alarm, and Griffin leaned over, threw open the door. "Get in!" he shouted.

Fitzpatrick rose, had the sense to drag the professor with her. "It's Griffin. *Hurry.*"

Francesca looked shaken, glanced back toward the priest, who finally roused himself and started toward the van. Griffin looked up, saw the gray car speeding toward them. "Move!"

Fitzpatrick opened the side door, shoved the woman in. She followed after her, and Dumas hustled into the front seat, just as a tremendous blast shattered the November air. The cannon.

"Get down!" Griffin shouted.

The gray car raced toward them, and Griffin saw a gun come out the open passenger window. He slammed the throttle, the van lurched forward. He heard the first shot, then the peal of bells from every nearby tower. The perfect cover for a shooting.

He glanced in his mirror, saw the car skid as it rounded the Garibaldi statue after them. As the mounted *carabinieri* spurred their horses, the crowd was just becoming aware that something was amiss, that there was more than just the bells tolling the hour.

Griffin stabbed the gas, careened around the hairpin turns down the hill. The gray car was still on them. He made a diversionary cross of the Tiber River on the Principe Amedeo Bridge. Their only hope was to lose the car in the maze of Renaissance streets.

Tunisia

Marc heard the guard's footsteps as he closed in on the hiding place beneath the desk. Kill or be killed. He braced his knife on his thigh, heard the phone ringing, the damned phone that was likely to ruin an entire operation. Unless Rafiq or Lisette could figure something out—the heart attack scenario wasn't flying. He heard Lisette calling out that her husband needed help. The faltering footstep of the guard, weighing duty over honor.

And then Marc's gaze caught on the phone cord draped down the side of the desk…

Hell. How'd he not think of that?

He reached behind him, unplugged the damned phone. *Silence.* The guard stopped midstep, mumbled something, then turned back the way he'd come. Through the one-way glass, Marc could see Lisette hovering over Rafiq, playing the panicked helpless woman to the hilt. The guard came out, and together they assisted Rafiq to the passenger side of the car, Marc's cue to leave once he photographed the schedule and returned it to the cabinet.

And he was just about to make his exit when he saw something in the monitor, the top left quarter that flashed on the interior of a warehouse on the premises. It was there and gone, its image replaced by another location, and he had to wait until it cycled back to the warehouse to see if he'd really seen what he'd thought was there.

Or was it his imagination?

Definitely not his imagination. The very sight drenched him with sweat. That was *the* warehouse they were blowing to smithereens. It took him a moment to rouse himself, realize that nothing was happening if he didn't get his ass out of there so they could figure out what to do next.

But as he slipped out of the guard shack, then on past the cement barricade, he couldn't shake the image from his mind.

That of a man heaped on a pallet, his face bloodied, his tux torn and dirty, his cowboy boots covered in mud.

Tex?

But he was supposed to be dead. Griffin had identified him at the morgue.

No, he realized. Griffin had made an identification of a man whose face had been removed…

Chapter Twenty-one

Francesca sat in the back of the van, gripping her briefcase as they went around yet another turn. The man called Griffin assured them that he'd at last lost the tail, and she finally felt as though she could breathe. Until the moment he answered Father Dumas' query as to where he was going to take them.

"My opinion," Griffin said, "they'll be safer in the States. We take the professor to the airport with Special Agent Fitzpatrick."

"You don't have any say," Francesca said. "I have a deadline. I stand to lose my entire grant if I don't have my research finished and to the academic press in time."

"Impossible," Griffin replied. "The men who tried to kill you up at the Passegiata will stop at nothing to get what they want. They've seen you. No doubt they're already investigating who you might be, if they haven't already discovered it."

"I am not leaving, and I'm fairly certain that you have no authority to make me."

Griffin looked at Dumas. "Maybe next time you can put in a good word and keep me from being saddled with stubborn women?"

"Come to church on Sunday and I'll see what I can do."

"Trust me. You wouldn't want to hear my confession."

Griffin checked each of the mirrors, then pulled over.

"Why are we stopped?" Francesca asked.

"To change my insignia. They'll be looking for the phone company. I'd rather not make it easy." He got out and walked around the van. A moment later, the side door opened, and he slid in two large magnetic signs, then removed two others that read "ENEL," for the electric company. A couple minutes later, he was back in the driver's seat, looking back at Francesca. "Convince me why we should let you stay."

"As I explained, I must finish my research to keep from losing my grant."

"You realize after this afternoon that it isn't safe for you to return to the Academy? Not until this matter is resolved."

She didn't even want to think what methods they'd use to *resolve* it. "But all my notes are there." When that didn't faze him, she added, "And I need to use the library there."

"What is it you're researching?"

She decided that Griffin didn't trust her, nor was he going to buy any simple explanations. It was true she had some research to do, but not for the reasons given. A partial truth was best in cases like this. "Historical burial sites."

"And the Academy has the only library suited for this?"

"No, of course not."

He looked over at Dumas, then back at Francesca. "The Vatican has a library, doesn't it?"

"Of course," she said.

"Won't it do?"

It would more than do, but she wasn't sure she wanted to seem too eager. "I believe so."

To Dumas, he asked, "Will she be safe there?"

"I will make sure of it."

"Then it's settled. You stay with Dumas. Now about this package Alessandra sent..."

Francesca said, "Alessandra was explicit on the code, and that until you answered to it, I wasn't to give out anything."

"There is no code. Alessandra's head was filled with fantasies."

"The code or no package," Francesca said.

Dumas smiled.

Griffin, however, looked more than annoyed as he said, "All for one and one for all. Alessandra had taken it upon herself to liken us to the three musketeers. Alessandra, Dumas, and me, of course."

"Three musketeers?" Sydney replied, looking at the both of them. Neither Dumas nor Griffin said a thing. "That means that Alessandra was working *with* you?"

Dumas shifted in his seat, his eyes downcast, as Griffin said, "Dumas recruited her."

"And you agreed," Father Dumas pointed out.

"Since by then it was too late."

Francesca's eyes narrowed as she looked at Dumas. "You're a spy? Housed in the Vatican?"

"Spy is a harsh word. As I explained earlier, I am looking out for the Vatican's interests, which happen to sometimes coincide with those of…certain governments that have embassies residing here," he said, casting a dark look toward Griffin.

Francesca rested her hand on the package Alessandra had sent. "I find it interesting that she chose to assist something she had come to detest. Governments and their machinations."

"Actually," Dumas said, "she came to us *because* of government machinations. She had overheard a few things by some men who attended her father's parties at the embassy, and—"

"And now it matters little," Griffin said, though his expression told Francesca it mattered very much. "What does matter is proving who killed Alessandra, and continuing the work she started."

In this at least Francesca recognized his sincerity, and she finally removed the package from her briefcase.

◇◇◇

Tunisia

Lisette and Rafiq stared at Marc, as he related what he'd seen. They'd fled the compound, supposedly en route to the hospital to have Rafiq examined for his chest pains, instead picking up Marc a few streets away. Lisette finally had to pull over. "You're sure of what you saw?"

"Positive," Marc said. "I couldn't believe it myself."

"You're sure it wasn't Dr. Balraj? It was Tex?"

"I couldn't see his face clear enough. Not enough time to get that close to the monitor. But it definitely wasn't Balraj. Besides, who the hell else would be wearing a tux and cowboy boots in the middle of the bloody afternoon in Tunisia?"

"Was he alive?" she asked.

"He wasn't moving."

Rafiq shook his head. "He was dead. Had to be."

"No," Lisette said. "Why go to the trouble of killing someone else to make us think Tex is dead, only to kill him, then hide his body in another country?"

Marc knew exactly why.

Rafiq answered. "He might not have been dead then, but maybe he is now. They needed time to torture him in hopes of finding out what we were about. If we thought he was dead, there would be no rescue attempts."

Lisette looked sick. "You don't think they have him in there because they know that building is our next target?" she asked Marc.

"We didn't even know it was our next target, which means Tex couldn't have known. Either way, we have to tell Griffin," Marc said, trying to recall exactly what he'd seen. If Tex was tied up, then he wasn't dead. But he couldn't remember seeing any ropes, primarily because he wasn't looking for them.

"They were best friends," Lisette said. "To get Griffin's hopes up…"

No one dared finish the thought. To get his hopes up, only to face the realization that if it was Tex in that warehouse, fortune would have to be smiling on them to perform a rescue. They were under orders that the warehouse and all its contents be destroyed by 0830 hours tomorrow. Any later and they risked that the biological weapons that were recently manufactured and stored there would be shipped out and used. According to Lisette, Adami's scientists were working primarily with bacteria. For that she was grateful. Should any biomatter escape the blast, the full desert sun would kill what was left, so the earlier the better.

Tex's life for possibly those of hundreds of thousands of innocents...

Marc looked at his watch. They had until tomorrow morning to destroy Adami's warehouse. Now that they had the delivery schedule, they needed to figure out who they were going to impersonate, and how they were going to get the explosives onto the compound. "We need to get to a secure phone. I've got to call HQ."

Chapter Twenty-two

Sydney watched as Francesca pulled a book from the package. A photograph of a pyramid was displayed on the dustcover beneath a title that read *Egyptian Influence on Ancient Roman History*. Griffin took it, flipped through the pages, then looked at Francesca in question. "*This* is what she sent?"

"It appears she bought it at the Smithsonian gift shop and had it mailed here," Francesca said.

"There's nothing in it. Why was it so important that she get it to us?"

"I have no idea. I'm only the messenger."

He flipped through the book once more, then handed it to Dumas. "See if you can find something in it."

Dumas opened it, doing a more thorough perusal of each page as Griffin started up the van, then pulled back onto the road. Dumas found nothing. Sydney was tempted to ask to see the book herself, but one look at Griffin's face when he glanced back at her told her he was not even remotely close to forgiving her for not flying home this morning—a feeling that persisted long after they'd dropped off Dumas and the professor at the Vatican.

Still, she thought, once they started the long and circuitous trip back to the safe house, someone was going to have to talk first, and Sydney figured it might as well be her. "Exactly who does Father Dumas work for?"

Griffin looked at her, his anger over her actions still evident on his face. He turned back to the road, let out a tense breath. Then, surprising her that he was even going to talk to her at all, said, "The Vatican first and foremost. After that, he is, for all intents and purposes—and to my objection—part of our team."

"I take it you don't trust him?"

"I trust him as long as the needs of the Vatican and ATLAS coincide. It's when they don't that I have concerns." He glanced in his rearview mirror, then over at her.

"His loyalties to the church aside, his placement in the Vatican is a valuable resource, one that can't be ignored."

"It never occurred to me that the Vatican, would be working covert operations."

"It never occurred to the Vatican, either, at least not officially, until Pope John Paul I decided to investigate the Mafia's involvement in the Vatican finances that uncovered the Banco Ambrosiano scandal. Unfortunately for him, the Mafia and the Black Network, another criminal organization, had infiltrated more than just the Vatican's bank. They'd also penetrated the most venerable walls of the Vatican's governing body, the Curia. There's no doubt why he died thirty days after becoming pope."

"So you believe his death was a murder?"

"Some historians might believe otherwise, but he was poisoned—not, however, before he handpicked a few of his most trustworthy associates to look after the Vatican's true interests. Dumas is the second generation of the team that Pope John Paul I started. They are covert, but not black ops. They are rarely called out on our business, and only as a liaison to the church."

"Why was Dumas called out on this operation?"

"That's the problem. He wasn't called out, though we had considered it initially. So either Alessandra brought him into this, or he is here for the church. That isn't necessarily a bad thing. It does present problems. It's clearly understood that Dumas has divided loyalties. Where our team must answer to the Director of Operations, Dumas must answer to God. And since God usually makes himself unavailable for personal interviews, the current pope stands in."

"And the pope is aware of Dumas' actions?" she asked, watching the side view mirror for any tails, and making sure she looked up at the corner buildings to read the street placards in case she ever had to navigate this place on her own. "He knows what you do?"

"The pope is aware of anything that directly involves the church. That does not necessarily mean he knows what we are doing."

Griffin turned off the Corso Vittorio into the Via dei Chiavari, then drove into a horseshoe-shaped parking lot. He pulled into a slot marked *"Riservato per SIP."* The telephone company, Sydney recalled, thinking of the phone company cover he'd used earlier. The van currently had the ENEL logo on it. That, of course, made her wonder if the sign was legit, or if he'd had it erected for his operation. At the moment, she was more interested in Dumas. "Hard to imagine a priest working covert ops."

"Don't let the clerical garb fool you. The man is as dangerous as any of our full-time operatives. And he's been a valuable resource at times. By the way, your bag is in the back. You left it at the Academy."

Only because she wanted there to be some sign of where she'd been. This didn't seem the time to point that out, and she grabbed her bag, exited the vehicle. "Then what is the problem with Dumas?" she asked, as Griffin walked up to the sign, casually removed it, then replaced it with one that read *"Riservato per ENEL,"* which matched the logo currently on the van. So much for the question of its legitimacy.

"The problem?" Griffin replied. "He saved my damned life two years ago in an operation that went bad. And I hate owing favors to guys I can't trust."

Trust. Now there was a word Sydney had difficulty embracing. She didn't trust herself, and apparently Griffin didn't trust anyone. Quite a team. Especially when it came to this case. Not that she was about to mention this to him. Instead she asked, "Do you get the feeling that the professor was holding something back?"

"Right now I'm more interested in why you aren't seated on a plane that should be across the Atlantic right now."

Too much to hope that he was going to let that slide. "Had I been, the professor and your spy at the Vatican would both be dead, and Adami's men would have the book that Alessandra sent."

"Or they'd never have been followed to begin with." He placed the SIP sign in the back of the van, picked up the book in question, then shut and locked the van door.

"Don't try to blame this on me," she said, as they walked over the cobbled street toward the dark green door of the apartment house. "If I had to guess, they saw Father Dumas enter the ambassador's residence, then saw him head to the Academy and followed us from there. There were sentinels posted, maybe even the same ones who followed you to my hotel."

"The outcome doesn't excuse the fact you should have been on that plane."

"Had I been, you wouldn't have rushed hell-bent to find me, thereby saving the day. You got to play hero." She glanced over at him, saw him clench his jaw as he rang the bell for Giustino to unlock the door. He jabbed the bell a second time, then held it far too long, clearly annoyed with her, and she realized he was right in some respects. "Look, I'm sorry. But Tasha was my friend, and just as you're not about to let Tex's murder go by without a fight, I wasn't about to let Tasha's go."

"You have no idea what you're talking about."

"Then by all means, clue me in."

He looked over at her as though contemplating just what it was he was going to tell her. But then suddenly looked away, and under his breath, said, "I could have you ordered back with one call."

"Yeah, you could," she said as the lock clicked and Griffin pushed open the door, revealing a whitewashed stairwell, with flagstone steps that wound upward in a square around the broken lift cage. At the moment she was thinking he should make that call. Somehow in the midst of all this, she'd forgotten just why it was that she'd gone off to Quantico. She'd lost her edge on that last case she'd worked, not trusting herself that she could do her job without endangering others. And now, because of her headstrong foolishness, she'd been shot at more times in the last week than in all her years of law enforcement service. And what bothered her the most was that a simple operation up at Adami's villa had resulted in the loss of one of Griffin's friends, and she couldn't absolve herself of that blame, either.

Griffin held the door for her, and she moved past him, then up the stairs, a number of emotions washing over her. Halfway up the first flight, she stopped, turned, looked him right in the eye. "Fine. Send me home. I'll go. You're right. I mean, maybe I shouldn't have jumped the gun on this, but I needed to do something and—" She stopped, unable to keep her train of thought under the intensity of his stare. She was no longer sure of herself. Hell, she wasn't sure she'd ever been sure of herself. And now, the way he watched her…"Goddamn it, was there something wrong with me last night? I haven't slept with a guy in close to a year, and I'd like to know if it's just me or—" Too late, she clamped her mouth shut, then looked away, her face turning hot, unable to believe those words had even slipped from her mouth. *Idiot.*

The resulting silence made her feel an even bigger fool, and she wanted to get as far from him as she could. But when she tried to head back up the steps, he grabbed her arm, held her there, his expression unreadable.

It was everything she could do to gather her thoughts. "Can we pretend like I never brought up the subject? Just put me on a plane, send me home?"

In answer, he pulled out his cell phone, flipped it open, pressed a button, and she figured this was it, he was making that call to have her sent back to the States.

"It's Griffin," he said into the phone. "Turn off the camera in the stairwell."

A camera in the stairwell? Great. Heat flooded her cheeks, and she wished she could melt into the walls or slither down past him and never come back.

He closed the phone, returned it to his belt, saying nothing, his grip on her arm firm, unyielding. Several seconds passed by before he said anything, then, "I do not like racing through the streets, feeling helpless because someone is walking into danger. Not in this country, not in our own. And I especially don't like the feeling I get when it's *you* walking into that danger."

She tried to smile, felt her lips tremble. "Does sorry work?"

"You're a distraction, and I don't like distractions." He stepped so close, his face was mere inches from hers, and she didn't dare move. Couldn't move. He glanced at her mouth, and just when she thought, *knew* he was going to kiss her, he pulled away, looked her in the eye. "I barely know you. I don't want to, Sydney. I can't be worried about you. You were supposed to be a rule follower…"

He took a step back, then down, and she tried to make light of the situation. "I've changed."

"I can't afford distractions."

"You mentioned that." She stepped away from him, brushed her hands over her clothes, surprised to feel her pulse racing. She wanted him. He didn't want the distraction. She was tempted to quip something about not worrying, because she damned well would be staying out of his bed from this point on. After all, they'd be separated by an entire ocean, never mind that her ego wasn't that fragile, no matter what stupid things she might utter about her nonexistent sex life.

Without another word, he indicated she should precede him up the stairs, and just like that the matter was dropped. As it should be, she figured. She had a life of her own, and it did not involve Zachary Griffin.

◇◇◇

Professor Francesca Santarella tried to get past the horrific details of how she'd come under such tight security. As if Alessandra's murder hadn't been bad enough, and never mind the attempt on their lives, Dumas had told her that the anthropologist whom Alessandra had chosen for her dig was also dead, apparently from a hit-and-run back in the States.

All twists of fate? Francesca didn't believe it for an instant, and in her mind the weak link in all this was Father Dumas. No one had shot at her until he'd showed up on her doorstep. He had also been involved with Alessandra, and apparently the dead anthropologist, Dr. Natasha Gilbert.

Perhaps it was some chance alignment of the stars that Dumas wasn't currently standing over her shoulder at the moment while she read the centuries-old documents before her. Somehow she doubted that Dumas would have let her near them if he'd known that the very subject of her research had been imprisoned under orders of the pope for his involvement with Freemasonry, then held until he gave up the names of every member in his lodge. The church was and always had been anti-Masonic, but she knew for a fact the arrest over Freemasonry had been but a pretext. The church wanted what her subject had hidden, the third key. But perhaps Dumas was not up on church history from the 1700s. He had looked at the time period she'd requested and gave his approval to the priest assigned to assist in finding the documents. The silver lining, if one could call it that, was that she was sitting here in the Vatican, reading transcripts from the secret archives, and was given more freedom than most in that she had no time constraints.

The only thing that hindered her was that Father Dumas had insisted on being her guide while she was here. She gathered that his activities with Mr. Griffin were known to none but a select few, and that set her to contemplate just what it was they did. Some sort of governmental agency, which made her wonder how it was that Alessandra had become involved. And why? Somehow it had never occurred to her that Alessandra might have had her own agenda.

Then again, no one had checked with Francesca to determine what her agenda might be, and that was something she had no desire to reveal. She was quite certain that if Dumas even suspected what it was, she would never have been allowed in here.

She glanced around, saw Father Dumas sitting in a chair not too far away, and decided that he was probably more guard than guide. He smiled when he noticed her look up, and she smiled back, then forced her gaze back to the transcripts in front of her. Her mind kept wandering to the message Alessandra had sent, what she'd tried to convey. The proof, she figured, was probably buried in these transcripts, and she scanned the text, hoping she was right. And if she was right, her next step needed some careful contemplation. Slipping out of the Vatican was one thing. Escaping the notice of Dumas, not quite the mild-mannered priest he portrayed, was quite another.

◇◇◇

"Sir?"

Giustino's voice cut into Griffin's thoughts about the latest turn of events on this case, and it took him a moment to realize he was being spoken to. He drew his attention from the security screen that covered one wall of the safe house, and looked over to see what it was Giustino wanted.

"Marc just called in on the secure line. He says it's urgent."

Griffin slid his chair over, took the phone. He hadn't even heard it ring, he'd been so wrapped up in getting Sydney home, and trying to figure out what the hell he was missing in this case. "Marc. Talk to me."

"I believe Tex is alive."

Griffin froze. The image of the faceless man at the morgue, his throat cut—He'd seen the ring, Tex's ring…If not Tex, then who? "Alive? Where? How?"

Marc told him what he'd learned.

"Why would they take him to Tunisia?"

"Perhaps for you not to follow, should you think he's alive?"

Griffin's first thought was to fly out to Tunisia, to look for Tex himself, but he knew that Marc could handle the matter as well if not better. "Do what you have to do to bring him home."

"A problem with that. The warehouse I saw him in? It's the one that we're going to take out. HQ wants us to proceed. I did not want to until I called you."

Griffin's pulse thudded at the realization of what Marc was saying. Tex had been considered collateral damage from the moment he was taken in Adami's villa. HQ wasn't about to stop the operation now for one man who was already considered dead. Should the bioweapons make it out of that warehouse, too many lives could be lost. And now Marc was looking for further direction, something outside the standing orders, direction he couldn't give—at least not explicitly. "Do *just* as I would. As ordered."

The slightest of hesitations, then, "Yes, sir."

"Marc?"

"Griff?"

"Let me know the moment you find anything further." Griffin hung up, not sure what to think.

Alive.

He clung to that small hope. Tex was alive.

Or was it a trap? Meant to lead them astray? The body in the morgue, no prints or identifiable features. Much like Alessandra's body. It took a week to get her identified. Here in the chaos of Rome…

"Marc thinks Tex may be alive," he told Giustino. "He thinks he saw him in the warehouse they have to take out."

"He will go in for him?"

"He's going to try."

Sydney walked into the room at that moment, just as Giustino said, "This I cannot believe. Tex? Alive?"

She turned to Griffin. "Did I hear right?"

"Yes."

"Then who is at the morgue?" she asked.

"I have no idea. But if what he is saying is true, they killed someone else who matched Tex's physical description to make us believe he is dead."

"Why would they want you to think he was dead?" Sydney asked.

"Who searches for a dead man?" He stared out the window, barely seeing the sunset gilding the scalloped cupola of Sant' Andrea della Valle. He didn't want to think what his friend had been going through since that night at the villa. "Assuming the information is correct, of course. It has yet to be verified."

"I will check the databases on missing persons," Giustino said, his expression somber. He sat at his desk, picked up the phone to call his *carabinieri* contact.

Sydney watched him a moment, as though trying to decipher the man's rapid-fire Italian as he spoke on the phone. "They had to think Tex had something they wanted. Information, maybe."

"Undoubtedly," Griffin replied.

"The Tunisia operation Marc is working on?" Sydney asked. "Maybe they know. Maybe they're trying to keep Tex there to protect it somehow."

"But Tex didn't know. We found out that information afterward."

She looked at the radio that Giustino had been manning. "Clearly they didn't know of the bug..."

"Not at first, but we haven't heard a word since we learned of the bio arms shipment."

"Which means they very well may have learned of the bug by now...From Tex..."

She'd only said what he'd been thinking. And it could be true. What Adami couldn't have known was what his team intended to do with that information, because that was something they'd only decided on after the fact.

After about a half hour, Giustino finally dropped the phone onto the cradle. "One of our investigators, he is searching for someone missing, who looks much like the victim in the morgue. This he discounts, because the pathologist, he tells him this victim, he is already identified. They are going to look more."

Griffin paced the room. "If it's not Tex, they killed this man and put Tex's ring on his hand, because he fit the general description. I need a positive identification. Now."

"You forget. This man's fingertips they are removed with his face, and the backlog for DNA is worse than in your country."

Griffin stopped, looked right at Sydney. "What about doing a forensic sketch, like you did for Alessandra?"

"That's a possibility," she said, "but before you go that route, it might help to look at the missing person's report. Maybe there's something in it—something no one noticed, because they weren't thinking it was anything beyond the routine."

"Have them fax you a copy," Griffin told Giustino.

Giustino made the call. A few minutes later, the fax purred to life. The moment the missing person's report dropped into the tray, Griffin picked it up. He spoke fluent Italian, but his grasp of the written language wasn't as good, and after looking it over, he gave it to Giustino to translate.

"The victim, Enzo Vitale, he goes for a walk with his dog that evening. He never returns. I see nothing else. He and Tex, they are very close in size, but there is no more to identify. *Niente.*"

To which Fitzpatrick said, "Something I didn't take into consideration. How many overworked officers bother to ask for minute details on a standard missing person's report? Especially when nine times out of ten, the victims turn up safe and sound?"

Griffin stopped at that. "Good point. Giustino? Call the family. See if there's some detail, some identifying detail they might have forgotten to tell the officer…And do it gently, in case it is this Enzo Vitale."

Giustino nodded, took the report, and made the call. When he hung up, he looked hopeful. "The wife of Enzo Vitale, she describes a heart-shaped mole about four centimeters below his navel."

Something only a wife would know. "Call the morgue."

Giustino dialed, related the information to the investigator on duty, then waited. Time stilled. No one moved, no one said a thing while Giustino sat there, the phone pressed to his ear. From the open windows, they could hear bits of conversation drifting up several stories from the piazza below, as diners arrived at Arnaldo's ristorante. Almost eight o'clock, and the three of them had yet to eat. After several minutes, Giustino sat up, said, "*Certo. Grazie, Commissario.*"

He hung up the phone, closed his eyes, seeming to sink in his seat, and Griffin had no idea if it was good news or bad, until Giustino said, "It is him. Enzo Vitale. They found the mole."

◇◇◇

University of Virginia

"Professor Denise Woods?" Carillo held out his shield and credentials for the petite woman to see.

"You're here about my missing student? Please tell me you've found him and he's okay?"

"Actually," Carillo said. "I'm here on a somewhat related matter. My partner saw you earlier in the week? Special Agent Fitzpatrick?"

"Yes. She's the one I gave the papers on conspiracy theory to. I've had so many people here asking about my students lately, I can't keep it straight."

"You've spoken to other agents?" he asked. Fitzpatrick had indicated there was more to this case than met the eye. "From which agency?"

"Come to think of it, they didn't really say."

"And what'd they ask you?"

"Same thing as your partner. Sort of. They were interested in my assistant. Wanted to know when was the last time I saw Alessandra, if she'd discussed anything out of the ordinary with me."

"And did she?"

"No. That was the gist of it, and they left."

"Anything else you can tell me?"

"About Alessandra? No."

"What about the other student?"

"Xavier, the young man Alessandra had befriended. Normally I don't encourage my assistants to become so closely involved in the projects of my students, but Alessandra had said she'd seen something in his work, something she'd like to explore further."

"What sort of something?"

"Two things, actually, the first being the conspiracy report I gave to your partner. What Alessandra saw in it besides the usual rubbish found on the internet, I'm not sure."

"And what was the other?"

"An odd thing on genealogy he's working on with another professor who is away on sabbatical. It was, in fact, the reason that Alessandra befriended him."

"My partner see that report?"

"Actually, no. I didn't think of it at the time, because she specifically asked if he was working on conspiracy theory."

"You don't still have it, do you?"

"Of course." She opened a file on her computer and printed something out. "Here it is, along with a copy of the conspiracy report."

"Mind if I copy it?"

"If it helps you in your investigation, it's yours."

"Thanks," Carillo said. "One other thing. You have the name of this professor on sabbatical that your student was working with?"

"Francesca Santarella."

Carillo handed Professor Woods a card, asking her to call if anyone else inquired into the matter, regardless of what governmental agency they said they were from. He left, sat in the car and sipped at his lukewarm coffee he'd picked up earlier that morning and read the papers he'd been given.

The odd thing on genealogy turned out to be a report on family trees and the skeletons one might find in their closets if they dug back far enough in their research. It was titled: "Six Degrees to a Serial Killer or King." Starting with the fact that everyone has two sets of grandparents, who each have two sets of grandparents, who have two sets of grandparents, and so on and so on. A tongue-in-cheek look at the pyramidal scheme of family trees. Even those who might lay claim to royalty no doubt had some nefarious relatives tucked in their closets. And to prove his point, the author researched his own history, discovering that, while there were no serial killers in his tree, he was directly related to the Prince of Sansevero, reported to be the first Freemasons Grand Master in Naples.

Carillo flipped through the report, and there were a couple of things that bothered him. The biggie was that the kid was missing after drafting such a report, whether it was this report or the other one he'd done on conspiracies. Now maybe it was merely coincidence that the kid happened to be friends with the daughter of the ambassador to the Holy See, who also happened to be missing—well, was missing, now dead. But Carillo didn't like coincidences, and this thing smacked of conspiracy all over the place. The other thing that bothered him was, as Professor Woods mentioned, under the list of references on his report, the kid noted a Professor Francesca Santarella. That in itself wouldn't bother him, since he had no idea who she was. It was her current address at the American Academy in Rome that made him look twice, something he might not have noticed if not for the fact Sydney was looking into the death of the ambassador's daughter. First thing he did once he found out that little tidbit was look up the ambassador's residence on a nice, big, fat internet map. That, of course, was the only reason he even knew that the American Academy was directly across the street.

And that was one hell of a coincidence he wasn't about to overlook.

He hit a number on his speed dial for the San Francisco office. Michael "Doc" Schermer picked up on his end of the phone. "I need you to check into something," Carillo said. "It's below the radar. That thing Fitz is working on. We need you to work your research magic, figure out what the common thread in all this is."

"Between you and Fitzpatrick, I should be getting paid double time."

"That's the beauty about government salaries. No double time. Saves the taxpayers' money."

"Yeah, well, I suppose they have to give me a lunch break sometime. What'dya got?"

"I'm gonna fax you over a couple reports," he said. "And I want you to dig up some information on a Professor Francesca Santarella."

About an hour later, Doc Schermer called him back. "These look like college term papers."

"They are."

"Some of this conspiracy stuff's swiped straight from the Net. I have to admit, the one he's working on with this Professor Santarella on six degrees of separation? At least it's interesting."

"And your point?"

"This stuff is pretty far out there. Any idea what you're looking for?"

"I was hoping you could tell me."

◇◇◇

Griffin, not trusting Sydney for an instant, handed her his cell phone, then listened intently to her conversation with her partner, Carillo, while she told him that she was booked on a flight out that very night. Suddenly her voice dropped, and she turned her back. Griffin should have put her on speakerphone, but he didn't want to tie up the secure line, and a good thing, too, because a moment later, it rang. Griffin grabbed it, hoping it was Marc with more information on Tex, now that the *carabinieri* had made a tentative ID on the man at the morgue as their missing person, Enzo Vitale.

It was Dumas. "We have a situation."

"What is it?" Griffin asked, shaking his head at Giustino to let him know it was not about Tex.

"The *professoressa*. She slipped out of the Vatican."

"Slipped out for what? A cappuccino?"

"Somehow I don't think that is foremost on her mind."

"Great. This is all I need right now."

"Something else going on?"

"Nothing," he said, not willing to share his hopes that Tex might be alive. Not yet. "Why would the professor leave?"

"According to Father Martinez, who was assisting her with her research, he noticed her taking numerous notes, and happened to walk past to see what had caught her interest."

"I don't suppose you happen to know what her notes said?"

"Actually I do. She only took the top sheet when she left. Father Martinez was able to bring up the remnants. The name Raimondo di Sangro came up. Apparently she was looking at transcripts that had to do with this prince in the 1700s, who managed to find himself jailed for matters that now would seem inconsequential, but back then were the height of scandal. Something to do with his involvement with Freemasonry."

"Freemasonry was a jailing offense?"

"Let us just say that back then the church held far more sway when it came to dissuading its congregation from embarking down the path of darkness. The other matter she was looking into had something to do with columbaria."

"Columbaria?"

"Ancient burial sites."

"She did say she was doing research on ancient burial sites. Anything else?"

"You have the same information I have."

"I appreciate the call."

"I know you would do the same."

Griffin wasn't so sure about that, but he muttered, "Of course. I'll let you know if we hear anything." He disconnected, trying to determine if it was even worth their effort to try to find the professor. "Santarella took off," he said to Giustino, who was busy perusing the book on the Egyptian influence on Roman history in hopes of discovering why it was sent.

"If she is stupid enough to leave on her own after being shot at, she deserves her fate."

"I tend to agree with you." He didn't have time to run after the professor. Not with Tex's situation unresolved, and not until he personally put Sydney safely on her flight out.

At least that was his thought until Sydney handed him back his cell phone, her look somewhat smug. "If I told you something you didn't know," she said, "would it change your mind about sending me home just yet?"

"I doubt it. But try me."

"Two things. One, that book. Carillo said the security video from the gift shop showed that wasn't the only thing Alessandra mailed."

"It wasn't?"

"She bought a postcard with a mummy on the front of it. On the back she wrote something and mailed it separately."

"Any idea what she wrote?" Griffin asked.

"As a matter of fact I do. She drew a triangle, then the word *Egypt* inside the null sign."

"A triangle?" He saw the image carved on Alessandra's face, tried not to think of it, failed, and it took him a moment to recover his thoughts. "Like the triangle carved on her face?"

"It could be a pyramid," she said. "Especially considering the word *Egypt* is next to it. Carillo thought the literal translation would be 'pyramid no Egypt.'"

"They were in Egypt," Griffin said. "Digging in a pyramid. Pyramid not in Egypt? But why mail the book?"

"Maybe as a decoy."

"More importantly, what does this have to do with Adami building and smuggling bioweapons?"

"Maybe she was trying to tell you that the dig was a ploy?"

The same thing that Tasha had suggested...It made no sense. "This second thing?"

"You'll never guess which professor's name Carillo saw on a reference page to a research paper written by a second missing person from UVA—a student who was last seen with Alessandra."

"Why do I not want to hear this?"

"Because the student also listed this professor's address as being at the American Academy."

Giustino set the book on the table. "What is that saying? The story fattens?"

"The plot thickens," Sydney said.

"I can think of a few other choice sayings," Griffin muttered. "None of them remotely polite."

Sydney gave a shrug. "I'm sure there's a perfectly plausible explanation, and I'd love to help you, especially with all the maps and notes tucked away in her office that probably have something to do with all this, but"—she made a show of looking at her watch "—have a plane to catch."

Giustino's smile turned into a full-blown grin, and Griffin glared at him before turning his attention back to Sydney. "Tell me about this paper Carillo found."

"According to Carillo, genealogy, something about some long-lost relative in Naples who was a prince. The other paper, the one I brought a copy of, was on conspiracy theory."

Hell. Dumas said Santarella was looking up something about a prince. "Like I said, what would either have to do with the smuggling of bioweapons?"

"Good question. Clearly the professor is hiding something."

He hated to admit she was right, but she was. He'd been bothered by the same thing, something he might have taken more heed of had he not been so distracted by Sydney's presence— which was another reason to get her on that plane tonight.

"Of course," Sydney continued, "you could always ask her."

"If I knew where she was."

"You mean Dumas lost her?"

"She was looking up information on a prince," he said, ignoring yet another smug look from her, "as well as something to do with the columbaria."

"When I was in her office, I saw a lot of stuff on her walls that had to do with the columbaria."

"What sort of stuff?"

"Maps, diagrams, photos, notes. I gathered it was sort of a specialty. What she was here to study. Maybe if we—if *you* stopped by her studio, you might find something that would give you an indication on where to look."

The thought bore merit. "Even if we did find something, how would we even know what we were looking at? It would have been nice to have an expert solidly in our own court. Someone we could trust without question."

Sydney walked over, picked up her travel bag, then placed it by the front door. "Too bad I'm leaving. I actually do have a go-to man when it comes to digging up obscure bits of information. If anyone can put a spin on some long-forgotten columbarium, Doc Schermer can."

"Doc Schermer?"

"My ex-partner Carillo's current partner."

"May I ask you something, Special Agent Fitzpatrick?"

"Fire away."

"Back in Quantico, when I mentioned that this case was not to be discussed with anyone, at what point did you disobey that directive?"

She gave a light shrug. "Couple hours into it when I called Carillo from my dorm room."

"Figures," he said, wondering how it was he'd so totally misjudged her. Then again, maybe had he given her free rein as she'd insisted, they might be further along.

Or she might be dead.

He'd had a number of good reasons for keeping things from her. Even now it was a risk. But like it or not, she was involved, not likely to change her mind, and he could use the help. Unlike Professor Santarella, Sydney Fitzpatrick knew most of the risks, was well-trained by the Bureau, and any knowledge she and her fellow agents brought to the table was a plus. He looked at Giustino, said, "I need two calls made before we move out. First, bring in someone to cover for you here. I don't want this unmanned while Tex is still out there."

"And the second?" Giustino asked.

"Call the airport and cancel Fitzpatrick's flight," he said, ignoring her catlike smile.

◇◇◇

Sydney rolled up the cuffs on her ENEL coveralls, trying to make them look more like they fit her, when they belonged to Giustino, who stood about four inches taller. When she finished, she smoothed out the uniform, and Griffin, also in ENEL coveralls, nodded.

"Not to worry," he said. "No one will pay much attention."

She could only hope, she thought as they walked across the street to the van where Giustino, dressed all in black, was waiting.

The moment she slid into the front passenger seat, Griffin said, "Do me a favor, Fitzpatrick. When we get to the American Academy, don't say a thing."

"Like the four words of Italian I know are going to do much good?"

"You sure you want to do this?"

"Absolutely."

A little after ten, they drove to the Academy, the ENEL electric company logo still on the van, a perfect cover for their plans this evening. Griffin dropped Giustino off around the corner from the entrance, then waited a short way down the street. About five minutes later, every light at the Academy went out.

They waited a couple of minutes before Griffin drove up to the electric gate and parked. It was still open, which meant it would remain that way until Griffin called Giustino to restore the power.

"You don't think we should have waited longer?" Sydney asked him.

"Trust me. The utility companies are notoriously slow. He'll be grateful to see us."

And sure enough, as the two of them, small toolboxes in hand, walked up to the open gate, the guard hurried toward them, smiling as he waved them through, saying, "*Non ha perso tempo!*"

Griffin rattled off something in Italian so fast that Sydney recognized only ENEL. Whatever he said worked. The guard returned to his shack, allowing Griffin and Sydney to enter the premises on their own. Their boots crunched the gravel path that circled the fountain, and just before they left the path, Sydney glanced back to see the guard standing near the open gate.

Flickering candlelight appeared in several windows, the Academy residents quickly adjusting to the power outage. Upstairs, just over the main entrance, the windows of Professor Santarella's studio were dark. Griffin and Sydney climbed the marble stairs, walked the short distance down the hall to studio 257. The door was locked. Griffin took a pick from his toolbox, slipped it into the lock, and had the door open in less than a minute. Sydney used a blue LED light for her search, while Griffin stood guard at the window, watching the gate. She wasn't even sure where to begin, there were so many papers and books strewn about, as though someone else had already been there and done a hasty search. She glanced over at the desk, where Francesca had been working on her laptop earlier in the day, thinking there might be something there. The laptop was gone. Which meant the professor had returned.

Or someone else had. No doubt, she thought, realizing that the professor wouldn't need to throw her things around to find them. She'd know where to look. Someone else had definitely been there.

But that didn't mean they'd found whatever they were looking for, and Sydney checked the long table, the desk, the walls. Nothing screamed, *look at me, the answer is here.* More like there were too many answers, and it would take days to search through them.

Griffin stepped back from the window. "We have to go. Now."

"I need more time."

"Now," he whispered. "Someone's out there, distracting the guard from his post."

She gave one last look around, saw the hand-drawn maps on the wall, the weird lines drawn across them. What the hell, she thought, and pulled both down, rolled them together. "Ready."

They walked out the door, and Griffin turned the lock, then pulled it shut. When she started toward the stairs they'd come up, he stopped her, listened. Someone was ascending, the quiet of the footfall enough to warn her it was someone who didn't want to be discovered. They hurried to the back stairs down the hall, past the kitchen. Griffin drew his weapon, then signaled for her to start down. They walked through the darkened archways of the cortile, slipped out past the fountain, and toward the guard in his shack. Sydney glanced back toward Francesca's studio, saw a dim light bouncing off the wall as someone searched the room.

Griffin saw it, too. They walked up to the guard, and Griffin waved, told him something in Italian about the power. The guard looked up, nodded as they walked out. "Probably Dumas," he said, when they'd gotten back in the van, as he picked up the phone to tell Giustino to restore the power in a few minutes. He didn't want to do it too soon.

"How do you know it's him and not the guys that came after us at the Passegiata?"

"Because the guard's still alive. Adami's men have no consciences."

"Good point."

Only when they were well away did he ask, "What was it you took from the wall?"

"A couple maps. Of what, I have no idea."

"Nothing else?"

"Nothing in the time we had."

"She's on too many radars. That doesn't bode well for her."

"I'm more interested in what's on *her* radar," Sydney said.

Griffin looked over at her, then back at the road. "You might make a good spy, after all."

"The word *spy* has connotations I don't care for."

"Secret agent, then."

"Special agent."

"FBI, through and through. Except when you're busy breaking the rules."

"Not rules. Guidelines," she said, unrolling the parchment. Pale yellow moonlight washed the paper, but it was too dark to see.

Sydney turned on the small LED she'd used in the break-in. The light was amazingly bright for such a tiny device, and he glanced over as she studied it. "Sort of looks like a map of the sewer system," he said.

"Why would a professor intent on ancient history have a map of the sewer system, unless it was the aqueduct, which I don't think this is."

Back at the safe house, she unrolled it on the kitchen table. "I'm beginning to think this might be maps of different columbaria," she said, seeing the arrows drawn on it and the notations, trying to decide what it was Francesca found so important that she went to the trouble of mapping it out on her wall. "Her writing's terrible." She squinted, tried to make out the tiny notations scrawled at various locations.

"I'd settle for finding which place she might be heading."

"If I had to guess," Sydney said, pointing, "it would be here."

"Why there?"

Sydney couldn't forget the image of Alessandra's disfigured face. "Because the note she jotted on here looks like it says 'pyramid skull.' Alessandra's killer used that symbol for a reason."

"As damned good a place to start as any. Call your Doc Schermer and see what he can dig up on this."

"When do we leave?"

"In the morning. The professor has to sleep, too."

◇◇◇

But the professor wasn't sleeping. She sat at her desk in the dark, even after the power had been restored, not sure if she should cry, scream, or laugh. How stupid to wait for dark to break into her own studio at the academy. Or go to the trouble of calling the guard away, to explain that she needed to enter without being seen, and could he just let her through the gate?

Someone had already been here.

The maps were missing from the wall.

And her laptop.

Neither was good without the other, but someone had them both.

It had taken her months and months to plot out the maps. They were important. But so was the info on her computer, and she seriously questioned her ability to find the final location of the Prince of Sansevero's crypt without it. How had she been so careless as to leave it on her laptop—believing that a lone guard at the gate would keep it safe?

If it was so damned safe, why'd she feel it necessary to sneak in herself?

"Idiot," she whispered. She should have grabbed the computer at the same time she grabbed the package Alessandra had sent. A lot of good that did her friend, getting involved with the government. Killed.

The thought of her own close call on the Passegiata with the men chasing after them brought her to her feet. Time enough to mourn her friend later. Right now she had to figure out what the hell she was going to do next. Her gaze strayed to the desk, where her laptop had been, her sight adjusting to the dark. A shaft of moonlight fell across the floor, washing the terra cotta tile in a pale blue glow. There beneath her desk, she saw what looked like a long dark shoestring upon the pattern of octagons…

Francesca crossed the room, reached down, picked it up. Not a shoestring, but the lanyard connected to a flash drive. She'd thought she'd left it in the laptop right after the FBI agent had knocked at her door this afternoon…It must have fallen off when whoever it was came in and stole her computer.

Not completely lost after all.

She slipped the lanyard around her neck, tucking the drive beneath her shirt, then grabbed her coat, locked her door, then walked down the hall. If anyone was looking for her, they'd search her studio or her apartment. She doubted anyone would bother looking in the TV room off the kitchen. As good a place to sleep as any, she figured. And then at first light, to the Columbarium of the Nile Frescoes.

◇◇◇

There was little traffic in the predawn hours, and Griffin made good time on their drive. After the immense Baths of Caracalla, the long narrow road forked, and Griffin veered to the right. He glanced over at Sydney, who was studying the map. "Well?" he asked, as he drove the van slowly down the Via di Porta San Sebastiano, which was almost pitch dark with its high walls and dense foliage.

"According to Doc Schermer's instructions, the entrance to the Columbarium of the Nile Frescos is somewhere on the left past the Tomb of the Scipios."

"And according to the map?"

"Assuming the professor is talking about the same colum-barium, I'd say it puts the entrance just over there," she said, pointing up ahead and to the left. Griffin drove past, caught sight of a staircase between the massive walls that lined the road, shielding the mansions and surrounding properties from view. He parked the van farther up the road, just out of sight. Sydney rolled up the map, put it in her travel bag, and then they walked back toward the staircase, where they hoped the entrance to the columbarium would be. The sun had not yet risen, not even a sliver of moonlight illuminated the road, the high walls on either side making it seem darker, more forbidding. They reached the break in the wall, where a Z-shaped staircase led up, and they ascended, waited in the dark just beyond the west bend. As the first light began to penetrate the needles of the umbrella pines beyond the Aurelian Wall, Francesca emerged from the street below and mounted the steps.

Griffin stepped out. "Fancy meeting you here."

Francesca froze in her tracks.

She looked from him to Sydney. "I suppose I shouldn't be surprised, considering you stole my computer last night."

"I'm afraid your computer was already gone by the time we got there."

She stared at him for several seconds. "So someone else was there?"

"Let me be frank," Griffin said. "What part of *your life is in danger* don't you get?"

"The part that tells me this can't be happening."

"It's happening. I don't suppose you want to share with us what is so important that you felt it necessary to avoid your protector and risk your own life as well as ours?"

The sound of someone else coming up the steps caught Griffin by surprise. He looked at Francesca, who didn't seem the least worried, as she said, "That would be Signore DeAngelis, the property owner."

A moment later, a man in his sixties turned the corner, slightly out of breath, his white hair looking a bit windblown, as though he'd been running. "I left it on the table," he said in Italian, holding up a large Byzantine key, before stopping short at the sight of Griffin and Sydney. He turned an accusing stare on Francesca. "You led me to believe you were coming alone, *professoressa*. The columbarium is very delicate, and we cannot have people just traipsing around."

"Yes, well—"

"These old columbaria," Griffin said. "They can be notoriously dangerous, and the *professoressa* asked us at the last minute to help her with her research." Griffin smiled, pulled a business card from his pocket, handing it to the old man. "As you can imagine, we are very interested in helping her complete her research so that she can get it to the publisher in time."

The man looked at the International Journal business card. "He is your editor?" he asked Francesca.

"One of them," she replied, which told Griffin she was desperate to get down there, and hadn't exactly been forthcoming with the property owner about her real purpose—whatever that might be.

"And this is?" the man asked, eyeing Sydney.

Griffin replied, "The artist."

"Artist?"

"My understanding is that flash photography can sometimes harm ancient works of art, and so we have brought a sketch artist to document the *professoressa's* research."

The man nodded. "Yes, this is true. We have never allowed cameras in there. You will show me your sketches?"

"She does not speak Italian," Griffin said. "American."

The property owner looked at Sydney, and in clear, precise English, said, "You will show me what you have drawn when you finish?"

"Of course," Sydney said, patting her travel bag. "I think you'll be pleased."

The man smiled, handed the key to Francesca, then said, "Do not forget to lock up the door tight before you leave. I must go, eat my breakfast."

"Thank you, signore." The three of them continued up the steps, while the property owner returned from the direction he came. After he was gone, Francesca said in a low voice, "How did you find me if you didn't take my computer?"

"The map on your wall. Special Agent Fitzpatrick has a friend who was able to discern the location of this columbarium based on the notations you had concerning a skull and pyramid. Now, about the real reason why you're here?"

"I explained that to you. Finishing up research for a grant."

"Then you won't mind if we come along."

"Surely you have something better to do with your time?"

"Your safety is our main concern."

She looked from him to Sydney, then shrugged. "Feel free. But you're wasting your time. Now that I've given you the book, I'm sure whoever you thought was looking for me, will have given up."

Griffin could only hope. "Lead the way, professor. You have promised some drawings to the signore, and we're eager to see what it is you'd be willing to risk your life for."

"Don't underestimate the power of history, Mr. Griffin."

"As long as you don't underestimate the power of a bullet ripping through your flesh."

She led the way up the steps just as the sun started to break over the wall. By the time they followed her down a long path through the trees, the sounds of morning traffic began to drown out the chorus of birds, and exhaust fumes started to mix with the spiced scent of the pines. Eventually they reached an iron gate, and then just beyond it a heavy wooden door. Griffin kept watch behind as she unlocked and pushed open the door, the hinges protesting as she ushered them into a long dark passage.

Chapter Twenty-three

It took several seconds for Sydney's eyes to adjust to the interior of what turned out to be a long corridor, and she stood there a few moments, afraid to venture farther until she could see.

Francesca turned on a large flashlight, its beam wavering off the stuccoed ceilings. "I certainly hope you brought a sketchbook," she said to Sydney. "Signore DeAngelis will ask to see the sketches when I return the key—and I may need to return here someday."

Griffin nodded to Sydney, and she pulled out her sketchbook as well as a pencil. "How many do you want?"

"Three or four should add some legitimacy," Francesca replied, then aimed her light at the ground, indicating they should follow. "Do be careful. The floor is uneven, and the staircase is narrow and steep—about forty feet straight down. There's an iron railing, but it's not very sturdy."

Although Sydney had no idea what to expect, she was unprepared for the immensity of the chamber as they descended. It looked nothing like the catacombs that she'd seen in pictures. The professor's flashlight revealed neatly stuccoed walls with row upon row of half-moon niches, about two feet in height and width, each of which had two terra cotta lids set into its base. Below each niche was a marble plaque with what Sydney supposed were the names of the deceased.

As they moved into the chamber, a soft light began to filter down from light wells that had been cut at one end of a vaulted ceiling. Fronds of maidenhair fern growing from the cracks in the ancient wall swayed as the air stirred around them, sending up sparkling dust motes into the shafts of light. Sydney looked around in awe. "It's beautiful."

"If you like mausoleums," Griffin said.

Sydney, ignoring him, opened her sketchbook, and started drawing. "How old is this place?"

"First century A.D.," Francesca said. "The columbaria were burial clubs where slaves and freed slaves gathered socially to commemorate and inter the ashes of their club members who had preceded them in death."

"And the lids in each niche?"

"The one thing besides the frescoes on the wall and the mosaics on the floor that the treasure hunters didn't bother to remove. Each niche contains two large terra cotta jars, out of sight, behind the walls." Francesca lifted the lid of one. "Cremated bones in each pot," she said, replacing the lid. "Bones are still here, but most of the decorations—freestanding urns or anything of value—were stripped during the eighteenth century and added to the pope's coffers," she said, glancing at Griffin as though he might be inclined to pass on that information to Dumas.

His response was to ask, "Exactly what are you looking for that couldn't wait?"

"A hidden chamber. Something that hasn't yet been discovered that has a connection to another ossuary chamber." She gave Griffin a patronizing smile. "That means bones."

"I'm so glad you clarified."

Sydney threw Griffin a dark look, turned the page in her sketchbook to start a new drawing. "You were saying?" she asked the professor.

"The purpose of my…grant is to prove the location of the final resting place of Raimondo di Sangro, Prince of Sansevero."

"And why would this be important?" Griffin asked.

"For history's sake. He is not buried in his own crypt, and there are some historians who believe that he is instead resting in a chamber elsewhere. And if you wonder at the historical significance of this, then you might also wonder at why the Vatican was interested in di Sangro's final resting place. They questioned a friar who helped di Sangro make his final arrangements and learned that he hid three…clues you might say, each one hidden in other burial chambers, which would eventually allow entry to his final burial chamber. The friar revealed only the location of this first key or clue, but so far it has eluded even the most ardent historians as well as the Vatican, and to this day remains unsolved."

"And yet," Griffin said, "you say you are looking for proof of the burial site, as in you have an idea of where it is?"

"A very good idea. Unfortunately, without the hidden clues, death will surely fall on those who search within."

"Another curse?"

"A reality. Trust me," she said, leading them deeper into the chamber. "According to the records I found at the Vatican, what I'm searching for is located 'past the great pyramids of the Nile, graffito behind the wall beyond the tomb of the harpists.'"

"Graffito?" Sydney asked.

"Graffiti," she replied. "Markings on the wall added by someone *after* this place was built. This particular chamber has already been searched because of that clue, by the Vatican in the late 1700s. Nothing was found, which is why we thought that the friar had to have been talking about the true pyramids of the Nile, and why Alessandra organized the search of the Egyptian tomb. Of course, we know now that her search there was fruitless, which leads us back here. It's the only place that fits. I've been here before, but I can assure you that I have never found anything remotely close to a clue."

"They're paying you *money* to research this?" Griffin asked, his voice filled with skepticism.

"Not to worry. It's a private grant, as opposed to the government paying you money to follow me around. But do feel free to save the taxpayers some hard-earned cash and leave."

Sydney wanted to strangle Griffin. If they were going to find out anything, it was not going to come about by antagonizing the professor any more than they already had. "Well, I for one am interested in what you're doing," she said as they followed Francesca to what looked like the end of the chamber, only to discover that it opened into another equally huge chamber branching to the right. Niches had also been set into its walls for several stories from top to bottom, an impressive sight. "How big is this place?"

"About three times the size of the chamber we are standing in. This particular columbarium is roughly in the shape of the letter E," she said, leading them toward the farthest branch of the E. "And the door that I'm searching for is at the end of the last chamber. When this columbarium was searched and stripped in the late 1700s by the Vatican after the questioning of the friar, the entrance to the lower chamber was never discovered. Someone had taken great pains to disguise it," she said, pausing at the entrance. "That is one more reason I think this is the right location."

"How was it found?"

"The present owner, Signore DeAngelis, was having repairs to his water pipes, and you can imagine his surprise when his plumbers broke into a huge chamber, complete with painted ceilings and frescoes. Thankfully he had the presence of mind to bring in the *soprintendenza archeologica* and various scholars to study it, which was how this particular entrance was found. Once they determined that the entrance had been sealed off sometime in the late 1700s, they decided to excavate it, and to restore it to its original state. Their consensus was that the chamber had been hidden to prevent further looting, perhaps the very looting for which the Vatican was responsible. The curious thing is that after the tomb was stripped, and before it was sealed, someone went to the pains to lay a new mosaic floor in a lower chamber at the end of this branch. No one really knows why."

"Hard to imagine why anyone cares," Griffin mumbled.

"You might not," Sydney replied. "But *I* find it fascinating."

"Well," Francesca continued, eyeing Sydney's sketch of the wall of niches, "the next century, the 1800s, was the era of the great fakes. Charlatans, like the notorious Marchese Campana, palmed off"—she wiggled her fingers in quotation marks, "'newly discovered' antiquities, which they sold to greedy collectors and museums. Even the British Museum got stung. My theory is that the fakery started half a century earlier, which would explain why the mosaic floor was relaid—to lend an aura of authenticity to fake urns and frescoes that went on sale to credulous buyers. They very well may have paraded them down here, using the place as a showroom. What I can't explain is why they sealed off the chamber after having gone to the trouble of putting in the new floor. Unless, perhaps, they were caught selling fakes and trying to hide the evidence."

Francesca led them through the door at the end of the chamber, where they descended another set of steps, not so steep as the last. At the bottom, Sydney saw the floor Francesca spoke of, an expanse of finely made multicolored mosaic tiles set in what seemed to be a random circular pattern. Aiming the beam of her light, Sydney took in her surroundings and was struck by the beauty of the place. The ceilings were still intact in all their original bright colors, and the walls between the niches had been frescoed with joyous paintings—crocodiles, ibises, hippopotamuses, and lotus leaves.

Flashlight tucked beneath her arm, Sydney sketched away. Francesca had other ideas besides standing there and soaking in the history of the place. She began lifting lids in each niche, those that she could reach, then shining her light carefully on those she couldn't, clearly looking for something.

Sydney and Griffin watched her for several moments, until she finally seemed to remember their presence. "Since you're here, you might as well help. I need every loculus checked, every lid of every olla lifted, at least of those you can reach."

"There are hundreds in here," Griffin said. "It'll take forever."

"Isn't it convenient that there are three of us?"

"And what is it we're looking for?"

"Something scratched on the wall or perhaps written on the inside of one of the lids. Something that tells me where this other hidden chamber is."

◇◇◇

Tunisia
0805 Hours

The delivery truck turned into the drive, then stopped at the barricade. The guard stepped out of his hut, walked up to the driver's door. Marc, dressed in coveralls matching the logo on the truck, handed a clipboard with an invoice attached. "Delivery."

The guard took it, looked at papers clipped to the board. "Oil?"

"Motor oil. High grade."

"Wait here." He returned into his office, then exited a few moments later with the schedule of deliveries in hand. "You're a day early. You'll have to come back tomorrow."

According to the schedule Marc had photographed, other than the oil that wasn't due for delivery until tomorrow, there wasn't anything scheduled until later in the week. It was the best they could do, and Marc pointed to his forged invoice. "Our paperwork says today. Tomorrow we have a full delivery schedule, and we won't be able to make it back here until next week." He waited.

The guard eyed him, and then Rafiq, who sat in the passenger side, twenty years added to his looks with gray hair and a mustache, thanks to Lisette's makeup skills. The guard turned his attention back to the paperwork, finally saying, "Open up the truck."

Marc exited, walked to the back of the truck followed closely by the guard, and slid open the rear door, revealing case after case of motor oil. The guard signaled for Marc to lower the lift, so that he could get up and inspect the cargo. He took a knife from his belt, slit open one of the cases, pulled out a can of oil, then punched the top of the can with his knife. He removed the knife, touched his finger to the tip, rubbing the oil, then smelling it, as he walked between the stacks of cases toward the front of the bed, where he was about to do the same to another case. There was a damned good chance that he was about to drive his knife into either a case containing the explosives or the combustible fluid needed to incinerate the bioweapons. The former was bound to raise his suspicions when his knife didn't come out covered in oil. The latter was a different problem. The slightest spark and they were toast.

The guard shoved the tip of his knife into the top of the case to open it, and Marc called out, "You want a case of the oil to take home?"

The guard hesitated, looked over at him. "Two cases."

"Two cases," Marc said, patting the two toward the front. He hopped up on the lift, then removed two cases. "Where do you want them?"

The guard walked over to Marc. "Bring them into there," he said, pointing to the guard shack. Marc followed him in, glancing at the monitors as he placed the cases on the floor before them.

"Not there," the guard said, pointing toward the desk. "There."

Marc lifted the cases and moved them behind the desk, where they would no doubt stay until the guard was off duty. In about forty minutes, the oil would be the last thing the guard would be thinking about, and Marc walked out, again trying to get a glimpse of the monitor of the warehouse. No sign of Tex. He wasn't sure if that was good news or bad.

The guard called for an escort, who drove up a few minutes later in a Jeep old enough to probably use half the oil in the truck at any given time. The escort was also uniformed in the same security coveralls, armed with a semiauto. He stood about five inches shorter than Marc, and when he removed his cap from his head, he swiped at his forehead with his sleeve as he looked over the paperwork. "Why are you a day early?"

Marc gave a casual shrug. "I only know I was supposed to deliver it today."

The second guard returned the invoice to Marc. "Follow me. If I am not with you, you will be shot."

Finally. Marc climbed into the truck, started it, and followed the Jeep into the compound. The compound was like a mini military base, with a handful of bunkhouses, perhaps where the guards and laborers slept, and a number of Quonset huts. The Quonset they needed was closer to the airstrip, which bordered the open desert. Fortunately, the oil was destined for the same locale, and guard number two stopped his Jeep in front of the tan Quonset, got out, and unlocked the door.

"Ready?" Marc asked Rafiq.

"Ready."

Rafiq got out and opened the back of the truck, while Marc took the clipboard in one hand, and a pair of leather work gloves in his other, and walked into the hut after the guard. He glanced around, noticing that the cameras were pointed toward the large doors of the interior, and the office area, where a second guard stood sentry. That, he figured, was the entrance to the actual lab, or where Tex was hidden, otherwise why have a man guarding an empty office? In the meantime, Marc wanted their escort guard out of sight of the camera. "We need to have this signed before we make the delivery," he said, stepping outside the door near the back of the open truck.

The guard took the paperwork just as Rafiq walked up and asked, "Where do you want us to put the oil?"

"That way," he said, pointing toward the interior.

Which was when Marc hit him over the head with the lead weight hidden in his gloves.

The guard crumpled to the ground, and Rafiq and Marc dragged him away from the doorway, into the back of the truck, where they stripped him of his uniform, gagged him, then tied his feet together and his hands behind his back. By the time he came to, Rafiq, being the shorter of the two, was dressed in his clothes, and pointing his gun at the man's head.

The guard looked around, his eyes wide, his nostrils flaring. His muffled cries barely made it through the gag.

"We're looking for someone," Marc said. "A man was brought into that warehouse yesterday. He was hurt. Did you see him?"

The guard nodded.

"Where is he?"

Rafiq lowered the gag.

"Die you pigs of hell."

Rafiq pressed his gun into the man's temple. "One more chance. Where is he?"

"He's dead. Like you'll be."

When he started to scream, Rafiq stuffed the gag back in his mouth, saying, "Another sound and you die. Be quiet and live. Understand?"

Apparently he didn't. He tried to kick out at them, and Rafiq hit him over the head with the gun butt.

Marc looked at his watch. Twenty minutes. Twenty minutes to find Tex. He moved a few cases rigged with explosives onto the dolly, and for benefit of the camera, Rafiq escorted him, directing him into the interior.

Rafiq stood guard, his hand on his weapon. "You're sure he was in there?"

"Like I said, it was a quick glimpse, but those cowboy boots sure looked like his."

"Where do you think he was?"

Marc looked around, saw the remaining guard glance their way, but then, seeing Rafiq in his uniform, relax. Marc nodded toward the far side, his heart pounding. If they didn't find Tex…"Over there. That pallet that looked like it was filled with sacks of rice. You'll have to go look while I unload the truck."

Rafiq ran his fingers through his hair, then put on the guard's cap so it sat low, covering his face. "I don't like this. What if we can't find him?"

"We have no choice. We go ahead as planned."

Rafiq nodded, then walked across the floor, past the shelves and pallets to have a look. He returned a few minutes later.

"Looks like maybe dried blood, but nothing else. If he's in here, he could be anywhere."

Rafiq was right. Some of the pallets were stacked on shelves up to the roof. There were dozens of barrels that contained the alleged biohazard material that needed to be destroyed. Anyone of those could hold a body, conscious or unconscious. He could be stuffed behind any number of boxes and cartons stacked around the premises, and they had yet to make entry into the actual lab.

"I'll finish," Marc said. "You take another look, while I set the charges."

Several minutes later, Marc was unloading the last of the cases inside the Quonset, placing them in precise locations meant for optimal performance. "Anything?" he asked Rafiq, hoping for good news.

"No. I'm sorry."

"Let's take out the other sentry. See what he's guarding. Maybe Tex is there."

Marc, his clipboard in hand, approached the other guard. "I think there is some sort of mistake on here," he said, holding out the clipboard.

"This area is forbidden," the guard said.

"Can you just take a look? I have a full truck, and this says only half. Should I just deliver it all?" He casually walked past the guard into the office, placing the clipboard onto the desk, noting a steel door just inside.

The guard followed him in. "You are not permitted—" And then Rafiq took him out as easily as they had the first guard.

Marc searched him, found an electronic key for the door. He opened it and saw a stairwell that led down. He grabbed two boxes of the explosives, and then he and Rafiq descended. Inside several men and one woman in white lab coats were working at tables in the vast underground space of glass-enclosed cubicles. One looked up in alarm, a sheen of sweat on his dark skin, and it took Marc a moment to recover his senses once he recognized him. In English, he said, "Dr. Balraj? We were told to deliver these supplies for your work."

Balraj eyed the boxes with suspicion, stepping out of his room. "What supplies?"

"Particulate matter. For aerosol," Marc said, having no idea if that sounded scientific enough when it came to bioweapons. He hefted the boxes, trying to get a better grip. "It was ordered from Aron Blackman Industries."

Dr. Balraj narrowed his gaze, staring hard at Marc, then at Rafiq, who now stood guard in the doorway. Aron Blackman was Balraj's assistant, the one who'd been killed in the hit-and-run. The doctor cleared his throat, saying, "I hope you brought the right size particulates."

"I'll put this out of your way," Marc said, walking past him to place one of the boxes at the far end of the lab, where a dark-haired woman in her late thirties worked intently over a microscope. As Marc passed her, he noticed her watching him in the reflection of the glass of her cubicle. As soon as he set down the box and turned, she was back to her microscope. The other scientists barely spared a glance, intent on whatever it was they were working on. Marc figured they didn't speak English, or they would have noticed the boxes were labeled "motor oil." Either that or they were used to supplies coming in mismarked due to the nature of their work. He returned upstairs, brought down several more boxes and placed them as well, while Rafiq did his best to look the threatening guard.

"Any other labs?" Marc quietly asked Dr. Balraj when he'd finished.

"Not at this facility. Everything is contained in here and the warehouse above us."

"I'd suggest you follow our lead. Rafiq?"

Rafiq stepped behind Balraj, pointing his pistol at the man's back. "You will come with us to help unload the boxes."

Balraj raised his hands, and this time the scientist closest to them looked up, saw the gun, and immediately returned his attention back to his microscope. Taking someone at gunpoint around here was no doubt commonplace, Marc thought as Rafiq indicated that Dr. Balraj should walk toward the stairs.

"Are there very many boxes?" Balraj asked.

"Why?" Rafiq replied.

"Perhaps you would care for some extra help?"

Rafiq looked at Marc, who said, "How many helpers did you have in mind?"

"Just one. Dr. Zemke. The woman at that last station."

Marc glanced over, saw her openly watching them. He gave a slight tilt of the head and Rafiq waved his pistol at her, saying, "You. Come." She rose, walked toward them, her gaze fixed on Rafiq, who ordered, "Up the stairs. We have work for you."

"Who are you?" she asked at the top of the stairs.

"Friends," Marc said. "Quickly. We don't have much time." Marc and Rafiq led the two scientists out of sight of the cameras to the back of the truck. "You haven't seen a beat-up American in a tux and cowboy boots, have you?"

They both shook their heads no. After he shut them safely inside the cargo area with the bound guard, he took one last look around, then glanced at his watch. "We have five minutes," he told Rafiq, who was busy stuffing his guard's uniform beneath the truck seat.

Tex or no Tex, this place was going up.

Chapter Twenty-four

Sydney had lost count as to how many loculi she'd inspected, and she stopped, shone her light around the chamber, trying to figure out if Francesca was stringing them along, or if there was a real purpose to what they were doing.

Griffin, however, appeared to be trying to redeem himself in the professor's eyes, faking his interest in the place, no doubt in hopes of getting the professor to slip up and reveal her true purpose. "Why is this chamber so different than the outer one?" he asked.

"This is where the founders of the columbarium had their loculi—niches. Prime real estate. You notice that in here the niches are lined in marble. There were also beautifully carved freestanding urns in those square niches in the far wall."

Then, surprising Sydney that he was even paying attention, he asked, "I thought you said they were slaves and freed slaves."

"Who saved all their money for their final resting places," Francesca said, sweeping her light over the marble-lined niches. "These are the loculi of the officers of the columbarium club."

"The officers?"

"Yes, it's ironic that the slaves and freed slaves' burial clubs were the one democratic institution in ancient Rome. They elected their own officers, and voted on how they wanted the place decorated. This group obviously was into Egyptomania."

Francesca's flashlight skimmed across the painting on the wall, revealing a glimpse of the great pyramids, palm trees, and cone-hatted pygmies dancing beneath them, beside a great river. Sydney stopped in her tracks. "I've seen this before," she said, slowly walking toward the fresco, unable to look away from the wall. "This was frescoed on Adami's ceiling. I'm sure of it. He knows about this place already."

"Adami?" Francesca said. "As in the philanthropist Adami?"

"Hardly a philanthropist," Griffin replied, frowning at Sydney, no doubt to remind her not to reveal too much of their investigation.

Sydney turned to a fresh page in her sketchbook. "I thought that the painting had something to do with Adami's Freemason lodge, because of a conversation I overheard about a pyramid."

"Possibly," Francesca said. "Egyptian symbolism figures strongly in Freemasonry. But during the first century A.D., the Romans were infatuated with all things Egyptian. You have only to look at that huge Pyramid of Gaius Cestius, just outside the Aurelian Wall at the Porta San Sebastiano." She led them further past the fresco. "In the early 1700s at the birth of Freemasonry, Egyptian symbols such as the Nile and the pyramid held sway, which may be why Adami chose to include them."

She shone her light across the fresco. "Many Freemasons would have you believe that they trace their origins to early Egypt. Here is a perfect example." She walked a few feet, sweeping her flashlight across a mosaic in one of the niches, a mosaic set in the pattern of a skull. "You are no doubt aware of the most famous of Masonic symbols, the angle and compass? Observe. This skull could be hanging from what could be interpreted as a Masonic angle, and it is resting on what well might be a Masonic compass in a mosaic in a columbarium from the first century."

"I thought the Masons were a modern invention," Griffin said, while Sydney's pencil raced across her page, trying to capture the detail of the skull mosaic.

"Historians insist that the Masons didn't come into being until the 1700s, the late 1600s at the earliest, yet here on a wall dating back to the first century A.D. are several symbols that are commonly found in Masonic iconography. Masons wanted to believe this proves their origins to early Egypt. All it proves, however, is that like the rest of the world before and after, Egyptian iconography was just as popular in the first century as it was in the eighteenth century."

Sydney examined the skull she'd drawn, then turned back to the page with the Egyptian fresco. "So what I saw on Adami's wall?"

"Probably nothing more than a typical Renaissance depiction of ancient Egypt." She looked around the chamber and sighed. "Unfortunately, I have a feeling that this fresco and mosaic may also signify the customary first-century depiction of ancient Egypt and nothing more. Of course, that depends on how you interpret the phrase, 'past the great pyramids.' It could mean any point beyond these frescoes."

"You mean you had a *specific* location to search?"

"Look," she rounded on him. "I'm not the one who insisted that you follow me. So yes, I had a specific place to search, and by assigning you a different wall, I hoped I might search this one in peace."

Sydney saw Griffin take a calming breath, probably telling himself that he'd be better off taking the professor to an interrogation room and questioning her as he would any other source he needed to squeeze information from.

Francesca retraced her steps, walking past the frescoed pyramids, past the river that was supposed to represent the Nile, past the palm trees and a stretch of what appeared to be barren hills, where two columns had been depicted flanking an opening in the hills where a harp stood. "The tomb of the harp."

Sydney looked at the pyramids, then at the harp. "There's a clue hidden here? Something leading to yet another chamber?"

"That's my hypothesis."

"And then what?" Griffin asked.

"And then I follow it to see where it leads. Nothing more." She stood there, staring at the wall. "As you can see, the problem is that there is nothing else. This is the farthest I've ever penetrated."

Griffin raised his hand in a gesture of silence.

"What's wrong?" Sydney asked.

"I'm not sure. A sound up the stairs."

Sydney heard something as well. An echo of a scrape, and Griffin said, "You locked the gate after us?"

"Yes," Francesca said.

"Is there any other way in here?"

"None that I know of."

Which didn't sound too positive, Sydney thought, as Griffin drew his gun, then looked around. "Let's hope it's the wind, or the owner coming to check on us. But just in case, we need some cover. Can you hide in these fireplace things?" he asked Francesca, flicking his light on the loculi that were off to the right of the Nile painting and the columns.

"Far too small."

Sydney looked around, and realized they weren't going to offer much cover at all. And then she saw a niche just beneath the stairs, about wide enough for a person to slip into. "Maybe we can hide beneath the stairs. That will afford some cover for at least two people."

Griffin glanced over, saw what she saw. In a low voice, he said, "Get the professor under cover." He shut off his flashlight and moved to the edge of the stairs.

Sydney guided Francesca to the niche. "Can you fit?" Sydney whispered.

"I think so."

Francesca tucked herself back into the crevice, and Sydney hesitated until Griffin said, "Hurry. Get that light out." He moved up the stairs until he was just inside the entrance to the outer chamber.

She scooted into the niche next to the professor. And then they waited several minutes in the dark, her mind conjuring up all sorts of possibilities, none of them ending up well. And just when she'd decided that someone had gotten to Griffin, she heard him say, "You can come out. I think I found our intruder."

Sydney stepped from the space and moved around to the bottom of the steps where Griffin stood holding a tabby. She heard Francesca shuffling behind her and assumed she was following her out. "We're trying to hide from a cat?"

"It could be worse," Griffin said. "It could have been a gun-wielding cat." He let the cat go, giving Sydney a strange look. "Where's the professor?"

"She was right behind me."

But when Griffin shone his light into the niche beneath the stairs, there was no sign of Francesca. Anywhere.

◇◇◇

Tunisia
0830 hours

The first guard waved at Marc, lifting the barricade so that he could drive the now empty delivery truck past. For whatever reason, the man didn't question that they weren't escorted to the gate. Not their problem. Their captive was starting to wake up, and they heard him kicking at the panels in the back of the truck. Unfortunately for him, or perhaps more fortunate, they were already out of the compound. Adami wasn't known to be the understanding sort of employer, probably even less so once he learned the fate of his warehouse. Marc only hoped that Dr. Balraj and Dr. Zemke were sitting well away from the guard's feet.

"Call the number," Marc said, as they turned the corner, out of sight of the compound.

Rafiq took his sat phone, punched in a number, but hesitated before hitting Send. His gaze locked on Marc's, his dark skin looking pale.

"Maybe he's not in there," Marc said. "Neither scientist saw him."

"Locked below, they wouldn't know. I can't."

Marc held out his hand for the phone. Rafiq handed it over.

Marc positioned his thumb on the Send button, gripped the steering wheel tightly with his other hand, and then couldn't help it. *Forgive me.* He pressed the button, tossed the phone onto the seat, then stabbed his foot on the gas pedal. There was a sixty-second delay in the first charge. The longest sixty seconds of Marc's life.

The explosion rocked the air, and a moment later, the second explosion that incinerated everything inside the warehouse hit. He glanced in his rearview mirror, saw a fireball rising in the sky.

◇◇◇

Sydney eyed the tunnel. No way was she going in. She'd had a fear about dark spaces ever since the murder of her father, and that little tunnel seemed awfully dark to her, not that she was about to reveal her secrets to Griffin. "You go after her," she said.

Griffin shone his light into the tunnel, then looked at Sydney. "After you."

"Somebody should probably stand guard here, don't you think?"

"Spider phobia?"

She was tempted to tell him the truth, but then heard Francesca call out, "There's actually a shaft of light coming in from above. You have to see this."

"Well?" Griffin said.

"I scoff at spiders. But you have the flashlight."

He moved beneath the steps, shone his light into the tunnel that was hidden from view until one moved all the way into the niche. Here goes nothing, she thought, dropping her sketchbook into her shoulder bag, then trying to tamp down the fear that she'd be in the middle of the tunnel and Griffin's flashlight would go out and she wouldn't be able to find her way.

His flashlight was not going to go out. That's what she told herself as she crawled after him, then came to a turn, and realized that it led to more stairs, these leading upward.

This stairwell was even narrower than the one they'd taken to descend into the columbarium. She could stand, but the ceiling was low and Griffin had to stoop as they ascended what seemed to be about two stories. And as the professor had promised, there was a bit of light coming in through the arched ceiling at the top of the steps where Francesca was waiting.

"What is this place?" Sydney asked, moving next to Francesca.

"It seems to be some sort of private viewing area of the columbarium we just left." She pointed over the ledge, and Sydney looked out, realized they were indeed looking at the chamber from above. A stunning view, and she started a new drawing to capture the center of the mosaic floor below. From this height, the center of the mosaic appeared to be a large circular labyrinth, unrecognizable from the ground level, due to the proximity.

While Sydney sketched, Francesca began an earnest search, directing Griffin to help. Sydney was nearly finished when Francesca called out. "There's something scratched on the wall below this painting."

Sydney drew her gaze from the lower chamber to the wall where Francesca was standing. Another skull. While the mosaic of the skull and symbols they'd seen in the lower chamber might loosely bear resemblance to something Masonic, there was no doubt in Sydney's mind of a Masonic connection with this painted skull. Above and below it, in much sharper detail than the first-century version, was a definite Masonic square and compass. And below it, as Francesca indicated, was something etched into the wall: "*Hic iacet pulvis cinis et nihil.*"

"Latin?" Griffin asked. "Meaning what?"

"'Here lies dust, ash, and nothing,'" Francesca translated, her voice filled with excitement. "It has to be the key."

"The key to what?" Griffin asked.

"That leads to the next clue," she said quickly.

"Then by all means," he said to the professor. "Lead us on."

◇◇◇

They returned the columbarium gate key to Signore DeAngelis, who was delighted when Sydney presented him with a sketch of the maidenhair ferns growing among the loculi. Griffin kept careful watch on Francesca, insisting that she would remain with him from this point on, as they walked down the stairs and up the street to where they'd left the van. The stone walls on either side of the street towered overhead, and they walked single file as cars zipped past them on the narrow road.

"So it seems you have found the first sign," Griffin said, when they'd reached the van. "Where is it leading to next?"

"Right now I have no idea," Francesca replied. "It will take more research. Perhaps another trip to the Vatican."

"So you can take off again? I think not."

"Maybe," Sydney said, as she slid into the front passenger seat, "we should return to the safe house. We might even hear something about Tex."

Griffin kept an eye on Francesca as he walked around the van, opening the side door, apparently to make sure the professor didn't bolt. "We can't afford to compromise the place."

"Can we afford to at least have lunch?" Francesca asked. "I'm starved. And at the very least, we can decide on the next course of action. I would very much like to find this second sign."

"Do you know of any restaurants nearby?" Griffin asked.

"Just up the road. The Hostaria Antica Roma. A rather apropos setting if I do say so myself."

The restaurant was about a three-minute drive up the road, and just as she said, very apropos, Sydney thought, if one didn't mind dining in a place that once housed the dead. "Part of the charm," Francesca said, smiling at their expressions when they saw what made up the walls of the patio setting: ruins of a columbarium, much like the one they'd just left.

The owner, Paolo Magnanimi, introduced himself when they walked in. He stood almost as tall as Griffin, his dark, handsome features lighting up when he recognized Francesca. "It has been far too long since you last visited my restaurant. Please sit down," he said, waving his hand toward the empty patio, it still being early for lunch.

When he started to reach for the menus, Francesca stopped him, saying something in Italian.

"*Sì, professoressa.* The best for you and your friends."

He left, and Francesca told Sydney, "I told him to bring us whatever is fresh from the garden for a vegetable, for pasta, the *tagliolini* in a fresh tomato and basil sauce, and for dessert, his exquisite tiramisu."

"About this second sign?" Griffin asked, apparently not about to let the matter of food get in the way of his mission. "What is it? And where is it?"

"If I knew that, I would have been there long before now."

"Then how do you intend to find it?"

"By researching the phrase scratched on the wall in the columbarium. If it is correct, it should lead to another burial chamber of some sort. There are three, each one leading to the next."

"And the final destination? The culmination of these signs?"

"As I said, di Sangro's final resting place. Until I get there, I can't be sure."

Griffin leaned back in his chair, looking as though he didn't believe a word she said, but was interrupted from saying anything as a waiter brought them each a glass and a bottle of sparkling water. When the waiter left, Griffin turned to Sydney. "Your friend, Doc Schermer. Do you think he can research this for us? This phrase found on the wall?"

"It's worth a try," Sydney said.

"Call him."

She looked at her watch. "You realize it is about two in the morning, there?"

"Call."

She took out her cell phone, called Doc Schermer's cell, hoping he kept it with him, since she didn't have his home number. He answered on the fourth ring, his voice thick with sleep.

"Hey Doc. It's Sydney."

"I'm guessing you must still be in Rome, otherwise you'd know it's dark here."

"First, sorry for waking you. Second, there're extenuating circumstances. I need you to look up some obscure facts having to do with a Latin phrase."

"Give me a sec."

Sydney heard what sounded like the phone being put down, some shuffling, probably booting up his computer. She covered the phone, asked Francesca to write down the phrase. Griffin handed her a pen and a receipt he found in his pocket. When Doc returned to the phone, she spelled out each Latin word, then said, "It means: 'Here lies dust, ash, and nothing.' Supposedly it was inscribed there by Raimondo di Sangro, Prince of Sansevero, as a clue to find his final resting place."

"Anything else I should know about the phrase?"

She repeated his request to Francesca.

"I'm looking for a connection to another burial chamber. Something with bones. And if it has a Masonic connection of some sort, that's even better."

Doc apparently heard her, and said, "Give me a few. I'll call you back when I find something."

"He's checking the info now," she said, placing the phone on the table after turning the ringer to vibrate.

They fell into a somewhat strained silence, finally broken when Griffin asked Francesca, "Why the Masonic connection?"

"Raimondo di Sangro was a Grand Master of the Masons, and as such was very fond of including Masonic iconology in whatever he was involved with."

"And the purpose of all this?"

"As I explained, simple research in trying to locate the final burial site of the prince."

"You expect me to believe that that's what this is about? Trying to find the prince's final resting place?"

"That's precisely what this is about," she said as Paolo showed two men to a sun-dappled table on the far side of the patio, his rapid Italian telling Sydney that his customers were locals, not tourists. One man shrugged out of his leather jacket, glancing over at them as Sydney's phone bounced around on the table, clattering against her water glass.

Sydney scooped up the phone, glad it was too early for much of a lunch crowd. She looked at the number. "That was fast," she told Doc Schermer, when she answered.

"Not sure if this is what you're looking for, frankly because there's not a lot out there on this Latin phrase, and any Masonic connection is tenuous at best."

"Let's have it."

"'Here lies dust, ash, and nothing' happens to be the English translation of the epitaph on the tomb of Cardinal Antonio Barberini, whose remains are interred at the Capuchin Crypt in Rome."

"And the Masonic connection?"

"Depends on how you look at it. Barberini's uncle was Pope Urban VIII, which sort of gives it an anti-Masonic bent. Of course, your di Sangro guy wasn't born until the next century, and Freemasons weren't officially around yet, which means the first papal bull against Freemasonry wasn't issued for maybe another hundred years after Barberini's time, which makes it even more—"

"Doc?" she said, knowing his penchant for delving into historical trivia.

"Sorry. Your Masonic connection is that Barberini was the Grand Almoner for France, which means he was in charge of carrying out works of charity."

"And how does that become a Masonic connection?"

"Like I said, tenuous at best. The Almoner is an office that exists to this day in Masonic Lodges in England, in charge of charity and welfare of the members."

Sydney repeated the info to the others.

Francesca leaned back in her chair, shaking her head. "How is it I never thought of the Capuchin crypt?"

To which Griffin said, "You think this is the connection you were looking for?"

"It certainly sounds like it. Your friend is correct. It might be tenuous, but that may very well be why di Sangro chose the Capuchin crypt. Brilliant, if you think about it. Di Sangro would have picked the Capuchin crypt for both reasons."

"How is that?" Griffin asked as Paolo brought their food to them, two large platters, one filled with Swiss chard, the other steaming paper-thin egg noodles, covered with fresh tomato and basil sauce.

"He was excommunicated and imprisoned for a time by the Pope for his participation as Grand Master of the Naples Lodge, so what better way to nurse a grudge than to choose a location for the next key with a connection to the papacy and to the Masons, almost as if he was thumbing his nose at them."

Sydney's mouth watered as the scent of tomato and basil drifted toward her. "We do get to finish eating before we leave for this crypt?"

"Trust me," Francesca said, as she dished the steaming pasta onto her plate. "You want to eat this before it cools. Besides, at this hour, there is no hurry." Francesca slid the platter of *tagliolini* toward Sydney. "Like many places in Italy, the Capuchin crypt closes for lunch and doesn't open until three. So eat up. We have a lot of bones to look through when we leave here."

Chapter Twenty-five

Francesca hid her excitement over the discovery of the inscription being connected to the Cardinal Antonio Barberini, and at half past two they left for the Capuchin crypt. When they arrived at the Via Veneto, the doors of the unobtrusive entrance to the Cimitero Cappuccino were open for business—if you could call leaving a modest donation for the staid woman sitting just inside the doors business, since the monks made most of their money from the postcard concession.

As Francesca shepherded them through the entrance, several British tourists with stunned looks on their faces were leaving the crypt. "They come for the skeletons," Francesca explained in a whisper, since she was fairly certain that Sydney had no idea what they were about to see. "The place is decorated with the bones of some four thousand Capuchin monks."

"You're kidding," Sydney said.

And Griffin asked, "And what are you looking for here? A sign in the bones?"

"Precisely," Francesca said, since in truth, she had no idea what it was she was supposed to find. She only hoped that whatever it was stood out to her, and she glanced over at Griffin, about to make up some story, when she saw him watching two men who had entered the anteroom at the back of a small group of German tourists. One man wore a gray jacket, the other a leather coat. Both were holding open guidebooks.

"What's wrong?" she heard Sydney ask Griffin in a low voice as the three of them entered the narrow crypt corridor.

"Those two men behind us," he said. "Do you recognize them?"

"The men from the restaurant."

Francesca whispered, "Surely they're just tourists."

"They spoke fluent Italian at the restaurant," Griffin said.

"Should we leave?" Sydney asked.

"Not yet. I'll keep an eye on them. You two play tourists and find what the professor is supposed to find so that she can finish her research and we can put her on a plane back to the States."

Back to the States? No way, she thought, moving down the corridor into the long, vaulted, brightly lit hallway, its walls and ceilings covered in detailed latticework, intricate designs of lacelike patterns that pleased the eye wherever one looked. She glanced at Sydney, watched the agent's face as she no doubt gradually realized that the exquisite filigrees adorning the walls and ceilings were all made of bones: butterflies were pelvises; rosettes were shoulder blades; the lacy lattices were ribs. Lanterns, hourglasses, stars, and coats of arms all made of bones, bones, and more bones.

"This," Sydney said, "may be one of the strangest, most maca-bre and beautiful places I've ever been to, and I have seen a lot of strange places."

"You'd be surprised," Francesca said, "how many other such repositories there are throughout Europe."

"Makes you wonder about the mind of the person who cre-ated this. Today he'd probably be committed."

Francesca led them down the corridor. To their left, the hall opened up to several alcoves. The hushed voices and a couple of nervous laughs of the visitors seemed to echo off the walls.

In truth, the crypts were mesmerizing in their surreal and eerie beauty, as long as one didn't look too closely and think about what the decorations were made of. The first, the Crypt of the Resurrection, held skeleton parts that formed a frame for the painting of Jesus commanding Lazarus to emerge from the tomb. Most of the visitors seemed to pay it little attention, and moved quickly on to the main attractions: the bones. As they passed on to the next alcove, Sydney asked her, "Anything?"

And what was she supposed to say, even if she did find what she was looking for? "Nothing. Sorry."

Next was the Crypt of the Skulls with its circles of bone flowers predominating in the vault. Brown-robed Capuchin skeletons— their bony fingers clasped, as if in prayer, seemed to be suspended in contemplation in their eternal niches, which were made entirely of skulls and thighbones stacked atop each other, their shape, liked arched fireplaces, reminding her of the niches in the columbarium. Perhaps that was what she was supposed to see?

She and Sydney had just moved to one side of the narrow corridor to allow others a view, when Griffin stepped in behind them and whispered, "The two men. Even if they were just coincidentally tourists who arrived at the same destination, they're definitely watching us. They haven't looked at their guidebook once, or at the bones."

Sydney didn't turn around. "What do you want to do?"

"We can't do anything now, or they'll know that we know. Keep on walking to the end, casually, and then we'll start weaving our way back out of here as quick as we can."

Griffin took Francesca by the arm, she assumed for her protection, and they moved on to the next alcove, pausing only long enough at each display so as not to alert the men that they were aware of their presence. The Crypt of the Pelvises was much the same as the last crypt, except here the wall behind the friars was nothing but pelvises stacked one upon the other. Next was the Crypt of the leg bones and thigh bones, which contained a depiction of St. Francis, wearing a crown of vertebrae. The last alcove, the Crypt of the Three Skeletons, held a small, delicate, child-skeleton suspended from the ceiling. In one hand, he was grasping a bone scythe, and in the other, he held balance scales that dangled downward. The scales of good and evil come Judgment Day, she thought as Griffin nudged them back along the corridor toward the one-way entrance.

They walked as casually as possible past the group of Germans, and she saw Sydney glance up at the ceiling, which was dominated by a large clock made entirely of vertebrae and phalanges, its hands perpetually on midnight.

"The symbol of eternity," said Francesca. "But look closely at the hands. You'll see the bone clock is made up of Roman numerals, I, II, III, IV, V, VI. Note that the Roman numeral six is at the top? Midnight is actually six o'clock."

"I wonder what the meaning is behind that," Sydney asked. "Midnight that isn't really midnight? A clock that isn't really a clock?"

"Find anything?" Griffin asked Francesca, the tone of his voice telling her that he completely doubted the veracity of their visit.

"Nothing."

"Good," he said as they strolled casually past their shadows, who were now making a show of consulting their guidebooks. "Then your research is over and we can get on with our lives."

"Forgive the bad pun," Sydney said, quickening her pace to match theirs, "but other than the guys following us, this is one dead end. I think we should get the hell out of here."

"I agree."

Francesca glanced behind her. Their two pursuers had dropped the pretense of reading their guidebooks, and were now pushing their way toward them. She had a bad feeling about this, something that intensified when Sydney said, "You know what really bothers me? Those are not the guys who came after us on the Passegiata."

"You're sure?" Griffin said.

"I tend to notice guys who are shooting at me," she said. "How many different groups are after us?"

"More importantly, how'd they know we'd be here?" he said, pushing through the door.

They hurried down the stairs, and Francesca thought that the Via Veneto might offer some protection since it was filled with people waiting for the bus or out for a late afternoon stroll.

Griffin turned to Francesca. "You have any ideas how we can lose them around here?"

She pointed across the street. "Via dei Cappuccini," she said, indicating the smaller street that intersected with the Via Veneto. "It leads right to the Via Sistina. Maybe we can lose them in the crowd, or down the Spanish Steps."

"Let's go." They crossed over to Via dei Cappuccini, which sloped a short way downhill where it ended in the Via Sistina, a narrow street, with shops, hotels, and plenty of pedestrians.

As they turned onto the busy street, Francesca looked back and saw the men following at a brisk pace about thirty yards behind them. "They're still on us."

And Sydney said, "Tell me you have a plan?"

"When in doubt," Griffin said, "Plan B."

"I hate Plan B."

"You don't even know what it is."

"And that's usually the problem," Sydney replied as they crossed to the opposite side of the street.

"You have a mirror in that purse?" he asked Francesca.

"Yes."

"Get it out."

She dug it from her purse just as they approached the Piazza della Trinità dei Monti with its huge Egyptian obelisk overlooking the Piazza di Spagna—the famous Spanish Steps. Tourists and Italians were descending the sweeping stairway, and at first that was where Francesca thought Griffin intended to take them. But just as they reached the end of Via Sistina, Griffin put his hand on her shoulder. "This way," he said.

They made a hard left onto a dark, narrow street that intersected in a sharp V at the end of Via Sistina. Not a pedestrian in sight. Only parked cars and trucks.

Griffin handed Sydney the mirror, then grabbed Francesca's hand, holding tight as they raced up the street, not stopping until they reached a set of steps jutting down from a building façade. In the deepening shadows, Francesca saw a gigantic gargoyle face that seemed to be swallowing the door at the top of the short flight of stairs. Griffin shoved Francesca behind the landing. "You, don't move," he ordered her. To Sydney, he said, "Watch the street. Let me know when they're almost on us."

"And then what?" Sydney asked, as Griffin ducked behind a delivery truck.

"Time to find out who they are and what they're planning."

And for the second time in as many days, Francesca wondered if she'd made a very big mistake. One that might cost her her life.

Chapter Twenty-six

Sydney crouched behind the truck beside Griffin, holding the mirror out just far enough to view their surroundings without being seen. A few seconds later, she saw the two men who were shadowing them. "They've stopped at the end of the street," she whispered. "Looking around, like they're trying to figure out which way to go…Guy in the leather coat is pointing this way…They're coming." She waited until they were just a few feet away, then she raised her hand, signaling with her fingers, three…two…one.

Griffin stepped out, grabbed the guy's leather jacket, pulled him back between the truck. Sydney saw a glint of silver as Griffin held a knife to the man's throat.

The other man took a hesitant step toward them.

Griffin shook his head. "Don't move. Who are you and why are you following us?"

The man looked around him in both directions, before saying in heavily accented English, "We are simply messengers. You have nothing to fear from us. I—we work for Father Dumas."

"And he works for God," Griffin muttered, clearly not letting down his guard on the simple belief that God made Dumas any more trustworthy. "Search him," he told Sydney.

She moved up behind the other man, patted him down. "He's clean."

"How about you?" Griffin asked the man he still had a tight grip on. "You carrying?"

"No."

"And what would that be poking me in my gut?"

"Maybe just a small gun." American, Sydney realized.

"Then you won't mind if my associate removes it, for your safety."

"No."

"Didn't think so."

Sydney pulled a not so small Beretta from his waistband, aimed the weapon at him.

Griffin stepped back, holding the knife at his side. "The gun tells me you don't work for Dumas. Why are you watching us?"

The guy glanced at Sydney, and the gun she held. "Really, Special Agent Fitzpatrick. There's no need for lethal weapons. I'm simply the messenger. If we wanted to kill you, you'd be dead."

She hid her surprise at hearing her name. "Then who was that shooting at us at the Gianicolo Hill yesterday?"

"An unfortunate misunderstanding from...some associates. We now have a strong interest in ensuring that everyone's needs are met on this venture."

"Needs?" Griffin asked. "What needs?"

"Let's just say that you are very close to acquiring something that we want. And to guarantee its safe delivery into our hands, we intend to offer you something—or rather some*one* that you want."

Griffin tensed. "I'm listening."

"Bring us the map, we return your friend."

"And how do I know my friend is alive?" Griffin asked, while Sydney was trying to figure out what the man was talking about. A map of what? Francesca's map of the columbarium? No. That made little sense. Adami was after bioweapons, not ancient burial sites.

"If you'll allow me to reach in my pocket," the guy said, "I have a mobile phone for you to call."

Sydney kept the gun trained on him. "Slowly," she ordered.

He lifted his jacket so that they could see inside, then reached in and pulled out a thin cell phone. He held it up, saying, "First, the rules. In exchange for your friend, we require that the map

be given directly to us. No copies or photographs of it allowed."
He glanced over at Francesca, who still waited by the stairs,
adding, "Not even for academic purposes. And we require that
you remain in contact via mobile phone. *This* mobile phone.
Agreed?"

"As I said," Griffin replied, "I'll need assurance that my friend
is alive."

"Allow me to make the call." The man punched in a number,
waited a moment, then said, "Signore Griffin is here with me…
Yes. It's been explained." He handed Griffin the phone.

Griffin held it to his ear, then "Tex? You're okay?" He listened
for a short time, then closed the cell phone. "I agree to your
terms on one condition." The guy said nothing, and Griffin
continued. "Call off your trigger-happy watchdogs. If anything
happens to any one of us, the deal is off."

"Of course. There is one other stipulation. You have twenty-
four hours. You will use this phone to communicate. The number
is programmed in. If we lose communication with you, or you
go beyond the allotted time, we will assume you have broken
your end of the agreement. Your friend will die, and I can no
longer guarantee your safety."

"I can't guarantee we'll find it in that time."

"That would be most unfortunate." He looked at his watch.
"It is a little after four P.M., and so, being in a generous mood,
we shall expect the map by five P.M. tomorrow."

Griffin dropped the phone in his pocket. "Anything else?"

"My gun."

Griffin glanced over at Sydney. "You want to give him back
his gun?"

"Not really."

"Tell you what," Griffin said. "When all this is over, we'll
turn it into the *carabinieri* for safekeeping. You can pick it up
from them."

Sydney smiled at the dark look from the man as he said "You
know they won't return it to me."

"A shame," Griffin said. "Now get the hell out of here so we can find that damned map."

The two men wasted no time in leaving, and Sydney kept the weapon trained on them as she watched them go. "Adami's men?"

"That remains to be seen." He stormed across the street, then dragged the professor up by her arm, demanding, "What *map* is he talking about?"

Chapter Twenty-seven

Griffin resisted the urge to strangle the professor, only because it would make it very difficult to get answers from a dead woman. "I said, what map?"

"I have no idea what he's talking about."

"The hell you don't. Now I suggest you answer my question, because I owe my life to the man they're holding. In fact, every citizen of America and, yes, even this country, owes their miserable life to that man."

The professor shook her head, tried to back away. "It's only a map. I have no idea why anyone else would want it."

"A map that has something to do with some prince named di Sangro?"

She said nothing.

He let her go, and she fell against the staircase.

"Honestly," she said, righting herself. "I didn't think it would be so...I had no idea."

"No idea about what? That your life was in danger? That others' lives were as well? The people shooting at you weren't a clue?"

"I thought the shooting had something to do with whatever Alessandra had gotten herself involved in."

"You're telling me Alessandra didn't know anything about this map?"

"No. I mean I thought it was her association with you and this—this other matter. The one where she went out on that spurious dig with the anthropologist."

"Anthropologist?" Sydney asked.

Hell. That was all he needed right now, for Sydney to realize that Tasha Gilbert was the anthropologist in question. He didn't need the grief that would cause once she discovered that it was Tasha who set up his meeting with Sydney back in Quantico. "We'll talk about this back at the safe house," he said to Francesca. "And if I have to hook you up to a polygraph to get to the truth, I will."

Of course, returning to the safe house presented a problem of its own. He had no idea whether its location was compromised. Had Adami's men followed them from there to the crypt? Or was there a simpler explanation?

He looked at the professor. "Who knew you were coming here?"

"No one."

"You didn't telephone anyone?"

"One. A friend in Naples."

"When?"

"Yesterday. After I left the Vatican. But I had no idea at the time that I was coming here. We hadn't yet been to the columbarium to discover the clue."

"Naples? What's in Naples?"

"Allegedly, the map."

Griffin ran his fingers through his hair, frustrated, angry, wanting to smash something. They'd undoubtedly followed her to the columbarium, and from there, followed all of them to the restaurant and then to the Capuchin crypt. "Let's get to the car," he said, realizing that even if the safe house wasn't compromised, it would be, the moment he walked into it with the damned cell phone Adami's goon had given him. It probably had GPS tracking on it, maybe even a remote-activated listening device as well—hell, what was he thinking? Of course it had a listening device, and he tried to recall everything the three of them had discussed since he'd taken possession of the phone. He didn't think they'd said anything Adami's men didn't already know, but even so, he took out the phone, held it up so that Sydney and

Francesca could see it, and put his finger over his lips to indicate they weren't to talk. Sydney nodded, then leaned over to whisper to Francesca, in case she didn't understand why.

It took them about fifteen minutes to walk back to the van. Once there, he handed Adami's phone to Sydney, signaled that he was going to make a call with his own, then walked off about twenty feet, standing near a group of tourists who were busy talking, the better to cover his own conversation. He called Giustino. "I think your location's been compromised. And if it hasn't, it's about to be."

◇◇◇

Sydney knew better than to demand that Griffin stop and answer her question as to who this anthropologist was. Nor was she about to demand any answers from Francesca, even though she was fairly certain the professor knew far more than she was letting on. The damned phone Griffin had given her to hold was probably remotely picking up their conversations, and she wasn't about to risk anyone's lives by speaking now. Besides, Tex was alive and they had a chance to rescue him, and Griffin understandably needed to concentrate on that, as well as the security of Giustino and the safe house. For now, she did her part, kept an eye on the side mirror, the passing cars, making sure there was no immediate danger. Whatever this map business was about, Francesca Santarella seemed to be in the thick of it, and like it or not, they had no choice but to stay the course.

The trip to the safe house was quiet. The professor had the presence of mind not to say a word, a good thing, because Griffin looked ready to do some serious harm.

At the safe house, Giustino buzzed them through the door. He was already packing up equipment when they walked in. "What happened?" he asked Griffin.

"We have to go to Naples. Adami has Tex."

Sydney pulled out the cell phone that Griffin had given her, holding her finger to her lips, then saying, "They gave us this and said if they lose contact via this phone, they'll kill Tex."

She gave the phone to Giustino, who examined it, walked to the front door, saying loudly, "I watch your phone while you get your things together." He opened the door, set the cell phone just outside on the landing, before he closed the door again. "No sound comes through reinforced door. The phone may pick up your conversations, even if turned off."

"What if it rings?" Sydney asked.

"If it rings, I hear it on the monitor."

The very mention of the monitor reminded her of her encounter with Griffin on the stairs, and she studiously avoided looking at him. Instead, she leaned against the wall, keeping an eye on the closed-circuit monitors of the area surrounding the safe house as Giustino said, "Tell me about Tex."

Griffin directed Francesca to a chair at the dinette table, glared at her until she finally sat, then turned his attention to Giustino. "I spoke to him myself. Typical Tex. He says he's fine, and not to do what anyone's asking. They took the phone away from him after that."

"Where?"

"I have no idea. But at least he wasn't in the warehouse when it blew."

"Then what is happening? Why do they take him?"

"I'm baffled on this one." He looked at Francesca, who still seemed to be shaken over the night's activities. As well she should be, Sydney thought. And Griffin said, "They want some map. Perhaps the professor wouldn't mind explaining to us what it is we need to know?"

"I—Where would you like me to start?" she asked, her voice breaking.

"The beginning would be nice," he said, taking a seat at the table opposite her.

"Alessandra had contacted me after she had gone to work on an excavation in Egypt. She said the government, you, I presume, thought the whole dig was a setup to cover illegal arms dealing."

"She told you this?"

"Only because she believed that the government had made a mistake, but she wanted to verify it. She thought the dig was absolutely authentic."

Sydney tried to remember her conversation with Tasha at dinner that night in D.C. Something about returning from some dig, and her apparent paranoia. And Sydney wondered, what were the chances it was the same one? Not that she was about to interrupt Griffin's interrogation to ask.

"I thought you hated big government," Griffin said. "Why did you agree to work with her?"

"Because she'd overheard something said by the men she was supposed to be watching, something that had to do with a third key."

Griffin's reaction was barely noticeable, a slight tensing of the shoulders, and Sydney figured he was thinking of what she'd been able to pick up at Adami's gathering at his villa. "What about this third key?" he asked Francesca.

"It's supposed to be the means of finding—well, of finding this map. Alessandra was certain that this is what the men were actually searching for in Egypt, but something made her think that perhaps they were searching in the wrong place. That they'd misinterpreted the location, and she wanted proof. She sent a postcard from the Smithsonian with a note. The pyramid. Not in Egypt. I'm sure she felt that one couldn't disrupt an entire government operation based on conjecture about some map that many scholars think is merely legend."

"A map to what?"

It seemed several heartbeats before she finally answered, as though it was a secret she still didn't want to share. "Some believe it's the key to the lost Templar treasure. Some, however, believe it is the key to something far more dangerous. Something that could kill millions."

Chapter Twenty-eight

Griffin was certain he'd heard wrong. "The Templar treasure? Dangerous? Forgive me if I don't follow. We're talking gold, right?"

"Gold?" Francesca's expression dismissed this possibility outright. "Do you have any idea what is said to be found in the Templar treasure? Put aside its historical significance, or the questions it could possibly answer about religion, questions that entire wars have been fought over. This goes beyond mere gold." She looked at each of them, waiting for some response, and when no one spoke, she added, "Do none of you read the Bible?"

"File your complaints with Dumas," Griffin replied. "About the Templars and these religious artifacts. I was under the impression that the treasure was lost in the raid and destruction of the second temple of Solomon."

"Not lost. The treasure itself has been captured and moved many times, cursing all who come across it. One can either believe in God's hand, or fate, or perhaps the misfortune of being in the path of the Black Plague, but each time someone has attempted to possess the treasure for their own benefit, the downfall of their civilization has followed shortly thereafter. What remains is trying to retrace the last years of the treasure's whereabouts. Rome in 70 A.D., Carthage in 455, Constantinople in 533—"

"Carthage?"

"As in Tunisia."

Hell, he thought. No wonder Adami had set up shop there. He'd been searching for this treasure a lot longer than they'd thought. "Go on."

"The last word was that the treasure was returned to Jerusalem, only to be hidden once again when the city was ransacked by the Persian Sasanians. After this point, it was never seen again. Except for the rumor that the Templar Knights found it and became the guardians."

"So the rumor that the treasure is sitting in the vaults of the Vatican is false?"

"If it were at the Vatican, then ask yourself why Dumas is busy searching for it."

A good point, he thought. "And Adami would be after this for what reason?"

Sydney answered. "Wouldn't the acquisition of religious artifacts worth billions factor into Adami's game plan? If you're going to sell weapons to terrorists, and you want to keep warring factions at each others' throats to inflate your prices, then it seems to me possession of these artifacts would up his ante."

"You both are missing the point," Francesca said. "I am not talking about the gold, precious stones, or scrolls. I am talking about the Ark of the Covenant that was found by the Templars. *Everything* documented in the Bible and history beyond proves that wherever the Ark landed, death and destruction followed. I am talking about what might have been contained *in* the Ark, or possibly hidden along with it. The deadly plagues. The *biblical* plagues that Moses brought onto the land at God's behest."

Griffin and Sydney stared in disbelief. Even Giustino looked up from the monitors, waiting for an explanation.

"Surely," Francesca said, "you didn't think Adami was in this strictly for the advancement of art or religion or academia?"

That was the farthest from Griffin's mind. Carlo Adami, an arms dealer and secret intelligence broker, was first and foremost a master manipulator, willing to sell out to the highest bidder, no matter what country was involved. He was loyal only to himself. The man craved power, and anyone who held important religious artifacts would wield a lot of power, stirring up radicals into a bloodlust over territories and beliefs. And if those religious artifacts contained something that could be used as a bioweapon? Was it even possible? "*What* exactly are you talking about?"

"Carlo Adami was funding the study for the search. My friend was the recipient of the grant and gave periodic reports to him, unaware, I'm sure, as to what his true motive was. Regardless, several years ago, this friend of mine, a biblical archeologist, came across some papers in the Vatican archives detailing information about a map leading to the Ark of the Covenant, a map held by the Ark's guardians, the Templar Knights, papers he is certain were misfiled and not meant for public view. And therein lies the problem." Francesca leaned back in her chair, crossing her arms. "The Vatican was not very forthcoming when he tried to research further, and the documents he'd been researching were promptly removed. Some scholars insist that this third key is merely legend. No map, no gold, no artifacts, nothing at all. They think that the entire concept was invented by di Sangro as a ruse to anger the Vatican in revenge for ruining his name, and to keep them from finding the treasure."

And here was that di Sangro prince again. "What do you believe?"

"You were with me when I found the first key in the very columbarium that I know for a fact was searched and ransacked before, including by the Vatican in the 1700s. They were searching for the first key back then. How can I not believe?"

Griffin pushed his chair back, trying to figure out what the hell was going on. "How do you know that what you found in the columbarium was the first key, if you found no second key at the crypt? And why is it so important?"

"It's difficult to explain."

"Try."

"Di Sangro ensured that without all three keys, if someone tries to remove this map, that person will be killed."

"This has something to do with a so-called curse at the tomb of the Valley of the Kings?" Griffin asked, thinking of what Tasha had told him when she'd first returned from the dig in Egypt.

"That's a separate curse entirely, and, as most of the Egyptian curses go, a fable to ward off grave robbers. What di Sangro constructed in his own crypt is no curse. It *will* kill you."

"What was di Sangro's motive?"

"Familial duty. The city of San Severo, his birthright, was owned by the Knights Templar. Add to that that di Sangro was the first Grand Master of the Freemasons in Naples in the 1700s, it explains why some scholars believe he was also an appointed guardian of part of the Templar treasure."

"Why waste time searching through these long-forgotten chambers of death for keys that may or may not exist? What's to prevent someone from just going in and taking the damned map?"

"According to my research, historians believe he constructed his crypt to fall upon itself if anything is moved without benefit of the three keys."

"And you believe this?"

"Di Sangro was considered the Leonardo da Vinci of the eighteenth century, and his job was to ensure that this map did not fall into the wrong hands—which makes perfect sense if, in fact, it does lead to something as deadly as a biblical plague and that plague could be used at will to kill one's enemies. If someone should discover where this map had been hidden, then tried to remove it, death would be imminent."

"Can we get past the curses and legends?" Griffin asked. "There's got to be something more substantial."

Giustino shook his head. "For Americans, legends are *difficile* to believe, probably because your country is so very young."

"Giustino?" Griffin said.

"You want me to be silent?"

"Anything," he said, fast losing his temper, "that will allow her to finish her story in a timely manner."

"That," Francesca said, "could take hours. You don't under-stand—"

"*You* don't understand," he said, deciding the hell with keeping his cool. "We have less than twenty-four hours. I'll give you five damned minutes to tell me what is going on." He looked at his watch.

Francesca bit her lip, and looked around the room, as though trying to decide whether he was serious. No one moved, no one said a word. "I can't possibly give you any more than a very rudimentary explanation in such a short time."

"Not a problem," Sydney said. "He's a rudimentary kind of guy."

Griffin made a show of consulting his watch. "You have four minutes and thirty seconds."

"Fine. As I explained, Raimondo di Sangro, Prince of Sansevero, first Grand Master in Naples, was imprisoned and ordered by the King of Naples and the Vatican to reveal the names of each and every member of the lodge. Their ultimate goal was to learn who was in the inner circle and who might have knowledge of this fabled treasure, which had been hidden by the original Templar guardians when King Philip of France had every Templar in France imprisoned to take control of that treasure in 1307. The Templars went underground and were never heard from again—until the Freemasons emerged in the 1700s."

"I don't want a damned history lesson."

"Then you don't want the damned map, do you? Now if I might continue?" When he said nothing, she proceeded. "Di Sangro was brought in by the Vatican, questioned about his ties to Freemasonry, and forced to reveal the names of other Masons. Worried that his fellow Masons might give up some of the secrets of the inner circle, di Sangro moved the treasure to a new location, then entrusted the first key to his mentor from the Jesuit school he attended as a boy. Di Sangro gave explicit instructions about how and where the key was to be hidden, and how it should be passed on only to the next guardian. And that is a very, very basic explanation."

"And who was this next guardian?"

"No one knows. The priest never gave up the information after he completed this quest of hiding the first key."

"Then tell me what you do know."

"According to my earlier research and confirmed by what I found in the Vatican archives, the Jesuit priest told his inquisitors truthfully that di Sangro had given him the first key to hide, and that key was hidden in the ossuary—the bone chamber—'past the great pyramids of the Nile,' and to look for the 'graffito behind the wall beyond the tomb of the harpists.' It was assumed that he was referring to Egypt, the Valley of the Kings, primarily because the Vatican's search of the columbarium in Rome was fruitless. The priest also warned them that the map was well protected, and without all three keys, the finder would be crushed. According to the Vatican archives, he said he did not know the location of the other two keys, only di Sangro did."

"Maybe this priest or di Sangro gave it to someone else? The next guardian."

"As far as we know, both he and di Sangro died before the next guardian was chosen, and I don't believe he would have ever entrusted the information to anyone else."

"And so what you found in the columbarium?"

"I'm sure it was the first key."

"But no second key at the crypt."

"If it's there, I can't possibly say where or what it could be."

"Do you know the location of the third key?"

"The *general* location of di Sangro's hidden burial chamber is in Naples, but no one has been foolish enough to attempt to access it without having the three keys."

"So this map everyone has been seeking has been sitting in some chamber for years on end, free for the taking?"

"If one has all three keys."

"And what if the keys and this so-called curse or trap are merely a ruse?"

"Would you be willing to risk your life or another's because you thought it was merely a ruse?"

"I'm not even sure the map exists," Griffin said.

Sydney crossed her arms, gave a slight shrug. "Doesn't matter what you think. Adami thinks it exists, which sort of makes it a moot point."

Hell, he thought. Pyramids and bone chambers, and triangles carved on faces...*Someone* believed it was true. And if there was a trap, Adami had the advantage. Send in Griffin. If the trap worked, Griffin was dead...and so was Tex. "Get McNiel on the line," he told Giustino. A moment later, Giustino handed him the phone. "Mac? Griffin. I have a...development on this third key." He told McNiel what Francesca had said.

There was a long stretch of silence on the other end, and he was certain that like him, McNiel was having a hard time absorbing this. "How sure are you about this?"

"I'm not sure at all," Griffin replied. "But as Fitzpatrick mentioned earlier, does it matter? Adami believes it to be true, therefore what choice do we have?"

More silence. Then, "When are you leaving for Naples?"

"First light."

"If there's any truth to this, that map isn't to leave in unfriendly hands. Keep me informed."

Griffin disconnected, then looked at Giustino. "You have almost everything ready to go here?"

"A team is on its way, *adesso*. We should be out within the hour."

To Francesca he said, "Naples?"

"Naples."

And just when he thought that was the end of any discussion on the matter, Sydney looked right at Francesca, and said, "You never did mention the name of this anthropologist you were speaking about..."

Great, he thought. How the hell was he going to get out of this one?

Chapter Twenty-nine

Sydney watched as Griffin quelled the professor into silence with one look, then asked Giustino to take the professor into the kitchen so that they could talk. If that wasn't telling, the fact he could barely look Sydney in the eye was.

"Well?" Sydney asked.

"Your friend," he said. "Dr. Natasha Gilbert was the anthropologist who had worked with Alessandra."

"*Tasha*?" she said, and still had a hard time believing it. She wasn't even sure what to say, what to think. It didn't matter that she'd suspected this from the moment she'd heard Francesca mention that an anthropologist had been working with Alessandra. Too coincidental for it not to be she. Once again Sydney thought back to the beginning, the night she and Tasha went to dinner, the conversation they'd had.

She recalled thinking that something was off. Tasha had seemed jumpy, had purposefully deflected any personal questions...

Sydney got up, walked to the window, stared out, seeing nothing. With the clarity of hindsight, she realized that Tasha had been worried about something, no doubt this dig she'd gone out on. Tasha probably had no idea the depths to which it ran, or the dangers involved. Nor was she trained to deal with such matters. Griffin, however, did know, and Sydney turned, glared at him. "How could you not tell me?"

"What good would it have done, except make you worry?"

"Oh, I don't know. Make me trust you a little more from the get-go? What the hell else haven't you told me?" He simply looked at her, his face unreadable, and that infuriated her even more. She paced the room, tried to think..."How long did you know she was involved with Alessandra's case?"

"From the beginning."

She thought of the implications, tried to determine what all this meant. "And yet you *let* me suggest her name for that drawing?"

He hesitated, looked away a moment, and she wondered what kind of bullshit excuse he was going to give her. "The information was classified. I couldn't tell you."

"Couldn't or wouldn't? Maybe if you'd trusted someone else besides your goddamned self—"

"At least I trust myself."

"What's that supposed to mean?"

He didn't answer.

Suddenly she wondered if he'd known how much confidence she'd lost in her own judgment ever since her father's murder investigation. And then she recalled that he'd done a complete background on her, decided he knew *exactly* what he was saying. "You're a bastard."

"You've established that on more than one occasion. It doesn't change the fact I could not tell you."

"I went to dinner with her, for God's sake. She was clearly worried about whatever this was. I could have talked to her. Maybe found out something, *helped* her."

"It was out of your control, Sydney," he said, his voice so quiet, she barely heard him. "Just like everything that's going on right now is out of my control. All we can do is work with what we have right here, right now."

And he was right. They had one objective right now, and that was to find Tex. "Fine. But when this is over, it's over. I never want to run into you or anyone from ATLAS again."

"At least we agree on something."

◇◇◇

They took the early morning train to Naples, and Sydney was glad for the chance to relax, even if only for the next couple hours. Griffin continued to query the professor on this prince of Sansevero and his missing map, and when that line of questioning was done, he moved on to why she insisted on keeping something like this from him when she knew that Alessandra had been killed over it.

"I don't expect you to understand." Francesca sighed, leaning her head against the train window, staring out at the long unbroken series of arches of the Roman aqueduct, with the green cascading plants sprouting from the ancient bricks. "I cannot sit idly by and allow your government to get in the way of something I've devoted my life to discovering."

"And yet you'd risk your life, and the lives of the rest of us around you?" Griffin looked at Sydney. "Watch the professor. I'm going to check the train, then find us some coffee."

He left, and Francesca leaned back in her seat, seeming resigned to her fate. "I suppose you must think I'm a calloused academic, obsessed with myself and my glorious goal of publish or perish."

"What I think," Sydney said, "is that your goal is getting in the way of your common sense. These people who are after whatever this is, they'll kill you and anyone around you without batting an eye."

"You don't understand."

"You're right. Your friend was murdered, brutally, and then my friend was killed as part of the investigation looking into that murder. We won't even go into the number of attempts on my and Griffin's lives as a result, never mind the attempt on your and Dumas' just, when? Day before yesterday? Does that mean nothing to you?"

"Of course not." Francesca had the grace to look somewhat humiliated. "But this is my life's work."

"And your life's work won't mean a thing if you're dead."

"But my work will still be here."

"I'm sure that means a lot to Alessandra and my friend Tasha."

"I did not ask Alessandra to become involved. She and I merely shared some of the same academic interests, which happened to involve ancient burial sites."

"How do you know it wasn't your interests that got her killed?"

Francesca's brown eyes glistened. "I've thought of nothing else. Or maybe I've tried not to think it…"

Someone jostled Sydney from behind, trying to move through the aisle, and she turned to see a teenage boy with an accordion, who filled the space with his presence as he pumped a lively off-key rendition of the Venetian Boat Song—a little too lively for that hour of the morning. Behind him was a young girl with long dark braids, who moved shyly forward, her calloused hand outstretched, and a sweet, professional smile playing about her pretty face as she begged for coins. Sydney judged her to be about the same age as her own sister, Angie, just eleven, and her heart went out to the girl, her instinct to dig into her purse. Before she could, Francesca said something in Italian, rather rudely, judging from the tone of her voice.

To Sydney, the girl said, "You are American? I tell your fortune, yes?"

Francesca looked about to protest, but Sydney waved her back, dug into her bag, and pulled out a few Euros, handing them to the girl. "What's my fortune?"

"It smiles on you, nice lady."

To which Francesca said, "*Va via!*" She waved her hand impatiently, and the boy and the girl moved on, but not before the girl turned around, looked back at Francesca, then Sydney, her dark eyes sharp, unyielding, the smile from her young face gone.

When they were out of earshot, Francesca said, "Professional beggars. Bad idea to encourage them."

After a silence, Sydney asked, "What is the Vatican's involvement in this affair? Father Dumas? If he was working with Alessandra, he must have known about this map."

"I'm quite sure he does," Francesca said. "This map is said not to exist, yet the most powerful Church in the world has been searching for it for the past two centuries, perhaps even longer, since it appears that someone had to have been a guardian before di Sangro was appointed. That they would imprison di Sangro because he is a Freemason? I have always found that suspect, especially considering their interrogation of the Jesuit priest who hid the first key. They were interested then, and they're interested now. Whether or not it is for the same reason that your government wants it, I don't know. And if you have any suppositions about my callousness, put yourself in my shoes. When I find what I'm looking for, then I find out why Alessandra was killed."

"I am in your shoes," Sydney said. "In a fashion."

"How so?"

"Let's just say I insinuated myself in this investigation to find answers as to why my friend was killed. I might be employed by the government, but my loyalties belong to Tasha, because in a way, it's my fault she's dead. I was the one who recommended her services to Griffin in order to discover Alessandra's identity after she was killed."

"Her identity?"

"She was missing her face and her fingerprints at the time."

Francesca paled. "Missing them...?"

"Her face was carved off, or a piece of it in the shape of a pyramid was removed, and her fingerprints removed as well. My friend was a forensic anthropologist. I was the forensic artist who was supposed to work with her."

Francesca stared mutely out the window for several long seconds. Finally she said, "Was your anthropologist friend killed the same way?"

"No. A hit-and-run, no doubt intended to deflect our attention from the two cases, so we wouldn't think they were connected."

"A hit-and-run...? I—I didn't think any of this would lead to..." She took a breath. "I can't believe this..." Looking shaken, she closed her eyes, crossed her arms tightly about her, as though the thought of so much death was too much to bear.

Griffin walked up just then, bearing a plastic tray with three espressos. "If any of Adami's crowd is on this train, I haven't noticed them," he said, taking a seat besides Sydney. He turned his attention to Francesca, then back to Sydney. "What happened?" he asked, nodding toward the professor.

"We were discussing Alessandra's murder," Sydney replied, taking one of the plastic cups from the tray. Francesca took hers, but didn't drink. Griffin asked no further questions, and the remainder of the trip passed in a relative and uncomfortable silence.

An hour and a half later, the train slowed to a stop in the Naples station. Griffin handed Sydney her bag that contained her sketchbook and the two maps she'd taken from Francesca's wall, then slung his backpack over his shoulder. "We can get a cab in the taxi line just outside the station."

They walked down the *binario* into the station, wading through the mass of passengers moving in all directions. Sydney saw the accordionist and the young girl moving through the crowd. A loud argument between two men turned into a shoving match, and everyone seemed to surge back at the same time, trying to avoid the fight, which made it more difficult to get through the crush.

As they left the station, they joined the taxi line, which moved swiftly, thanks to what looked like a sea of official yellow cabs waiting to pick up their fares. A cab pulled up, and Griffin held the door open, allowing Francesca to slide in first.

Sydney was about to get into the cab when she felt the slightest of tugs at her back. She turned, glimpsed the dark braids as the girl from the train darted through the crowd, and she knew without a doubt that her bag had just been picked. Doubt turned to wonder when she checked her bag, found her money still there. She looked around her, saw the boy with the accordion, and decided that the girl had to be close. Sure enough, she saw the girl through the crowd, looking right at her, as though daring her to give chase. Whatever, Sydney thought, about to get into the cab, when she caught sight of what was in the girl's hand. A rolled parchment. "The professor's maps," she whispered to Griffin.

"What?"

"Pickpocket."

"Professor, get out of the cab."

The driver shouted at them as they abandoned the cab. Griffin followed Sydney toward the entrance to the station, and Francesca raced after them.

"Why would she take the maps?" Sydney asked.

"Maps?" Francesca said. "Why would a street girl take maps, when she could just as easily get your money?"

"Maybe she figured they were something valuable," Sydney said. "You did give them a nice antique appearance."

"They were *my* maps?"

"Let's hope that's all it is," Griffin replied. "I'd hate to think someone else already had us pegged."

There were still too many people about to find such a small girl, who was no doubt an expert at remaining hidden. But the accordion-wielding accomplice stood out easily, and Sydney pointed him out, saying, "They were together."

"Then we wait here," Griffin said.

And they did just that, waiting near the newspaper kiosk.

After several minutes, Sydney found the girl, darting in and out of the crowd, no doubt filling her pockets as she did so. "There, by the magazine kiosk."

Griffin nodded, started that direction. He looked everywhere but at the girl. A moment later, he had her by the scruff of the neck. Sydney and Francesca walked up in time to hear the girl say, "These papers, I only take them from the *signorina*, because she is nice. I take them to protect her."

"Protect her from whom?"

She pulled the maps from the back of her shirt, holding them out to Sydney.

Clever, Sydney thought. She took the maps from the girl, then told Griffin, "Pay her."

"For our own property?"

"You heard her, she thinks I'm nice."

Griffin dug into his pocket, pulled out a few Euros and held them out.

The girl looked at the money, then frowned at Griffin. "This is all, when I return your valuable papers out of the kindness of my heart?"

"You are lucky I don't send the *carabinieri* after you for this."

The girl's smile brightened as she reached for the money, then said, "And how much I get if I tell you that you are followed?"

Griffin didn't let go of the money. "That depends on the information."

Sydney looked around, but trying to see if they were truly being followed in this crowd was impossible.

The girl, however, clamped her mouth shut, and Griffin let go of the money, which she quickly pocketed, as he took a few more bills from his wallet. "Tell me what you know, and I'll decide what it's worth."

"The white taxi, do you see it?" she said, pointing across the piazza to where several limousines and a few odd-colored taxis were parked farther beyond the official taxi line. "He follows you."

"And you know this how?"

"This man, he is also on the train from Roma. He watches the signorina," she said, nodding toward Francesca. "I see him, he talks to the driver and pays him money, but then he does not get in. The driver? He watches all of you while you wait in the taxi line." Griffin handed her two bills, and she added, "My brother, he followed them. It is extra if you want to know what this man said to the driver."

"And that was?"

"To let him know where you are going. When he passes that information, the man will pay him again."

Griffin held out the Euros. "I don't suppose you caught this man's name?"

"No, signore. The man, he carried a big gun."

"What should we do?" Francesca asked.

"I want you and Sydney to get back in the taxi queue. I intend to find out if this is part of Adami's crew. If it isn't, then I want to know who else is watching us." He looked at the girl, and said, "One hundred Euros to you and your brother, if you create a distraction that will draw that taxi driver from his cab for at least sixty seconds."

Chapter Thirty

The dark-eyed street girl left to get her brother, while Sydney and Francesca returned to the long taxi line. Griffin kept an eye on them, as he took out Adami's cell phone from the special pouch that Giustino had given them. The case helped to ensure that their own conversations were muffled, but the GPS would not be inhibited.

Griffin hit Redial. A man answered. Not Adami. The voice sounded much like the leather-clad man from the Capuchin Crypt.

"This is Griffin."

"I see you are in Naples."

"Did you follow us on the train?"

"Why would I need to do that? The phone has GPS. We know where you are. And your friend here has every confidence in your abilities."

"My sources tell me that someone is paying a pirate cab to follow us. It's not yours, is it?"

There was a rustling sound, as though he covered up the phone to speak to someone. A moment later, he came back on. "Signore Adami informs me that we sent no one. We will be meeting you at the appointed hotel."

"What hotel?"

He gave him the address. "There will be a room waiting for you under your name. When you have the map, I will meet you there."

"Who would be following us?"

"I can assure you it is not we." And then he hung up the phone.

Griffin replaced the phone into the pouch. A moment later, the street girl dragged her brother by his hand, his accordion strapped over one shoulder.

"My brother, Mario."

In Italian, Griffin told them that he needed a distraction, one that the driver wouldn't know was directed at him, but that would allow Griffin uninterrupted access to his cab for at least sixty seconds. The two kids grinned, apparently thinking this an easy prospect.

Griffin moved around the kiosk as Mario and his sister raced across the piazza toward the pirate taxis, so called because the vehicles' owners either failed or refused to be regulated by the government, which forced them to remain on the fringes, hoping to pick up a fare from anyone who didn't want to wait in the long official taxi queue. The pirate cabdriver who was allegedly being paid to watch Francesca, definitely had his attention fixed on the two women, who were about halfway through the rapidly moving line. Griffin crossed the piazza toward the driver, figuring he had no more than five minutes to take care of business, before they hit the front of the line. And just when he wondered what it was the two street kids had planned, he looked up to see Mario slapping the hoods of the pirate taxis, darting in and out between the cars, while his sister chased him.

As Griffin came up behind the suspect cab, Mario ran in front of it, drumming the hood with both hands, laughing. The driver leaned his head out the window, yelling at Mario. Mario laughed, ran off a few feet, then returned and did it again. This time the driver opened his door, only to have it hit Mario's sister, who seemed to appear out of nowhere. She started crying loudly, and when the driver told her to shut up, she started wailing that the man had hit her. Mario then called out for the *carabinieri*, that his sister had been hurt, which immediately set the driver on alert. He looked around, tried to quiet the two kids, no doubt worried that the police might show up.

It was the opening that Griffin needed. From a small case from his backpack, he had removed a jet-black device no bigger than a dime, and maybe twice as thick as a nickel. Flipping it over, he pushed a tiny switch with his thumbnail to turn it on. He glanced over at the trio, the girl still crying, the driver trying to shush her, but desperately watching the taxi line, seeing his chance at easy money evaporate the closer the two women got to the front. Griffin casually walked past the taxi, tossed the bug into the open door—not his preferred method, but right now, the most efficient method—and continued past it, judging that it probably landed on the floorboard of the front passenger seat. The driver wouldn't be looking for it, his attention would be fixed on whatever cab he was following.

Griffin made eye contact with Mario, as he started across the piazza toward the taxi queue. And just as suddenly as it started, Mario grabbed his sister, telling her to quit being such a big baby. That she wasn't hurt. The two kids ran across the street and waited for Griffin by the newspaper kiosk.

"We did good, yes?" Mario asked.

"You did excellent." Griffin removed a hundred Euros from his wallet, then handed them to Mario. "*Grazie.*"

The girl smiled at the sight of the money. "If you want help with your tunnels, come to San Gennaro—Duomo of Naples." Suddenly she grinned. "I saw it on the signorina's map." And then, before Griffin could question her further, she and Mario darted off into the crowd.

Heaven help the next unwary traveler, he thought, rejoining Sydney and Francesca as they reached the front of the line, about to get into a taxi.

Griffin gave the man the name of the hotel. About ten minutes later, the cab pulled up in front of the hotel, its seventeenth-century edifice giving testament to a past grandeur that had faded due to neglect or lack of money over the last couple centuries. The property was either owned by Adami, or the owner was in his pockets, which meant that anyone who worked within was suspect. They exited, and Griffin paid the driver. The pirate cab had indeed followed them, was parked just down the street. Griffin escorted the women toward the hotel's front door, at the same time, removing the listening device from his backpack, something that resembled a portable music player, replete with little white headphones that completed the look. He put one earpiece in his right ear, said, "It sounds like he is making a call… He is. Saying our taxi dropped us off at the hotel, and where should he wait to collect the rest of his money…"

They entered the lobby, crossing a marble floor, the brown and white swirls having lost their gleam long ago. Only the wood-paneled walls and the counter were polished. Griffin gave his name to the lone man at the reservation desk, and was given a key, then directed to the elevator. Inside the lift, he lost the signal completely. "Let's hope the room faces the front street," he said. But judging from the direction they had to take when they stepped off the elevator, it did not.

"Why hope for a room at the front?" Sydney asked, as he unlocked the door, and they entered. There were two double beds, a table and two chairs cramped into a space that barely fit the furniture. The only thing that saved the room was the tall French window that overlooked a narrow alley, the light pouring in giving the illusion of spaciousness.

"The digital listening device I planted in the cab. Direct line of sight brings a clearer signal." He moved to the window. Could just make out the main street from his view of the alley.

Francesca moved straight toward the bathroom. The moment she closed the door behind her, Sydney said, "I get the feeling she's still hiding something."

"As long as she doesn't take too long in revealing it. All we can do is watch and wait. Unless you're any good at reading maps," he said, nodding at the rolled-up parchment in the bag she'd tossed onto the bed.

"Tunnels leading to ancient burial sites aren't my forte."

"Mine either. But I have it on good authority that we want to head toward the San Gennaro. At least that's what your little street urchin told me."

"Quite the entrepreneur, that one."

"Quite."

A few minutes later, Francesca emerged from the bathroom, took a seat in a chair by the window, tapping her fingers on the small table. "How long will we be here?"

"That depends," Griffin said. "How much time do you need, Professor?"

"Enough time to contact—to get a computer and look up my notes, and try to pin the last coordinates from the map."

Griffin stepped closer to the window, pressing the earpiece tighter. "Quiet," he said. "The cabdriver is talking."

◇◇◇

Sydney glanced toward Griffin, decided he was listening to the cabbie, maybe even missed what Francesca had said about contacting someone. She moved closer to the professor. "Contact who?"

"No one. A misstatement."

"I don't think so."

"I know the risks. Please let me handle this my way."

Apparently Griffin had been listening to her. "Had we done that from the beginning, you'd be dead."

"It's dangerous. I realize that."

He pressed a button on the receiver, removed the headphones, and turned up the volume so that they could hear what had been recorded. Sydney understood little, as they were speaking Italian, but of course Francesca understood every word. Sydney did, however, recognize the name of the hotel where the taxi driver dropped them off. Then another voice saying, "*Grazie,*" and then the sharp ping of gunfire, muted by the tiny device, but still recognizable.

Francesca's face paled. She sank back in her chair. "Why? They said they wouldn't hurt anyone if we brought them the map."

Griffin wrapped the earphones around the receiver, dropped it into his pocket. "I don't believe these are Adami's men. Someone else is following us. Who, I have no idea. But whether it's them or Adami, any witnesses are liabilities. That includes anyone who has contact with them, even cabdrivers or government agents. Are you starting to understand how serious these people are, professor?"

She nodded.

"Now is there something you wanted to tell us about your contact in Naples?"

"I'm supposed to meet a colleague who knows the history of Sansevero. He e-mailed me the other morning, saying that he had found the right tunnel, but he ran into a dead end, and he thought if he could find another entrance, it would lead to the right chamber."

"This e-mail, it was on your computer when it was stolen?"

"Oh my God."

Griffin handed her his personal cell phone. "You need to call him now, and tell him to leave his house, office, or wherever else he's known to hang out. Then have him meet up with us somewhere not even remotely associated."

"What if—"

"No time for what-ifs," he said, urging them toward the door. "If we're lucky, we buy your friend a bit of time while they search for us. Let's not make it too easy."

They were just exiting the stairwell into the main lobby, when Sydney saw a man at the registration desk. She put her arm out, stopping Francesca and Griffin from moving forward. "Time for Plan B. I'm sure I saw that man on the train."

"What is Plan B?" Francesca asked.

And Griffin said, "In this case, I'd say the service entrance." They turned back into the stairwell, wandered through a hallway then through a side door, exiting into a narrow street that was blocked by a delivery truck unloading towels and linens to the hotel. Griffin gave Francesca a secure phone to call her contact, and when she finished, he asked, "Where are we meeting your friend?"

"A café not too far from here. We can walk."

The streets at the center of town were narrow, cobbled, and filled with pedestrians, small cars and scooters. The café was about five minutes from the hotel. The inside was dark, and Sydney's eyes hadn't yet adjusted to the change in lighting. Francesca led them to the back, where they took a seat at a table, but had a clear view of the door. About ten minutes later, a man walked in, his features silhouetted by the light from outside. Francesca stood, called out his name, and that's when Sydney realized the identity of the professor's so-called colleague.

Xavier Caldwell.

The missing student from UVA.

Chapter Thirty-one

Francesca rushed forward, so relieved to see Xavier that she nearly knocked over the table as she embraced him. "You're okay. Thank God."

"Of course I'm okay. Why wouldn't I be?" He looked past her to the two agents, before holding her by her shoulders and searching her face. "What is going on? Where's Alessandra? I've been trying to call her for two weeks."

Francesca wasn't sure how to tell him, wasn't sure how he'd react. She would have liked more time, and hated that she had to break the news this way. "She's...She's been murdered."

His face blanched, and she reached up, grasped his hands from her shoulders, then guided him to the table. "That's impossible," he finally said. "She was fine when I last saw her. She said—She told me—I can't believe it."

"I didn't believe it at first, either, but it's very real, and these people with me are working to find out who killed her."

"Who are they?" he said, as he took a seat at the table.

She gripped his hand tighter, knowing he wouldn't like this news any better. "Government agents."

"What?" He tried to rise from his seat, and she pulled him back down.

"Don't worry. They're on our side."

"The government's never on our side."

"You have to trust me," Francesca said. "Trust me that they're here to protect us and everything will be fine."

"Alessandra's dead. How can everything be fine?"

"Because she wanted this as much as you. You honor her by continuing with what she started."

He gave a slight nod, seemed to calm, then turned his attention to the two agents, his expression guarded. "Who are you?"

Sydney held out her hand, and said, "Sydney Fitzpatrick, FBI. I'm here because my friend was killed looking into Alessandra's murder."

"This friend was an agent?" he said.

"A forensic anthropologist."

He shook her hand, said, "I'm sorry about your friend."

"Thank you."

"And you? Who are you?"

"Zachary Griffin. I was a friend of Alessandra's, and she asked me to help her. Unfortunately, I was too late."

Xavier covered his face with his hands. "I shouldn't have left her. Maybe I could have done something…"

Grief was better than blinding distrust, Francesca figured, and she turned to Griffin. "I think we could all use some coffee."

He left to order the coffee.

"Xavier, I need you to listen to me," Francesca said.

"Can't I have a few moments?"

"We don't have time. A friend of theirs was kidnapped by these people. Your life is in danger. All our lives."

"What do you mean?"

"The people who came after Alessandra and Sydney's friend? They're after me, and they stole my computer. It had the e-mail you sent to me. Griffin thinks you're in danger."

"Why come after me?"

"Because they want what I have, what we're looking for—and they're willing to kill anyone who gets in the way of their plans." There, she said what she hadn't been willing to admit before. It did little to ease her guilt over the needless deaths. No, not deaths. Murders—something neither she nor Alessandra had foreseen. Alessandra's murder had been totally unexpected, as had the attack up at the Passegiata. And while she couldn't bring

Alessandra back, she could damned well find the answers and thereby ensure that Alessandra hadn't died in vain. But after the murder of the taxi driver, she realized that every step she took from that point on was as dangerous as walking on the highest, crumbling cliff with nothing but jagged rocks below. And now everyone she encountered on that walk was subject to the same torturous death, whether they were truly involved or not. "If you come with us, your life is in danger. I can't ask that of you."

"But if I *don't* go with you, it seems my life is in danger."

"I think so."

"Then I go with you. For Alessandra," he said, his voice catching.

"For Alessandra."

He looked away, brushed at his eyes, and just when Griffin returned, said, "I think I'll go see what's taking that coffee so long."

Xavier got up, walked to the front, then made a right toward the restroom instead.

As soon as he disappeared around the corner, she turned to Griffin and Sydney. "I would rather he didn't come. He's too young. He hasn't even graduated college yet."

"I think," Griffin said, "that we can arrange for safe passage home, once we get him out of Naples. Until then, he's probably safer with us than without."

"All right," she said, as the waiter arrived with their coffees. She dusted hers with cinnamon, then sipped at the steaming foam, trying to relax, telling herself that all would be fine. But then, they still had the tunnels to negotiate, and she looked at Xavier's backpack, and the laptop she knew was within. And suddenly panic set in. She reached for the lanyard around her neck, worried that she'd lost the flash drive. But no, it was there.

That thought quickly fled to worse thoughts when, several minutes later, Sydney said, "Xavier is going to come out of there, isn't he?"

◇◇◇

The last thing Griffin needed was to chase after a college student *and* a professor, because he didn't doubt for a second that if Xavier took off, Francesca wouldn't be far behind him. He stood, gave Sydney the signal to watch over Francesca, then walked to the restroom, finding Xavier standing just outside it. His eyes red-rimmed, he leaned against the wall next to the payphone, and Griffin felt a twinge of guilt for not trusting the kid. "You okay?" he asked.

"Yeah." Xavier took a breath, stood a bit straighter. "I'm fine."

"It's not easy losing someone you're close to. I know," he said, trying but failing to keep from thinking about those he'd lost, and now there was Tex and he wondered if he was safe…

"We weren't close. Not like that. I mean, I liked her, she just wasn't interested, you know?"

Griffin merely nodded, since it seemed the right thing to do at the moment.

"She was sort of married to this thing. Wanted to know all the answers. I admired her a lot."

"Me too," Griffin said.

"You knew her?"

"For about a year. I worked at—for her father at one time."

"I didn't know her father. I met her at the university…All these crazy ideas I had, all this conspiracy stuff I wrote about for my class at UVA, no one believed me. When she talked about it, it was like she knew, really knew this stuff went on. She was the only one who didn't think I was crazy."

Griffin glanced at the door, hoped no one would wander their way and interrupt the kid's flow. "What sort of things did she talk about?"

"I appreciate what you're doing, but that doesn't mean I'm going to trust you. The professor said you work for the government."

"In the end, I work for myself."

"What does that mean?"

What it really meant was that when the shit hit the fan, the government wasn't about to take the blame for anything Griffin and his crew did, not something he was about to relay to Xavier, or anyone else for that matter. "That means I'm my own boss. I answer to me." As if, he thought. "I do what's right, and what is needed to finish the job."

"And your job is?"

"To find out who killed Alessandra, and rescue my friend. And to do that, I need to know what she was involved in, who she was involved with."

"That's it? You're only here to help solve her murder?"

"That's it." As long as one didn't count that if the map did exist, and it led to the Templar treasure, and there really were some sort of bioweapons that could come from finding it, and that if it fell into Adami's hands, he'd use it to manipulate world governments even more than he was currently doing. Something else that bothered him about this was that they had yet to learn who Adami was working for. "But there is one thing you need to understand. I need your cooperation in all things if you want to stay alive. We're working against some very bad people, who won't hesitate to kill you, if given the chance. We have very little time." He looked at his watch. "Six hours before they kill my friend if we don't find whatever this is that is buried and bring it to them. So any background on what you and Alessandra were working on can only help."

Xavier nodded. "I was helping her with some of the research when all these weird things started happening. We assumed it was the government," he said, with a dark look.

Since Griffin wasn't even aware the kid had existed until now, he seriously doubted the government was involved—at least not the legitimate government. "What sort of weird things?"

"Like we were being followed, or I'd hear clicks on my telephone, like someone was listening in. And then someone shot into my apartment, and the police called it a gang-related drive-by, but I'm not so sure. Alessandra said that she was being followed, too, and that's when she asked me to stop, back off, you know? But by then, I was too far into it. My cousin works for the Department of the Underground here in Naples, and with his help, I found all this information on the tunnels, and we figured that the prince had to have used the underground caverns to hide the map. My job was to come to Naples, and explore the tunnels to find the one that we'd pinned down, then wait for Professor Santarella to meet up with me here as soon as she got back from some dig she was on." He looked away, tried to compose himself. "I've been here for two weeks, and the entire time, Alessandra's been dead, and I didn't even know it…"

"What happened the last time you saw her?"

It took a moment for Xavier to shake off his grief. "By then there was no doubt that she was being followed, and so we borrowed my girlfriend's car, you know, to throw them off. Alessandra dropped me off at a restaurant, and I slipped out the back, took a taxi to the airport. She stayed on, because she had to do some more research in the States. She was supposed to meet up with that forensic anthropologist who had been working out on that same dig. The one where Alessandra had discovered that they were searching for the first key. Then she was supposed to meet up with some scientist to find out…well, if there was any way this stuff could be true. The biblical plague thing. And then she was going to follow me out here."

"Did you hear from Alessandra after you arrived in Naples?"

"One call when I got here to let her know I'd arrived safe. She said not to worry if I didn't hear from her for a bit, because she was going to lay low, and if her phone was being tapped, she didn't want to lead anyone to me. But I do know this. Whatever it was she was looking for, she'd found it, and she was sending it home, so it would be there when she got back."

Which verified why Adami's men had been watching the ambassador's residence. "Were you on a cell phone when you called her?"

"No, I used a payphone at the airport. But I called her cell phone."

Alessandra's phone had no doubt been compromised, and they'd heard every word. He wondered how long they'd been watching her. "And do you have any idea what she was doing after you left for Naples?"

"Like I said, research. She wanted to talk to some scientist about the viability of some virus or plague laying dormant for a couple thousand years, and what would happen if it was suddenly released into the wild, or disturbed. She wasn't sure if what she was looking for might contain these old plagues, or if they were maybe somewhere else."

"Do you know the name of this scientist?"

"Dr. Raj? Raja? Something like that."

"Could it have been Balraj?"

"That was it."

"Any idea where they were to meet?" he asked, even though he knew the answer.

"Yeah. The Smithsonian," Xavier said.

"Why the Smithsonian? The Templar display?"

"She wasn't there for the display, not really. She'd seen all that stuff before, but she knew there was lots of security. She wanted someplace public, just in case she was being followed."

And a lot of good that did her. The real security guard was probably killed the moment that Alessandra and the microbiologist entered the Smithsonian, and Alessandra's killer needed a cover. "Any idea if she found what she was looking for? This information on the plagues?"

"You might check with Francesca, since she's the one that Alessandra sent the flash drive to."

"She sent what?"

"You know. A mini hard drive? Francesca said she found it stuffed into the spine of some book that Alessandra had mailed to her."

Griffin wondered how many times he'd be blindsided on this case, and it was all he could do to keep his temper in check. Last thing he needed was to spook the kid, because he wanted to throttle the professor. "Go drink your coffee. We don't have much time."

Xavier walked out, joined Sydney and Francesca, and Griffin watched Francesca's face as Xavier took a seat beside her. Relief. That boded well, he decided, and he called McNiel and related what Xavier told him about why Alessandra wanted to meet with Dr. Balraj, the query into how many centuries a plague or virus could survive under optimal conditions.

"You think this map really exists?" McNiel asked.

"A good chance, considering the research the professor did at the Vatican. She no doubt knew Alessandra was inquiring into the viability of dormant plagues and viruses, since she's the one who told us that the map was believed to lead to them. It certainly explains Adami's interest."

McNiel gave a sigh of resignation. "Do what you can to rescue Tex, but that map is not to fall into Adami's hands. If it ends up a suicide mission, I want that map destroyed. Clear?"

"Yes, sir."

"I'll send a chopper out from Rome and have them stand by at the Naples airport."

Griffin disconnected, knowing there was no way he could break the news to Sydney. Her world was not so black and white as his. How was he going to tell her that their mission was to destroy the map if it left their hands, even if it meant Tex's life? Or their lives?

Her instinct would be to save Tex. He would deal with that when the time came. Now, he had to worry about what Francesca knew, what she was holding back, and if she assumed Xavier had kept all her secrets. He returned to the others, sat down across from the professor, smiled. "You didn't forget to mention anything that might have come from Alessandra, did you?"

Her gaze darted from him to Xavier, then back. "What do you mean?"

"Say, a flash drive? Perhaps one that has information about this map on it?"

"I—I didn't think it was important. I couldn't access it, so I figured it had been damaged…"

"Let me make one thing *perfectly* clear. As long as Tex is being held captive, *you* do not get to choose what is important. And in case that isn't clear enough, should I find out you are with-holding any other information, I'll ship you back to the States. In handcuffs if I have to."

She reached into the collar of her shirt, pulled a lanyard from around her neck, one that had escaped his notice until now. Hanging from it was a flash drive, which she handed over. "You'll see. There's nothing on it. Just a copy of my notes on the tunnels."

"We need a computer," Griffin said.

Xavier hefted his backpack to the table. "I have one."

Xavier took out his laptop, booted it up, and slid it toward Francesca, so that she could insert her flash drive into the USB port. She typed something on the keyboard, then slid the computer to Griffin. "As you can see," she said, "there's nothing on there but a copy of my notes on the tunnels, which I e-mailed to her. And then a photograph of di Sangro's family crest at his chapel, which, at the time, we thought was the location of the third key. But the key is supposed to be with him, and his body is not in the crypt. In fact, it has never been found."

"The actual crypt is supposed to contain the map," Xavier said. "That's what I've been searching for."

Griffin clicked on the icon for the flash drive. Two icons appeared in the folder. Francesca's documents on the tunnels, which he opened, scanned, then closed out. The other was an icon showing a photograph. He clicked on it. Nothing happened.

"As I told you," Francesca said, "I couldn't open it, either."

"It's encrypted," Griffin replied.

"Encrypted?"

He typed in a command to have the computer open the photograph. Appearing in the very center near the bottom was a long white box, with a blinking cursor, waiting for a password to be entered.

Xavier stared at it. "Great. What the hell is the password?"

Francesca leaned over, and before Griffin could stop her, typed in a password and hit Enter. Nothing happened. "This makes no sense. Where's the information from my flash drive? My notes?"

"Actually," Griffin said, putting his hand out to keep her from typing anything further, "it's part of the program."

"How would you know?" Francesca asked.

"I gave the program to Alessandra."

A look of distrust filled Xavier's face. "Why?"

"She wanted to embed some information and was worried about someone in her father's household gaining access to her computer should she visit. At least that's what she told me. What that was, I have no idea."

Francesca leaned forward, trying to get a better view. "Then how do we access what is embedded?"

Griffin pushed his coffee cup aside, then angled the computer so they could all see it. "She didn't give either one of you the final access code?"

"No," Francesca said. "Clearly the code isn't my password. Unless I made a mistake. You want me to retype it and see what happens?"

"Only if you want to chance destroying whatever information is on the flash drive," Griffin replied. "We need to be sure. This particular program gives us three tries. First one is gratis. You already took that. Second, the cursor stops moving, indicating you are about to be locked out. Third mistake is fatal. It erases whatever information she embedded into it."

The four of them stared at the screen, the cursor blinking, blinking, blinking in the empty box just begging for a password. Sydney sat up, looked over at Griffin. "She did pass on the final code. She said you knew it."

"Of course," Francesca said to Griffin. "She insisted I ask for the code, and that was how I would know you. Dumas told us the code this morning. You confirmed it. All for one and one for all."

"That can't be right," Griffin said. "There has to be a combination of letters and numbers, or the program wouldn't accept the password to begin with."

Francesca said, "Maybe substituting the numeral one for the word one?"

Two chances left, he thought. "Try it."

Francesca typed in the new variation, "Allfor1and1forall." The cursor stopped blinking.

"Damn it," Francesca said.

Not good, Griffin thought. Alessandra hadn't counted on dying, obviously, but she'd certainly taken the precaution to protect the information if she couldn't be there. "If not that, what code would she have used?"

"Maybe," Xavier said, "there isn't anything so drastic as a special code. She knew the professor and I were going to meet. Maybe we simply enter our individual codes together. They have the letter numeral combination." Xavier angled the computer his way to look.

Griffin stopped him. "Alessandra was too meticulous to combine two known codes. We have one try left. If we don't get it, it's over."

Francesca said, "Surely the government has something they can hook up to it, and figure out what the hell it should be?"

"Which," Griffin said, "entails time and resources we don't have at the moment. We need to think about this." And quickly, he realized. With less than six hours to search unknown caverns for something they didn't even know existed, the odds were not stacked in their favor.

Sydney reached for a napkin. "I've got it." He certainly hoped so. "I think Francesca was on to something, replacing the words with numbers, but if Alessandra was as meticulous as you say, and as paranoid as Xavier, she'd go further if at all possible. She'd replace everything."

Francesca said, "Like the word 'for' with the numeral four?"

"Even more so. Especially if she was entrusting that someone else was going to bring that code back, and there was the possibility of being overheard or intercepted. Think license plates."

"License plates?" Griffin asked.

"Anyone have a pen?" Sydney said. Xavier pulled one from the pocket of his backpack. She wrote on the napkin, then turned it for everyone to see. L41N14L. "L equals All and N equals And."

"Yes," Xavier said. "I can see her doing that."

"Well?" Sydney asked.

"Type it in," Griffin said.

Chapter Thirty-two

Sydney typed in the combination, let it sit there a moment, her finger poised over the Enter key. It seemed they all held their breaths. What if she was wrong? What if she was the one responsible for the loss of all the information? She glanced at Griffin. He gave a slight nod. Reassurance. She needed that, and she pressed the key, felt Griffin tense beside her. How long would it take to send the computer to forensics, recover the info, if she screwed this up?

Suddenly the picture disintegrated into pixels that dropped to the bottom of the screen. What was left was a white background, with a few lines of type, reading: "Observe with an attentive eye and with veneration the urns of the heroes endowed with glory and reflect with astonishment on the precious homage to the divine work and the tomb of the deceased and when you have given due honor, contemplate profoundly and distance yourself."

"What does it mean?" Sydney asked.

"It's the translation from the side entrance to di Sangro's chapel," Francesca said.

"Then we're on the right track."

"Yes, but we knew that. This is something else. Almost as important as the third key. Maybe it is the third key. I remember overhearing a phone conversation she had with her friend, the anthropologist, talking about this very thing."

Griffin ignored the dark look Sydney tossed him at the mention of Tasha's occupation. "This conversation you overheard," he said. "Do you recall what Alessandra or this friend of hers *thought* it meant?"

"A hidden meaning. Subtext," Francesca replied. "Now that I think about it, I wonder if that has something to do with the second key, the one we couldn't find." She gave Xavier a brief rundown on their trip through the Capuchin crypt, then added, "Di Sangro was all about hidden meanings. His entire chapel is filled with Masonic symbolism and iconology."

"So we have to interpret it right or we're caught in this trap he's set up?"

"Exactly."

And Xavier said, "We believe he modeled it much like the deadfall traps in the ancient Egyptian tombs. That may be why everyone thought Egypt was the location of the first key."

Griffin leaned back in his chair, pushing his coffee aside. "Deadfall. As in a wall falls on top of someone?"

"More like the entire tomb comes crashing down on the tomb raiders," Francesca said.

"That's my theory," Xavier said. "I also think that when you find this hidden crypt, it'll lead you to di Sangro's body. And the treasure map. But Alessandra said that maybe the plagues were hidden there, and that's why she wanted to connect with Dr. Balraj. She wanted to be prepared for either scenario. So whatever we find, extreme caution needs to be taken." He pointed to a location on his map of the tunnels. "This," he said, "is where we will enter. The basilica houses the entrance to the tunnels behind its altar. We have a lot of ground to cover. According to my cousin, who works for the city, all of Naples and the surrounding area sits upon a honeycomb of about a million square meters of caves, grottos, tunnels, and catacombs, all carved from volcanic sandstone, *tufo*."

Griffin's brows raised slightly at the number. "And where is this crypt located?"

To which Xavier replied, "Hard to say. Countless churches and cathedrals in Italy were built atop older churches, which commonly were built atop underground crypts for burial purposes. There's a lot of bones down there."

And Francesca said, "Everything I have heard on the keys directs us to a bone chamber of some sort. Since the first key was an inscription by a skull, and that led us to the Capuchin crypt, I have to think we may be looking for another skull, or if it is truly leading us to a Templar map, a skull and crossbones."

Sydney glanced over at the computer and the phrase from the chapel entrance. "How does this old quote help us?"

"That," Francesca said, "is what we hope to find out once we get to the right location."

"In other words," Griffin said, copying the phrase onto a napkin. "Like the missing second key, you don't have the answer."

Francesca shook her head. "No. Not yet. But if time is of the essence, then what choice do we have?"

"No choice," Griffin said.

Xavier smoothed out the map. "Here is the last place I was able to explore, using the coordinates we pieced together before—" He cleared his throat, took a breath. "—the last time I saw Alessandra."

Sydney wanted to reach out, touch his hand, tell him it would be okay, but she knew it was a promise she couldn't make, and he continued with "This is where di Sangro lived. And over here is a long section of tunnel that was known to have led to an underground marketplace back in the first and second century A.D. Di Sangro spent his fortune retrofitting his church, but it's believed he was also retrofitting the caverns below it near that marketplace. It's here that makes the most sense, because they could enter the tunnel without being seen from the outside, work as long as they needed, and no one's the wiser."

Griffin studied the map. "Do *you* think he went to the trouble of booby-trapping this chamber?"

"Legend aside, it would have taken a genius to design it, and the expertise of master masons to pull it off. Di Sangro was a genius in his own right. He ruined his own reputation, allowed himself to be shunned by society to protect the greater good, guarding this map. Which is a long way of saying yes, I do believe it. Without the key, anyone who enters the cache and disturbs the treasure will be crushed."

"And these other paths," Griffin said. "Where do they lead?"

"To here," Xavier replied, pointing to each direction on the map. "This is my best estimation of where we want to end up. My cousin and I have done some exploring at this location, but we hit a dead end going down into a cistern. This time, I think we need to go up further in the tunnel, not down."

Griffin leaned in for a better view. "It doesn't look all that far."

"Even so, I have to warn you, we'll be heading into an area that, if you're the least bit claustrophobic or afraid of the dark or heights, might make you uncomfortable."

Okay, probably not the time for Sydney to mention her fear of the dark. But that's what flashlights were for. Aloud, she said, "Heights? We're going underground."

"When you're hanging from a rope with nothing beneath your feet but unending darkness and over a hundred-foot drop, it really doesn't matter what you call it."

At which point she had to remind herself this wasn't about her and what she feared, especially when Griffin said, "You're welcome to stay behind."

"So you can get all the credit for rescuing Tex? Don't think so."

"To the tunnels, then." He smiled, but it was grim, and she gathered that traveling to the center of the earth wasn't his idea of fun, either.

◇◇◇

Xavier's cousin, Alfredo, met them at the basilica, handing them each a small pack containing extra rope, a hard hat with headlamp, gloves, water, and a flashlight from the back of his utility van. He eyed each of them, judging their sizes, then gave each a bright orange jumpsuit with reflective strips across the chest and back and sleeves. Apparently he had plenty to spare.

"It's a steady fifty degrees down there. Chilly. These will help keep you warm, and protect your skin and clothes from those tight spaces."

Sydney took the pack, realized it was too small to put her travel bag with her sketchbook into it, and decided to leave the travel bag behind in Alfredo's van. She pulled on the jumpsuit, then started toward the entrance to the catacombs beneath the basilica, when Griffin stopped her. "Take these," he said, handing her a folding knife and a semiauto from his backpack, the Beretta they'd taken from their earlier assailants.

From the weight of it, it felt fully loaded, and she ejected the magazine, saw there were fifteen rounds. "You think it's Adami's men following us?"

"Like his man said when I called him at the train station to ask that very question, he has no need to follow when he knows where we are going, and where we'll end up."

"If it's not his men, then who?"

"Someone who knew enough to follow us on a train to Naples—which makes me wonder if it isn't whoever stole the professor's computer. We're assuming we lost the man at the hotel, and we got to Xavier first, but as of now, we have no way of knowing that Xavier or his cousin were not being followed."

Sydney glanced over at Xavier and Alfredo, who were helping Francesca with her jumpsuit. Suddenly the thought of walking through tunnels or rappelling into the vast depths of a cistern no longer bothered her.

Being murdered and left behind in some long-forgotten chamber, knowing that her bones might not be discovered for centuries, was far worse. "I'll keep an eye out," she said, replacing the magazine, then putting the weapon in the pocket of her coveralls. She started toward the others.

"There's something else. Something I haven't told you."

He stepped in close. But then Xavier called out that they were leaving, and Griffin moved away, saying, "It can wait."

His face held that stubborn, closed look she was beginning to recognize, the one that told her he wasn't about to reveal his secrets to her or anyone else. "Let's do this," she said.

"You sure?" he asked.

She wasn't. Not sure of anything. Especially not him. Even so, her answer was to pick up the pack that Alfredo had given her and walk over to where the others stood waiting.

Sydney eyed the larger packs carried by Xavier and Alfredo. The equipment hanging from both reminded her of what a mountain climber might carry, and then some. "How long are we going to be down there?" she asked.

Alfredo shrugged. "Judging from the distance, and depending on how much obstruction lies between here and di Sangro's tunnel, not more than a few hours."

She could only hope that's all it was. A few hours of walking through the caves she could live with. As long as they were back in time. She and Griffin looked at their watches at the same moment. Not quite five hours before they had to deliver this lost map to Adami.

They filed into the entrance of the tunnels below the basilica. Sydney saw the yellowish rock, and decided it wasn't as bad as she'd first imagined. They continued on, for what seemed an eternity, the temperature cooling as they descended, then remaining steady. The perfect wine cellar, she thought, grateful for the jumpsuits Xavier's cousin had provided. In all, their journey consisted of winding through a labyrinth of switchback steps, long passageways, and endless tunnels that seemed to lead down.

And down.

The intense quiet felt surreal. Their breathing seemed to echo off the walls, and the only other sounds heard were their footsteps as they trudged along the rough-hewn floor, and the rattle and clang of equipment hanging from Xavier's and Alfredo's packs.

Alfredo broke the repressive silence, telling them that the passageway they were walking through was discovered after a devastating earthquake in the 1980s. He pointed to narrow openings seen along one side. "Crypts," he said. "After the earthquake, they found huge piles of bones, probably from burials dating back to the 1500s."

To which Griffin said, "We're sure one of those isn't the so-called bone chamber we're looking for?"

"No," Xavier answered. "What we're looking for is a specific sign. The crossbones. I found something that looks like it much farther on, but that's the dead end I was telling you about. That's what we're hoping to find this time around. The secret tunnel into the bone chamber."

They passed through other tunnels where the archways were shored up with thick timber, something Sydney hoped had been reinforced over the years. And then they had to crawl through low cramped tunnels that led to narrow ledges with sheer drops, and she didn't dare look down. Every now and then, however, she thought she heard something behind them. Because of the echoes, she couldn't tell if it was her imagination playing tricks— not that she was about to take a chance. Especially when a small pebble skittered past her feet. "What was that?"

Alfredo seemed unconcerned. "Could be we knocked something loose on our way down. Sometimes the earth shifts, and things just fall."

Sydney looked over at Griffin, who gave a slight nod, as if to say, like her, he was on guard. They slowed their pace, staying to the rear.

Finally they entered a low-ceilinged cavern, and Xavier swung his light out before them, revealing a vast squared-out area where, in the center on the ground, there appeared to be a large hole.

"That's where we're going," Xavier said, pointing.

"Into the hole?" Sydney asked, changing her opinion of the entire affair in an instant, and not in a good way.

Xavier laughed when he saw where she was looking. "Not down. That massive cistern is one of the dead ends. The one I told you we already checked out. We're going through that tunnel. There's supposed to be a hidden passageway up there, which I hope is actually the secret tunnel that leads to the bone chamber." He shone his light past the cistern, then above, where carved in the yellow *tufo* was what appeared to be an upside-down skull and crossbones. "If that's not a sign, I don't know what is."

"Are you sure it's not just some old graffiti?"

"Actually there is a lot of old graffiti, especially down that cistern," he said, pointing to the large hole in the ground, the one she was grateful they weren't going into. "But since we're specifically looking for the signs di Sangro's men left for us, then this has to be the way."

Griffin moved toward it. "Why is it upside-down?"

"Not sure," Xavier said. "Possibly to keep others from recognizing it or paying any attention. I believe there is a hidden opening that leads into another chamber, something that isn't readily identifiable as a door. With the crossbones on top, maybe they didn't want to be too obvious."

"Or," Griffin said, "it's a warning."

"A warning?" Sydney replied, turning her head, trying to view it from different angles. Xavier swung his light across the carving, into the opening, and she could have sworn that a shadow appeared in the form of an arrow. "As long as it's not telling us to go down. Please tell me that's not a crude arrow pointing down."

"Like I said, there's not a lot down there," Xavier said, aiming his lamp on the wide opening on the floor of the cave. "A big cistern that leads to nowhere. We've already explored it. You can see the top of the ladder anchored at the edge."

Griffin walked over, looked down the opening. "How far down does it go?"

Alfredo answered. "Maybe an additional thirty meters beyond that ledge," he said, shining his light into the cistern. "It's actually a marvel of engineering. Narrow at the top like a bottle, then widening as it gets deeper to make sure it's structurally sound and doesn't collapse in on itself," he said, moving to Griffin's side, and shining his flashlight down. "Like Xavier said, that's not where we want to go. Follow the crossbones." Alfredo turned, shone his light on the carving of the inverted crossbones.

The light drew Sydney's gaze to the top of the tunnel's entrance, where she saw the skull and crossbones waver in the light, then disappear in a shadow as he aimed the beam up the long tunnel. "This way," Alfredo said, starting forward, his voice echoing up the passageway.

Xavier and Francesca followed him in, but Sydney hesitated again, trying to decipher what she'd actually seen.

Griffin stopped beside her. "Something wrong?"

She whispered. "I swear there's an arrow up there."

"An arrow?"

Instead of trying to explain, she took her own light, moved it across the entrance of the tunnel and over the skull and crossbones in a sweeping fashion, much as Xavier had done. Perhaps it was the way the thing was carved in the tufo, merely a coincidence in the play of shadows, and she glanced over at Griffin.

"You think that's an arrow?" he said.

"Pointing down."

And before either had a chance to look further, there was a sharp crack of gunfire. It echoed around the cavern, making it impossible to pinpoint it.

Yellow tufo dust fell from the tunnel entrance. "Run!" Griffin shouted into the tunnel at Francesca. "Turn off your lights!"

Alfredo froze. Francesca and Xavier pulled him up the tunnel, away from the gunfire. Griffin and Sydney each took one side off the tunnel entrance, tried to press themselves into the walls for cover. It wasn't much, but it was better than nothing, she thought, switching off her light, pulling her glove off with her teeth, then drawing her weapon from her jumpsuit pocket.

She glanced toward the path they'd taken from the basilica, saw a muzzle flash, then another. The gunshots echoed across the cavern. At least two shooters, maybe more. She closed one eye to preserve her night vision. Hoped the reflective stripes from the jumpsuits didn't make them more of a target. Aimed. Fired.

Chapter Thirty-three

"We're sitting ducks here," Griffin said. "We're going to have to try to make it up the tunnel. Follow the others."

Sydney fired off two more rounds, hating herself for even thinking about what she was going to say. "No."

"No?"

"We need to go down."

"No. We don't separate."

"If we go up, we're leading them right to the others. Xavier knows his way around here. He thinks there's a hidden passage up there. The arrow pointed down, and we may be their only chance for escape."

"It was an anomaly. Shadow play." A shot hit the *tufo* above them. Dust rained down.

"From everything I've heard on this di Sangro guy, he was far too intelligent to let some shadow get in the way. The skull and crossbones is upside-down, so it makes sense the arrow would clarify."

He fired off a round, then, "How sure are you about this?"

"You have a better idea?"

She heard him taking in a deep breath, as though coming to a weighty decision. "We go down."

God, let me be right, she thought.

He fired again.

Answering gunshots. Sydney pressed herself into the wall, then leaned out, fired a couple more rounds.

"Ready?" Griffin said.

She looked over to where she thought he was on the opposite side of the tunnel entrance, imagining she could see him in the dark. "Yeah."

"Cover me, wait a second, then follow." Griffin fired twice, then ran into the main cavern.

Sydney fired. Again and again. Figured she had about seven rounds left. Someone or several someones were running down the main entrance. She waited a heartbeat, jumped out, fired a volley, then ran like hell.

Griffin flashed a light on then off. He was perched halfway into the entrance of the cistern in the floor, one hand gripping the ladder anchored to the *tufo*. He dared the light again, then tossed her a rope, looped at one end. "Put this around your middle and pull tight."

She tucked her gun into her waistband, grabbed the rope, slipped it on, pulled. "I already hate this idea."

Griffin was heading down. "If you fall, try not to take me with you."

"I really, really hate this idea."

"You said that," he replied, then disappeared from view. The light from his headlamp cast an eerie glow from the depths of the cistern. It was just enough light to let her see the flexible-sided ladder, which, in her mind, didn't look sturdy enough for one person, let alone two at once.

Shouts from the tunnel entrance, one saying, "This way!" gave her all the impetus she needed to get on the ladder and start down. She sat on the ledge, grabbed the top of the ladder, then felt for a rung with her foot as she let herself over.

Griffin called up, "Keep your body close to the ladder, and your hands no higher than your face."

She took the first step down, trying to ignore the vibration of the cables that reminded her of all the nothingness between her and the bottom of the cistern. The damned thing held Griffin, surely it could hold her.

Foot down, hand down. Foot down, hand down. The ladder swayed beneath her weight, and she glanced up, saw an even brighter light sweeping over the top of the cistern entrance.

"They're going down!" someone shouted.

The word *down* echoed through the chamber below them. Griffin no doubt heard it. "I'm turning off my lamp."

The world around her went black.

Her arms were wrapped around the ladder, and she clung tightly as it swayed in the darkness. Afraid to move, afraid to breathe. The dark petrified her. "I can't do this."

"Keep going," Griffin said.

"I can't."

"I really don't want to die down here."

And neither did she. *Do it. Do it. Do it.* She lowered one foot, found the next rung, even in the dark. She could do this. She could. Hand down, foot down.

"*There!*"

Sydney looked up, was blinded by the light.

She felt the rope around her waist tighten.

"Take my hand." And then she felt Griffin's strong grasp as he took her hand in his. "Feel for the ledge with your foot."

"I can't see."

"Trust me."

"I don't even trust myself." But she stuck her foot out, tapped, felt the ground beneath her feet, allowed him to pull her toward him.

A shot cracked through the cavern, echoed off the walls around them.

Griffin pushed her to the ground, away from the edge. Whoever was after them would have to climb down the ladder to get them, unless she and Griffin made it easy by standing out toward the edge of the ledge.

Something they weren't about to do.

"Come on out, we'll spare your lives."

Laughter, then another voice saying, "I have a much better idea."

"The ladder," she cried, realizing the men were pulling it up and out of the cistern.

Griffin held her arm. "Stay back," he whispered. The ladder scraped against the ledge, then the mouth of the cistern.

"Leave them," she heard from above. "Let's go after the others up in the tunnel. After all, they know what we want. To follow the skull and crossbones."

"We come back in a few years, and make crossbones out of the two down there?"

More laughter, and the sound of receding footsteps. Then a shout followed by several shots fired.

And then nothing.

◇◇◇

Griffin sat side-by-side with Fitzpatrick, the darkness surrounding them completely, the quiet almost deafening. The cold started to seep in, now that the adrenaline rush had left, and he felt Sydney shivering next to him. It had been at least ten minutes since Adami's men—no, not Adami's men—whoever they were, had pulled up the ladder, leaving them down here on the ledge of the cistern. And seemingly an eternity since they'd heard the gunshots that could only mean one thing. The others were dead. And even if a rescue team arrived, how would anyone know where to find them?

"You okay?' he whispered.

"Fine…" Her breathing was strained, but at least she wasn't shivering anymore. "I'm fine."

"Let's hope the others made it out safely." His words rang hollow. He'd lost two friends, Alessandra and Tasha, because he'd let his guard down, and he'd failed to rescue Tex. And now the professor and Xavier and Alfredo—never mind the mess he and Sydney were sitting in the midst of. He knew better than to let outsiders in. He should never have let Sydney leave the States. He should have marched her off the plane the moment he saw her walk on. "Maybe they're getting help now."

"Can I ask you something?"

"What?"

"November. Giustino said you had a hard time with November. What happened?"

He didn't answer right away, wasn't sure he wanted to. Still, she deserved to know. "Two years ago, I was on a mission with another operative. I did something I shouldn't have. I gave up the lead. We were ambushed, and that agent was killed."

"Because of a decision you made or a decision he made?"

"She."

"She...Your girlfriend?"

"My wife."

"Your—I didn't know. I'm sorry."

"We hadn't been together in a while. She'd just filed for divorce."

He could tell she didn't know what to say. And who would? Especially now, with history seeming to repeat itself. Ambushed.

He leaned back against his pack, closed his eyes, could almost see his wife's face. Almost. "I still loved her. I think that's why I let her take over, just to show her that I—" He took a deep breath, tried to shake off the anger, the hurt, the helplessness. She was pregnant. Three months, according to the autopsy. They hadn't slept together in far longer than that, and now, to this day, he wondered who the father was, if he even knew what he'd lost..."Dumas found us. She was dead. I would have been if not for him."

"I'm sorry."

"Me too."

They sat there for a couple of minutes, not saying anything after that, and then Sydney said, "I'm sorry about everything."

"For what?"

"For Tex. For leading us into this hole. For everything."

"It's my fault. I'm the one who let this happen from the very beginning."

"How so?"

"I knew the moment I walked into Tasha's office, right after she called you to arrange that dinner date, that something was wrong. She was jumpy. Not like herself at all. Just like you said she was at dinner. I should have done all the things you thought about. Talked to her, found out what was wrong."

She sat up straight, drew away from him. Silence reigned. Then, after several seconds, "You knew she had called me?"

"I just said that."

"You *knew*?"

He tried to figure out what had changed, what he'd said. "We discussed this at the safe house. I told you about Tasha when you asked—"

"I can't believe this."

"Believe what?"

"Do you realize how long I blamed myself for her death? And Tex? The guilt I've carried around for the two of them?"

"Now you know how I feel."

She stiffened. "You played me."

"We needed you."

"You could have asked."

"We needed your skills, *without* the Bureau knowing the particulars."

"I would have done anything for her."

"Would you have? Even had you known it was regarding a black op?"

She was silent. He suspected not. And perhaps curiosity finally got the better of her, as she asked, "Tasha was part of ATLAS?"

"Yes."

"A government agent?"

"Yes."

"Alessandra?"

"No. But her father was aware of our operations. Dumas was the voice of the Vatican when it came to ATLAS, and reported to her father. Not Alessandra's part. Her father wasn't aware that she knew ATLAS even existed. She was the one who insisted her father not be told. She was adamant."

"But you're going to tell him?"

"When we figure out who killed her, yes."

But in the silence that followed, he wondered if he'd ever get the chance.

"You're a goddamned son of a bitch," Sydney said.

"I think we've established that."

"No. We haven't. Nor have we established that if you'd just told me in the beginning, Tasha might have come forward with what she was hiding. Which means I might have stayed home, because she wouldn't be dead, and I wouldn't have spent all my time searching for the identity of a victim you already knew the identity of."

"We didn't know it was Alessandra."

"Well, you suspected. I would never have gone to the Smithsonian, the guard would never have followed me, and Tex would still be safe and sound, because Adami's damned cousin wouldn't have recognized me at the party, because he saw me at the hotel when he came after you, because I would be *home* for Thanksgiving vacation. Where I should be right now, picking out the turkey from the butcher. In a few days, they'll be sitting around the table, wondering what happened to me. I was stupid for getting involved. I went to Quantico for a reason, to hide, to make sure I didn't endanger anyone else, and I've gone and done the very thing I wanted to avoid."

He heard her moving, was certain she'd crossed her arms. "But I'd be dead."

"You don't know that," she said.

"He recognized you because you saved me. And we know Adami was searching for this third key, because you had the instinct to move closer and listen in. And what happened to Tex was my fault not yours."

"How so?"

"I failed to convince him to follow my orders."

"Yeah? Well whose fault is it we're sitting in a damned hole and can't get out?"

"Who's to say we wouldn't be dead if we had followed the others up the tunnel? Maybe you saved our lives. Again. Have you thought of that?"

She didn't answer, and he knew immediately that she was thinking of the others. The shots fired, that they didn't make it.

He reached over, found her hand, held it in his, and realized she was getting cold again. He rubbed her fingers in his, and when she tried to pull away, he said, "You need to stay warm, preserve your strength."

She didn't argue, didn't pull away this time. Not that it eased his guilt any. He might have been able to do something to help the others, but somehow he'd allowed Sydney to convince him to go against his instincts. He'd placed his trust in her and he'd let the others suffer as a result. And once again came the thought that history was repeating itself.

He had no one to blame but himself.

He didn't trust anyone else, she didn't trust herself. They were quite a pair. "I take it you have real issues with the dark?"

When she didn't answer, he wondered if she was ever going to speak to him again, until a few moments later, she said, "If I told you I sleep with a night-light on would you laugh?"

"Doubt it. Why?"

"Nightmares. From when my father was killed."

He recalled her dossier, the background he'd done on her. She'd been only thirteen when she'd witnessed her father's murder. "If it makes you feel any better, I'm afraid of enclosed spaces. Claustrophobic."

"You're kidding?"

"Do I look like the sort who kids about that stuff?"

"Can't tell. It's too damned dark."

"The only reason I was able to climb into this hole is because it's huge. If it was small, enclosed, you'd be on your own. The narrow tunnels we came down through? Just about killed me to do it. And back in the columbarium? In that tunnel underneath the steps? Trust me. I was not doing well."

"Great. I don't like the dark, and you don't like enclosed spaces. You know what that means? We're up shit creek."

He couldn't help but smile.

"You think we can recover that ladder?"

"I'd rather not have my head blown off, trying to find the damned thing."

"You think they're up there?"

"Who knows."

"I think they think we're toast, so why bother."

"Maybe we are," he said.

"I'm not ready to die…Wasn't Xavier talking about how soft *tufo* is? Maybe we can dig our way out. Assuming you can handle climbing through some skinny tunnel."

"I really, really don't like enclosed spaces."

"Now you're starting to sound like me." Sydney switched on her light.

"What are you doing?"

"Looking for a shovel. Or maybe something we can toss up, try to hook that ladder." She reached for her pack, then stood, slowly. "Uh, Griffin? You might want to take a look at this."

He turned. Saw what she saw. What they hadn't had time to see when they were being shot at. The rock behind them wasn't the solid mass of tufo it appeared to be. In fact, had Sydney not moved to the side, shone her light just so in looking for the shovel, they might never have noticed the outcropping that hid the tunnel behind it. "You think that arrow you saw in the cavern above was pointing to this?"

"Xavier said he looked down here. There was nothing," she said. "But if he continued down that ladder past this ledge into the cistern, he could very well have missed this. The ledge isn't very big, and from where the ladder was situated, you'd never see this."

"Beats trying to dig our way out." Griffin scooped up his pack, and followed her between the outcropping and the tunnel hidden in the V of it. "One problem I see."

"What's that?"

"It barely looks big enough to fit through."

"Yeah, well unless you have a better idea…"

He wasn't kidding about the tight spaces. He hated them. But he'd trained himself over the years to get past the absurd fear that he'd get stuck. He would have never made the ATLAS team otherwise. And hell if he was going to let Sydney show him up. "After you."

"By all means. Brawn before beauty."

He hesitated, took a deep breath, then entered. Though tall enough, it was narrow, so narrow in places that Griffin's shoulders hit the walls, and he had to turn to his side to pass through. The entire passageway was much rougher than the tunnels off the cavern above, as though this particular area had been excavated more hastily, and perhaps, judging from the outcropping that hid it, on the sly to keep it from being discovered. At one point, they had to snake through on their bellies, and he concentrated on his breathing, the better to keep his mind off the confining passageway. "Hard to imagine anyone going to this much trouble for a burial chamber."

"If we get out of here," Sydney said from behind him, "I never want to be in another fifty-degree underground chamber again."

"I'll second that." After several more feet, the floor in front of him dropped sharply into a wide cavern that looked like a massive honeycomb of stalactites and stalagmites.

He crawled out, slid down a few feet to the cavern floor. Sydney did the same.

"Amazing," she said. "I thought water seepage made the columns, but these look too uniform, like they're all carved."

She was about to take a step forward when he reached out, stopped her. "Don't move."

"What's wrong?"

He pointed between the columns into the interior, his headlamp sweeping across strangely shaped mounds. It took several moments for his sight to adjust, to see what was beneath the *tufo* dust that covered everything. The realization of what he was seeing hit him. Urns and chests, each strategically placed around the center columns. "Hell," he said, not daring to let go of Sydney's arm.

"But that means the map has to be here."

"Yeah? And we never discovered the second key. So if it is all true…"

One false step and they were dead.

Chapter Thirty-four

Francesca tried to catch her breath, leaning against the rough wall of the tunnel, while Xavier and Alfredo felt around with their hands. The passageway they'd taken led up, and they'd run the entire way.

"What exactly are you looking for?" she asked, her voice low.

"I just don't understand it," Xavier said.

"Understand what?" she replied, not liking the worry in his voice. She had enough to worry about right now, like what had happened to Sydney and Griffin. Were they still alive? Bleeding and injured down in the cavern? The two agents had sacrificed their own safety so the three of them could get away. But how the hell were they going to get help to them if they couldn't avoid being shot by the men who were chasing them?

"There should be a sign," Xavier said. "A skull and crossbones that tells me this is the right passageway, just like the one in the tunnel below that led us up here."

"You mean this might not be the right way?"

Alfredo slammed his hand against the stone wall. "It's certainly looking that way."

"Calm down," Xavier said. "Maybe the signs change. Maybe it's not supposed to be a skull and crossbones. Maybe that's one of the things we're supposed to learn."

"For God's sake," Francesca said. "This is not the time to make that discovery. We should have known this before we even set out."

"Yeah?" Xavier whispered harshly. "And when was that? Between the five minutes I'd learned you wanted to meet me and the announcement that Alessandra was murdered? You've had a hell of a lot longer to look at the flash drive she sent, so get off my case."

"I'm sorry," she said. "What can I do to help?"

"Not a lot. By all calculations, this should lead to the passageway that di Sangro plotted out."

"You're sure?"

"I'm sure where it's not, and it's not here."

"Actually," Alfredo said, "if I had to guess, this passageway leads right back to the basilica. We've gone in one big giant circle."

"I wonder if that's what Sydney saw down in the main cavern."

Xavier stopped pressing on the wall. "What are you talking about?"

"Right before those men shot at us, she called Griffin over. I think she realized something was off down there."

"Well," Alfredo said. "Whatever it was, we have to be grateful, or more than likely we'd all be dead," he said, as he and Xavier continued to push on the rock wall with their gloved hands. "We'd have been sitting ducks if those men had followed us up here right away. All we can do now is hope that your agent friends were able to fight them off and discovered the right passage, and we can get the hell out of here before those guys find us."

A scuffling sound echoing up from the passage below sent her heart racing. "They're getting closer."

"Look there!" Xavier said, pointing his flashlight beam toward a crevice in the wall, narrow at the base but widening as it rose. The light bounced off the tunnel walls into a ceiling that seemed to disappear into a deep blackness. "We'll make them think we're gone."

Alfredo began climbing up the V-shaped crevice. He reached down for Francesca's hand, pulled her up, as Xavier boosted her from the floor, then followed. Inching their way inward and upward, they didn't speak. Suddenly Xavier reached over, gripped her arm, his fingers digging into her in warning.

She needed none. She heard the two men coming up the tunnel, and she held her breath, praying they wouldn't hear anything. Beside her, Alfredo's foot slipped, knocking loose a bit of *tufo* that skittered down the crevice into the tunnel below, and she thought this was it. They were caught.

◇◇◇

"You hear that, Vinny?"

"You shut up long enough and I might."

Francesca's heart pounded at the realization of just how close the men were to their hiding spot.

"It's coming from up there," the first man said.

"It's them. It has to be." Francesca heard what sounded like a gun being racked, as though one of the men was checking his weapon, checking to see if he had enough ammunition. "Hurry. They might be getting away."

"What's your rush? Even if this tunnel does lead out, we have someone posted on almost every street corner around the basilica. They can't get farther than that."

"Yeah, well we need to be there when they find what they're looking for." A light bounced off the tunnel walls. She closed her eyes, pressed her face into the rock. *Please don't let them find us...*

"Why do you suppose Mr. Westgate wants to get this thing?"

"Because Mr. Westgate's boss wants to get power over Adami."

"How's some stupid map gonna get him that?" Vinny asked. "They both got more money than God. Seems to me that if we were smart, we'd get the map for ourselves."

"And have both Adami and Mr. Westgate's boss after us? You got a death wish?"

"Just thinking aloud."

"What the hell?" She heard their footsteps stop, heard some shuffling. "They're gone! I could've sworn I heard something coming from up this way."

"They must have gone out a different tunnel." Francesca dared a look over Xavier's shoulder, caught a glimpse of the light beam as it swung the opposite direction.

"Now what?"

"The only thing left. We go after the two down in the cistern."

◇◇◇

Griffin stared at the mass of urns before them, certain they were filled with gold—not that he was about to disturb the *tufo* dust to find out. Even so, he couldn't help but wonder if they were the first in centuries to look upon this chamber. The treasure reported to be a deathtrap by the mad genius.

"This is what they're killing for," she said. "Gold."

"I'm fairly certain it's more about where it's reported to have come from, assuming it really is Templar treasure from Solomon's temple."

"You believe that?" Her voice was quiet, filled with awe, perhaps at the thought that they could indeed be standing amid something historic. "Do you think the Templars became Freemasons, all as a duty to protect this?"

"The gold or the map? The bigger question is what's the secret of getting out without being crushed, or releasing some disease. There's a reason di Sangro chose to hide this treasure, even at the cost of his reputation. He took an oath."

"My. You were listening in class."

"Very funny," he said. "If Francesca is correct, and others in the past knew the treasure existed, the danger would have to be very real in order for someone to leave this amount of gold alone. Sort of makes you wonder about the loyalty of whoever set this up. Who was it who walked away from all this, and wasn't tempted?"

"I'm thinking whoever put him here."

She pointed to the interior of the cavern, her headlamp shining on a wide rock formation near the center, where, surrounded by even more urns, it appeared as though a man sat resting, his back to a large chest, his hands crossed over his midsection, as though someone positioned him after he died. Together, they walked over, touching nothing, carefully weaving around the rock columns, the chests and urns, their footsteps echoing off the cavern roof. Griffin looked around, trying to decide if there was any truth to the possibility that the place was an elaborate trap, meant to snare di Sangro's perceived enemies. As they approached, it became apparent that the dead visitor, a male, had indeed been resting there for quite some time, perhaps a century or more, judging from his clothing. Like the monks in the Capuchin crypt, this man seemed well preserved, no doubt due to the constant cool, dry temperature of the underground cavern. "Prince of Sansevero?" Griffin asked.

"A good guess, since his clothes seem a bit too fancy for a mere laborer," she said, nodding at the bunch of lace at his throat. "And he's wearing a Masonic ring."

"The shield behind him, that would be the crest we saw on the computer," Griffin said, nodding toward a blue and gold crest beneath a crown. "Definitely royalty."

"Royalty or not, what if he died because he couldn't find his way out?" She pointed to the numerous openings throughout the cavern.

"Any one of those could be the way out, or simply part of the maze we're already lost in."

She looked down at the corpse again, eyed the ring, careful not to touch anything. "Okay. Let's say this is Raimondo di Sangro. It might be my imagination, but could we be looking at a very obvious skull and crossbones, sort of what was carved over the tunnel in the upper chamber? That is supposed to be the sign the Templars took up after they were hunted down. Maybe this one happens to be pointing at something with his right hand?"

Griffin saw exactly what she meant. Every finger but his right index was folded. "Pointing to the way out? Or better yet, to this missing key?"

"Or the way that leads to death? And what's with all the sand piled up behind him and these urns?"

"Good question."

"We need to think about this," she said. "Francesca told us that Alessandra and Tasha were talking about subtext. Freemasons were all about symbols and the hidden meaning…"

"The skull and crossbones led down. If this is a trap, it's a trap for the unwary, for those who aren't supposed to be here. Assuming what the good professor told us was correct." He glanced over at the tunnel opening, the one the corpse seemed to be pointing toward. It was tall, cleanly carved, and wide enough for two to walk abreast. The others were of varying sizes, and all far more claustrophobic-looking. "It could be any one of these. Seven openings, including the one we just came through. Maybe they all lead to the same place?"

"That shadow arrow I saw up there clearly pointed down. And yet the entrance was hidden from any who dared venture into that cistern, and now we have Dead Guy here, pointing to God knows where."

"Pick one?"

"And hope we don't end up as two more bone markers, pointing out the road that led us to our deaths?" she asked.

"Or end up as pancakes."

She looked over at the tunnels, then grinned. "How much you want to bet it's going to be the smallest, darkest tunnel?"

"Some secrets should never be shared."

Her smile faded. "Yeah. And some things, especially about friends, should never be secret, but it's a little late for that, isn't it."

Moment of levity over. Not that he blamed her. "Look, I know it's late, but I'm sorry about what happened. If I could change things, I would."

She refused to look at him.

"Truce?"

This time she looked right at him. "Fine. Only because we need to get out of here. But understand this. Any chance we had of liking each other ended the moment you let her lie to me, and *then* never told me."

"You're taking this far too personally."

"Personally?" She stood up straight, putting both hands on her hips. "Personally?"

"She was working for the government. It was a job. She was doing it."

"Don't try to put this on Tasha. You're the one who couldn't trust anyone. Maybe if you didn't have that little flaw, things might have been different."

He wanted to rail at her, but all he could do was say, "You're right."

She stared at him for several seconds, as if refusing to believe he wasn't going to argue. Finally she said, "Fine. Truce. Now where the hell is this map, and how do we get out of here?"

"I'm not sure we should be searching for anything but the way out, since we have no idea what the trap is. Death by crushing or disease. We can always come back."

"What about Tex?"

"We can't save him if we don't save ourselves." Griffin eyed the wide tunnel. "Is he or isn't he pointing to the way out?"

"Maybe we're being too literal."

He looked back toward her, saw she was kneeling on the ground before the corpse. "Please don't touch anything."

"Do you realize he's sitting next to a leather tube? Like something you might carry a map in?"

Griffin leaned down, saw what she was looking at. Sure enough, next to the corpse, between it and the large chest, was a leather tube, maybe two feet in length, and three inches in diameter. Out of everything in the chamber, this was the oddest. It wasn't gold, didn't look valuable at all, and he was half tempted to pull it out. But on closer inspection, he realized that the tube was acting like a stopper. Move it and the sand would be released…"Like a ballast." He looked around, pointing. "Move his body, to get to the chest beneath him, the gold piled behind him, and the sand is released."

"It'd be nice to come back after the place was surveyed by engineers first."

"We don't exactly have that luxury." He looked at his watch. They had two hours and twenty minutes left to trade the map for Tex. Hell. What was he thinking? There would be no trade. The map was not to leave their hands.

A feeling of helplessness swept through him. Not only was Tex's life in the balance, at the moment, their lives were as well.

Sydney reached out, touched his arm. "We'll figure this out."

"How?"

"Francesca said that there were three keys."

"And we know of only one of any certainty."

"No, we know the third is the inscription from his door. And we were at the Capuchin crypt where the second was, so maybe we can apply that knowledge?"

She was right. They'd been everywhere that Francesca had been. Maybe they could work this out…"Okay," he said, wanting to pace, to think it through, but knowing any unnecessary movement could prove fatal. "Alessandra went to the trouble of saying the key is below Sansevero, and here, allegedly, is the prince of Sansevero, or a man bearing his crest. And he's sitting on a tube that might or might not be the missing map. Yank it out and run?"

"Run to where? If he was that smart, and he took the trouble to set up this elaborate trap, then there has to be something more to this. What was that inscription on the door again?"

Griffin took out the napkin that he'd written it on, and read, "'Observe with an attentive eye and with veneration the urns of the heroes endowed with glory and reflect with astonishment on the precious homage to the divine work and the tomb of the deceased and when you have given due honor, contemplate profoundly and distance yourself.'"

She blew some dust off the top of one of the urns. "Urns filled with gold coins. 'Urns of the heroes'?"

"Assuming this saying is filled with subtext, then yes."

"'Contemplate profoundly and distance yourself,'" Sydney said, repeating the inscription from the door. "Distance ourselves as in not being too literal, or as in get the hell out of here, because of a deadly plague or major collapse?" She walked a few steps away, careful not to stray from the narrow path, and cocked her head, stared at the corpse, his leathered face. "What was so important that we had to go to the Capuchin crypt before we came here? What's the commonality between this place and the Capuchin crypt?"

"Besides all the gold? About three thousand nine hundred and ninety-nine more sets of bones. Clearly a warning that death is imminent."

"Or that time is endless, especially if you take into context the first key, 'here lies dust, ash, and nothing,'" she said, walking up, looking at the pocket watch the skeleton held. "It reads exactly twelve, just like the Capuchin crypt. Well, sort of. The clock made of bones that wasn't a clock. Endlessly where midnight should be, considering it only had six numbers on it."

"Maybe it has nothing to do with time," Griffin said. "If his pocket watch were a compass, the two hands would be pointing due north." He looked toward the tunnel directly opposite the watch's hands. It was the smallest passageway. "A deliberate position of the body and the watch? Or mere coincidence?"

"Anyone could read anything into any of these clues," she said, looking around. "You think there's any truth to this trap thing? That if anything's moved, it'll set it off?"

Again he took stock. "Move his body to get to the chest beneath him, the gold piled behind him, and the sand is released. Like you said, our safest course of action would be to leave and return with a very knowledgeable bunch of engineers."

"Yet here we are."

A shout from the tunnel they'd entered stopped them. If there was any doubt as to the intent of the newcomers, the sharp crack of gunfire dispelled any hope they were there for a rescue.

◇◇◇

Francesca's limbs were stiff and sore by the time they finally climbed down from the crevice, not daring to leave the relative safety of the dark until they no longer heard the echoing of the footsteps in the tunnel below, and even for several minutes after that. The route they took back was not the same as the one they'd taken, Alfredo leading them a different way after overhearing the two men talk about others posted outside. But finally they were out and Francesca squinted against the bright sunlight as Xavier helped her from the secret passageway that led to the street behind the Cappella Sansevero. The moment she was free and clear, he and Alfredo slid the massive stone door closed, rendering it invisible to any who might pass by. She wasn't sure they'd be able to find it again if necessary.

"This way," Xavier said, leading her around the corner.

She followed, only to stop short on seeing the dark-clad man standing at the edge of the building. "Father Dumas."

"*Professoressa*," he said, with a slight nod to his head. "You are a hard woman to track down."

Xavier looked from one to the other. "Who is this?"

Dumas gave a slight bow and introduced himself.

"A friend of Alessandra's," Francesca said. "Exactly what sort of friend, I'm not sure."

Xavier frowned. "I don't recall Alessandra mentioning him before."

"Be that as it may," Dumas said, "I am what she says. And if the two, or rather three of you had any sense," he said, apparently noticing Xavier's cousin for the first time, "you would realize that you are in danger. Where are the two agents?"

"In the tunnels," Francesca said. "We were ambushed."

"That's not surprising," Dumas said. "You were followed here."

"Tell us something we don't know," she replied.

"There are several of Adami's men in the area, as well as some others I do not recognize, and if you insist on going that direction, you will run right into them."

She hesitated, not sure what to believe. "And how do I know you're not one of them?"

"You do not. Again, where are the two agents?"

"Below. They covered us so we could escape. Two men were down there, shooting at us. We would've been killed had we not hidden and had Xavier and Alfredo not found the passageway out. We need to get help."

"Did the agents give you anything? Did you find the key?"

Francesca stared in disbelief. "Did you not hear a word I said? They're in trouble."

"And if they moved anything without having found the key, they're about to be smashed into bits, with nothing you or I can do about it. So answer me again, do you know if they found the key?"

"Sydney thought she knew where it was…"

Dumas held her gaze for an instant, mumbled a quick "God be with them," then said, "I'd suggest we put some distance between us and here." Dumas pulled her back from the street. "I recognize those two near the corner." He nodded toward the pedestrians crossing the square, then the two men lurking at the fringes. "I saw them outside the train station."

"You've been following us too?" Francesca said.

"Someone needed to."

"I think we should split up," Xavier said. "Make it harder for those men to track us."

"No," Dumas replied. "It's too dangerous. Griffin and Sydney could be dead for all we know. And if not, they soon will be."

"But what if they find their way out?" Francesca asked. "We need to watch out for them, warn them."

Dumas seemed ready to protest, and she added, "If di Sangro wasn't the monster many have painted him to be, there was an escape route, and Sydney and Griffin are making their way through it now."

"Then we must look for them," Dumas said. "But together. We've come too far to split up now."

Indeed, she thought, not trusting Dumas at all. How was it that he'd arrived just where they'd exited? Divine intervention, or something far more earthly? "Together, then," Francesca said. "Xavier. You and Alfredo work your magic, and let's find where those two will emerge before Adami's henchmen do."

Alfredo knew the streets of Naples like the back of his hand, and between that knowledge and Xavier's calculations, they estimated a few block radius of the original tunnel entrance. The main problem as Alfredo saw it was that nearly every house in this area had access to the tunnels. Most accesses, however, were unused, many long-forgotten, others in complete disrepair. He decided, however, to concentrate their efforts not too far from di Sangro's old basement, deciding that the prince probably had several routes out of his family's home, for the sole purpose of keeping his affairs secret. They set up across the street, keeping in the shadow of a delivery truck. Xavier double-checked his map and nodded. "There. That's where I think they'll emerge."

He pointed, and just as his hand came up, Francesca saw two men walking right toward that location. She recognized one from the hotel lobby. "If that turns out to be the escape route, they're going to run right into those men," she said, pulling Xavier's hand down in case the men should look up and in their direction.

"What should we do?" Xavier said.

"Dumas?" Francesca asked.

"I'm thinking."

"We need a distraction," she said.

"Short of calling them over here, what do you suggest?" Dumas said.

"Exactly that. Xavier and I can pull them off, we owe them that much. When they follow us, you get over there, watch out for Griffin and Sydney. If they make it out, you give warning. Give us an hour to meet back with you."

"Where?" Dumas asked.

The only place she could think of was the café around the corner from the hotel where Griffin had the room. She knew he had to eventually make his way there to rescue his friend. Alfredo and Dumas would return to the café, then call the police if they weren't back in an hour.

Dumas nodded, and she put her hand on his arm. "You need to not stand out," she continued. "If any of these men are the ones who shot at us up on the Passegiata, they might be looking for a priest. Perhaps you can remove the clerical collar?"

Dumas reached up, pulled it off, unbuttoned the top collar of his shirt, and instantly transformed himself from man of God to man about town.

She turned to Xavier. "Ready?"

"Yeah," he said, though he didn't look too sure.

They hurried across the street, heading toward Adami's men. She took Xavier's map, pretended to be looking at it with him. "We have to get their attention," she whispered. "We need them to follow us away from the chapel, and then we've got to lose them."

"Shouldn't be a problem."

"Let's hope not," she said, looking up over the top of the map. "Because here they come." And then she lowered the map, looked the men directly in the eye, gave her best impression of surprise, then screamed. "Oh my God! They found us!" She grabbed Xavier's hand. "Run!"

◇◇◇

Sydney ducked behind an urn filled with gold, drawing her weapon. A bullet ricocheted off the urn next to her, cracking it. By some small miracle, it didn't break. But sand started sifting through between it and the urn beside it.

Griffin crouched beside her, hefted his gun in his hand. "We need to get out of here. That sand moves, we're as good as dead."

"We're as good as dead anyway, if we don't know which tunnel to take."

They crouched even lower as another shot rang out. "And which one would you take?"

"Let's give the guy credit for being a mad genius. He sent us down a specific path. That means he's logical. The bone clock at the crypt. His watch with the same time, and clocks that aren't clocks could be considered compasses. The tunnel that points north."

"Then I'll cover you, and you go for it."

"And what are you going to do?" she asked.

"Hold them off. At least one of us gets out of here alive."

"Are you nuts? You're going to sacrifice yourself?"

"You think of a better idea?"

"Not at the moment. But hell if I'm going to let you lord it over me from eternity. And if they kill you, what's to stop them from following me up the tunnel? I'll be a sitting duck."

Griffin peered around an urn, aimed, fired. The shot echoed throughout the cavern. "We're about to run out of ammo, which makes it a moot point."

Sydney glanced back at the corpse. "I have an idea," she said. "I need you to go to the north tunnel."

He didn't move.

"I am not her. Trust me on this," she said. "For once."

"Why?"

"I can reach the tube without exposing myself by scooting on my belly behind that chest. You can't. If you're already at the tunnel, you can cover me."

"And then?"

She took a breath, smiled. "And then we save the last couple shots to see if di Sangro knew what he was doing. We bring this place down."

Chapter Thirty-five

Sydney kept an eye on the two men, wondering if she'd truly lost her mind, thinking she could spring di Sangro's trap. What if it was an elaborate hoax, like the curse in the pyramids to ward off grave robbers? Or what if the sand was merely there to keep some deadly plague hidden and out of sight?

Griffin fired off two rounds. "This plan of yours…I'm not sure we have enough ammo to break these urns and try to keep them at bay."

"I've already thought of that." By her calculations, she had maybe three shots left. "Just watch for my cue, and get ready to cover me."

He crouched beside the urn. Sydney nodded once, then popped up, shouting as she fired two rounds. One of the men cried out, hit. She ducked back. Hope he's dead, she thought, then glanced over toward Griffin. He was halfway across the cavern, crouching behind one of the manmade stalagmites. She turned back to her targets; both had moved closer. Great. The man she'd hit wasn't dead, just grazed on his shoulder. One shot left. Griffin nodded. She popped up, took her last shot, prayed Griffin made it, then dropped flat to the ground. She scooted past the skeleton, then yanked on the tube beside it. It was wedged tight. She pulled harder. The moment she did, she heard something move. Shift. Sand slid to the floor from the rocky shelf behind the body. No time to wonder. A shot hit the urn above her head. The report echoed off the walls.

This was it. Keeping well to one side, and out of sight, she held the tube up over the urn that had been cracked, yelling, "I give up. Don't shoot!"

A sharp report echoed across the cavern. The urn broke apart. Sand poured forth from behind it, and she yelled, "Now!"

Griffin fired off his last rounds. Tube in hand, Sydney scrambled toward the north tunnel.

Suddenly a low rumbling noise seemed to shake the very stone itself. The floor beneath them vibrated. Dust rained down, into her eyes, rattled against her helmet like dried rice. She hesitated.

"Move," Griffin yelled.

She sprinted toward Griffin and the tunnel. He grabbed the tube, lifted her in. He climbed in after her, and she caught sight of the two men, no longer watching them. Both looked up at the ceiling.

"Forget them," he said.

She scurried forward. The space, though wide, was barely high enough to crawl on hands and knees, and at some points, not even that high. After twenty or so feet they rounded a corner, and the path began a sharp incline. Sydney scurried up, her eyes watering against the dust. Bits of tufo stung her face, her back. Suddenly the floor rippled beneath her, the air tasting of crushed rock. She started sliding down. Griffin grabbed her by the shirt, braced himself. A pressure in her ears pushed then released, as though the air was sucked out of the tunnels. A second later, she looked down, the dim light from her helmet revealing the blocked passageway below. The entrance was gone. No space at all. The rumbling continued as rock below them seemed to settle. There was no way back.

Only up.

Almost straight up.

"How the hell—"

"Like Santa in a chimney," Griffin said.

◇◇◇

Francesca and Xavier fled around the corner, then down one of countless narrow streets, this time into the midst of the open-air market, crowded with locals and tourists alike, all talking about the minor earthquake they'd felt. The two ducked behind a cart filled with ice and fresh fish, then dared a peek around the edge to see if they were still being followed.

"You see them?" Francesca asked.

Xavier nodded, trying to catch his breath. "Yeah. Don't think they saw where we went, but give it a minute or two and they'll trip right over us."

"We really need to get out of this. Preferably in one piece." And without anyone else around them getting hurt, she wanted to add. She was tired, too tired to run. Playing cat and mouse was a lot harder than she thought, and any momentary admiration and envy at seeing Sydney Fitzpatrick in action made her truly appreciate her own choice of going into academia. She ignored the thought that it was that very pursuit for historical significance that had started this mess, and she leaned against the cart, tried to catch her breath. That was when she saw the catwalk between the buildings, barely visible behind the awning that covered the pushcarts of fruits and vegetables spread out before it. The vendor called out in Nepalese that he had fresh produce for sale. "You have any idea where that leads?" she asked, pointing to the catwalk.

Xavier looked over. "Back to the basilica. Why?"

"I think we need to slip through there."

◇◇◇

The two men chasing Francesca and Xavier stopped in the middle of the market square. "They can't have gone far," the first said.

"Over there. That's where I saw them last. By the fish."

"If we find them, I vote we finish them here, now."

"Idiot. There are too many witnesses. We do it right. Stick our gun in their ribs, frighten them, get them to tell us where their friends are. Then we take the map and kill them. Adami has no idea we are here, and Mr. Westgate doesn't want to lose the map to him."

"What about the witnesses?"

He didn't answer, apparently because the question needed no answering. There were to be no witnesses. Period. Francesca dared a look from where she hid. The man started toward the fish cart, then stopped just in front of it, looking around. "You see them?"

"No."

"Fresh fruit!" cried the vendor across the street.

The man ignored him.

"Fresh fish!" called the vendor beside the two men.

They started to move away, but the first man stopped. "I am looking for my friends," he asked the vendor. "A man and a woman. Americans."

"The woman, red hair?"

"Yes."

The vendor narrowed his gaze. "Your American friends, they almost knocked my cart over."

"They are in trouble. My apologies. Which way did they go?"

"Through there. I heard them say something about the basilica," he replied, pointing across the street toward the catwalk.

"*Grazie.*"

He gave a shrug, then turned away, calling out, "Fresh fish! The freshest!"

"Hurry," the first man said. "They may have a car parked at the basilica."

"Fresh fish!"

Francesca's breath caught. They ran right past her. She waited until their footfall faded down the catwalk before she emerged. She dug all the money she had from her pocket, then handed it over to the fish vendor the moment the two henchmen disappeared from sight at the other end of the catwalk. "*Grazie, signore.*"

The vendor smiled. "My pleasure, *signorina*. If you are smart, you and your friend will go to the end of the street, then turn south. My friend has a horse and cart for tourists. He can give you a ride to wherever it is you need to go. Tell him that Pietro sent you. He will help."

They thanked him again, then raced down the street, where, as promised, his friend waited and gladly took them on at the mention of Pietro's name. Within minutes they were seated in a covered carriage, the sound of the mare's hooves clopping down the cobbled street at a brisk trot. Xavier offered the man some money, but he refused, saying he was going that way anyway, and their thanks was enough. Fifteen minutes later, he dropped them off a half block from the coffee shop where they were to meet Dumas.

◇◇◇

Sydney watched as Griffin took the rope from his backpack, the one they'd used the first time, then looped it around her waist. That done, he shimmied up a few feet into the tunnel to show her it could be done, his back wedged against one wall of the tunnel, his feet against the other. She followed him up, thinking it was rough enough to allow some hand purchase, and wasn't as hard as she first thought. Nor as easy, she realized. Especially after another shift of stone, as though the earth finally settled. She looked down. Nothing but blackness, an unsettling feeling, not having any idea how far they'd traveled. Or how far she'd fall if she slipped. The very thought made her dizzy.

"Don't recommend that," Griffin said.

"Now you tell me. How much farther?"

"Hard to say. Another ten feet?"

She could do ten feet.

After about fifteen, she figured he'd lied to her. Probably a good thing. She'd lost her right glove when she'd pulled it off during the firefight down in the cistern. And now her nails shredded against the rough surface, the rock dug into her fingertips. She was stretched out, one foot on each wall, her hands gripping the sides.

A low rumble pulsated along the tunnel walls.

"Griffin?"

"Just the earth settling. Don't worry."

But the rumbling didn't stop. It grew louder, deeper, vibrated through the stones into her bones. She braced herself against the walls, tried to hold on. Rocks hurtled down, hit her helmet, her arms. The earth shuddered one last heave. Her bloody hand slipped, and she plunged down into the blackness, nothing beneath her feet.

Chapter Thirty-six

Francesca and Xavier met Dumas at the café, and Francesca's pulse shot up again as a third fire truck zipped past. Alfredo had left to get his van, in case they needed more equipment for a rescue. He had not yet returned. A second building midblock had collapsed, just sank into the earth, and, from the talk around them, the citizens of Naples were blaming it on yet another crumbling tunnel, long forgotten, finally giving way.

Xavier shook his head. "How does a man set a trap that lasts over two hundred years?"

"Like da Vinci before him," Dumas said, "di Sangro's genius was unparalleled."

"But to what end?" Francesca wondered aloud. She'd studied every nuance about the prince and even she was having difficulties comprehending that his trap was real. Or perhaps she didn't want to believe it. To do so meant that there was no hope.

"From what I gathered from the documents that you uncovered at the Vatican, di Sangro's sole purpose was to protect that which he sought to hide, from those he hoped to hide it from. Why else leave such enigmatic clues?"

"Enigmatic?" Xavier said. "Or purposefully deceitful? Maybe he really was the monster that some historians thought."

"I don't believe so," Dumas said. "Misunderstood, as those who are too far ahead of their time often are. But in this instance, he had a purpose. Perhaps one the Church didn't see as clearly as he did at the time. To protect mankind."

Francesca watched the crowd surge forward, no doubt trying to see what, if anything, or anyone, was left in the collapsed building. "If di Sangro went to such trouble to give specific clues on the door of his chapel, warning of a trap, or how to avoid it, then there could equally be a specific escape route." She turned to Xavier. "Where was it you thought his tunnel came out?"

"Originally? Where we came out."

"Any other guesses, now that we know that wasn't the right way?"

And Dumas, staring at the fallen building, said, "Let's hope it wasn't there."

Xavier took out Francesca's map, spread it across the tabletop. "This is the cistern they went down, and here's where we came out…" He pointed to the area where the building fell through. "It was obviously to one side of the cistern, probably off that ledge near the top, some hidden passageway. If di Sangro had a route planned out, it would be on the outskirts of the cave-in." He drew a circle with his finger around the building. "Somewhere in this area, or this one. Perhaps they were lucky."

"As much as I don't like it," Dumas said, "we will need to split up again, the better to cover both areas."

"Then that's what we need to do," she said. "We need to find them before Adami's men do."

◇◇◇

"*Sydney!*"

Blackness. Pain. It was several moments before Sydney dared breathe, dared move. And several more moments before she realized that she was suspended by the rope, hanging, spinning. "Griff?"

"You're okay?" His voice sounded a million miles away.

"Yeah. Sort of…Oh my God. The map!" She reached back, felt it still strapped across her shoulder, looked up, tried to see him, but her eyes filled with dust, still raining down from above.

"Can you climb?"

"I'm sure as hell gonna try." She reached out, touched the wall, tried to stop the turning, then braced both her feet against the tunnel walls. As soon as she started climbing, the rope seemed to loosen from around her chest, and she felt like she could breathe again.

"You're doing good. Keep going."

She had to stop to rest, tried to ignore the pulsing pain in her hand. "You know this is hell on my manicure."

"Didn't think you were the manicure type."

"You know me. All about fashion and accessories. A real girly girl."

Toward the top, however, the passageway widened, and she couldn't find purchase, her hands and feet slipped. She finally had to stop. "I can't make it."

She could hear Griffin breathing above her. "Just a bit more."

Her foot slid on the tufo. "I'm losing my grip. It's too wide." And just when she was sure she couldn't hang on another second, just when she knew she was going to fall again, drag him down with her, the rope pulled tight beneath her arms.

"I've got you," he said. "I'm going to pull you up."

"Whose idea was it to get on that plane to Italy?"

"We're almost to the surface. Just a couple more feet."

He helped her to the top, then over the edge, and she collapsed next to him. She'd been climbing on sheer adrenaline, of which there was none left at the moment. As she caught her breath, she looked over at him. "I'm going to have rope burn in places no rope should ever be."

He laughed. "That'll be foremost in my mind next time I decide to climb through tunnels in Naples."

"Figures," she said, staring up at the ceiling, at the shadows.

"You want, I could—"

"Is that light up there?"

"Where?"

She pointed straight up.

"I'll be damned," he said.

"Where are we?"

"Sort of looks like an unfinished basement, if I had to guess. Maybe the opening was blocked until the cave-in."

She closed her eyes in relief, opened them again, worried that the light from the windows above would disappear, that it had all been a dream. But no, it was still there. And in that moment, she reached out, felt the round shape of the tube from the cavern. "What time is it?" she asked.

Griffin looked at his watch. "We have less than an hour before Adami expects us to contact him."

Together they moved to the window. Griffin opened it, about to help Sydney out, but stopped at the sound of the sirens.

"What's going on?" Sydney whispered.

She peered out the window they'd almost climbed through, saw general chaos with people running in every direction, then froze at the sight of dark-clad legs walking toward their window. She looked up, saw Dumas looking down at them.

◇◇◇

"Need a hand?" Dumas said.

Griffin hesitated. He glanced over at Sydney, then turned his attention back to Dumas. "As it turns out, yes." Griffin held up the window, and Sydney handed him the tube, then allowed Dumas to help her out. Griffin followed.

Dumas eyed the leather tube that Griffin now carried, but said only, "This way." They followed him down the street to a small car parked about two blocks away. "The *professoressa* and her friend were most insistent on helping draw off the men searching for you. A favor returned, she said. They are watching for you on the other side of the collapsed building. His cousin has returned to start a search-and-rescue operation for the both of you. He should be back shortly."

"These men the professor and Xavier drew off? How many?"

"Two chased after them, and just before the collapse I saw another two. Conjecture, of course, based on their inordinate interest in the known locations of that particular tunnel entrance.

I recognized Adami's men. These others, I do not know them. Someone else is after this thing."

"There were at least two down in the tunnels that we know of. I doubt they're coming up."

They piled into the car, Sydney in the front passenger seat, Griffin in the back. "What about Francesca and Xavier?" he asked.

Dumas pulled out and into traffic. "The young man, Xavier, seems to have a grasp of these streets that will serve them well. I will meet up with them after I take you wherever it is you need to go. First I intend to see if we are being followed. I take it you found the key? That is what is in the tube?"

Griffin saw Sydney's shoulders tense as she said, "What makes you say that?"

"The collapse," Dumas replied. "After the *professoressa* fled the Vatican, Father Martinez brought me the documents she'd been researching. It was there I found the passage about di Sangro. Depending on how you interpreted it, it could mean one of two things. Whosoever found the key and moved it would meet a most untimely death, turning their corpses into dust, or, whoever finds the key must choose the right time and direction to avoid such a fate."

"The eternal clock in the Capuchin crypt," Sydney said. "We chose to interpret it as a compass that indicated north. That's the direction we fled."

"And a good thing you did," Dumas said, expertly weaving in and out of traffic with the finesse of a local cabbie. "How did you guess in time?"

"Lady Luck," Griffin said, as he leaned back, far too exhausted to explain. But he couldn't help but think of their near escape.

"Or perhaps," Dumas said, "God was watching over you."

"As were you, it seems."

Dumas didn't reply, and Griffin felt only slightly guilty. He had no doubts as to Dumas' loyalty. The church first, their mission second. That he'd come here to warn them was something, at least.

Dumas slowed as a bus pulled out in front of him, then glanced in his rearview mirror. "I am not sure what your plans were, but it seems I underestimated the number of men following you. The man in the car directly behind us made a point to let me know he is armed."

Griffin shifted in his seat, looked out the back, recognizing the man in the front passenger seat as one of the two men who had followed them from the Capuchin crypt. So much for his plans for quietly leaving Naples with the map.

"What is it you'd like me to do?" Dumas asked.

"Drive us to the hotel," he said, not wanting to give Adami's men any inkling that he intended to do anything but trade the map for Tex. Returning to the hotel would allow him to regroup, come up with an alternate plan. Or destroy the map if need be…

Dumas did as he was told, stopping the car in front of the hotel.

Griffin opened the car door. "You're not even curious as to what this is?" he asked, tapping on the leather tube.

"I'll find out in good time when you return it to the Vatican."

"The Vatican?"

"The papal seal on the end?" he said, reaching out, touching the tooled leather. "That shows it is Vatican property. And the records the *professoressa* found confirm it. But I am a patient man if nothing else."

Good thing, Griffin thought, because this map wasn't going anywhere near the Vatican.

◇◇◇

Sydney pushed through the door the moment Griffin inserted the key. "Let's open that thing up and see what's in there," she said, walking to the table by the window and clearing the hotel's literature from it. She looked up to see why he hadn't immediately followed her. "Well?"

"This thing's over two hundred years old at the least."

"And at a constant fifty degrees, probably preserved better than if it was in some museum." He didn't move. "What? You think it's going to disintegrate the moment you unlatch the top? At least take a look before we have to hand it over. If it seems crumbly, we wait. If not, I say pull the damned thing out and let's see it. I'd like to see what we almost died for."

He pushed the door closed, then walked over to the table, in no particular hurry.

Sydney tried to keep the impatience from her voice. "Anytime."

Surprisingly, he handed the tube to her. "You rescued it. The honor should be yours."

And suddenly she wasn't sure she wanted it. What if she opened it, and she was the one responsible for destroying a piece of history? That thought lasted until the moment her hand gripped the still supple tube. Now that the danger was seemingly over, and they were no longer running, she had a moment to admire the intricate hand-tooled leather. The case itself was probably worth something, she thought, running her finger over the elaborate papal seal tooled on the top. She slid the thin leather strap up, allowing the top to be lifted. The edge of a rolled parchment was visible just inside, and she touched it with her finger. "It feels sturdy."

"Slide it out."

"Shouldn't we be wearing gloves, or something?"

"Now you're worried?"

"Maybe we should wait for Francesca. She is the expert, after all."

Griffin's answer to that was to grab several tissues from a box on the bathroom counter, then return and hand them to her. "Happy? Take the damned thing out."

"I'd be happier if we had a camera," she said. "What about the camera on your phone?"

"No. No photos."

She looked up at him, wondered why he was so adamant, but figured he had his reasons. "It's your mission," she said, using the tissue to keep her fingers from touching the parchment as she carefully slid it partway from the tube, revealing a fleur-de-lis on the top corner. That was the only marking on the outside of the parchment. With Griffin's help, they unrolled it onto the table, weighting it down with a telephone book on one side and an empty ice bucket on the other.

"This sure as hell doesn't look like any key or map," she said. It was a drawing of a large labyrinth, and with it what appeared to be a legend down the right side, unfortunately in some language that Sydney could only guess at. There was a coat of arms in the bottom left corner, with the Templar cross situated above another fleur-de-lis. "What do you think it's for?"

"I have no idea."

They stared at it for several minutes, and when nothing seemed to present itself, Sydney said, "You get the feeling that out of all the things down there, maybe this wasn't the thing to grab?"

"Like we had a lot of time to think about it?" The muted ring of Adami's cell phone sounded through Griffin's pack. Sydney's heart skipped a beat with each ring. *Tex,* she thought as Griffin pulled the pouch from his pack and then removed the phone, opened it.

He signaled for Sydney to move next to him, and he held the phone so that they both could hear.

"You're back."

"Yes," Griffin said. "Where's Tex?"

"I see you have the map?"

See? "We have it."

"Do not leave the room until we get there."

"And when will that be?"

"Enough time for the both of you to take a shower. You look a bit dusty." He disconnected.

Griffin tossed the phone onto the bed. "How did we not figure he'd have cameras set up in this room?"

"We had other things on our mind. What should we do?"

He looked around the room, perhaps trying to see where the camera was situated, then moved in close. "There's nothing we can do," he said, lowering his voice. Then, louder, said, "Adami's on his way. I for one am going to take a shower."

He disappeared into the bathroom, and while he was gone, she tried to determine why he was against taking a photo of it. Then again, if this room had cameras, Adami would know the moment they tried to snap a photo.

Griffin stepped out of the bathroom a few minutes later, towel-drying his hair, dressed only in his pants. He draped his shirt over the chair. "Dumas hasn't called?"

"Not yet."

He walked over to take another look at the map, when there was a knock at the door. Griffin strode over, peered through the peephole, then backed away. "It's Dumas. He's with Francesca. And there's someone standing beside them."

"Who?"

"Our friend from the Capuchin crypt," he said quietly, then pointed at the map.

She lifted the ice bucket, allowing the parchment to roll up on itself. She rolled it tighter, then dropped it into the tube.

"Hold on," Griffin said loudly, grabbing his shirt. "Let me throw on my clothes."

"What do you want me to do?" she whispered.

"Hug me for good luck."

It took a moment for his odd request to sink in, and then she thought, cameras. She stepped into his arms, felt his skin, warm, moist against her, as he whispered, "Take it in the bathroom, pretend to be taking a shower, and destroy it." She looked up, about to protest, but he held her tight, his whisper filled with urgency. "We're out of ammo, and Tex or no Tex, if we can't get the map out of Naples, I'm under orders *not* to let it leave our hands—even if we are killed in the process. We have to destroy it."

His words sent a chill through her. She couldn't believe he would willingly let his friend die. But she knew the hopelessness of the situation the moment she looked into his eyes, saw the pain, the resignation. As much as he wanted Tex safe, it had always been about the map, keeping it from the enemy.

She took the tube, carried it into the windowless bathroom, closed the door, locked it. She turned on the water to the shower, then looked at her reflection more ghostly than real through all that steam, and in that moment, she realized the full weight of Griffin's dilemma. He was under orders not to let Adami have the map. But could she really think that he'd choose the map over Tex's life? Even then, he couldn't just turn over the map, when they knew what it might lead to. If there was any truth to this whole biblical plague thing—and so far everything she'd seen led her to believe it was all true—then everything they did from this moment on could mean countless lives saved…

Griffin's bosses wanted the map. Impossible with Adami's man outside the door.

But the impossible meant the map had to be destroyed. She took out the knife Griffin had given her, removed the map from the tube, unrolling it on the bathroom counter. She poised the knife over the map, intending to cut it to shreds, before flushing it, and it occurred to her what sort of history she was about to decimate.

But it wasn't history that came to mind. It was Tex. One life or thousands of lives?

How did one choose?

◇◇◇

"Dumas," Griffin said, opening the door. "I see you brought company."

Father Dumas gave an apologetic shrug. "The *professoressa* said that you'd want to see this man. He says his name is Silvio and that Adami sent him. He wants to know if you have the map."

"I do. Where's Tex?"

Silvio, his hand in the pocket of his overcoat, no doubt holding a weapon on them, barged into the room, looking around.

"Signore Adami will bring your friend, once I call to confirm the map is here. Where is it?"

"Surely you saw the map on the monitor?"

"Until I verify that it is real, no exchange will be made."

"It's in the bathroom with my associate. I'd get it, but the door's locked and she's taking a shower."

Silvio pulled his hand from his pocket, revealing the pistol he'd been hiding. He pointed it at Griffin. "I'd suggest she hurry. We are to meet Signore Adami out front with the map in hand in exchange for your friend. And he wants to know that he has the only copy, or the deal is off."

There was a moment of silence, and then Griffin shouted Sydney's name.

"I'm washing my hair," she called back.

"Hurry."

Griffin leaned against the bathroom door, heard the blow dryer start up, and wondered what the hell Sydney was doing in there.

Adami's man stood in the center of the room, his arms crossed. "You're sure she's going to come out?"

"She has to. There are no windows."

"What's taking her so long?"

"She's a girl. That's what they do."

The man's phone rang. He flipped it open, said, "*Pronto.*" Then, "Adami is here. He wants reassurance that the map is here. Now."

"No cameras in the bathroom?"

"We are not without some scruples," he said, which was when Griffin wondered if there really were cameras in the room at all. Griffin had purposefully taken a shower just in case there were cameras in there, in order to steam the things up. He was not about to destroy the map and let anyone see it being done. Adami had no scruples, and he doubted that anyone who worked for him did either. Definitely not this man, who demanded, "Let me see the map or Adami leaves with your friend."

"Sydney! The map. I need it now."

He heard the blow dryer shut off.

A few seconds later, the door opened a crack, and Sydney stepped out, holding the tube, her hair looking damp, as though she hadn't bothered to dry it all the way.

"The map," Griffin said, nodding toward Sydney.

"Show me."

Sydney unbuckled the lid. His heart skipped a beat as he peered in, saw a bit of yellowish white. It was there, he realized, watching her tipping it upside-down to slide out the parchment partway. He wanted to throttle Sydney. She was supposed to have destroyed it. Francesca sucked in her breath at the sight of the fleur-de-lis on the outside corner. When she tried to move closer, Dumas put his hand out to stop her, and Sydney tapped the rolled parchment back into the tube and handed it to Griffin.

The man said into the phone, "It appears to be the map…"

"Satisfied?" Griffin asked.

"Signore Adami will be once he is assured there are no copies. I'll need to search the room and the bathroom, as well as any of your possessions."

"All yours," he said, indicating the man could check the hotel room.

Adami's man walked through the room, looking in Griffin's backpack, the armoire, then behind it. He ripped off the sheets, checked beneath the mattress, around and beneath the bed, then in the drawers of the small bedside table, as well as the desk. And that confirmed it for Griffin that there were no cameras. They would have known that he and Sydney came straight in, opened the map, and then took it into the bathroom. He no doubt knew they were dusty because he had someone posted out front, and that person had seen them walk in. The man pocketed a small pad of paper he found in the desk drawer.

Griffin looked Sydney in the eye, trying to figure out what she was up to, why she didn't destroy the map as ordered. "He wants to check the bathroom, to make sure there is nothing hidden in there."

"Have at it," she said, pushing the bathroom door wide open.

Adami's man walked inside, looked around, peeked behind the door and into the shower, then came out. Into the phone, he said, "All clear." He listened a moment, then told Griffin, "He's waiting downstairs in the car."

"I want to know my friend is safe before we go down there."

"You don't call the orders."

"Then you don't get the map."

He nodded, said into the phone, "He wants to talk to his friend…" He handed the phone to Griffin.

"Tex?"

"Griff? I told you not—"

And then Adami saying, "Bring me the map. You have five minutes, or your friend dies."

Chapter Thirty-seven

When Griffin refused to hand over the map to Adami's goon, instead giving it to Sydney to hold, she had a feeling it was just in case any fighting had to be done. Griffin would be free.

She slipped the parchment tube's leather strap over her shoulder, allowing the tube to hang across her back, as Adami's man ushered all through the door.

And all she could think was that Tex was alive.

But then the reality of the situation hit her as they walked down the long hallway to the elevator. What guarantee did they have that Adami would keep his end of the bargain? None, whatsoever, which meant she'd gone to all this trouble for nothing, a point brought home when Griffin caught up to her, his whisper harsh. "What the hell? Do you realize the danger if Adami gets his hands on that map? I sent you in there to destroy it."

"He won't get it. Besides, I couldn't do it like that." She glanced back over her shoulder, saw Silvio, his gun in his coat pocket, the barrel jutting slightly through the wool, close the room door, then follow them. "I couldn't just let them kill Tex outright."

"Adami's not going to release Tex," he whispered. "And now, thanks to you, we need damage control. We can't let him have that damned map."

"That's what I'm trying to tell you. I—"

"You two shut the hell up," Silvio called out. "Onto the elevator, and no more talking." They rode the elevator to the ground floor and the lobby. Silvio motioned for everyone to exit the front door, as he held it open. Out front, she saw a black Mercedes. A taxi pulled in behind it, honking its horn, perhaps in hopes of getting the larger car to move forward. It didn't budge, and the tinted rear window of the Mercedes rolled partway down.

Adami peered out at them, smiling. "Signore Griffin."

Silvio moved to the car, standing beside it, keeping watch. Griffin dropped Sydney's arm, started toward the Mercedes, just as Adami looked over at the priest and said, "Ah, Father Dumas. I suppose I should offer my thanks to you for keeping me so well-informed."

Griffin paused, looked over at Dumas.

The priest shook his head. "A lie," he said, when he finally found his tongue.

Griffin turned back to Adami. "You expect me to believe that Dumas works for you?" he asked, taking another step forward.

Adami gave a shrug. "Perhaps indirectly. He managed to keep the ambassador apprised, and the ambassador, in turn, kept me *very* well informed of most of ATLAS' next moves. The death of his daughter, and his return to the States, unfortunately, left me on my own these past few days, or you wouldn't have had the advantage you had in Tunisia."

"*You* killed Alessandra?"

"If you hope I'll confess to murder, you're wrong. I believe the man who killed her, Niko, met an untimely death in some apartment in Washington," he said, looking right at Sydney, before turning his attention back to Griffin. "But I suspect you may know more about that than I, seeing as how it was your FBI agent who killed him."

"You're saying the ambassador willingly gave you information on our operations?"

"He's not the only one. You might want to ask him who he reports to."

"I'll certainly look into the matter," Griffin said, trying to peer into the Mercedes.

"The map," Adami said.

"That map belongs to the Vatican," Dumas replied.

Adami narrowed his gaze, and a vein pulsed in his temple. "What is it the church is so fond of saying? An eye for an eye? This map will almost make up for the warehouse I lost along with the year's worth of work, as well as the personnel within. You're lucky I don't lay claim to each life lost. But a deal's a deal, and I am in a benevolent mood."

Benevolent? Or counting on finding the lost plagues and rebuilding his bioweapons? What better source than something that hadn't seen the light of day in two thousand years? Something that hadn't been studied, something that might be deadlier because of its very isolation? And that was when Sydney realized the foolishness of her plan—and why Griffin had insisted on destroying that map.

The window rolled down the rest of the way, and Sydney saw Tex, still dressed in his tuxedo. Adami held a gun pointed at Tex's gut, just low enough that most passersby wouldn't see. Tex looked out the window at Griffin, cocked his head slightly. His face was bruised, dried blood crusted around his eyes and his mouth. His breathing was shallow, and he looked like hell.

But he was alive, Sydney thought.

Griffin returned his attention to Adami, took another step forward, his hand held to his side, and Sydney wondered if he was going to pull an empty gun trying to bluff Tex out of that car alive. Griffin and Sydney had no ammunition. Dumas carried no weapons. She was sure Adami wouldn't hesitate to kill Tex right there, was probably going to do it anyway. That was precisely what Griffin had thought, and she watched as he turned, leaning as though he was merely looking into the car. His strategic placement told her he was going for Adami's guard, Silvio.

She looked at Tex, saw he was also watching Griffin, then saw him close his eyes, a look of utter defeat overtaking his features. He expected the worst. When he opened his eyes again, he looked right at Sydney. Shook his head. Glanced at Griffin, then back at her in warning. *No,* he mouthed silently.

Sydney's pulse pounded with each passing second. She wasn't sure what Griffin was planning. To dive past the goon and through the window, grab the gun? Surely he wasn't foolish enough to think that Adami was the only man armed in there? The driver was surely armed, as was the man Adami had sent to fetch them. Griffin would be dead before he ever had a chance to pull Tex out. Worse yet, the moment they handed the map over, Tex was dead. He clearly knew it, was warning them off.

Once again why Griffin had wanted her to destroy the map.

She needed to stop him. But Griffin edged closer. Before she could get his attention, a young couple, laughing as they walked arm-in-arm, crossed in front of Sydney, blocking her view, and she had to step aside as the man leaned forward to toss a smoldering cigarette into the ashtray on top of the garbage bin near the door. She felt helpless. As out of control as the smoke that swirled up, and drifted away.

Adami said, "Time is up..." He raised the gun to Tex's head.

She had to do something, or Griffin was going to lose Tex, and maybe his own life.

"Here it is," Sydney shouted.

"No!" Griffin said.

She slid the strap from her shoulder, opened the tube, and slid the parchment out, unrolling it slightly, revealing the lower left corner with the fleur-de-lis and Templar cross, and the very edge of the labyrinth, before she let the map roll shut. But she didn't move forward, just stood there by the door.

"Hand it over," Adami said.

"First," she said, "you hand over Tex."

"You're in no position to argue."

"But I am," she replied. "I'll bet two-hundred-year-old paper would burn pretty damned quick if lit." She held it over the ashtray, allowing the smoke from the cigarette to drift right up to the paper. Francesca cried out. When Adami's goon started forward, Sydney lowered the parchment toward the cigarette. "I wouldn't try it," Sydney said.

"Stop!" Adami ordered. Silvio stilled, and Adami dropped the gun slightly, as though weighing Sydney's resolve against his. "As I said, the map for your friend."

Sydney said, "Have your man open the door."

"Agreed. Silvio, the door." Silvio walked around to the far side of the car and opened the passenger door. "Now your turn," Adami said.

She didn't remove the parchment. Instead she picked up the cigarette, and held it closer to the paper. "Tex first."

Adami motioned for Tex to slide out. His hands were tied behind him, and he moved stiffly. "Hand me the map, and I will allow Griffin to assist him from the car."

"Get your man away," Sydney ordered.

"Silvio," Adami said. "In the car."

Silvio walked back around and opened the front door, got in. Just before he closed the door, she saw the driver, his gun pointed toward the passenger compartment. "Tell your driver, and anyone else with a gun that if I so much as hear a click, this thing is going up in smoke."

"Lower your weapons," Adami called out.

Sydney looked at Griffin. He ignored her, walked to the other side of the car. As he pulled Tex out, she dropped the rolled parchment into the tube, leaned forward, handed it to Adami. Tex was in Griffin's arms, and he dragged him back, away from the car. Sydney let go of the leather strap, tossed the cigarette into the gutter as Adami rolled up the window. "Go!" he said to the driver.

The Mercedes took off.

Griffin looked at Sydney, defeat and anger written across his face.

Chapter Thirty-eight

Griffin shook himself. Sure, with Sydney's help they'd rescued Tex, but at what price? The map was lost and he had no one to blame but himself for their failed mission.

"Easy does it," Tex said, as Dumas cut the cords at his wrists. When he was free, he rubbed the circulation back, glaring at Griffin, "I spent how many days tied up in some room of his, and you let him get that map? You do realize what it leads to? Why he wanted it?"

"It's not his fault," Sydney interjected. "There's something I—"

"*Now* isn't the time," Griffin told her.

"Hell if it isn't," she said. "When Adami figures out that that map isn't quite what he bargained for, we're going to be in a world of hurt."

"What are you talking about?" Griffin asked.

She lifted her shirt.

Francesca sucked in her breath. Tex whistled. "That what I think it is?"

"When Griffin sent me into the bathroom to destroy it, I figured why not cut out the important parts? Give him what's left over?"

"Jesus Christ," Griffin said. "We need to get the hell out of here. Now!"

"Xavier is waiting at the café for Alfredo," Dumas said. "My car is there." Dumas took one side of Tex, Griffin the other, just in case he needed help, but Tex held his own as they raced around the corner.

"Where are they?" Griffin asked.

Dumas looked about the piazza. "There!" he said, pointing to a table at the café.

Alfredo and Xavier saw them and ran across the cobbled piazza, Alfredo carrying Sydney's black bag on his shoulder. He held it out. "This was left in my van."

Griffin took the bag and handed it to Sydney. "Right now, the farther you are from us, the safer you'll be," he told Alfredo. "Adami will undoubtedly be coming after us and the map."

"Where should we go?" Alfredo asked.

"Take Xavier to the nearest *carabinieri* office. Have them contact the *vice-comandante generale* in Rome. Give them my name and they'll know what to do."

"Very good," Alfredo said.

"And thanks for your help. Both of you."

The two took off toward Alfredo's van, and Dumas directed the others to his car parked nearby. He unlocked it, then threw Griffin his keys. "You're better at evading," he said, getting into the front passenger seat.

Francesca and Sydney got into the back. Tex was just about to slide in beside them when Griffin looked up, saw a black Mercedes drive past the intersection. The telltale sound of tires skidding on pavement told them that he and Tex had been spotted. "Hell," he said, digging out his phone and tossing it into the backseat for Tex, before he got in. "HQ has a chopper on standby at the airport. Get it here."

Tex called HQ as Griffin hit the gas, sped off. Traffic was incredibly thick on the main street. He pulled in at the first opening, not pausing to see if Adami was following.

"May I see it?" he heard Francesca ask Sydney.

Griffin eyed Sydney in the rearview mirror. "Do *not* pull that thing out under any circumstances."

Francesca wasn't about to let the matter drop. "I have to know how you did it?"

"Did what?" Sydney asked.

"Fooled Adami into making him think he had the map?"

"Technically he did have it. Just not all of it."

"But I saw it!"

"Only what was left of it. I unrolled it just far enough so he couldn't see that I'd cut out most of the labyrinth from the middle and the list of words of what I presumed was some sort of key or legend."

Francesca gave a horrified gasp. "Do you realize what you've done? The history you've decimated?"

"And the lives she saved?" Griffin replied, braking to avoid a motorcycle that pulled out in front of him.

That, at least, shut Francesca up, but any chance of peace was lost when Dumas slammed his hand on the dashboard. "What about the lives I may have lost?"

Griffin checked the mirrors, saw the roof of a black vehicle about four cars back. "You sure it can't wait for Sunday confessional? I could use your help trying to save the lives in this car right now. He's behind us."

"But what he told you about the ambassador."

"What the hell? You didn't think I believed that shit?" When there was no answer, Griffin glanced over, saw the look of self-loathing on the priest's face. "For Christ's sake. You mean you *knew* the ambassador was relaying info to Adami?"

"No. But I *should* have known."

"How?" Griffin said, looking into the mirror. Adami's driver veered into the opposing lane, passed two cars, then jumped in again. "He was as much a part of ATLAS as you and I."

"Yet you didn't pass on information, thereby endangering the team."

Griffin felt Sydney's gaze on him. "No, but my failure to pass on information caused issues." He hit the horn, trying to get the car in front of him to pull aside.

"That makes us quite the pair. You trust no one, and I put all my trust in God."

To which Tex said, "This kumbaya shit is all well and good, but I could sure use a shot of Johnnie Walker and a shower, and if Adami catches up to us, I'm not getting either."

Griffin checked his mirror. The black Mercedes was closing in on them. He whipped the wheel, made a hard right turn down a narrow street. "Find out where that chopper is, Tex."

Tex made the call. "They're tracking our cell now."

Griffin turned left down an alley, then down another street that opened into a plaza. He blasted the horn. Pedestrians fled. The Mercedes was on their tail. Silvio leaned out the window, pointed a gun at them. And then the welcoming thrum of helicopter rotor blades filled the air. Griffin looked up, saw the military helicopter hovering above an Egyptian obelisk in the plaza's center.

The chopper maneuvered down, and two uniformed *carabinieri* leaned out, submachine guns in hand. He saw Giustino behind the crew, talking to someone on his headset. "The cavalry's here," Griffin said.

"Adami's backing off," Tex replied.

"They're leaving!" Dumas cried, and he made the sign of the cross.

◇◇◇

Not until they'd landed safely at the *carabinieri* helipad, and Giustino guided everyone into an office, did Griffin agree to let Sydney pull out the map. She spread it out on the table and he studied the portion of the labyrinth she'd cut out, as well as the words listed down the side. "Not bad, Fitzpatrick," he said. "But it would've been nice to have gotten us the whole thing."

"I was working on a time crunch."

Francesca ran her fingers against the cut edge, looking sick to her stomach. "Ruined. Almost half of the labyrinth is missing. To be so close…"

"These words," Sydney asked her. "Any idea what they mean?"

It was Dumas who answered. "Possibly Old French, archaic. They'd need to be researched. That of course can be done once it is rightfully returned to the Vatican."

"Like hell it will be," Griffin replied. "And even if it does belong to the Vatican, you think the Pope will do a better job protecting the world from the threat of a plague released by a madman?"

"With God's help."

"What were you saying earlier about putting all your trust in God? Maybe a little trust in ATLAS' capabilities?"

Dumas gave a heavy sigh. "Agreed. There has been too much death where this thing has been concerned."

"Maybe you should put it away," Griffin told Sydney, taking out his phone to call headquarters. "Less temptation for everyone."

Sydney removed her sketchbook from the bag Alfredo had returned. She opened it to slip the map in, and Father Dumas saw one of the sketches of the loculi in the columbarium. "May I?"

"Sure," she said, handing him the sketchbook. "I wish I'd had more time there. It was an amazing place."

Giustino was talking to a fellow *carabinieri* near the door, arranging vehicle transportation for Griffin and the others back to Rome. He looked up, stopped when he realized Griffin was trying to make a call, and signaled for the other officer to step out with him. Even so, Griffin moved to the far side of the room for some privacy. The thought of telling McNiel about Ambassador Harden weighed on him, but he had no choice.

McNiel answered.

Griffin heard several people talking in the background. "You're up late."

"Damage control," McNiel replied. "The thing we tried to avoid by keeping Alessandra's murder from the press? It's happening now. Ambassador Harden unwittingly started a firestorm at his daughter's funeral, stating he wouldn't rest until he learned who had killed her. We barely got him away from the press, before they started asking if he knew if his daughter was having an affair with Congressman Burnett. It'd be nice to bury this thing without exposing ATLAS."

"About that," Griffin said, watching as Sydney pointed out the details on one of the sketches, talking avidly about the columbarium to Dumas and Tex. "It might be too late. Who's there with you?"

"I'm sitting here with the directorate and half the ATLAS oversight committee. What do you have to report?"

"Good news and bad. I'll give you the good first, which you *can* relay," he said, emphasizing the word as a warning. "We found Tex. He's safe."

"Thank God." He heard McNiel repeat the information. Heard the congratulations being passed around the room. After a moment, McNiel said, "And this other news?"

"Ambassador Harden. He's been passing on information to Adami. And Adami hinted that Harden was reporting to someone higher up."

A long stretch of silence on the other end, then finally, "Yes, of course we heard about the warehouse and the bioweapons being destroyed. Everyone here is ecstatic."

Translation: McNiel wasn't about to reveal to anyone in that room that he knew there might be a mole. "Unfortunately," Griffin continued, "Adami got part of the map. A very small piece if that's any consolation. But it also renders the part we have as unusable. There was nothing we could do."

"Clearly we know your next mission."

Recover the rest of the map to stop Adami. Griffin realized the others had grown silent, and he glanced up, saw them all staring at him. Tex had an odd look on his face. "I should go," he said. "I think we should get Tex to a hospital."

"Tell him I'm glad he's safe."

"I will."

Griffin disconnected. "What's going on?" he asked them.

"This," Sydney said, lifting up the sketchbook, showing him her drawing of the mosaic on the columbarium floor. And then she held up the parchment and what was left of the labyrinth beside it.

The map. There on the columbarium floor the whole time.

Outside, he heard the helicopter starting up. He shook himself, ran from the room. Giustino and the other officer were just getting on. "Giustino!"

Giustino stopped, looked back.

"Any chance we can commandeer that helicopter one more time? There's something important we need to see in Rome. And time is of the essence."

◇◇◇

The following evening en route to Fiumicino Airport, Rome.

Sydney shifted in the front seat of the car, trying to get a glimpse of the Colosseum, its arches lit against the black night sky. "Are you sure we don't have time to stop? It's the Colosseum, after all. When in Rome…"

"Not a chance," he said. "You have a plane to catch, and I intend to make sure you're on it."

"There is no way I'm going to miss it. It's not as if I have a reason to stay this time. I know who killed Tasha, and you now have a complete copy of the map—though Francesca wasn't too happy to learn you ripped up the floor of the columbarium after you got your photos. I think she would like to have had her own photos to publish, since as far as she knows, no one has ever seen the floor from that high up to determine the pattern on it."

"She can't complain too much, since she will be helping us research the Old French so that we can decipher the labyrinth and find out where the map leads to. Once we have the location secure and stabilized, she can publish the photos anywhere she wants."

"And the scientists you rescued? Do they get any credit?"

"What they're getting is new identities to ensure their safety and keep their work from falling into enemy hands. According to Dr. Balraj, Dr. Zemke did more to set back Adami's plans than Adami ever realized. She was genetically engineering a super-plague that was more of a super-dud. It looked virulent in the lab, but its DNA was faulty."

"No one ever suspected her?"

"One of his scientists did, but she managed to convince him that the test sample he was viewing had been contaminated. She said it was a matter of days before they would have realized that she was working against them. Regardless, Adami had enough material down there to cause some serious damage, even without creating a super-plague. Her fear is that Adami will find this new source and start over again."

"Any chance he'll succeed?"

"Since he has very little of the map, I'd say no. Not that we're about to take any chances, should he have another lab equipped to pick up where he left off. Thanks to Dr. Balraj and Zemke, we have a fair idea where that lab might be," he said, slowing behind a bus that pulled out from the curb. "Our next step is to recover the lost part of the map from Adami, before he or his associates attempt to discover the location it leads to. And once we discover that location and what the map leads to, our team of scientists will go in and assess exactly what it is we're dealing with. In other words," he said, glancing over at her, then back to the road, "nothing that we can't handle on our own, which means *you* are no longer needed."

"You could at least wait until *after* I'm on the plane to gloat."

"Trust me. I won't be gloating until you are well across the Atlantic. Past experience tells me I'll need all my wits about me to get you on that plane and home for Thanksgiving."

"Aren't you the funny one." She leaned back in her seat, thinking that if truth be told, she was glad to be going back to San Francisco. "What about you? Who are you spending Thanksgiving with?"

"I'm not—" His phone rang and he pulled it from his pocket, answered it. Suddenly he slowed, turned a corner, and pulled over, and Sydney knew that whatever news he was being told, wasn't good. When he disconnected, he looked troubled. "That was McNiel. They picked up Harden this morning. Apparently he was denying any involvement with Adami, until they finally mentioned that his daughter had been a part of ATLAS. McNiel says he turned white as a sheet, then broke down."

"So it was true," Sydney said. "The ambassador was feeding Adami info."

"Info that probably got his daughter killed. But Harden also implicated someone pretty high up the political ladder. He asked for a lawyer, and promised that once he had a chance to speak with his counsel, he'd tell us the name of the person he was working for."

"That's good, then."

"Except that he and his attorney were both killed in a vehicle collision on their way to Langley a few hours ago."

It was a second before the implication of it all hit her. "I take it that it wasn't an accident."

"McNiel's fairly certain it wasn't. Unfortunately for the parties involved, Harden's lawyer had a written confession in his briefcase, and it survived intact. Harden implicated Jon Westgate."

"Who is that?"

"He used to be a low-level crime boss who hailed from Adami's hometown in New Jersey. And you'll never guess whose number popped up several times on Westgate's cell phone. Martin Hoagland."

"Hoagland?" Sydney repeated. "As in Congressman Hoagland?"

"The same. He always felt he should have headed the committee for ATLAS."

Sydney couldn't believe what she was hearing. "This was out of spite?"

"Trust me," Griffin said, pulling away from the curb, then back out to the main street. "If Hoagland did it for anything, it was for control. He and Adami are cut from the same cloth. Power and domination."

"And what better way to dominate world powers than having inside intel into an organization such as ATLAS."

"Exactly," he said. "Only now he'll have to attempt doing it from a federal prison cell."

At the airport, Griffin and a *carabinieri* contact escorted her through the security entrance at the airport, where she'd be flown home on the ATLAS jet.

Their contact waited a discreet distance from the door that led out to the tarmac, and Griffin held out his hand. "I never did thank you for what you did to help Tex."

She shook hands with him, said, "I sort of owed you one. I'm only sorry it wasn't as dramatic as that night at Adami's villa. Now *that* would make for a good war story at the bar. You're sure I'm not allowed to talk about any of this?"

"Sorry." He looked down at her hand, seemed to realize he was still holding it, then let go. "You know, if you ever get tired of the Bureau..."

She smiled. "Sorry. I have a job."

"At the FBI Academy?"

"I like it. For a reason."

"To hide."

"Wrong. It's giving me time to think where I want to go next."

"If you change your mind," he said, handing her bag to her, "you know how to reach me."

"I do."

They stood there for several seconds, the silence turning awkward, until Griffin said, "I don't need to personally walk you to that plane, do I?"

"I'm going. I'm going." She started toward the jet, thinking about everything that had happened since she'd left Washington. She was damned lonely at times, and hell, life these past few days had been more exhilarating than anything she'd done in a long time. She glanced back, saw that Griffin had turned to leave, was walking toward the security door where the *carabinieri* contact was waiting.

"Griffin!"

He stopped, turned, a bemused expression on his face. "You have a real problem getting on planes."

Suddenly she was uncomfortable, not sure what he'd say. What she was even going to ask. She'd be on that plane tonight, alone.

He tilted his head, waiting.

"You never did say what you were doing for Thanksgiving…" she finally ventured.

"No plans."

"Well, if you find yourself in San Francisco, you could stop by my mother's house. She cooks a mean turkey, and with your connections, I'll bet you have no trouble finding the address."

Griffin stood there a moment, his hands shoved in his pockets, as though mulling it over. Suddenly he smiled. "Tell her to set an extra place. I'd like that. A lot."

Fact or Fiction

One of the more infamous conspiracy theories is that of the Freemasons running a shadow government in the U.S., and controlling the global economy. Proof of this can be found on the back of a dollar bill: the Illuminati's "all-seeing eye" over the pyramid, which forms one half of a six-pointed star, with five of those points touching the letters to form the anagram that spells *MASON*. According to these theorists, that same shadow government that originated with our country's founding fathers who were Masons, is still in power today.

Conspiracy theories aside, in this day and age it would be damned difficult to infiltrate and corrupt an entire country's government, installing criminal networks in with the politicians and the national bankers, all to control the global economy.

Or would it?

In the early 1980s, the Italian government and banking system nearly toppled because of the infiltration and corruption from one Freemason lodge, Propaganda Due, or P2. P2 became a clandestine lodge from 1976 on after being expelled by the Grand Orient of Italy. Counted among its ranks in the lodge before and after the expulsion were prominent journalists, parliamentarians, industrialists, and military leaders, as well as the heads of all three Italian intelligence services. There were also high-ranking members of the Catholic Church listed in the membership, which perhaps explains how the Holy See's bank became involved in the scandal with Banco Ambrosiano, becoming a major shareholder in a bank used by both the Mafia and P2's shadow government—as well as the American government, which used the bank to funnel covert money from the United States to the Contras, among other things.

Add to that the mysterious death of Pope John Paul I in 1978 after a mere thirty-three days in office, allegedly linked to his investigation into the bank's ties to the Mafia. Then a few years later, the murder of the chairman of the Banco Ambrosiano, found hanged beneath the Blackfriars Bridge in England, his pockets filled with stone and masonry—perhaps a not-so-veiled warning as to what happens to Freemasons who violate their oath of secrecy. His death was originally ruled a suicide—and rumor has it that it was investigated by Freemasons, hence the botched initial investigation. In other words, you have the makings of some great fiction—if not for the fact it was real life. For this novel, I was counting on the possibility that not all the P2 players were caught, and intended to start up again where they left off.

Anything can happen in a circle to which only a select few are invited. Such is the history of Freemasonry, the largest secret organization in the world. But where did they come from? John J. Robinson, author of *Born in Blood: The Lost Secrets of Freemasonry,* argues—quite convincingly—that after the King of France (assisted by the pope) hunted down the Templar Knights in 1307, the Templars went underground and emerged several centuries later as Freemasons. If true, what happened to the Templar Treasure? And what was listed among the contents of this legendary cache? Unfortunately when it comes to the treasure, history is murky. Was it simply accumulated wealth from the Templars' vast banking and land holdings, or, as some historians surmise, the treasure from Solomon's Temple, which contained some of the most amazing religious artifacts known to mankind, including the Ark of the Covenant?

That, of course, got me to thinking about the Bible and the plagues brought down to earth by Moses, so that the pharaoh would free the people of Israel. Scientific evidence has been offered to show that the plagues were possible, and that there was a natural explanation—whether one believes or not. Some historians have surmised that the Ark may contain the staff that Moses used to bring forth the deadly plagues. Is it possible that this ark, built to specific standards as indicated in the Bible, contained the original source or location of these plagues, so that Moses could bring them forth at the right time?

More importantly, can a deadly plague remain dormant for centuries, only to emerge as dangerous or even more so than it once was? My medical sources and research state yes. (For further reading on this subject, try: *Plague Wars: The Terrifying Reality of Biological Warfare,* by Tom Mangold and Jeff Goldberg.)

But back to the Templars and Freemasons. I bring up the historical figure of Raimondo di Sangro, Prince of Sansevero, and perhaps my own contribution to the idea that the Templars emerged centuries later as the Freemasons. In 1750, Di Sangro, a genius (mad genius according to some), became the first Grand Master of the Freemasons in Naples, and because of this was excommunicated by the pope. (And why is it that the Church is so dead set against the Masons?) How does this connect di Sangro to the Templars? Quite simply, the principality that gave him his namesake, the town of San Severo, was sold to the Templar Knights in 1233. If the Templar Knights emerged as the Freemasons in the 1700s, it is certainly conceivable that a man, a Freemason, whose principality was owned by the Templars, could be hiding a treasure that they intended to guard—a treasure still being sought to this day.

Beyond that, the prince's body has never been found, he did plan to enlarge his crypt, and his entire chapel is filled with Freemason iconography. Adding to the mystery are the vast miles of tunnels beneath Naples equal in size to the entire Vatican city, and even more still unexplored to this day—it certainly sparks the imagination that there might be a chamber or two left holding secrets that we may never know about. Why not a missing treasure or map?

To receive a free catalog of Poisoned Pen Press titles, please contact us in one of the following ways:

Phone: 1-800-421-3976
Facsimile: 1-480-949-1707
Email: info@poisonedpenpress.com
Website: www.poisonedpenpress.com

Poisoned Pen Press
6962 E. First Ave. Ste. 103
Scottsdale, AZ 85251